A Soul Mate's Promise

Robin H. Soprano

Dream, Wish, Believe

Robin H. Soprano

A Soul Mate's Promise by Robin H. Soprano
Copyright © 2014 by Robin Soprano
Cover layout by Alexandra King
A Soul Mate's Promise by Robin H. Soprano
410p. ill. cm.
ISBN 978-1-935795-31-5
LCCN 2014916430

All Rights Reserved. No part of this book may be reproduced, stored in a retrieval system, or transmitted in any form or by any means, electronic, mechanical, photocopying, recording, or otherwise, without permission in writing from Michael Ray King Publishing

Michael Ray King Publishing
PO Box 353431
Palm Coast, FL 32135-3431
www.clearviewpressinc.com

Printed in the United States of America

DEDICATION

To my Mother and Father, who always told me; I can do anything. I know they are guiding me from above.

To every one of my friends, too many to list, who have cheered me on to pursue my dream. Thank you I truly could not have done this without all of you.

To the special few that have talked me down from ledges when I was banging my head against the wall. Your words of encouragement and support even in the smallest way, helped save me from a dark hour and kept me motivated. And to breathe...

Thank you:

Suzanne Kework.
Margherita Perry.
Kathryn Batta.
Michael Ray King.(Author /Publisher)
Jorja Dupont Olivia.(Author)
Lori Elen Maguire.(Author)
Jennifer Probst. (Author)

Nancy Quatrano. (Editor) You heard my heart and helped the world understand it. You are the echo of my voice. Thank you for also making me laugh at my mistakes instead of crying!

To my husband Paul – Thank you for letting me do my thing and letting me fly.

~ *Anima Gemella* ~

~ He is more myself then I am
Whatever our souls are made of, his and mine
Are the same ~

Emily Bronte ~

CHAPTER 1

Three years ago, I woke up at two in the morning and reached over to find Richard missing—again. Unable to stop the tears that had become far too frequent, my dog Toby jumped up on the bed to lick my face and try to comfort me. My heart felt like broken glass, the pain in my chest nearly suffocating me—almost beyond what I could bear.

What had once been a marriage and life full of promise and love became a nightmare of loneliness and desperation for me.

The man I'd met, loved and married had disappeared in the seductive power and wealth that his parents left him as his inheritance.

A bird in a gilded cage, I realized late that I hadn't changed—but that he had. And I couldn't live with the changes.

* * *

Up and about at the crack of dawn, Toby rouses me so we can go for our morning hike on the beach and watch the sun come up.

This is my peaceful time of day, where I do most of my thinking. My divorce is just about final, just some discrepancies about money to be ironed out.

I don't know what's so difficult. I just want to move on and I need money to do it. Richard and I were married for twelve years, nine of those before the evil inheritance. I think on some level Richard feels bad things didn't work out. He moved me so far away from my home in the Northeast that I never recovered. He thought he was going to give me the world but it came with too high a price for me.

We grew apart. His life was corporate chaos, and the more involved he got the more I felt like a nuisance to him. When we tried and failed to have a baby, the marriage just crashed and burned. I went to a dark depressed place after two miscarriages, and Richard was too busy to notice. On one occasion he told me to just get over it and toughen up! When I emerged from my grief-filled fog, I asked Richard for a divorce.

I guess I knew in my gut that we were just not meant to be. He felt the same, so he left. He told me I could stay at the mansion—he knew I had nowhere to go. He promised that soon the details would be figured out.

I suspect that he feels responsible; he was supposed to take care of me. I gave up everything for him: my job, my family, and my friends! When we moved south he told me that he would be the breadwinner. I didn't need to worry about a job. Not like I could easily find one way out here on the god-forsaken island that he'd inherited, anyway.

I loved being a veterinarian's assistant and I miss that work. For me, no job and being alone so much was not a good combination After a while, I was actually happier when he wasn't home since my sadness seemed to make him angrier every day. When he was at home we had one fight after another over stupid nonsense.

Shortly after we separated, and he moved out, Richard started seeing Camille James, his business associate. I gotta say, I knew it, and really, wasn't shocked or upset.

I think they're right for each other. They are both cold type personalities. I crave affection and I love to give it, too. When I would try to cozy up to Richard he would push me away and say, "stop your annoying me!" His words broke me down every time.

I want more out of life, I want to be appreciated and cherished by someone.

*   *   *

Here on the island property is a cute, smaller cottage-style house that sits closer to the beach. It has a tin roof, and the white paint is a little worn away from the salt air. The back of this house faces the back yard of the mansion, a few yards apart with grass separating them. A little stone path between them shows the way from door to door.. I was told by my mother-in-law that in the old days it was used for a maid's quarters. For a few years my in-laws rented or loaned it to clients for vacations or business trips. But now, a very nice older gentleman by the name of Antonio Patroni lives there.

Years ago, before I knew the Boumonts, he was a security guard for them. One night Antonio stopped a robbery at the mansion and got shot; the outcome left him in a wheelchair. Antonio did managed to shoot one of the bastards, and off to prison they went!

A few years before that accident, his wife had past on and his two sons already had lives of their own. My in-laws left him the little cottage in their will in recognition of his service and sacrifice.

I adore Antonio. He is just sweet, old Tony to me. He's my only neighbor and we have become kind of dependent on each other; he has become like a father figure to me, and I've become like the daughter he never had.

Over the years, Tony has dried some of my tears over a good glass of wine and good advice! He came to the States by ship from Palermo Italy when he was in his twenty's. He is 70 now with salt and pepper hair and dark eyes that look deep into yours and he has a laugh like Santa Clause. I'm blessed to have him as a friend.

* * *

Finished with our walk, Toby and I head straight to Antonio's. He's already yelling and waving at us from his deck. "Good morning, Mia Caro!"

I smile big because I love his accent. He reminds me of my family who are also Italian, though passed on. I miss them dearly, so we have some common ground, he and I.

"Hows-a- my gal today?" he asks like he's singing.

"Oh fine," I say as I make my way up to the deck. Toby runs ahead to give Antonio a big hello lick and get a pat on the head.

"Did you make coffee?" I ask.

"Of-a-course," he says, "helpa you-self."

I go in and pour myself a mug and go back out on the deck and have a seat next to Antonio, Toby's already chewing on his morning treat. I take a look over the calm ocean and take in a deep breath.

"What's happening with the divorce?" he asks.

"Well, not too much," I start, taking a sip of the fragrant brew in my mug. "The attorney says I'm entitled to half of everything. But truly, I just want enough to get out and make it on my own. But because I gave Rich money for the new part of the firm, the lawyer says I should get profits. I think Rich and Camille are just spitting fire about it!" Antonio looks at me with an eyebrow arched.

"You listen to what the lawyer says, Caro, he knows what is best to do."

I look over at him, and nod. "Thanks by the way for getting me this lawyer. I wouldn't have known the first thing about it. And apparently, he is one of the best in the area!"

"Ahh, no thanking me. You just listen to him Gracie, and have faith. Now, let-a me see your beautiful smile!"

I look over at him and cross my eyes and stick out my tongue. He laughs his big hearty laugh and pats me on the knee.

"So, what's on your agenda today, Tony, you need to go to the store or anything?"

"Nahh," he grunts, "calm day today."

Before he continues on, his phone rings. "You want me to get that?" I gesture with my thumb.

"Please, *gratzi*." He nods.

I run in the house and grab his cell off the kitchen counter. "Hello?"

A deep voice on the other end replies, "Gracie, hi!"

"Hi, Joey!" I say. "What's up?"

"Where's Pop?"

"Oh, we're out on the deck. I'll get him for you–just a sec. So Joe, how's things in Cali? You and Mary alright?"

"Yes, thanks. Everything is fine, though Mary's getting grumpy with the pregnancy."

I chuckle. "Oh yeah Well you just give her anything she wants."

"Oh, you got that right!" He laughs. "She will kick my ass you know, and I really would like to be alive for the birth of my son!"

"Good! You need an ass kicking every now and then, it's good for you! Oh by the way have you come up with names yet? Please tell me you won't name him Jesus!"

"Ahh, cute Gracie," he says as he laughs, "like we haven't heard *that one* before!"

Still giggling, I hand the phone to Antonio. "Here, it's your son Joseph."

"What's so funny?" he asks.

"Oh, nothing," I say, "Joe and Mary are thinking about naming the baby, Jesus!"

"AHHH!" he grunts waving the phone in the air. He lightly spanks me on the rear with his hand. "You all crazy!"

I returned into his kitchen to get more coffee. I over hear the usual comebacks and move further into the house. Walking through Antonio's house I always look at the pictures in the living room of his wife Marie, his son Joe, and Joe's wife Mary and the winery they live on in Napa.

I know he had another son who is estranged from the family. Antonio doesn't really talk about him much, just told me once that he was military, Special Ops.

The soldier-son went all over the world. When Antonio's wife Marie was dying, and his youngest son didn't return home in time for good-bye's, Antonio could not let it go, though Marie had begged him to.

"He broke my heart," Antonio told me once.

"Gracie!" Antonio calls me, breaking me out of the memories.

I walk back out on the deck and sit down. The sun was all the way up and the air is getting warmer.

"Hey, you off the phone? You want more coffee or breakfast?" I ask him.

"Huh? Oh, no, no I'm good" he says with a far-away look in his eye.

"Tony, is everything okay?"

"Huh? Oh yeah yeah," he says. "I umm.. that-a was Joey," he says

"And?" I encouraged.

"He tells me my son Salvatore got hurt, but he's alright—CIA gave him a discharge to get well and he wants to come home. Joey thought it would be best for him to come here so we can mend our relationship."

"Wow, Tony," I said. "How bad is he hurt?"

"Just a shot to the shoulder–he will be fine but he needs physical and mental therapy. It's mandatory when you work in the Government or military."

"Oh," I say, feeling bad for Tony because I know how he feels about Sal. "Soooo, he'll be here when?"

"Day after tomorrow," he answers as he looks out towards the sea. Drifting in his own thoughts he suddenly seems smaller, much older than he did a half-hour ago.

"Umm, Tony?" I prod softly, trying to get his attention back. Are you okay with this?"

He gazes back at me, a small smile playing on his lips though his eyes remain creased with concern.

"I no have a choice, Caro—he is-a my son." He turns his eyes back to the ocean and I go to sit on the lounge chair in front of him touching his hands lightly.

"Tony, this might be a good thing for you guys to get back in touch. I don't know–repair a father son bond?" I squint, hoping I've said the right thing.

He turns his gaze back in my direction and smiles. My Tony is back, even if only for a second.

"Yeah or we will kill each other!"

My eyes go wide at first, then I laugh. "Try Tony, maybe it'll be a good reunion!"

Tony sticks his chin out and nods once. "We are a lot a like, him and me. Stubborn."

"Yes," I agree with a laugh. "But, you have an excuse–you're old and crazy!"

CHAPTER 2

Antonio's son Sal arrives later today. Thunderstorms rumble across the grey sky.

I promised Tony that I would make a baked ziti and a pot of sauce with meatballs and some cookies for them so they would have some meals for the week while they settled in, that meant we had to hit the store before I could begin cooking. And, since Antonio asked me to stay for dinner so at least their first meal together might be less stressful, I planned to cook and be the gracious hostess, although I wasn't all that keen on the idea.

So, after a quick run to the grocery store, and the little wine shop we have on the beach-side I got everything I needed. Toby and I headed back home and over to Antonio's.

When I get there, he's happy to see me, but I can feel the tension in the air.

To lighten the mood, I grab an Andrea Bocelli CD, *A Night in Tuscany*, and play it on Tony's CD player. Music fills the house along with the delicious smells of garlic and simmering tomato gravy coming from his kitchen.

With everything on simmer, I pour two glasses of Chianti for Tony and me and walk out on the deck where he is sitting with Toby at his side. The rain has let up for now but we can still hear thunder in the distance.

"Here ya go, have some wine, its good for you," I say as I hand him the glass.

"Gratzi, mio caro," he says with a smile as he takes the wine.

I sit down next to him. "Here's to a happy reunion!" I offer and we clink our glasses.

"I gotta tell you, Tony, I think I'm a little nervous myself for you guys."

Antonio looks up at me. "Don't worry Gracie, we will be on our best behavior."

"Okay." I say, "I'll drink to that. You promise me now because I don't like fighting and neither does Toby."

"I promise, Caro." he says with a hint of a smile.

A few hours pass and so do the thunderstorms and Sal still hasn't arrived, but Joey calls to see how it's going.

"We still haven't seen Sal and haven't been able to get him on the phone," I tell Joey. "I made enough sauce and meat for your brother and father to eat for a week."

Joey thanks me and explains I should just let the two men work out their differences and not worry about it.

"I can't tell you how happy I am that my dad has you to watch out for him. You're the best thing to happen to him in many years."

"And he's the best thing to happen to me, too," I tell Joey. Then I give the phone to Tony and they talk for a few more minutes while I go into the kitchen to shut off the stove.

"How about we just have that dinner, Mia Caro?" Tony says when he joins me.

"Sounds like a great idea. I'm sure we'll hear from Salvatore soon. Maybe his plane was delayed."

I pull out another CD of Italian Favorites, and as soon as Rosemary Clooney starts "Mambo Italiano," I pull the baked Ziti out of the oven and put it down on the little dinette set in his dining room.

"This house is so cute," I tell him as we are getting ready to eat. The cottage has seen slight remodeling over the years to keep up the charm and functionality of it. At about 1300 square feet, the two-bedroom, two-bath structure has a detached garage, hardwood floors and a small, but functional fireplace. The kitchen isn't big enough for a table, but the house has a great room for lounging and dining.

After Tony moved in, he had ramps put in to accommodate his wheelchair.

He looks around and I see a smile cross his face and light his eyes. "Yes, this house serves me just fine," he says. "Is the kitchen hard to cook in? You must be used to that big gourmet kitchen you gotta next door."

"Nope," I tell him, "I like your kitchen–it's cozy and quaint. Mine feels too industrial sometimes. I was going to have it remodeled but that's pointless now." I take a sip of wine, determined not to go down that sorry path again.

"Okaaaaay," I sing, to change the subject. "Tell me about Salvatore? Where has he been? What's his deal?"

Antonio smiles at me and shrugs his shoulders.

"My son, he always fought me, he makes up his own rules and he can have a bad temper."

"How old is he?"

"He is-a- forty-one now."

"Oh he's my age!"

"Yes, Joseph is two years older than Sal. They were born shortly after Marie and I moved to the States. They went to school up in NJ, then went their separate ways. After school, Sal went into the military, there was Desert Storm first, and when we got hit with 911, I knew he would be off to Iraq."

Antonio shifted in his seat and cleared his throat. "After that he went into Special Ops. We couldn't hear from him much because he was Secret Service. But he had plenty of time to know his mother was-a sick. He kept saying he would come, then never did. Just like now."

"He's just late, Tony." I try to sooth him. I can tell he is getting aggravated because there is no word from Sal yet and he is saying things like, "See how he is? He don't call to tell-a- me if he is okay."

I grab his hand. "Don't worry, he'll be here!"

After dinner, Antonio goes outside on the deck to have a cigar. He takes Toby with him. I clean up and can still hear thunder in the distance.

I pack up the trash and get ready to take it out to the garbage. I hear the click clack of dog paws on the wood floors. Toby's back and circling me, waiting to see if he is going get any leftovers. Suddenly he stops, his hackles go up and a low thunderous growl roars out of him. He is standing close enough for me to feel his whole body vibrate.

"What is it Toby?"

He trots to the front window and cocks his head to the left and then right.

"What's a matter with Toby?"

"I don't know?" I shrug. "I was picking up a garbage bag to take out side, he must hear a deer or something, I'll be right back. You want some coffee Tony? I made your favorite cookies too, chocolate chip biscotti's!"

"Si, caro, but let me make it, you did enough."

It's just getting dark as I make my way out the side door to go to the garage. Toby comes running up behind me.

"Slow down, boy!" I call to him. I round the side of the house where the garbage cans are. And Toby is in front of me growling at something.

I look up and there is a shadow of someone. Bigger and taller than me, standing there like a marble statue. I suck in my breath and it gets stuck in my throat.

A calm and smooth voice says, "Can you please tell your dog I'm not an ax murderer?"

I try to speak, but stutter instead. "I ..I.. how do I know you're not?"

"Because I don't have an ax in my hand?" he answers.

Toby continues to growl as he moves closer to the stranger.

"Can you please call your dog off?" he asks again.

"Who are you?"

"I'm Sal, Antonio's son."

Toby gets closer to Sal and is about zipper level to his jeans.

"Please, the dog!"

"Oh my God! Sorry!" I yell.

"Toby, it's okay shhh.. it's okay."

Toby takes a few whiffs but stays alert. I squint in the darkness. "You're late!" I scold him. "Your father's been very worried. Why didn't you call instead of sneaking around?"

"I didn't know I needed to." Who the hell are you?" he demands.

"First of all," I start, "You should have called your father when you landed. Second, my name is Gracie. I live next door. I'm a friend of your father's."

He looked over his shoulder at the mansion, then back to me.

"Oh. okay, Princess," he says putting his hands up in surrender, "you and the mutt gonna let me pass?"

"Yeah, sure. Let's go inside." I motion toward the house. "He's *not* a mutt by the way. He's a full-bred German Shepherd. His name is Toby." We round the corner of the garage when I decide to set things straight. "And for the record, I'm *not* a Princess, far from it."

I yank open the door and Toby leads the way. Sal follows me inside and through to the kitchen where Antonio is making coffee.

"Look who I found?" I chime. "He says he belongs to you."

Antonio looks up at his son and they stare at each other for a minute.

Sal lifts his chin. "Hey, Pop."

Antonio examines his son for another moment. "Okay let-a-me see what they do. Gotta you in the shoulder, huh?"

"Yeah Pop, it's really nothing, I'll be fine."

"Okay, okay. Come sit down." Antonio spoke softly, "What happen you're late? This-a-lovely gal made us a wonderful meal, you missed it. Where were you?"

Sal put down his duffle bag. "We couldn't land because of the storms. They had us circling. I thought I'd never land!" he said, shaking his head.

As the two men are getting acquainted, Toby is still sniffing Sal and his duffle bag thoroughly. I sit down at the counter stool and take in the sight that is, Salvatore Petroni.

He's about six feet tall and has on old jeans, faded in the knees and fraying at the hem of each leg. His sneakers are clean and white. A dark red and blue flannel shirt with the sleeves cut off hugs his big frame.

Since it's not buttoned all the way up, I can see a massive chest with just a little bit of hair. He's sporting a plain, dark blue baseball hat with the bill pointed down low, so I can't see his eyes.

For a military guy, he has quite a bit of hair, it seems to me. Medium to dark brown and in waves slightly past his collar. One arm is in a black cloth sling. His other arm, totally defined with muscle.

He isn't dark olive skin tone like his dad, so he must take after his mom's side of the family.

He takes off his ball cap and tosses it onto the chair.

He looks in my direction. He has his father's eyes—big dark brown, velvet eyes which seem to cut right through me. He steps toward me and offers a crooked half-smile. "I'm sorry. I didn't mean to scare you. I must have missed a very good meal, but I'll get to eat the leftover's, I suppose."

"Huh? Oh yeah, that's fine" My voice comes out sounding like I'm a two-year old with a cold. I clear my throat. "We were just going to have coffee and cookies. Would you like some?"

"Did you make the cookies too?" he asks.

"I did, chocolate chip bicotti's—your dad loves them!"

"Yeah, I know," he says, "they are my favorites as well, but I need a shower first.. You two go ahead. I'll be back in ten!"

Sal goes off with his bag in hand to the other side of the house where the spare bedrooms are. I stand for a moment staring after him like a lovesick puppy.

"Gracie!" Antonio calls, snapping me back to the moment.

"Huh? Wha..what?" I stammer.

Antonio laughs and cocks an eyebrow at me. "Hey, you like what you see, caro?"

"Huh? No, no," I say, giggling to hide my embarrassment. "Let me get dessert out.... and don't you worry about what I'm looking at!"

Antonio laughs his hearty Santa laugh, then mumbles something in Italian under his breath.

* * *

Salvatore emerges from the guest room wearing black cotton lounging bottoms with a draw string at the waist and a white sleeveless Tee shirt.

He doesn't have the sling on and I can see a cluster of stitches where he was shot and patched up again.

From behind the kitchen counter, I watched him approach us, barefoot, walking around and stretching his arms. His hair is damp and pushed back off his face hanging in loose waves to his neck. A little five o'clock shadow clings to a square jaw line and a handsome cleft chin

He sits down at the table and I hand him a mug of hot coffee. When he takes it from me, he flashes a big smile that travels to his eyes.

"Thanks!"

I almost faint—or is it throw up? I feel a pulling sensation deep down in my chest and stomach like I've just done a roller coaster ride. *Do I know him from somewhere?*

Does he feel something, too? I feel his eyes on me the whole time we sit there. As if he is trying to get in my head or trying to remember something. It's unnerving and intriguing at the same time.

Father and son chit chat for a while until I just know it's past time for me to go home. I get to my feet so fast, I knock over the kitchen stool, which bangs on the floor like a gunshot. Sal flinches and my stomach lurches again.

"Listen guys, I think it's time for us to go. Sal, I'm glad you finally made it. Can I get you guys anything else before I leave?"

Sal looks at me with his dark eyes. "So you live next door?" he asks.

"Yes," I reply, then turn to rinse my coffee cup at the sink.

"And you came here and cooked dinner for us?"

"Yes," I say, turning back to the counter. "I make lots of stuff and bring it to your father. Your dad has been wonderful and kind to me. I'm lucky he's in my life."

"Oh really?" he asks with that sexy little half-smile playing on his lips., "Tell me."

I look right into his warm, chocolate-brown eyes they were hypnotic. "Your father has helped me a lot over the past couple of years. I don't know what I would have done without him."

Antonio gazes up at me. "This gal is a wonderful gal, like a daughter to me. She has a big heart!"

"Okay," I say, noting that the heat rising in my face means I'm as red as a boiled lobster right about now. "Thanks, Tony, and that's my cue. Gotta get going before we get all mushy. Good night, guys!"

Salvatore stands and reached for my hand. I almost jump back, shocked by the shivers his touch shook my spine.

"It was nice to meet you, Gracie," he says, his voice smooth as melted butter.

"Same here," I answer. "I guess I'll be seeing you around?" He's still holding my hand and I'm finding it difficult to focus on chit chat.

"Do you need me to walk you over to your place?" he asks.

"Umm, no," I say with a little shiver, "it's all right. I've got Toby!"

"Ah, yes, Toby," he says, looking to his dad while pointing to my dog. "That dog almost ate my junk for dessert. Yes, I'm sure you'll be safe."

Nervous giggles bubble up in my throat. I manage to pull my hand out of his gentle grasp. "Yes, okay...gg- good night!"

"Good night, Gracie" he replies.

"Good night, mio caro."

Toby and I leave them and trudge back to our lonely, cold mansion.

Once showered and settled into bed, I can't help but wonder about Salvatore. Call it intuition, but I feel like I know him—or used to...

* * *

The next morning Toby and I are on the beach earlier then normal.

A cloudy humid day, the heat overwhelms me so we come straight back home without chasing a single gull or wave.

Sticky from the heat and salt air, I dove into the pool and let the cool water refresh me, then headed up stairs for a quick shower.

After I dry off, I pull on a flowing loose-fitting sundress that fits comfortably around my body, I'm a little too curvy for today's waif like magazine models and I always try to hide it. I stroll over to my vanity, roll my eyes, and wrinkle my nose at the sight of my hair. Running a comb through my long unruly mess of a mane, I fight against the humidity frizzies. I dry it the best I can and let the damp ringlets fall around my shoulders. I decide a little bronzer on my cheeks, and liner and mascara around my eyes will be good enough for a muggy day!

I look around the room for dirty laundry and decide to get some of it done. And, honestly, even though it's just me and Toby in this mausoleum my soon-to-be-ex called a house, it really can use some cleaning, too.

The place would do well with a staff, but that's not happening with me living here alone. But, maybe the Ice Queen Camille will hire some maids to keep it up when she moves in – just real quick with the dust mop all around and I'll be happy with that. Yeah Thank god for hard wood floors and just a few carpeted areas.

Done with all that mundane stuff, I get a huge mug of coffee, check the PH of the pool water and settle on a chaise on the lanai.

After a minute or so I hear a whistle and look over in the direction of Tony's house, he is on his deck. I wave and Toby whines, so I grab my mug and head over to check on him.

"Ahh, La Mia ragazza bella... you look very nice-a-this-a morning Gracie, you walk early today yes?"

"Yes, we had an early start. Thanks for the compliment, Tony. Toby had me up before the crack of dawn today, but it's so humid I needed to shower as soon as I got back." I climb the stairs to his deck and look at him. "So...how did last night go?"

"Thankfully, it was uneventful. Salvatore got up and left already, too. He decided to go check out his new surroundings find the two doctor's office's he needs to visit for the next eight weeks of therapy."

"Well I'm glad everything so far is calm. You need anything today?"

"No, Caro, I'm going to wait for Sal to come back and hear what he has to say."

"Okay, then. I'll be around. Shout if you need me!"

"Gratzi. See you later."

I smile at him, call for Toby and head back over the stone path that leads to the mansion.

When I get back to my lanai, my cell phone is alerting me that I missed a call and two texts from a dear friend, Celine Mathews.

CHAPTER 3

I hit the call back button. "Hello?" she answered.

"Hey Celine, what's up lady?" I chime. She answered in her usual devilish way only Celine can.

"Not Lance. HA! That's for sure!"

She always makes fun of her husband and I chuckle at her joke. Celine is southern born and raised in an upper class, well-to-do southern family. She is older then me by about ten or twelve years, and her husband is about fifteen or more years older than she
is.

"Oh Celine!" I gasp, "your so bad, poor Lance!"

She yells back at me, "Oh please baby girl he's getting as ornery as he is old, and senile too! I'm starting to take over some of the task's he's supposed to do as city councilman, our PR guy told me its for the best right now, we don't need to stir the pot. So, she continued, "I need a break from my crazy life, whatcha doin' over there on hell island today?"

"Oh the usual, nothing, then a little later some more nothing." I crack in a sarcastic tone.

"Okay then!" she quipped, "I'm headed in your direction with a Cosmo mix, can we sit and talk and get drunk?"

I laugh and tell her I'd be here waiting on her!

Celine married within her social status and has two children who are off and doing their own thing.

As soon as they hit eighteen she told them, "I love you both but my job is done!" and sent them off to colleges far away. She isn't cold hearted, she just wants her children to become self sufficient human beings. So she cut those apron strings right off. Her kids come and visit on holidays and vacations and she loves it.

Celine also started a life of her own. Let's just say she and Lance have a understanding...she has her flings and he understands, He once told her, "Don't fall in love till I'm gone." Celine replied, "Funny huh, I've *never* been "in love."

I met Celine not too long after I came to Saw Grass Island. My mother-in-law insisted I join the Southern Women's Society, to meet, as she put it, the "nice elite" -well bred stock of the area.

They were not very welcoming and I fit in as well with them as a humane society stray does at the Westminster dog show. I tried to be friendly, but they would toss me phony smiles and kept me an arms length away. One night at a SWS function I was getting out numbered in a heated discussion, that's when a very thin pretty woman with brown hi-lighted short hair grabbed my arm and pulled me to her side, in a very warm southern accent whispered to me, "Watch out, it's feeding time for those sharks and you're the bait. I had met Celine and never regretted it.

She saved me from the sharks and what promised to be a dreadfully stuffy evening and we became good buddies, for which I am tremendously grateful.

She taught me who to trust and who to watch out for. Taught me not to get too involved in their bullshit politics and religion.

But she knows I'm no dummy. I have a lot of common sense and street smarts which she tells me is one of the reason why she is drawn to me. What you see is what you get for us both. We don't put on airs and we don't try to impress anyone.

* * *

A couple of hours later, Celine pulls up in her red Jaguar XF. I open the door to meet her and Toby trots out to the car to say hello. I hear her tell Toby in her high, twinkley, southern-style baby voice, "Well, hi there, Toby! How's my big ol' luuug ..you-a-goood baby arentcha!! Yes you is..."

"Hey, Celine!" I yell from the doorway, "come on in!"

"Okay, just let me get more Toby love," she tells me,. "Okay, boy let's go inside to Momma. Yesss, you-a-good baby..."..

Celine enters and hands me a half-gallon of cranberry juice cocktail and a big bottle of Grey Goose vodka.

"Here, Darlin', mix'em up and let's get happy!"

I giggle and go to the kitchen.

"What's shakin', Sweetie?" she asks. "Any divorce news?"

"Yep," I begin, "we are now fighting over money. Rich has it and doesn't want to give it, which I don't understand. He seemed amicable about everything in the beginning-it's like someone else is in charge of his brain these days."

Celine looks over at me and raises an eyebrow. "You just getting that now?"

"No, no, I mean, things were going pretty smooth but now there's a bump in the road for no reason that I can't understand."

I hand Celine her Cosmo, we clink glasses, and both take long gulping sips. Celine cocks her head to the side.

"I'll tell ya what the problem is, Gracie. That cold hearted slut Camille James. She's suckin' his dick now, so she's in charge of his brain. I've known that girl since she came here to go to college. Slept her way through all the corporate men who could help her up the social ladder. Nothin' but a gold diggin' whore if ya ask me!"

I take an other sip of my drink, the smooth flavor of vodka warms my throat. "Why should she care what I get or don't get? It's none of her business..."

"Well, it will be, if she marries Richard!" Celine says.

I shake my head. I've got a good friend for company and a great drink in hand. I'm not wasting my time on Richard's stubbornness nor his choice of new companion. "Can we talk about something else?" I suggest.

"Sure baby," she says with empathy nod, "let's go out by that gorgeous pool and have a seat."

We walk out on the lanai and take a lounge chair each, cocktails in hand. I see Tony out on his deck reading the paper, so I wave and he waves back.

"How's he doing?" Celine asks.

"Oh, he's doing good. His son Salvatore is here and living with him now-for how long I'm not sure. He got shot in the line of duty, he's fine...but, the military gave him some kind of disability discharge, I don't have the whole story yet, but I gotta tell ya he is one handsome man. When I looked into his eyes I felt something strange - like I knew him from somewhere!"

"I'll tell ya what you felt baby-*horny*! Seriously, how long has it been?" Celine asked with a grin and a wink.

"Oh my god!" I reply, almost choking on my drink. "Celine, really, I felt a connection I can't explain."

The grumble of a motorcycle coming down the long cul-de-sac road gets louder and louder and we give each other a quizzical look.

Toby stands and begins to growl. Sure enough, a motorcycle pulls in the little dirt driveway of Tony's house.

"Celine that's him, that's Sal!"

Like a gladiator in a stallion-powered chariot, Salvatore Patroni sits on a silver and black Harley Davidson Electra Glide. He isn't wearing a helmet but has on his baseball cap, dark sunglasses, a black tee shirt and snug fitted jeans.

He parks, gets off the bike and starts walking to the deck where Tony is sitting. Celine and I get to our feet to get a better view.

"That's him!" I say, glancing over at Celine, who looks as though she is about to drool.

"Oh my! Baby girl, you *gotta* get you some of that!"

"Some of what? *Him*?" I ask, raising my voice an octave higher. "What are you talking about?" I continue, "I've gotta get through a divorce! I don't want to start up a relationship. Men are not on my to-do list right now."

Celine barks back at me. "Who's talkin' bout a relationship? You need to get laid, let him blow your socks off among other things! Just get yourself some release and let him put a smile back on your face. You deserve it!"

"Oh I couldn't...could I?" I ask, feeling like I'm swimming in a pool that's way too deep for me.. "And what makes you think he would want me anyway?"

Celine reaches over and hooks a finger at the elastic top of my sundress, glances down at my breasts and grins at me. "Oh Darlin'... you really have to ask?"

CHAPTER 4

After too much drink, loads of laughs and some dinner, Celine decides she will spend the night at my place and go home in the morning.

That night as I lay in bed, my mind is on over load and I can't shut it down. I'm thinking about Richard and his ridiculous charade, then I'm considering ways to slap that bitch Camille, and finally I wonder if I can bear to get involved with the very handsome Salvatore Petroni.

I look at the clock next to my bed and it's two in the morning. I let out a big sigh, get up, step over Toby who is laying on the floor almost under my feet, then hear the thumping of his tail on the hard wood floor.

"Hey, big boy...I'm going out on the balcony. You wanna come too?"

Feeling overwhelmed I decide first to head into the bathroom and take a Xanax to calm my nerves. I walk to the edge of my bedroom and open the door. I walk across a landing to French doors that lead out to a small balcony that over looks the ocean.

From here I can see the whole yard and part of the beach. To the left, I can see Tony's house and his deck. I take a seat at the railing.

I watch a little lightening shoot across the sky. I sit there and begin to cry. This is becoming a habit. My late night panic-filled crying attacks take a toll, but I let it out in the hopes of feeling better.

*　　*　　*

Salvatore Petroni was sitting in the shadows out on the deck of his father's house. He couldn't sleep because of the things he was sorting in his head. Adding to the mix, the auburn hair beauty next door, when he heard something. He looked around, then up. He could just about see that it was Gracie, sitting, staring out at the ocean.

Is she crying? Quietly he went back in the house to grab the binoculars he'd seen on the kitchen counter. As he reached for them in the dark, his Dad wheeled himself out into the living room.

" Crap! You scared me! Why aren't you in bed, Pop?"

"I could not-a sleep tonight."

"Yeah, me either."

"What are you doing, son?"

Sal looked at his father and gave him a concerned look. "I think I hear Gracie... crying? I was gonna get the binoculars..."

Antonio cut him off..

"Yeah, yeah, it's Gracie. She has bad nights sometimes. She has gone through a rough time— she's a little lonely and heart broken."

"Why? What's her story?"

"Eh...her and her husband didn't work out. She has no family left except a brother, ahh Steve, I think is-a his name, but he is out all over the world. Green Peace or-a-some-a-ting, I don't know. Gracie is a very sweet gal, and she deserves better than what she got dealt. She will be okay, she's strong."

"Should we go check on her, Pop? I feel like we should check..."

"Let her be," his father interrupts, "she gets it all out and goes back to bed. I watch her from-a-here."

They went out on the deck with the binoculars just in time to see Gracie wipe her face and go back inside, with Toby right behind her.

"See son? She be alright. Maybe we ask-a-her to come tomorrow for lunch huh?"

"Okay, Pop, sure, what ever you say."

*   *   *

Toby wakes me up with a cold nose to my cheek and a long whine.

"Okay, okay, I'm getting up!"

Shuffling to the bathroom I brush my teeth, take my vitamins, put on my blue terry cloth shorts and a white Tee shirt, slide on my sneakers and head for the stairs.

As I am making my way down, the smell of coffee hits my nose, smelling good and for the first time in years, making me think of this mausoleum as a home.

I enter the kitchen and Celine is bright eyed and raring to go.

"What are you doing up so early? I figured you sleep through to the afternoon!" I tell her as I reach for a mug to pour the coffee into.

"Nah," she says, "I've got stuff to do, people to yell at!"

"Wow, you're full of energy this morning!" I laugh.

"Darlin', listen to me good. Be the kind of woman that when your feet hit the floor each morning, the Devil says, "Oh shit she's up!"

I grin and nod. " I love that! You just make my day with your words of wisdom. Where do you come up with this crap?"

"Facebook," she replies with a giggle. Her smile fades a little as she points a burgundy-colored fingernail at me. "You know what, baby girl? It's not crap. That should be your everyday mantra. I know you're not dumb, but, you need to grow a pair of balls and make shit happen for yourself, like the divorce for one thing. And secondly, you need to go flirt with Antonio's son. Richard's moved on-now it's your turn, baby!"

"I know, I hear you," I snap. "Stop mother-henning me."

"Mother what? I could be just your older sister at the most, now cut the crap! So, where you off to so early, the sun is just about up?" she asks.

"Toby and I like to go for a walk on the beach every morning and watch the sunrise. It's our Zen," I say, raising an eyebrow.

"Zen this!" she says and flips me her middle finger.

I bust out laughing...I always told her it was funny to see a woman of her class, loaded up with her fine jewelry, flipping the bird!

"Okay darlin'" she says still giggling. "Have a good walk. "You want a coffee to go?"

"No, but save me some for when I get back. Will you still be here?" I ask.

"Nope, I gotta boogie on outta here and start my day, check in on the old man. Maybe he kicked the bucket!"

"Oh, Celine!" I yell, "that's terrible!" I know she is half-joking, but still...

"Oh, don't get your panties in a bunch!" she says, waving her hands at me.

I narrow my eyes and smirk at her. "I can't ...I'm not wearing any!"

"Thatta girl!" she says with a grin.

I walk her to the front door and watch her drive off. I can feel the house sigh sadly that the laughter is gone and I shrug off a chill.

"Ready Toby? Let's hit the beach."

Toby runs to the back of the house, paws slipping on the floor like Scooby-Doo does when he runs in place before he can get a grip.

We head over to the French doors that lead out to the pool and lanai area, then through the screen door. On the grassy yard we jog over to the little wooden walk way that leads down to the white sandy beach.

The September sky is doing amazing things for a sunrise spectacular. A mix of peach and lavender streaks light up the horizon as the sunlight just begins to filter through.

Soon, even here, we'll be changing into fall without the heavy humidity of summer. I always appreciate the cooler air.

We're just about ready to walk back home when I see Salvatore come onto the beach. He has on what looks like might have once been sweat pants, cut into shorts, and sneakers. He's without his shirt, but the baseball hat and sunglasses are in place.

As soon as he hits the sand, he starts into a jog. Toby spots him and runs over and I start to walk his way, my heart pounding like I'd been running, myself. We meet halfway between the tideline and the dunes. Toby still unsure, gives him some more growl-n-sniff.

"Good morning, Sal"

"Hi," he answers. "Ummm...when is your dog going to trust me?"

"He is just really over protective of me," I say with a smile. "Just give him some time. So you're jogging the beach this morning?" I gesture with my hand.

He takes off his hat and runs a hand through his brown curls and chuckles.

"Yeah, I guess I am. Thought I might take a look around. Care to join me?"

I look up and smile at him. "We were just on our way back, but thanks anyway. Toby gets me up very early since I don't sleep well at night anyway."

"Yeah, I know what you mean," he says, "I don't sleep very good either. Oh, Pop wanted me to ask you if you would like to come for lunch later if you can."

"I can," I answer, nodding my head. "Should I bring anything?"

"No, I'm gonna go over later to the store and pick up some things. Just come by about noon."

"Okay, noon it is, I say. "Enjoy your run. Oh, is your dad on deck?" I ask, still smiling.

"Yeah, he's there probably waiting on you and Toby here to pass by."

We stand there awkwardly smiling at each other.

"All right," I say, breaking the awkward moment. "I'll go sit with him a bit"

Walking back over the little wooden ramp and towards the houses, I catch my breath. I see Tony and wave.

"Good morning, Caro!" he yells to me. Did-a-you see my son? Did he ask you to come over for lunch later?"

"Yes he did! Thank you. I gotta run some errands first. Do you need anything?" Toby and I climb the wooden stairs so I can stop yelling at Tony.

"No nothing I can think of. Where-a-you go today?" he asks with a concerned look.

"Well, I need some food for Toby, my Jeep needs gas and the attorney left me a message to come and sign some papers."

"What are the papers?"

"Umm, I'm not sure but he said standard stuff so he can get into the bank accounts, and as he puts it, 'Nail Richard to a wall.'" I use my fingers on each hand to mimic the quotes and Tony smiles.

"Caro, bring me a copy of-a-those papers. I want to look them over, too."

"All right. What would I do without you?" I give him a big bear hug and kiss him on his cheek. "Okay, I'm off! I'll see you guys in a few hours!"

As I start to make my way down the steps, I almost get trampled by Sal running up from his jog.

"WHOOOA! Oh, sorry!" he says, breathing hard through his mouth. He grabs my arms to steady me. "Are you okay?"

"Yeah, yeah, I'm fine!" I say, smiling. "You came up pretty fast, you in a hurry or what? That was a really fast jog!"

"Oh, I'm so sorry," he keeps apologizing. "I didn't mean to.. I didn't think you'd be right here..just momentum and adrenaline, I guess...I'm so sorry...hey, you leaving already?"

"Ahh..yeah..I have to go into town and do a few things before I come for lunch.

"Oh,.. hey, ah... where you going?" he asks. "I have to go into town as well, do you want a ride? I can take you if you want?"

"That's okay," I say, "I don't think I would do so good on the back of a motorcycle."

He gives me a sexy smirk and cocks his head to the side knitting his eyebrows together. "Really? I think you would do *very* well on the back of my bike, but," he says, raising his cleft chin in my direction, "there is a car we can use."

"Yes, your father's van."

"No, there is a car..." he says with that devilish smile.

"Really?" I ask, confused. "Where? I haven't seen a—"

Sal cuts me off with a lift of his finger and looks up at his dad who is watching us.

"She doesn't know about the beast, Pop?"

"Ohhhh, nooo," Antonio says with a little laughter in his voice. "No son, I never showed her."

"Showed me what?" I ask.

Salvatore blinks at me. "Oh, you need to follow me!"

I follow him to the garage, he opens the door and I see a big blue tarp covering what I assume is the car he's referring to.

"You ready?" he asks.

I shrug my shoulders, wondering what in the world could be hidden under the cover. "Umm, I guess so."

He pulls off the tarp and there sits a little sports car.

"Well? What do you think? Pretty cool huh?"

"Umm... what is it?" I ask bunching my eyebrows.

"What is it?" he exclaims with a smile and look of surprise. "This is a 1995 Dodge Viper!"

"A Viper?" I repeat. "I kind of remember those, do they still make these?"

"No," he says with a grin, "but I did hear that maybe they might start production again."

I look at the little charcoal-gray coup with only two seats. "Very small," I say.

He glances my way and points to the car. "These cars are now classics. It has a very interesting history–they didn't make very many because they were not very practical."

I walk around the car to get a better look. It has side exhausts and big scallop scoops on the front fenders running into the doors and a light gray interior with a black dashboard.

Sal begins to tell me he worked on it for a year or two with his dad and brother. They made some changes and had ordered some stuff for it, like a roof.

"What? The car didn't have a roof?" I ask.

"No," he laughs. "They didn't come with one in the early years. No windows or door locks, either."

"What?! Shut up! No way!" I yell. "You're joking!"..

"No, I'm not. It's just a big engine with seats – a simple car, a very *fast* car for its time. You either love them or you don't. We modified a lot on here and specialized and customized. The three of us had fun working on it. We never fought about any of it. That was a great time for all of us. My mom hated this car, she thought it was too loud and fast and we would get hurt in it."

"Fast, huh?" I ask. "How fast?"

"Well, it's four-hundred horse power—which in the early 90s was something. It has a six speed manual transmission and Lamborghini helped with the design to get some of the weight off the engine. The making of this car was very impressive for back then. It's unique—I like unique things."

As he proceeds to tell me about the car, he strides up next to me, very close, so close I can feel the heat radiating from his body, smell the scent of him mixed with the salt of the sea from his run. He opens the hood for me.

"It opens backwards?" I ask.

"Yep, unique!" he says.

I peek at the engine that says *VIPER* in bold letters and looks almost too big for the car. "That looks like something out of a sci fi movie."

He laughs, shuts the hood, then leans on the side of the car so he can face me.

"You know," he goes on, "some people have considered this to be the sexiest car of it's day, describing the body as passionate, voluptuous and complex."

"R-R-really?" I stammer, raising an eyebrow as I try to stay cool and composed. I'm getting turned on just listening to him chatter about the Viper. *Is he flirting and comparing me to this sexy little sports car? Could I be that lucky?*

"Some thought the Viper shouldn't have been sold legally in the United States."

"Oh? How come?".

"Well, because it's like a stripped down car, no anti lock breaks, and all that safety stuff."

"The inside looks different," I say. "The steering wheel looks small in a way".

"Yeah, that's because there's no air bags, just steering wheel."

"No air bags? You better hope you don't ever get hit in this thing!" I groan.

He smiles, then laughs. "Now you sound like my mother used too, minus the accent!"

"Well?" he asks, "what do you think? You wanna go into town in the beast?"

I look up at him, my eyes wide in surprise. "Definitely, *yes*!"

"Okay then," he laughs. "Be ready in half an hour, can you do that? I'll meet you right outside your front door."

"See you in thirty." I answer.

CHAPTER 5

Camille sat in an area of Richard's office at BOUMONT & SON INC. The affluence oozed from the expensive décor made her all but shiver with delight.

Though she'd come away looking something of a gold digger for nabbing Richard away from poor little Gracie, it didn't keep her up at night. She was a southern woman and she was entitled to get what she went after. And if the debutante bitches at the Southern Woman's Society didn't embrace her, what did she care? They hadn't exactly treated little Gracie much better.

I got what I need– I'm on the top and laughing all the way to the bank!

She looked over at Richard reading over some papers.

"Darling," she said, "would you care to go to the club for lunch this afternoon? Or should I have Jessica make a deli run and we can have a quiet lunch in?"

"Hmmmm?" he replied not looking up at her. "Oh, ahh lunch, just get some sandwiches sent up. I've gotta get this deal worked out before next week's deadline," he said flatly.

"Fine. What would you like then, turkey or a Rueben?"

"Oh, a Rueben sounds great," he said. "Make sure it's not too greasy. I want rye bread with no seeds, and lightly toasted, not too much of the Russian dressing, and make sure it's hot." he demanded. "Last time it got cold and gummy and I just couldn't eat it."

Camille arched a well-defined brow. "Really, darling I'm not going to *get* it. I'm sending the secretary. I can tell her all of that but do you honestly think it will happen? Why don't you get something more accommodating to your needs?"

"Camille, why don't *you* call it in for me according to my needs. This way it just has to be picked up!"

"Okay Richard, okay," she said under her breath.

Camille was learning pretty fast that Richard had a very high maintenance personality, which sometimes exhausted her, but she could overlook anything if her bank balance improved. She got on the phone to the deli and just about begged for Richard's sandwich to come out the way he wanted. Once the lunch order was placed, she hit the call button to Jessica's desk, and asked her to go pick their lunch up and deliver it to their offices.

Camille took a deep cleansing breath and braced herself for her next question.

"Richard, she asked softly. "What's happening with the divorce proceedings?"

Richard looked up, his eyes wide.

"Oh crap, that's just an other thing on my plate to deal with. I'd just as soon give Gracie what she wants and be done with it. Could be final in a matter of days at that point."

"Richard, you can't be serious!" Camille gasped. "She has never done anything for the company, she doesn't even understand what we do here. She didn't even like hosting parties for your clients– you used to say that she was going to say something to embarrass you —and.. you want to give her a percentage of our profits? For what? Honestly, I'm clueless!"

"Well," he surmised, "she gave me money to open the other office downtown. I never paid her back and it's half in her name. I did that while we were still good, or so I thought. I have people working on it. Don't sweat something that you shouldn't be concerned about."

Oh, but Camille *was* concerned. *That little bitch wants out, let her get out without a dime. She didn't go to college like I did, and work hard to get where I am. No, Gracie is not part of the plan.*

* * *

Up and over the bridge, and into town Sal drives us in the Viper, roaring down streets. At the stoplights, Sal revs up the engine and people on the street stare at the shiny unique sports car that was loud, passionate, voluptuous and complex!

I giggle every time and feel the engine vibrate through my whole body. Sal's brother Joe had placed a C.D. player in the car a while back, and we decide to crank up some Van Halen's Greatest Hits.

One of my favorite songs is, "Right Now" with Sammy Hagar, and we blast it out of the car for the whole town to hear! It's really nice to just let loose and have some fun. I'm singing along, enjoying the wind in my face when Sal looks over at me.

"Am I driving too fast for you? Am I making you nervous at all?"

"Oh, no! You're fine!" I shout over the music and engine throb. "Who knew running errands could be this much fun?"

He laughs and shakes his head. "Good I'm glad you're having fun. Now, where to first? The pet store?"

I nod my head.

He turns up the main drag and pulls into what we call a town center. When we park the car, I remember a story. No idea why, but I blurt it out to Sal.

"I was going to ask for a job here once and Richard talked me out of it. I thought it would be cool to work with the animals and stuff. He thought it would be embarrassing for his wife to work here and that I really didn't need to work. I shouldn't have listened to him. And I don't know why I just told you that story., Sorry didn't mean to air my crap on you."

He chuckles. "No, no, it's all right, although I can't imagine what you could do to be embarrassing to him."

"Well," I say, "he didn't want me working unless it was something substantial. I hated being home alone all day.. Richard's mood swings exhausted me. I was never right. Dammed if I did and dammed if I didn't."

"What did you guys have in common in the first place?" Sal asks.

"You know what, Sal? I really can't remember, and I really don't care anymore."

We go into the pet store and Sal maneuvers the shopping cart around the store. He lifts the heavy bag of dog food into the cart, then wrestles it into the little so called trunk. I got all warm and fuzzy having him help me. I feel flutters–he even makes sure my seat belt is secure.

"Oh, umm, I have to go to my attorney's office. Leonard Burnes over on Windmere Avenue. I'll show you where."

"I think I know where that is. My rehabilitation doctor is over there, I had a session already."

"How is your shoulder doing?" I ask. "You were very lucky that's all the damage you took. It must be scary always being in the line of fire."

"Well," he says with a shrug. "Like a cop or fireman you just do it, don't think or you'll choke. The world is a crazy mad place these days."

"Yes, it is"! I agree. "I'm glad we have heroes like you protecting us everyday."

His face transforms into stone he's obviously uncomfortable. "Thanks... I don't feel much like a hero."

"Oh yes you are," I insist. But his discomfort is growing. "I'm sorry Sal, I don't want to upset you, See? This is what my Ex used to say I embarrassed him about by not knowing when to keep quiet. I'm sorry."

"You have nothing to be sorry for, Gracie. You said nothing wrong, it's just a little hard to talk about sometimes. How were you supposed to know? It's really kind of nice talking to you about it. You make me feel calm. I don't know why, but you do. Pop says you have a kind heart. I guess I can feel it too."

I just sit there in a stunned silence. I stumble when I try to speak. "Wow, thank you Sal. That's really nice of you to say!"

"Hey," he says, "sometimes I don't stick my foot in my big mouth like Pop might have told you."

"Nope, he hasn't really told me much about you. Why don't I just let you do that from now on, Sal, sound good?" I ask.

"Yeah, I'm good with that," he says, and gives me a very handsome cleft-chin smile. And to my surprise makes me chuckle.

Sal turns the key in the ignition and once again the Viper roars to life like a waking lion. And, we are off. We pull up to the first traffic light and I feel Sal's warm brown eyes on me.

"You know what, Princess? You've got the best laugh! It's very contagious."

"Thank you." I smile shyly "So tell me," I ask. "This Princess thing, is this now my nickname? Because, truly I'm so *not* a Princess. Far from it, or is that the irony of the nickname?"

He just smiles. "Hmmm, I don't know," he shrugs. "My first impression of you, it popped in my head. But after talking with you, and knowing that Pop thinks very highly of you, I see it differently. Don't take it the wrong way, but you remind me of a damsel in distress. I don't know why, but, *Princess* seems to fit. I'll stop if you don't like it."

"No, no, it's okay," I say. "A damsel in distress huh? Maybe more like under a lot of stress."

He pulls up to the door of the office building and asks me if I want his company, but I decline.

"Okay," he says, "I'll be right here then."

The door says "Leonard Burns Divorce Attorney" and as I walk into the office, I take a deep breath. Sometimes I'm still not sure this is really happening, at least not until I wake alone in Richard's house and realize it has never been *my* house.

A young girl at a small glass desk with a computer and a headset looks up at me and smiles. She was very pretty, in a new age or Goth kind of way. She had a small diamond stud on the side of her nostril and black nail polish on her long fingernails. She's dressed very professionally, and her makeup looked like a super model's. I border on being envious of how together she seems when I'm always feeling like I'm falling apart. "Hi, I'm Gracie Boumont," I say. "I'm supposed to sign some papers for Leonard? He told me to just swing by any time today. Is he here?"

"Yes Mrs. Boumont, I have your papers right here. And no, he's not in right now, he's at court."

"Oh, okay. Could you run off copies for me so I can have them for my own files?"

"Yes of course," she says with a smile that makes the stud in her nose twinkle. "I did that already. A Mr. Antonio Petroni called. He asked if I could do that for you. Is that your dad?"

"No," I reply with a smile of my own. "But he acts like one."

She hands me a ton of paper with legal mumbo jumbo written on it. It may as well be in Chinese. I take a deep breath and will myself not to break into a sweat but it isn't working. The anxiety is a knot in my chest and it's hard to breathe

"Are you all right, Mrs. Boumont?" the young woman asks.

I nod and look at her. "Yes, it's just all this legal talk I just don't understand. Makes me very nervous."

"Oh, don't worry, Mr. Burns knows what he's doing. That's what you pay lawyers for, right?" she asks. "These papers let Mr. Burns go to the court and get permission to collect your husband's financial information. See the yellow tabs? Just sign on the lines where I indicated for you. Don't worry, Mrs. Boumont. Come in the little conference room right here and make yourself comfortable."

When she calls me Mrs. Boumont for the second time in five minutes, I cringe. "Call me Gracie, please."

"Okay, Gracie," she says, "would you like a bottle of cold water?"

"Yes please, that would be great," I mutter, following her into the room directly off the waiting room. She leaves the door open which is a relief because I swear the walls are closing in.

As she leaves to get the water, I look at the stack of papers in front of me on the table that's polished so well that I can see my reflection. I don't look very good and take another deep breath. *I can do this...*

Before I start searching for the all-important yellow sticky tabs, Sal walks in. I look up at him a little surprised

"What are you doing? I thought you were gonna wait in the car? Are you okay?"

He shrugs and gives me that lopsided grin. "Yeah, I'm fine. By the look on your face, I should be asking you that question. I was sitting in the car and I just thought you might need some moral support."

Just then the Goth secretary comes back with a bottle of spring water and hands it to me. She ignores Sal, though I have no idea what woman could do that.

"Are you feeling better?" she asks me, her concern clear.

"Why? What happened?" Sal asks as he kneels beside my chair and puts his hand on my shoulder.

"She got a bit shaky and short of breath. I went to get her water. Sometimes that helps," the secretary replies, looking as though she wished she was somewhere else.

"Really, it's nothing," I interrupt. "I'm fine. I just get anxiety attacks sometimes and I just got too nervous about all this paperwork – and what it all stands for, I guess." I take a big sip of the water which is nice and cold going down my throat. "I'm fine really, feeling better already." I can't quite pull off a smile, but my breathing is steadier.

Sal pulls out a chair, sits down next to me and looks up at Goth Girl. "It's okay, I got it from here."

Sal looked me over. "Okay Gracie what happened, I understand anxiety. That shit can be awful. Are you sure you're okay?"

"I'm fine, honest." I'm struggling not to let my frustration show. Since the divorce thing started, my self-confidence has decreased as the anxiety increased. "No big deal. I just got overwhelmed." I wave my hand over the stack of neatly-typed paperwork. "I probably should read all this, but will I understand it all? It just freaked me out. I'll be fine."

"Alright," he says in a husky whisper, "you've got a good point. You have a lot to lose if you make a major mistake, but let's take a look." He points to the papers.

He pulls them in front of him and reads through the first few pages, then shrugs and looks at me." This isn't really for you to understand," he says. "In law, they use a hundred pages to say what could be said in one or two. This is a motion to the court that makes your application for divorce all official. Now the lawyers can duke it out. You aren't signing away any rights or anything."

I look at him and drink in his smile. His dark brown gaze bores into my soul.

" Princess," he whispers, "take a deep breath. It'll be fine".

I smile. He's made me feel better. I give him a chuckle and take a big gulp of the water. He holds the paperwork aside at each tab and I sign away. Each signature is more sure than the one before it. One last deep breath, and I finish the last few pages. I tidy the sheaf of paper and push back my chair.

We leave the conference room and I put the papers on Goth Girl's desk. She gives me a relieved smile.

"I guess I'll see you soon," she says, handing me a folder with my copy of the motion.

Sal comes up behind me and takes the folder, offering me the rest of the spring water. "I'll trade you –I'll take the paperwork, you drink more water. You okay to go?"

"Sure," I say, "I want out of here."

Outside, a warm salty-aired breeze blows through us. Sal points at the parking lot were he stashed the Viper. We make a beeline for it and jump in. *Having no roof has good points when you want to behave like a teenager, I guess.*

"Princess you need to go anywhere else? Or do you just want to go home?" he asks with a grin.

"I'm good! I thought you had some stuff to do, too."

He gives me a closed lip smile and a wink as he starts the car. "Nah, I just wanted to take the beast out. Pop starts it now and again but it needs to be driven. I thought well, two birds one stone have some fun. So you like the car or what?"

"Yeah, it sure is a fun ride, but I couldn't use this for everyday."

"Oh, I don't know, but I got the bike, too. And this, I figured it would be enough to serve my purposes." He reaches over and tugs on my seat belt to make sure it's tight.

"I'm used to my Jeep—it's big and roomy. I can fit stuff like an eighty-five pound German Shepherd in it and it has a roof..." I say with a laugh.

"Hey!" he says with an exaggerated frown. "I have a roof, I just didn't put it on today."

We laugh as we drive off. Before we get home Tony calls Sal on his cell with a request for a loaf of Chibatta bread. We hit the little grocery store on the island.

"Maybe some food will make you feel better," Sal says as we're getting back into the car, this time using the doors.

"I am hungry, but I'm all right. Thanks, by the way. You helped me out of a major panic attack back there. What made you come in?"

He shrugs. "I don't know, I just got a powerful urge to go in and check on you. Glad I could help Princess."

Again, I sense that somehow Sal and I have a connection that I don't understand. I look out through the windshield and contemplate the thought.

"So you get panic attacks a lot?" he asks.

I nod. "Lately they're not as bad or frequent as they used to be, like when Rich still lived home. Sometimes I wake up in the middle of the night though, and it scares the hell out of me."

"What do you do about it?"

I glance over at his strong hands, easily steering the Viper along the winding road. "I get up, walk it off, go out on my balcony look out over the ocean. I have a prescription for Xanax which helps. Some times I take a sleeping pill."

"Does it really help you?" he asks, taking his eyes off the road to look at me.

"Sometimes," I say, "but I don't like to be alone in the middle of the night when it happens. I feel like I can't breathe. It's scary but having Toby there helps." I look up and we're pulling into Tony's little driveway.

"Home sweet home!" he says with a grin. "Let's go eat!"

"That was fun Sal. We'll have to run errands like that again soon," I tell him.

"Yes...or..." He hesitates and my heart goes thump. He climbs out of the Viper cockpit and comes around to open my door. "Maybe we could go out? You could show me around, get a drink one night or whatever."

It's all I can do not to pump my fist in the air like a school kid. I don't look at him as I climb out of the low seat. "Yeah, I'd like that, Sal."

I stand by the garage door while Sal lifts the dog food onto his good shoulder and delivers it to the back door of the lanai. He jogs back and we take the file and the bread and climb the stairs to the back deck.

Toby spots me instantly and almost runs me down before I squat down and let him give me hello licks like I've been gone for days instead of two hours!

Inside on the table is a big antipasti platter of meats and cheeses, all kinds of olives, bright red roasted peppers and roasted garlic cloves with sliced roma tomatoes. I put the bread on the table as Sal opens a bottle of Sangiovese wine. My stomach grumbled loudly. Tony grinned at me.

"Ah, mio caro, you-a-hungry? Good! Manga.. eat, eat!!"

Sal cut up the bread, and I was making myself a sandwich and scooping olives and stuff onto my plate in no time!

"Hey look at that! Sal said, a girl who actually eats! You don't see that very often."

Tony laughed. "Oh yeah she's a good gal she lova-to-eat not shy, it's a good thing."

I take a bite of my sandwich and smile when Sal notices I'm not shy around food. "I'm no fun when I'm hungry and I don't want to be cranky."

"You are-a-beautiful, Gracie, just the way you are...You agree, Sal?" Tony winks.

Sal looks up from his plate. "Yes, Pop, she is quite unique. One might say, passionate, complex and voluptuous."

I almost choke on my food, and grab for my glass of wine to wash it down before I do. "Geeez, thanks guys!"

Tony shoots Sal a look intended to knock him off his chair. "Hey, hey.."

"Pop no, it's a compliment. I'm sorry, Gracie. Did I offend you?"

I cut them both off with raise hands. "Absolutely not! I need the boost. Thank you!"

Tony mutters something in Italian then looks to me " if-a-my son talks outta line you have-a-my permission to smack 'em in-a-the head, yes?"

"Pop!" yells Sal.

I laugh "This is great—makes me feel like home. I miss my family."

Tony reaches for my hand. "You are home, Caro. Ti adoro, la mia casa `e la tua casa."

I almost cry and again gulp my wine to get myself collected. I adore him as well and he knows this.

After lunch, I sit on a lounger and tuck my legs underneath me. I expect Toby to join me but he is busy sniffing around the deck. After a few minutes Sal and Tony come out to join me. Sal sits next to me at the end of the lounge chair. In less than a minute, he is almost nose to nose with Toby, who maneuvered himself in between us with a whiney growl.

"Okay, enough." Sal chuckles. He puts his hands up. "What's the deal with your dog? Why doesn't he like me?"

I giggle. "You gotta give him time. He's just used to me and Tony. I guess he's a little over protective."

"You guess? This dog is like a trained Navy Seal! Where'd you get him?"

"You know it was the strangest thing," I began. "Not long after Rich and I started to break up, I was walking on the beach one morning and this dog ran up to me. No collar on him, and I thought, how weird a full breed shepherd pup wondering alone on the beach. He followed me home. After a few hours, I realized he was trained and everything! Your dad told me to give him a name and some love, so I kept him. I took him to the vet and they said judging by his teeth, he was about one year old and very healthy.

"Oh really?" Sal says with a smirk. "And Pop told you to keep him? Hmmm..." He glanced at his dad from the corner of his eye as he spoke. "Interesting."

I wonder what that look is about, but I'm too cozy to really care. "Yeah, I'm glad I did, because he has been a wonderful companion for me." Reaching down to give Toby a little scratch between his ears. "Really, Pop? He was just wander..."

"Ahemm!" Antonio clears his throat, cutting off Sal's sentence., "..Ahh..does-a-anybody want something sweet? Ahh.. ahh.. I gotta ice-a-cream inside. Sal, go get-a-the ice cream..."

"Oh, none for me, I'm so full, and I'm enjoying my wine," I say, still curious about what's going on between them.

"Yeah, me either Pop," Sal says, still giving his dad a questionable look.

"Okay, then no ice cream," he cuts in. "Did you bring-a-the copy's of your papers from Leonard?"

"Yes, I have them,." Sal says as he gets to his feet. In a moment he's back with them and hands them to his father.

I sigh loudly. "I almost had a panic attack when I looked at them."

"Ah," Tony shrugged. "Don't worry, Caro. It's all right."

"Sal actually helped me to calm down," I say, giving Sal a smile.

"Did he?" Tony asks as he's reading the paperwork.

"Yeah, it was nice," I say with a little laughter in my tone. "Very gentlemanly, coming to my rescue and all."

"Oh really, Son? You helped her huh? Good...good...."

The two men exchanged looks a few more times. I don't want to pry so I ignore it.

We drink wine, laugh and chatted the afternoon away. Tony's asleep in his chair by the time the sun disappears.

"Maybe you should put him to bed," I whisper to Sal.

"Yeah, Pop's just can't hang like he used to," he jokes. We chuckle quietly.

"I guess I should probably go," I say, struggling to get to my feet from the lounge. Toby gets up, too. "Tell Tony thank you for a great afternoon. Everything was wonderful."

"Hey, ahh, Let me walk you to your door. Please."

"Okay," I say with a shrug, "if you really want to."

Sal walks me with Toby flanking behind, over the stone path, back to my lanai and over to the French doors that enter the backside of the house.

I put the key in, unlock the door, and flip on some lights. As I turn to thank him, Sal snakes an arm around my waist and gently pulls me into him.

Looking into my eyes he slowly dove in, bent his head and gave me a warm, soft kiss. I'm stunned, then my blood seems to boil at the same time my knees get weak and I relax and lean against him. As the kiss gets more intense and deeper, I put my arms around his neck. I don't want it to stop. After a long moment, he puts his hands on my face and slowly pulls away, keeping our foreheads together.

"Are you okay with this?" he whispers.

I can't speak. I nod my head. In the pale light, he smiles, bends to take my lips with his again. This time, I gave as deep as he did, I taste his tongue in my mouth. When he finally steps away, he reaches up with his fingers and brushes the hair out of my eyes.

"That was nice. I'll see you tomorrow? Early, on the beach?" he whispers, as out of breath as I am.

"A..aa..a yeah, okay," I stutter.

He takes a slight step back and grabs my chin with his thumb and index finger and raises my face a bit to look into my eyes. He smiles and lets out a little chuckle. "Sleep good tonight, Princess."

* * *

Over at Antonio's, Sal came back up the deck and saw that his father was awake. They stared at each other for a long minute.

"Son, you walk-a Gracie home?"

"Yeah, Pop, she's home."

"Did you kiss her."

Sal looked away from his dad. "Pop, let's get you to bed." Sal started over to his wheelchair.

Antonio put up his hands and pushed at Sal. "I don't need-a-help. I asked you a question!" he spoke louder.

"Yeah. Yes!" Sal snapped. "Yes, I kissed her."

Antonio nodded his head, looked up at his son and waved for him to come closer. Sal leaned down a little. "What, Pop?"

Antonio reached up and smacked him across the face.

Sal stood holding the side of his face. "Shit that stings! Pop what the hell was that for?"

Antonio pointed a shaky finger at his son, his face furious. "You watch it with her, she is-a-good gal. She has had lots of heartbreak and my son is not-a-gonna come and add to her sadness. What now, you here for good? Or you go away again and-a-don't come back? Then she cry to me over you, *you*, he nearly shouted.

"No, Sal, if you feel for Gracie, do the right thing, and no games with her. I don't know how much more she can take!"

Sal rubbed at his face and hair. "I know, Pop, I know..."

Antonio cut him off. "You tell-a-her your life and intentions and let her see if she wants to continue...she is not a fling!"

"I know, Pop," Sal said. "I wouldn't do that, I..I.. I don't know, I really like her, something about her, she's calming to me, and I want to just help her, be near her. Protect her." He shook his head as though trying to clear it. "It's a strong feeling too, she's familiar somehow."

Antonio knitted his eyebrows together with a look of concern. "I have never seen you have a serious relationship–you feel-a-that strongly about her in this short time?"

"I never had time to really settle down. You *know* that, Pop! I've been out *saving the world* as you say. Dessert Storm, then Iraq, then everywhere that no one knows about. How could I possibly get close to anyone? I'm Secret Service. Sometimes I couldn't trust the very people I was working with for Christ sake! Look, I'm done. They gave me a nice pension for life and job well done for the country. They *told* me I was done."

"Do you want to be done? Son, you have made that your life's career, its in-a-your blood. "It would be nice if I can believe you." Antonio's face softened. "You are forty-one years old and I would love-a-to see you settle down, and-a-Gracie, she would make you happy, but you gonna have-a-to want it. Are you done? Are you out for good?"

Sal reached out to his dad's wheelchair and started pushing him into the house. "Come on lets get to bed," he said. "And yeah Pop, they told me I was done..."

"Ahh, that's-a-not what I asked you, Sal. I don't care what they say, I want to know what *you* say. Would you still be there if-a-they didn't tell you to leave? Is it a break or are you out?"

"Pop, I'm tired, I don't want to talk about it. Can't I just take one day at a time–clear my head and re-group?"

"Yeah, sure son," Antonio said, "but you involved someone special into your world now, do the right thing."

*   *   *

"No! No! When will you be home? Don't leave me!!"

I was out of breath, my heart pounding. I was running, but heavy skirts surrounded my legs.

I reached for who appeared to be Sal. He was on a horse, wearing a blue coat and white breeches with black boots. He was yelling something to me. I couldn't hear–there was havoc in the street. People were yelling, men were marching.

"Don't go!" I yelled to him.

He circled back to me, the horse stomping all around. I grabbed the reins and he reached down to touch my face.

"I must go my love, it is my duty. I will fight for what's right, I shall return to you, I promise!"

I watched as he road off with other men on horseback. I knew he wouldn't return. I felt it. I must stop him!

"NO!" I yelled, "I WILL NEVER SEE YOU AGAIN—NO PLEASE!" But he could not hear me anymore. I tripped over something, fell. I'm out of breath ....

I sit up in bed panting, gasping for air, my chest heaving.

Where am I?.. Trying to focus I reach over and turn on the light. Toby grunted.

I'm wiping sweat off my forehead and unraveling the sheets that are twisted around my legs. By the time I'm untangled, my breathing and heart rate has slowed down.

"Whew! What a weird nightmare!" This dream seemed like more then just a dream. It still played in my mind with the paralyzing fear and choking sorrow.

I go into the bathroom to splash water on my face but before I can dry off my face, the images are back and I can smell the air, smell the horses.

Such sadness…I am overtaken by sadness and begin to shake. "Oookayyy…Gracie, I say aloud, "get it together." I sit on the cold tile floor of my bathroom for a bit.

Toby comes in and whines as he looks at me with those big, whiskey eyes. "I'll be okay," I tell him with a weak laugh. He doesn't believe me, I can tell.

I look over at the counter at my prescription Xanax. Still a bit shaky, I get to my feet, dump a pill in my trembling palm and pour a glass of water.

I go out of my bedroom door and out on the balcony, for some air. The moon is full and bright, shining on the ocean. The sea air felt cool on my skin. I take some deep cleansing breaths, still feeling strange from the dream – or whatever it was.

The pill is working as I knew it would. I get back in bed. As I lay there waiting for sleep, I still can't get the images out of my mind. As I try to breathe through it, I recognize what I'm feeling. *It's grief. Massive, inconsolable, grief.*

CHAPTER 6

When I wake in the morning I'm jolted out of sleep with memories of the dream – and Sal's kiss.

I toss back the covers and do my usual morning routine, dressing in some yoga pants, a Tee shirt and sneakers. By the time I get down the stairs, Toby's already circling at the door.

"Alright buddy, just a minute," I shush him as I approach. We leave the lanai and start over the little wooden overpass to the beach only to run into Sal, standing right in the middle with a hand on either side of the wooden railings blocking the way.

"Good morning, Princess." The smooth tone of his voice makes my stomach swirl.

"Good morning, Sal," I reply, struggling to meet his gaze.

We stand for a moment looking at each other in the pre dawn light - then he gives me that little-boy grin and snakes one of his arms around my waist and with just a little force pulls me into him.

He gently reaches up and pushes a windblown curl out of the way as he holds my face in his hands and bends his head to give me another kiss. I totally surrender and it takes my breath away.

He pulls away and looks into my eyes. "Ready for a walk?"

I'm lightheaded and clutch for the railing.

"Whoa, Gracie, you okay?" He puts his hands on my arms to steady me.

I shake my head to get the ringing to stop. "Yeah, I'm fine," I whisper. "I don't know. I got a little dizzy there."

Walking quietly, he takes my hand. "Gracie, I hope I'm not moving too fast, but I have strong feelings for you and they kind of hit me out of the blue. I have to tell you, it's kind of strange but I feel like I've known you forever. I can't explain it."

I look at him and smile. "I know, I feel it, too. I have a pull towards you, have since I first saw you, I think. The thing is, I'm going through a divorce, and I don't know where I'm going to end up or where I should go. I feel like I'm in limbo and I don't want to drag you into the mess that is currently my life."

He stops walking, and looks at our hands, then raises mine up to his lips and kisses my knuckles. His exhale is warm on my skin.

"Gracie, let's just take one day at a time right now. I'll be here for you. I want you to consider me your friend and I will be patient. I have a lot of time on my hands now and I've got my own issues, but I have to tell you, being around you calms me. I feel centered and whole."

I can't believe my ears. "Really? Me? I center you?"

He chuckles. "Yes, you. Is that so hard to believe?"

"Well, yes." I say with a shake of my head. "I guess I never had anyone say that to me before."

"Well," he says with that grin that melts my heart, "first time for everything, Princess."

* * *

Walking back from the beach, fingers entwined, Sal says, "I hope you're hungry Princess, Pop's got breakfast going."

"He does?" I laugh, enjoying my new-found peace. "I usually cook him something or we just have coffee together. What's the occasion?"

Sal shrugs. "He felt like cooking and told me to tell you it's something you love."

"Oh I love everything! I say laughing as we approach the deck. Toby runs ahead of us barking and waging his tail to get into Antonio's door. "Easy boy, Sal said. As he opened the door for him. He's in there waiting on you.

Mio caro, good morning. I make-a-you favorite.

"Good morning Tony! What did you cook? Is that? Oh My God you made peppers and eggs!"

"Yes! He says laughing, and some rosemary potatoes too!"

"Smells great Pop."

With Toby underfoot, wagging and nosing around his friend Tony's wheelchair, Sal and I help Antonio move the food from the kitchen to the table.

I roll my eyes to the ceiling as I scoop up eggs and peppers and pile them on a fresh roll. Then I take a bite. That walk over the dunes this morning landed me in heaven! "Mmm…. Tony, this is so good! I haven't had this in a while," I say around a mouthful of potatoes.

"It's been way too long for me, too!" Sal chimes in. "With all the traveling I did for work it's nice to have home cooked food. By the way, did I tell you how great your baked ziti was Gracie?"

"Thanks I'm glad you enjoyed it. I enjoyed making it."

"Do you like to cook, Gracie?" he asked.

"Yes, I do," I answer after I swallow more food., "But I don't really do much of it, anymore. Cooking and baking was a good stress releaser at one time, but your father and I were both gaining a little weight and I cut back. Not good for me or Tony to get too chubby."

"What-a-you talk?" interrupted Tony with a wave if his hand and a frown on his face. "We no get-a-fat! I enjoyed all of the food you make."

"Thanks, Tony. You're very sweet." I finish the last bite of my egg sandwich and pick up my coffee mug. "I think for me, the saddest time is around the holiday season. There is no one to cook for. A house just isn't a home if there is no one to cook for." I sigh and look down at Toby who is laying at my feet. I look up at Sal and Antonio who are looking at me with big, brown puppy-eyes.

Talk about dumping cold water on a great morning! I clear my throat and give them both a grin and a wink. "Can I have more peppers and eggs please?"

Sal beats his dad to the serving spoon and I hand him my dish.

"I'm sorry. I didn't mean to sound so pitiful. I was raised around a big Italian-American family. Big family and loud holidays is what I'm used to. Now my parents are gone, my brother travels all over the world with his Green Peace stuff, and any other relatives are spread out all over the country. I just miss the holiday family overload, I guess."

Sal and Antonio nod their heads in understanding and Antonio chatters on about how his wife made all the holidays special. For the next hour we just share stories and eat, enjoying laughter and happy memories.

Sal remembered a story from one specific Christmas. He said that he and his brother Joey snooped and found their presents. Neither one of them were happy about what they were going to get, so some arguing resulted and eventually his mother found out what they'd done.

Just a little red-faced, he laughs and pokes Antonio in the arm. "She was so pissed in fact, that she made us open up our gifts on Christmas morning, then loaded us in the car with them and drove us to an orphanage. Mom made us give our presents to kids who were less fortunate." Sal shakes his head and looks past my shoulder and through the doorway to the deck. "I will never forget that Christmas. That was one lesson I learned the hard way. Joey too. We were never ungrateful again!"

I've got tears in my eyes. "Wow! I love it! I think me and Marie would have gotten along great!"

Antonio nods.

"Yes, Marie would have loved you. It's-a-too bad you never met. That would have been nice."

I smile at my old friend. "That's how I feel about my dad. The two of you would have been buddies for sure!"

After I helped clean up breakfast and Antonio went out on his deck with Toby, I let Sal know I've got to go home and check my cell phone for messages. He offers to walk over with me.

When we enter, Sal notices the twelve-foot tray ceilings and crown moldings that befit the mansion.

"Want a fifty-cent tour?" I ask. He accepts with a grin and I begin in the large foyer with the eye-popping staircase.

I show him the kitchen, the living room, the huge dining room with a table for twenty. Then the library and study, which I use for my computer.

"And this," I point, "is the mud room."

Sal knitted his eyebrows together. I bite back a laugh, but his expression is one of confusion.

"The mudroom? What's a *mudroom*?"

A laugh bursts out me like a soda that's been shaken in the heat. "I asked the same thing when I came here. It's a special room to take off your muddy boots or dirty clothes so you don't drag dirt through the house-it's right next to the laundry room."

Sal's eyebrows go up and he widens his eyes. "Ooh, fancy."

"Okay, okay... upstairs," I snarl." I show him multiple bedrooms, a playroom and bathrooms that are never used. At the end of the long hallway we enter my bedroom. He walks in and looks around.

"Nice," he says. "Did you decorate this room?"

"Yes, I got to do this room and the adjoining bathroom."

He walks into the huge bathroom and turns on some lights.

"I like the colors you picked, Gracie. You have very nice taste. Plums and gold's-I like it."

"Thanks, Sal."

He walks around gazing at the light fixtures. "I notice you have some lights out. I can fix those for you, if you want."

"Really? That would be great. I don't like ladders much and besides, it's still too high for me to reach. I have extra bulbs in this closet."

I show him the stuff in the closet and then show him the maintenance closet at the other end of the hall where I keep the six foot ladder.

While he's busy, I grab my cell phone and notice I have two missed calls and a couple of text messages.

Celine called to tell me there is a Southern Woman's Society meeting on Friday at ten in the morning to discuss the annual holiday dinner fundraiser for Children with Cancer. I find myself nodding. Although I loath that meeting with those uptight bitchy women, I do love helping to give those sick kids a great Christmas. I text Celine and tell her I will be there.

The next text is from my best friend up north, Margaret Macantire. In high school, her nickname was M&M but I've always just called her Mags. I've known her since we met in the seventh grade. My dad used to call her a Wild Irish Rose and she called him, Big Daddy. I smile at the memories of those two teasing each other.

She's a true blue friend. Never held back to tell me the truth, about anything. She is the only one who told me not to marry Richard. She couldn't explain why, she just insisted that something was wrong with the whole thing. I sigh in resignation. She was sure right.

Her text read:

Hey You!!! You have been on my mind haven't heard from ya. Call me!

Maggie has always been there for me but she's got two kids with her husband Mike, so she runs constantly. And, it doesn't help we live so far away from each other now. But I'm feeling better today than I've felt in a long time, so I eagerly text her back.

Hey You!!! Miss you! I will call you later tonight, our usual hour. Be ready, lot's to tell you!

I can hear Sal humming in the next room and I smile as I hit the icon for the voice mail. My smile disappears the second I hear his voice. *Richard.*

Grace you need to call me–NOW

I feel my shoulders sag and my stomach knot. I know that nasty tone voice and don't look forward to calling him back.

The next voice message is a bit friendlier, but my can-do mood is gone.

Hi Gracie this is Leonard Burns. I was notified by Richard's attorney that they received the papers I forwarded for Richard to produce bank statements and records of all his accounts since taking over the business. Now, they will try to fight this but I don't want you to worry, it's how the game is played, and if Richard tries to contact you I advise you to not divulge anything. I would strongly suggest that you don't talk with him at all. Have him call me if he pushes on you. If you have any questions feel free to call anytime.

A cold, clammy sweat has come over me. The tightness is building in my chest and my breath comes in waves. I sit down on the bed and peek into the bathroom. I can see Sal's feet on the ladder and he's still humming.

"How's it going?" I ask, picturing his crooked smile in my mind. The tightness let's go a little.

"Umm, okay," he says. "One of the bulbs broke in the socket so I'm going to need some tools to get it out."

I take a deep breath and try to sound as normal as possible. "In that same closet should be some tools."

"Yeah, I figured there would be," he answered. "Not what I need, though. I already checked."

"Well, be careful, okay? It would just stay burned out if it was up to me, so it can wait if it needs to."

"No problem. I'll be done in a few minutes," he tells me. "Get your calls all handled?"

I shrug, even though he can't see me. "Just about. Need to return one more, then I'm done."

Then I did something very stupid and called Richard.

Richard answers by spitting out my name and I flinch. Even sadder, we both still have each other in our phone contacts. I sigh.

"Grace, *what* is going on? What the hell did you *do*?"

I take a deep breath, hold it, then let it out. "What do you mean?"

"What are these papers? Have you any idea what you've done? What the hell are you thinking?" I can hear the venom dripping off each word but I'm not going to flinch again. "Why is your attorney digging in my business? Just what do you think is there?"

I start to shake just a little and remember that this is why I want out of this marriage. I straighten my shoulders and raise my chin. "This is what the attorney advised me to do under our circumstance—"

Richard continues his rant until I begin to feel like a helium balloon with a hole in it..

"Look Richard, this is what I was advised to do and I listen to my lawyer."

"Oh?" he snarls at me, "you listen to your lawyer? That's because you have *no* idea how business works! You've probably screwed up everything now because you *never* wanted to learn anything! Seriously Grace, you *never* think!

"Richard! Stop! Just *stop* the dramatics. What do you have to hide?" I ask, something telling me that's what's really going on. "I can't talk to you anymore unless you're going to calm down. You're always so angry! You've been an angry person ever since you took over that business."

Richard's tirade only increased in volume and viciousness. I feel hot tears fill my eyes and my heart is pounding in my ears. Then the heavy feeling in my chest creeps in, I gasp for air and realize I shouldn't have called him back at all. I hit End Call.

I wipe the tears off my face, suck in as much air as I can and turn around. Sal is standing just outside the bathroom doorway, his face oddly blank.

"Gracie, are you okay? Jesus, Was that Richard yelling at you? I heard him all the way over here!"

I can only nod, and then the floodgate of tears cascades down my face and I feel like a real fool. I start across the room to go in the bathroom but Sal stops me by putting his hands on each of my wrists.

"Hey... , Gracie, calm down. Shhh... He pulls me gently against his chest. "You're shaking! Can you tell me what the hell that was all about?"

I pull away and he lets me go, but I can feel him watching me. I go to my sink and splash water on my face, then grab a towel that only serves to catch more tears. I've lost it and I'm not sure I'll ever get the tears to stop. When I manage to look up, Sal is just standing there looking torn between love and murder. I almost laugh except I might just laugh myself into an asylum, so I don't let it out.

"Princess," he says softly, "we're friends, right? Please tell me what's going on. Might help to talk it out."

I take a shuddery breath and fill him in on the call, Richard's tirade and how stupid I feel for calling him back. I reach to the counter for my prescription bottles.

"What's that for?" he asks. I hold out the one bottle and show him it's my prescription for Xanax.

"This helps calm down the panic attacks." I reach for another bottle. "This one is a mild sleeping pill to help me sleep at night. I take them as needed."

Sal takes the little yellow bottles in his big palm and looks at them. When he glances at me, his eyebrows are bunched together and he's sporting a serious frown on his lips.

"Gracie," he starts softly, "when did you start taking these?"

I shrug my shoulders "Right before Rich and I decided to separate. It's unbelievable what your nerves can do to you."

"No," Sal says, shaking his head, "it's unbelievable that Richard is such a selfish bastard. You gave him your heart and then he neglected it. He broke your spirit instead of building you up. He's a taker-he took it all from you and never gave anything back, and now you're disconnected. That's why you're getting panic attacks." He let out a slow sigh. "Princess, you are not crazy. You are not stupid. You're hurt, but this stuff isn't going to help."

Hearing Sal's words, I can't stop the new tears and I clutch the soggy towel to my sore eyes. He might think I'm not crazy, but I'm not so sure anymore. Why couldn't I see what he just pointed out?

"Shhh...Gracie, don't cry. Don't you see? Your heart and soul is so open because you're a very loving and generous person. I figured that out in just a few conversations with you. Look at the way you are with Pop—you have a good heart. It's just been crushed." He puts down the prescription bottles, then takes the towel out of my hands and gently wipes my cheeks. After he tosses the towel in the sink basin, he takes my face in his hands.

"Look at me."

I gaze into his warm brown eyes. In a low, calm voice, he says, "Good. Now breathe nice and slow. Good. Deep breaths. Come on, do it with me, Gracie. Breathe. Keep your eyes on me—I'm here. That's it. Keep going. One more deep breath. Good. Better?"

I keep my eyes on his and my body relaxes and my breathing straightens out. Maybe I *can* beat this awful stuff.

"Yes," I whisper, "better, thank you. How did you know to do that?"

He shrugs and shakes his head, then wraps me in his arms.

"You don't need those meds to calm you. You just need your heart and soul to be whole again. Can you promise me something?" He lifts my chin to tilt my face up to his and nods toward the prescription bottles.

"Promise me that you won't use these medications. I will help you. You need rebuilding not masking, and you have to promise me that you won't talk to Richard again – at least not without your lawyer there. Listen to your lawyer. Capisce principessa? He says with a cute smirk.

I nod, beginning to feel human again I almost smile. "Capisce!"

"Good!" he says, then gives me a chaste kiss, scoops me up in his arms and puts me down on the bed. I'm giggling when he grabs my hand and looks closely at me. "Feeling better?"

I'm tired from the emotion, the tears, the anger, but I do feel better. "Yes I am, thank you, Sal. That was really sweet what you did. If only Richard knew to do things like that, maybe our marriage would have turned out different. He hardly ever touched me."

Sal looks down at the floor and his lips form a thin line—then he lets out a big breath and lets go of my hands.

"Don't take this the wrong way, but, his loss is my gain!" Looking at me out the corner of his eye, he flashes me a sexy smile and wiggles his eyebrows up and down.

I can't keep a straight face and burst into a loud, gaspy fit of laughter.

"Ah there it is," he says. "There's that contagious laugh of yours! Listen, why don't you just relax for a while. I gotta go into town with Pop but why don't I take you out later, get some dinner? Or a movie? What ever you want. I'd like to take you on a proper date, how's that sound?"

"That sounds great!" I say, thinking this day has been quite a roller coaster.

"I'll see you around 6 then?"

I nod. "Sounds great," I say, wondering if I'm crazy to let this thing between us grow.

He bends down a little and gives me a good solid kiss before he heads down the stairs.

"Thanks again for working on the lights and.. and, everything!"

"My pleasure Gracie I'll see you later."

* * *

I go down to check on Toby who came in the house when Sal left. After a thorough petting and some Toby kisses, I ran back upstairs to call Celine. She answered quickly.

"Hello, Darlin! What shakin?" she drawls. I smile.

Like a teenager, I'm ready to rattle off my past two days. I fight the urge and take a breath and collapse on my bed.

"Are you sitting down?" I begin. "Oh my god have I got news for you!" I tell Celine all about the drive into town, and lunch, then the kiss, and the dream, and everything else!

"He's taking me out tonight–dinner and stuff. I'm a little nervous, but in a good way. I swear it's like we've known each other all along, he's so familiar."

Celine is quiet for just about a second. "I KNEW IT!" she yells. I knew you were gonna turn his head. Now listen to me baby, don't go thinkin' too much, just try to have fun and let him put some spark back those eyes of yours. Remember, he's got baggage, too. Did he ever tell you about any of it?"

"No," I answer, "but, I thought I'd bring that up at dinner before I go jumping into a romance."

Celine makes a tsk sound with her tongue. "What did I tell you? Just have fun–no strings!"

"Celine, I told you, I can't do that. That's just not me. I'm just not that kind of person."

Celine exhales loudly. "I know, baby, I just thought it would help. You're such a giving person and you got a heart of gold–I just want you to have fun. But do what you gotta do."

"I know you mean well Celine, but I'm to the point that I might not want to let anyone in. I could never go through the pain of this kind of rejection again."

"Well Darlin', have fun on your date tonight. Who knows? Maybe Sal's the one! Talk to you later and see you Friday morning at ten for the meeting."

"Oh yes, the meeting. Celine, I'll call you soon!"

Before I can say goodbye, Celine chimes in and says, "Soon? You better call me tomorrow and tell me every dirty detail of this date!"

I laugh and it feels damned good. "No problem, but I don't think there will be much to report.."

CHAPTER 7

Toby and I hopped in the Jeep and headed for town to fuel up with groceries and gasoline.

While driving through town I spotted Antonio's van in the lot at the medical building, and I figured Sal was there for his orthopedic doctor's appointment. Though tempted to wait for them, I also feared that Toby would polish off the groceries, so I headed for home.

Toby was sprawled on the kitchen floor as I put away groceries. Twice I stopped in my tracks realizing that I was humming and grinning like a little kid. I have a date! My insides felt like a family of butterflies had moved in.

* * *

I get out of the shower and wrap a towel around me. I pad into the closet and sigh at my limited selection of stunning outfits.

Finally, I figure a pair of really nice dark jeans and a loose blouse that ties at the shoulders should work fine. I decide to finish off my look with a pair of four-inch platform sandals. I leave everything on the hanger and check the time. The clock reads, 4:00 PM. I have two hours till date time. I'm having more fun today than I've had in years. Hell, maybe in forever.

I have no idea why, but it took me a full two hours to get ready. I had a glass of wine in between applying makeup and putting on my jeans, just to calm the jitters.

With Toby fed and filled in on my plans for the evening, I let him out for a few minutes. That's when I hear the beast come to life! My heart's pounding with excitement and I see Sal leave the garage to make his way around to my house. I call for Toby to come inside, then wait for the doorbell.

I answer the door. There's Sal freshly showered and smelling of cologne. He too has on a nice pair of dark blue jeans with a white tailored shirt and a black vest. His hair is brushed back off his face, hanging in loose curls to his collar. I just stare in awe, hoping I'm not drooling, but even if I am, I can't do anything about it. His laughter breaks the spell.

"Hello, Gracie, you ready to go?" he asks. Before I can answer, he grabs me around the waist and gives me another toe-curling kiss. When he lets me go, I can feel my face turning the color of a ripe watermelon.

"You look beautiful! I've been waiting all day for that kiss," he says with his little half smile.

We drive the Beast along A1A and enjoy the beachside breeze. Sal pulls into Bistro Mediterranean, which sits right on the beach.

When Sal opens the door and ushers me inside, I catch my breath. It's like something out of a fairy tale, with small, candle lit tables set with black tablecloths.

A pretty blonde woman at a hostess desk welcomes us with a warm smile.

"We have reservations," Sal says, holding my hand at his side. He gives her his name and she consults the book on her desk.

"Right this way, Mr. Petroni." Her accent isn't Italian, but she certainly has one that rolls the "r" and makes it sound musical. I giggle and Sal squeezes my hand.

"After you, Princess." He lets my hand go and I feel a light touch at the small of my back as he guides me through the tables.

We follow the hostess to a quaint little table overlooking the ocean. The pinks and violets of the setting sun in the sky is very romantic.

"You really are beautiful tonight," he whispers as he settles his cloth napkin in his lap.

I roll my eyes and turn bright red judging from the heat in my cheeks. "Sal, you're embarrassing me!" I laughed waving my hand at him.

"Sorry," he says with a big smile playing on his lips, "but you really have got to learn how to take compliments."

Before I can take a sip of my water, the tuxedo-clad waiter comes up to the table and introduces himself as Gerard. In his French accent, he asks if we would care for cocktails or a bottle of wine.

Sal looks up at him and starts speaking French like a native. All I can do is listen and stare like a deer caught in headlights. I check to make sure my mouth isn't hanging open.

Sal looks over to me. "Gracie, would you like red or white wine tonight?"

Wine? All of that sexy talk is about wine? French is almost as sexy as Italian, I decide. "R-Red. I would like red."

Sal continues in French. I can only make out *Boujoules* or *Bordeaux.*

"Very well *monsieur.*" The waiter answers with a bow and leaves us.

"Okay," I start with a wrinkle in my nose, "I know you speak Italian, but French too?"

Sal laughs. "I speak a bunch of different languages: Spanish, German, Russian, Farsi, French. Had to learn it for my work."

The waiter comes back with our bottle of wine and makes Sal test it before pouring it for us. Sal approves and Gerard fills our glasses and puts the bottle on the table. He leaves us to look over the menu.

"So you had to learn to speak all those languages for work? What exactly was your job with the military?"

Sal takes a big gulp of his wine and sits back in his chair like someone has let the air out of him. "I was Special Ops. I can't really tell you much, but I had to go to a lot of different countries and stay there for months. Sometimes a year."

I raise my eyebrows. "You can't tell me much? What the hell were you, like 007? James Bond stuff?" I joke.

There's no smile on his face. "Close. I guess you could say that."

The waiter returns to find me in stunned silence again and asks if we have questions about the menu.

"Oh?" I say, "I didn't even look at it yet."

Sal looks at Gerard and has yet another French conversation. Hearing several words that I can figure out, I gather Sal is ordering our dinner.

Gerard responds with, "Superb *monsieur*, I'll bring you some bread."

Sal picks up his wineglass and smiles, but I sense he's uncertain. I smile back. I wonder if he's not as confident about this date as he'd have me think.

"I hope you don't mind but I ordered for both of us. I talked with Pop, he said you're not very picky. I ordered a couple of appetizers to try and then a surf and turf entrée. Will that be okay?"

Now I grin at him. "Well, you did good with the entrées but what else did you order?"

"You'll see," he says with a wink. "I think you'll be fine with it."

I press on with the conversation about his job. I want to know where he has been, what he's seen. I want to know everything about him.

"Sal, did you ever have to kill anyone?" I ask in a whisper, expecting him to laugh his head off.

"Yes, Gracie," he answers in a very quiet voice. He holds my gaze with his, his promise to be honest with me ringing in my ears.

"I have killed." He blows out a sigh, a look of sadness crosses his face and is gone so fast maybe I imagined it. "I don't like to talk about it."

I watch as the look on his face turns serious and dark. I get a little nervous because he looks like he disappeared for a moment.

"Hey," I say, hoping to bring him back to me, "it's okay. You don't have to talk about any of it. I'm sorry, I'm just curious. I want to know all about the man who calls me beautiful and gives me passionate kisses when I least expect it."

Sal smiles and raises his wineglass. "Here's to us and our new start in life."

We clink glasses and like the genie in the bottle, Gerard appears with our bread, followed by another server with two dishes. Gerard takes them from him and places them on our table. "Enjoy!" he says.

I look down at the plate and see escargot. Sal is looking at me with eyebrows raised, waiting for my reaction.

"I *love* escargot!" I nearly shout.

He draws in a breathy sigh of relief. "I thought you would, but I took a big guess. Pop was right – you do have a love for good food!"

"Yes, I suppose I do," I say as I pick up my tiny fork and aim for the butter and garlic soaked snail. "My parents owned a small Italian restaurant in New York City when I was very young. I think when you're raised around the cultures that a big city offers you, I guess you just get accustomed to a different variety of foods. I am *not* finicky when it comes to food. I have had some friends that just could not eat or even try new things, which is a little sad, I think."

I'm relieved to see that Sal's relaxing again now that we've gotten away from the topic of his work history. Odd that I can be so comfortable with a person who has killed people, and yet somehow, I understand him and I'm not afraid of him.

He asks me all about my life growing up, and what kind of student I was and how many boyfriends I had. I answered his questions until we finished our meal and all the wine.

"Don't get dessert," he says, "there is somewhere I want to go."

"Okay!" I say sounding a little too giddy and definitely buzzed.

Sal pays the check and with his arm firmly around my waist to help steady tipsy me on my four inch heels, we leave the restaurant laughing like children. His laughter stirs something deep inside me that assures me I will always be all right with him. Before we step off the curb, someone calls my name. "Grace?"

Thanks to the wine and the company, I don't freeze, but my stomach lurches just a little. Sal's arm tightens as we turn toward the voice. I'm sobering up fast.

We stand staring at Richard and Camille. I'm ready to run, Sal holds me tight against his side.

"What are you doing here?" Richard asks.

"Ummm, we had dinner?" *What else would we be doing at a restaurant?*

"Hello." he says to Sal, and sticks out his hand. "I'm Richard Boumont, Grace's husband."

I thought Camille was going to swallow her tongue.

"Really, Richard," Camille chimes in, "you're practically divorced. Hi, I'm Camille James, Richard's fiancée. And *you* are?"

I quickly answer. "This is Salvatore Petroni."

"Oh?" says Camille. "How long have you been dating? You two seem pretty close."

"It's still in the getting-to-know-you stage but—"

Sal cuts me off mid sentence. "Yes, we are close. I'm working on some of Gracie's trust issues. You know the ones that come with betrayal and cruelty?"

Camille's standing there with her mouth hanging open. Richard on the other hand, apparently hasn't heard a word that Sal's said.

Richard is still repeating Sal's last name. "Petroni..Petroni. I know that name. You're not Antonio's son are you?"

"Yes, I am," Sal answers.

"I thought you were like off in the military for life or something. Never met you before."

Sal nods slightly. "I was a Marine, I served, I'm done. Now if you two will excuse us, we're going to finish with our date. Good night."

"Grace, call me tomorrow," Richard calls to my back. "We have things to discuss."

I stop and turn and Sal stands beside me. "No, we don't Richard. I have nothing to talk to you about. Talk to my lawyer."

Sal turns us and we walk in silence back to the car.

We get in the car and Sal motions to me with a lift of his cleft chin. "You all right?"

"I'm fine." I say with a chuckle. "That was fun. I'm glad you were with me, it helped, but, I think it's killing my buzz."

"Well, I think I have just the fix!" he says. He drives up the road a few miles and pulls into Guido's Gelato.

"Oooh," I croon, "I love gelato!" "I thought you might." He parks the car, helps me get out of the low seat and we walk inside to a flavor list that's longer than the constitution.

"What would you like, Gracie?" Sal asks me.

"Okay," I say. "You ready for this? I want a scoop of the cappuccino flavor and a scoop of strawberry cheesecake!" I look at him with my mouth in a yummy smile.

"Gracie, you have dimples! I never noticed them before."

I put my hands on my cheeks and feel their heat. Sal grabs my hands and pulls them away from my face.

"Stop, they're adorable," he says. "Don't be embarrassed. I never want you to be embarrassed with me. You have no reason to be."

We get our treats and head outside. I'm two spoons into mine when I lean over to see what's in his cup.

"What is yours?" I ask with a mouthful of my weird combination.

He smiles and says, "Amaretto."

"Oh, I like that, too!" I tell him. "I like the liqueur, it was always a favorite of mine." Sal laughs.

"Is there anything you don't like, Gracie?"

"Ummm... not really?" I laugh with him.

"Ahh good, you're laughing," he says. "I like when you're laughing". He points to the beach. "Walk with me, Princess?"

"Oh.." I say, wrinkling my nose. "I don't think I have the right shoes for walking on the sand."

Sal looks down at my feet and back up at me with a look of determination. He hands me his gelato, then kneels down and taps one of my feet.

"Lift" he says. He slid off one of my sandals then does the same with the other foot. Then he rolls up the bottoms of my jeans and pats my feet. He removes his shoes too and places our footwear in the car.

"Okay," he says, swiping his hands together. "Problem solved."

We walk out to the beach, both of us quiet as we eat our gelato's.

"Gracie, what was the biggest thing Richard did during the time you two were married that made you upset with him?"

"That's a difficult question," I say. "Well, it just wasn't one thing. But if I had to put it in a nutshell, I guess after a while I felt I was a problem to him, like an obstacle in his way. I think he thought I was holding him back because I wanted my husband home with me and he put business first." I stopped walking and faced the ocean.

"He would bring clients home for dinner or he would take them out. In the beginning I would go with them, then he decided it was better if I wasn't around. He said I was an embarrassment because I couldn't keep up with the business conversations. I would get tired and yawn out of boredom no matter how I fought it. Clients would joke and ask if they were keeping me up. Rich didn't think it was funny.

"He would never come to my defense. He always thought I was the one who wasn't trying hard enough or I should take the time to learn the business. But I never had any interest in it and he couldn't understand that. It wasn't any problem when we married, only after he inherited the family business. Then I was supposed to be some corporate wife of an up and coming tycoon." I could feel Sal's eyes on me.

"This would cause fights?"

"Oh, big ones," I answer. "I was always wrong, in his eyes." I start to walk again, Sal at my side. "Maybe I could have tried harder, I don't know. At some point maybe I realized it wouldn't make any difference and then I'd have lost myself, too."

"Gracie did he ever hit you?" Sal asks softly.

"No, just the verbal fights. I would cry and that would piss him off even more. I truly don't know him like I thought I did. The things he would get mad at me for were so stupid. The way he would yell at me sometimes scared me. I thought he was going crazy and needed help."

We start to walk back toward the dunes. Sal tosses our empty cups in the garbage pail. "All of this happened after he took over the company, you said?" Sal asks, reaching for my hand again.

"Sort of. I saw some early signs, but yeah, it got really bad after that.."

"Sal, why did you want to know all this?"

"Because I want to make sure I don't make any of the same mistakes, but I think its pretty safe to say that I don't think I can. Now I can't say people don't have fights, but I would never disrespect you like he did."

I stop walking, Sal turns to look at me, I'm so overwhelmed with emotion, I look away. Sal searches my face, then captures it in his hands and gently draws me into him.

His kiss is electric and as he presses me against him I can feel him harden through his jeans.

As our tongues seek each other, I'm almost gasping for breath, but it's not anxiety driving my breathlessness. When we stop to take a breath, he brushes the hair out of my eyes like he has done before. That little gesture is such a small thing, but it's the act of caring that impacts me.

Sal can be as affectionate as I used to be, long to be. I'm falling for him and it terrifies me.

Still and quiet Sal just holds me, the waves crashing on the shore and the wind surrounding us.

"Lets get you home Princess, before we're doing something you might regret."

I laugh. "You have been the perfect gentleman."

"Thank you," he says with an exaggerated bow. "I've got to take my time with you and be patient. You can trust me." Then something makes him laugh. "If you told Pop I wasn't, he would kick my ass!" We laugh together for a moment. "Come on lets go," he says, leading me back to the car.

We got back to the Viper and started for home. On the way he pulled out a Nickel Back CD. "I love these guys, you?"

"Yes very much!" I answer.

Soon the car is filled with the song Far Away; Sal holds my hand the whole way home. I feel so completely safe.

*   *   *

"I'll be right back." I say once we're back at my place and he's pouring us Amarettos. "I'm going to change my clothes."

I run upstairs and change into my yoga pants and a tee shirt and clip my frizzy hair back.

Downstairs, I spot Sal. His shirt's untucked and the vest is on the arm of the couch. I like how he looks in my living room and I just look at his back for a minute. Then I come up behind him and wrap my arms around his waist.

He turns, smiles, and reaches down to the side table. "Here you go," he says, handing me a little glass of the amber colored liquid over ice. We clink our glasses.

"Salute," we toast in unison.

"Let's go sit over on the couch," I say, pointing with my thumb.

He sits squarely in the middle and I curl up on the corner tucking my legs up under me. Sal takes a long sip and closes his eyes..

"What time do you go to bed?" he asks.

"When I'm tired," I answer. "But tonight I'm waiting till after midnight. I have a close friend I grew up with back north. We call each other at midnight. It's our special time."

Sal's eyebrows form that frown I'm learning to recognize. "Why is it a special time?"

I smile. "She has two daughters and a husband. At the time when I was married too, we found it hard to catch up if everyone was around, so we'd wait till everyone is asleep. This way we are not disturbed."

"Ahhh." he says, "I see. So am I here to keep you awake till midnight?"

I giggle and sip my drink. "Busted," I say with a laugh.

"So, what are your plans for tomorrow?"

"Well, twice a month I take Toby over to the nursing home and to the children's hospital too. Everyone loves to pet or play with a dog and Toby loves the attention."

"That's really cool, Gracie."

"Yeah, I love to see the kid's faces. It makes them so happy. Staying at a hospital for a kid can be so devastating and boring. Going to the nursing home, well, it makes some of the elderly calmer. Would you like to come with us?"

"Oh, I would love to but tomorrow I got a couple of appointments. But another time, definitely."

I incline my head toward him. "More doctor's appointments?"

"Yeah," he says. "No big deal."

"Sal, why do you need all these appointments? Is there something else going on? You can talk to me. You know a lot of all my crap."

He tosses back the rest of his Amaretto like a shot and puts the glass down on the coffee table. Leaning forward, he puts his elbows on his knees and takes a deep breath.

"No, I will tell you someday, but not right now. Can I ask for you to trust me when I say I'm okay and you just don't need to know all this right now?"

"Alright..." I say, feeling sad that again I've made him unhappy somehow. "I'm sorry, I didn't—"

"No, no, no..." he says softly. "Stop. No need for you to be sorry, it's perfectly fine for you to ask me anything. Just some stuff I might not be able to answer at this time."

He reaches a hand over and grabs my arm and pulls me to him. "Do you trust me? Gracie?"

I look him in the eyes. "I want to..."

He exhales through his nose, then coaxes my chin upward. "I won't lie to you, not ever. Will you believe me? Please?"

I take in a deep breath, feeling as though I'm on the edge of a very high ledge, being asked to let go of my lifeline. I let out the breath I have been holding and look at him. "Okaaay... I'll trust you, Sal."

"Good. I want you to believe it."

He draws me into him and kisses me as we slowly fall back in the sofa, his mouth is sealed over mine. His hands rub up the sides if my ribs and around my back.

Suddenly his hands still and he lifts his head. He looks right into my eyes as if he is searching for something.

"Gracie, if I fall for you, are you going to break my heart?"

I suck in a breath. "I could ask you the same question."

He smiles at my comment. "I think we have a lot of trust issues to work on. I know your heart is broken, Gracie. I want to help you heal, teach you to trust again. We will take it one day at a time."

He gets up and pulls me to me feet. "I'm gonna go now, before this goes too fast. Besides, you have a phone call to make in half an hour."

We said our goodnights at the door after another nuclear kiss.

I watch him pull out of my driveway, then I let Toby have a quick sniff and pee before we head upstairs to get ready for bed. After slipping into my jammies and climbing into bed I send Maggie a text.

READY?

And right on cue, my cell phone rings.

CHAPTER 8

"I miss you, Mags! I got lot's going on but how is your world?"

"Oh, crazy-wonderful," she says. "Kids and Mike keep me busy and for now, knock on wood, there is no drama. Two teenage girls Gracie, creates too much drama. I don't remember us having all this drama at their age–did we?

I laugh because a quick replay of some maddening situations runs across my mind.

"You know, I think we did, Mags, but every generation has their own, I think."

She sighed. "Yeah, I suppose you're right. Then we grow up and have adult drama. Speaking of adult drama - what's going on with dick head?"

"Really? You want to go there already?" I let out a sigh and fill her in on Richard's latest outburst with me.

Maggie bursts into laughter. "Good! I hope it's killing him. And still yelling at you I see. Same old, same old there. I guess some shit never changes."

"No," I reply. "Oh, and to top it off I went on a date tonight and we ran into Richard and Camille. What a downer that was!"

"Okay..What? Wait a minute, Gracie. Just when were you going to tell me you are dating someone? How dare you not fill me in? Who is he? How long have you be seeing him? Come on, spill *now*!"

"Okay, okay! Geezz, don't get your panties in a bunch!" I tell her about my first date in way too long. "Long story short, his name is Salvatore Petroni. Antonio's son."

"You're kidding!" she cut in. "I thought he lived in Napa California?"

"No, no. That's Joe. This is his other son, Sal. Until a few weeks ago, he was career military. Special stuff that I don't know much about. But, this is why I wanted to catch up with you.

"Listen Maggie, when Sal and I first met it was like deja vue. I felt like I knew him and he said the same about me. We have been spending some time together, but here's the really weird thing. I had a dream about him but it felt like more than a dream. I can't explain it but that dream haunted me the whole next day. Even now when I think about it my stomach turns."

"Tell me about it," she prompts.

She doesn't interrupt me even once, but when I'm done, I hear her let out a breath.

"Gracie," she says, "maybe it was some kind of premonition. You've been through a bad deal – hell, you've been through a rough few years. If you have any more dreams try to stay calm and focused. Maybe something is trying to tell you something!

"So, tell me, how does he kiss? Did you have sex yet? What does he look like? Text me a picture!"

"Oh, you're impossible, Maggie."

"I know, that's why you love me!"

I fill her in on Sal's kisses, our plans to take it slow and build on a good friendship. She tells me to have fun, just like Celine did.

"Will do my best." "Remember what your mom used to tell us?" Maggie asks softly. "Always

82

keep them on their toes girls, make them wonder about you!"

We both broke into laughter remembering my mother's helpful tips on dating when we were teens.

"Yes, I remember. I miss my parents, Mags. Some days I could really use their help."

"I know, sweetie," she says. "I miss your parents too, they were the best!"

"Okay, Mags I'm hanging up before I start crying - I'm sick of crying. Good night, kiss the girls and punch Mike in the arm for me!"

"You bet, Gracie. Hey, keep me filled in and oh, a picture please! Don't forget."

"Shut up, Maggie. Go to bed!"

Giggling, she says, "Sleep well my friend. Love you."

* * *

Toby and I wake in the morning to the moans of the wind whipping around the mansion. Every now and then it howled, making Toby cock his head to one side, then the other. He looked so comical I started my day with a giggle.

Getting up to check the weather outside I open the balcony door, only to have the wind rip it out of my hands. "Holy crap" I gasp. Nice way to bring in October first, over cast and windy. *Looks like fall at least.*

Sal is waiting by my lanai door when Toby and I come out for our morning walk on the beach. "Good morning, Princess and Toby!" he says with a big, toothy smile.

"Morning! You been waiting long or are you stalking me now?" I look at him and bat my eyelashes.

"Cute," he says. "Hey Toby, how's the big boy?" he reaches out to pat Toby on the head. Toby snorts and takes off ahead of us. "Is your dog ever going to like me?"

I shrug. "Maybe he's jealous."

As we walk onto the beach, Sal takes my hand. "I want your cell number. I forgot to ask for it last night."

I realize I don't have his either, so we key in each other's numbers. I'm listed under *Princess*. Shaking my head, I smile. "Really?"

He laughs. "What? That's who you are to me."

I laugh. "Yeah, well, you're Crazy to me - but that's not how I put you in my phone."

He stops and tugs at my wrist just hard enough that I stumble into him. He catches me with a kiss.

"Now, that's a proper good morning," he says. "Did you talk with your friend last night?"

"As a matter of fact I did!" I miss Maggie, I love when we catch up, we make each other laugh, its like free therapy!"

"Good! He says, I like you a little more frisky."

I laugh and push him away and continue walking, the wind whipping the sand at us so hard it stings. I can see some surfers off in the distance, loving the waves.

He takes my hand again, that small gesture makes me float. I wondered if he notices.

"So tell me something. After the divorce, are you going to use your maiden name or keep the Boumont? And while I'm asking, what was your maiden name?"

I take a deep breath and ponder for a moment. "Hmmm... well," I begin, "I haven't thought much about it. It's probably easier to keep Boumont. I won't have to change things like my license and passport and all that stuff. Also, as much as I hate it, the name can open some doors. That's always helpful."

"Yeah, I suppose," he mumbles.

"My maiden name is D'Anella."

"Gracie Anna D'Anella?" It sounds like a song lyric when he says it. "That's a beautiful name.

It fits you because you are beautiful, inside and out."

He makes me feel so special Even the way he says my name makes me feel special. Tucked close together in the sand, we sit and watch the waves roll in and laugh at Toby running away as each one crashes just off the sandbar.

"Poor baby can't swim. I thought it was the waves that threw him off, but I tried to get him in the pool, and he's not having any of it. I'm lucky I get him in the shower to bathe him."

Sal's eyebrows draw together. "I thought all dogs can swim?"

"Oh no. Some just never get the hang of it. In Toby's case, he has a fear of it, he won't go near it. When I go in the ocean he barks and whines at me until I come out. He's afraid even for me!"

Sal takes my hand in his. "Do you miss working with dogs?"

I nod. "I'll tell you something-they are nicer than most humans."

We laugh, kiss and play with Toby until we spot Antonio out on his deck. He's waving his hands, then holds up a mug and points at it.

"Pop's up, he must have made coffee. Come on let's go, you ready?" Sal asked as he helped me up from the sand and brushed it off my butt. He whistled at Toby and we all started back to get some breakfast with Antonio and begin our day.

*   *   *

Miles south on the beach, at the massive high rise condominium The Boumont, Camille James sat at a big dining room table eating breakfast, with her cell phone in her hand. She shared the penthouse suite with Richard who of course owned the building. She was delighted to have a small staff to care for the two-story home which had every amenity including a private infinity pool.

She was in the midst of a text conversation when Richard came in for breakfast.

"Camille, who could you already be talking to so early in the morning?"

"Oh, just a girlfriend, darling. Just girl talk is all."

Richard picked up the newspaper and Rosa came quickly in to pour him some coffee.

"Breakfast today, Mr. Richard?" Rosa asked in her Cuban accent.

"Just some whole wheat toast and fruit will be fine." Richard replied evenly.

Camille resisted a smile. Good old Richard. No good mornings, or thank yous or pleases for him. Pleasantries were not a necessity in his world unless it was around business.

She put down her phone and looked at him.

"So, how do you feel about bumping into Gracie last night?"

Richard took a sip of coffee and snapped down a corner of the paper to look in Camille's direction.

"I feel fine, why? She was drunk and acting characteristically juvenile, giggling like a schoolgirl on a date. She should behave more properly when in public. She still carries my name. She should be more...respectful."

"Oh Richard, that was no date, those two are a couple. So she was a little tipsy. It's called fun, Richard."

He cocked an eyebrow. "What do you mean they're a couple?"

Camille put down her coffee. "You couldn't tell? That guy Sal was holding her like he was protecting her. I suspect they've known each other for a good while."

"It's possible," Richard pondered. "He is Antonio's son. She spends a lot of time over there."

Camille cleared her throat, changing the subject. "How are things going in accounting? Did Gracie's attorney get what he needed?"

Rosa came in with Richard's toast; he waited till she was gone to answer.

"Mostly yes, but I was told of some accounting mistakes. Some monies are missing. Not too big of a deal - I'm sure it's just human error. Don't worry Camille, it's not your concern." He went back to his paper and his breakfast.

Camille sat staring across the table at the paper, relieved and angered at the same time. Her mind raced. How she hated it every time Richard told her things were not her concern. But how she loved the good life and penthouse living.

She picked up her phone and continued with her text conversation.

* * *

With a tender kiss and a quick hug, Sal is off to an early appointment and I'm just finishing cleaning up our breakfast mess in Antonio's kitchen. I turn from the sink and almost end up in Tony's lap.

"Oh Tony," I gasp, clutching my chest, "I didn't see you!"

"Caro," he says, "come-a-sit. I want to talk with you."

I follow him into the living room and face him. His expression is so serious, my heart skips a beat. "Everything okay?"

"You and-a my son, is he treating you good?"

I smile. "Yes, he treats me very nice. Sal has been the perfect gentlemen."

"Good," he says with a nod. "Because I will kill-a-him if he is not!"

I break into laughter and assure Antonio that his son and I are taking it one day at a time.

"That's-a-good idea. You are both broken, maybe it's a good thing you two found-a-each other. I wasn't too happy about it at first, but both of you have changed. Tell me mio caro, have you been sleeping better?"

"Yes I have, although, I did have an intense dream." I tell Antonio all about the dream and he looks concerned.

"Some-a-times, caro, dreams are a way the mind and soul heal. Tell me, do you still take the pills to help-a-you sleep?"

"No, I made a promise to Sal I wouldn't use them anymore."

"I don't know if-a-my son tell you, but he no sleep so good either. But he has been doing better too, he is not so short tempered, he seems calmer, I think-a-because of you, Gracie."

I feel my face getting red but I can't keep a smile from my face. My heart is full with emotion. "Thanks, Tony, I think we are helping each other, but, Sal doesn't tell me much about his life, and he wants so much for me to trust him. And, I do to a point. I hope he can trust me enough to let me in."

"My Son has seen a lot Gracie, I think-a-something happen to him and he needs time, he don't talk-a-to me either. I ask him and he just say nothing. He will get there and I can-a-see my son adores you. How can he not mio caro"

I get to my feet. "Okay, okay. I'm blushing and you're going to make me cry. I've got places to be and kids to cheer up! Want to go with me?"

"Si, yes!" Antonio replies. I come! We can use-a-my van."

"Great," I answer. "I'm going to go home and get ready, Toby and I will be back here in say an hour or less?"

"I'll be ready!"

* * *

Antonio's van is equipped for his wheelchair and all the gears are up by the steering wheel so he can maneuver the van all with his hands. I learned to drive it a while back just in case he needs to get somewhere but doesn't feel up to driving.

We arrive at the nursing home first and parade Toby up and down the halls, saying hello to some of the staff. We pop into a few rooms so the patients can pet Toby or toss a ball to play fetch.

Some of the residents even have treats for him and Toby also knows where they hide the human treats, too. On more then one occasion Toby has found cookies, candies, even a cigarette or two.

About two hours later, we go across town and into the City of Jacksonville to the children's hospital.

"This is the best," I say to Antonio as we come through the automatic doors into the lobby area. "I love watching these kids light up when Toby comes in."

"Yes it is, Gracie, yes it is. You go on ahead, I'm gonna go get-a-some balloons in the gift shop. I meet-a-you upstairs."

When Toby and I get up to the fifth and begin our walk down the hall to the game room, the doctors and nurses call out to us.

"Where you guys been?"

"We thought maybe you weren't coming today..."

I laugh and wave as Toby leads the way, trotting down the hall like he owns the place. When we get to the game room, an older doctor on the floor is watching the excitement. "I don't know who is more excited, the kids or Toby. It's a nice thing you do here for them, Mrs. Boumont," he says.

Again I cringe at being referred to as Mrs. Boumont. "Gracie, please call me Gracie," I insist.

"Hi, kids! How is everyone today?" I ask in the cheeriest voice I have.

"Fine," they answer collectively.

I look around and many are not fine. They've got scars and shunts. Some have no hair or run about in special wheelchairs. But they always have big smiles. Some visits, they tell me what procedure they just had done and how brave they were. Some days I have to try really hard not to cry.

"CIAO BAMBINO'S!" Antonio calls in his big Santa Clause booming voice.

"How's-a-everyone today?" The kids all go running to him as if he really is Santa! They share their same stories with Antonio as he hands out the balloons. He talks to some of the kids that, like Antonio, are in wheelchairs, too. I notice a tear or two in his eyes as well.

For a couple of hours we talk, color, play games and do tricks with Toby. But they tire easily and we can't outstay our welcome. We wish the kids healthy blessings and say our good-bye's.

* * *

"I'll drop-a-you at your front door so you and Toby don't get wet," Antonio says. "The weather is getting nasty."

"Really, it's not so bad. A little wind and rain, that's all. Thanks Tony, for coming with us and driving. The kids love you!"

"Oh I love-a-to go, it makes me feel good."

He pulls in my driveway. "Okay caro right to-a-your front door."

I get out of the van and Toby jumps out behind me and heads to the door. I'm still saying good bye and thank you to Antonio when I hear Toby growl.

"What's the matter, Toby?" I ask, walking to see what's wrong. My stomach drops to my feet and my heart begins to thump. I turn back to Antonio and yell, "Someone's broken in!"

"Get back in the van, Gracie. Don't go in-a-the house! Come back. Come sit in the van."

I scramble back into the van. Toby is still standing near the door, stiff as a board with his hackles and ears up on full alert. Antonio is already talking on his cell phone.

"The police are on their way. Stay here, Gracie, don't move. Capisce?"

"Y-y-yeaa..." I stutter. Antonio reaches in front of me to get to the glove compartment and takes out a gun. I can feel the color drain out of my face.

"You have a gun in here?" I squeal.

"I always carry a gun, Gracie. You stay put!"

He wheels himself out of the driver's seat and to the side door that slides open. The van has a chair lift that lowers him down and out the door. With just a push of a button, he comes around my side.

"You might want to call Salvatore, give him a heads up."

He's so calm I swallow to get my panic under control. I nod rapidly several times. I find Sal's contact on my cell.

"Hello, Princess—

"Sal! I think someone has broken into my house and your dad has gone in there. He's got Toby and a gun!"

"Where are you?" he yelled.

"I'm outside in the van. My front door was busted in..hello?..hello? Sal?" "Shit, the call dropped!"

But it didn't. I look up and there is Sal running toward me.

"Gracie, are you okay?" he says on an exhale breath.

"Yes. But Tony's in there with a *gun* and my *dog*!"

Sal opens the door and reaches a hand to touch my face. "Breathe, Gracie. Pop's a good shot and chances are no one is in there. Did you call the police?"

"Yes, your father did."

"Stay put!" he commands. "I'm going in." Sal turns to go in my house and reaches around to the small of his back and pulls out a gun of his own.

"You, too?" I yell at him.

He turns and puts a finger to his lips to hush me. I snap my lips shut and clench my hands together in my lap. Oh god.. "be careful" I mouth to him. I close my eyes, I can hear my heart beat in my ears. I remember to breathe and turn to look at the house.

Finally two police cars and four officers arrive and I let out a long sigh. . A cop approaches me while I sit in the van with the door open.

"Hello, Mrs. Boumont?" I grind my teeth at the sound of my name. " Gracie. Please, just call me Gracie."

"Okay, Gracie. I'm Officer Dan. Can you tell me what happened?"

"I came home to find my doorknob busted and the door open. Antonio Petroni and his son Sal are in there. They're armed - tell the others not to shoot them!"

The officer smiles. "We know Antonio. It's fine. Has anyone come out?"

"No. I'm worried." I give my head a shake to stop the ringing that's started in my head.

"Have you heard gun shots?"

"N-n-no."

"Well, that's a good sign then," he said. "Whoever it was that broke in is probably gone. But it's a big house, so let us check it all out for you, It's gonna be fine. Just stay right here and be calm."

I nod and thank him. The other policemen all file into my house. Officer Dan follows behind them while conversing with someone on his walkie talkie.

Fifteen agonizing minutes later, Sal and that same officer come out to get me. Sal reaches for my hand.

"Come on, it's clear. Come inside. We have to show you something." Sal puts his arm around my waist and guides me into the house.

At first glance everything seems normal and untouched. "Gracie," Sal says calmly, "go into the study."

Like a robot I do as instructed. I enter the study where a small cabinet that housed a safe is tuned over and smashed. The safe was broken into and is empty.

Do you know what was in here?" Sal asks.

"I didn't have anything in it. Richard told me he didn't either. I think that's been empty since my father-in-law passed away. I was told he used it for important documents and some of my mother-in-law's jewelry. So as far as I know, it's been empty for a few years."

Officer Dan looked at me. "Where is the stuff now?" he asks. "Who has it?"

"Richard does, I guess." I look at the floor. "We're in the process of divorce. "He uses safety deposit boxes because of something just like this happening."

The officer writes his notes and then looks at me again. I don't see any judgements and somehow that makes this a little easier.

"Okay, ma'am we will call Mr. Boumont and ask him some questions."

Antonio's voice booms from the hallway. "Some-a-one knew where the safe was! They went right to it, nothing else just—a-that! It's someone who knows-a-this house!

I look up at Sal who is nodding in agreement. Officer Dan gets a strange look on his face. "One more question ma'am, and we have to ask, do you know of anyone who would want to harm you or has anyone threatened you at all lately?"

"No not at all." I answer.

"How's the divorce going? Friendly or ugly?" he asks quietly.

I shrug and feel Sal move a step closer to me. "Is there such a thing as a friendly divorce? Richard and I are working things out through the lawyers. He isn't to happy right now.."

He looks at me a long moment, then he closes his notebook. "Okay, we're going to check for finger prints and see if we can find some answers for you. Since nothing's out of order in here, if you'll contain your movements to the kitchen, that would be best. We're going to have a crew working this."

Sal took my hand. "Come on, come with me." He sits me down on a barstool by the counter and hands me a bottle of water. "Drink this."

I open the bottle, take a long sip and stare into space.

"Gracie, look at me." I only move my eyes in his direction. The rest of me is somehow suspended, disconnected.

"You okay?" he continues. "Talk to me, you look a little pale."

"I'm.... I'm..okay.... but I totally feel violated."

He touches my arm with his fingertips. I look at him. "I want to know something," he says, "why was your alarm not set?"

"Not set?" I say like a parrot. Then it dawns on me and I sit straighter. "You're right, Sal, it wasn't going off! I always set it. *Always!*"

Oh my god, Antonio's right! Whoever broke in knew more than just where the safe was. Just then, Antonio joins us in the kitchen with the same thought.

"Gracie, the alarm was set? Yes?"

"Yes Tony," I say, looking at him and two of the officers. "I always set the alarm."

Antonio and Sal glance at each other in that silent communication they seem to have, then

Antonio follows the other two officers out of the room.

"You sure you're okay now?" he asks.

"Yeah, I'm good," I assure him. Can't have him thinking I'm always going to be a basket case, can I? "I'm glad you and Antonio are here with me, though."

Sal takes my hands and kisses them. "Listen, I'm going to stay here with you tonight so you're not alone."

"Oh?" I say, a little surprised. Umm, you don't have to..."

"Gracie, I am staying here with you or you are going to stay with us over at Pop's. Either way you are not staying alone. I agree this is an inside job and we don't know what the hell we're dealing with. You are not alone anymore. You have me."

He comes over to me around the counter, wedges himself between my knees and gently takes my face in his hands so we are eye to eye.. "Princess, you are not alone. Not anymore. I won't let anything or anyone hurt you, do you understand me?" I nod. "Good," he says with a smug smile on his lips. "Now which is it, here or over there?"

"Here I guess."

"Okay then." He coaxed up my chin and brushed his lips with mine.

"Hey, Casanova, Antonio cut in abruptly, you gonna stay with her tonight?" Sal slowly broke our kiss, never moving his smoldering eyes from mine he smiled.

"Yeah pop I'll be right here."

CHAPTER 9

The police are winding things up and I'm in the sitting room, curled up on the couch with a cup of tea. Sal and Antonio are in the kitchen with Officer Dan, so I watch as the weather changes from a dreary drizzle to a dark, nasty thunderstorm. Since I'm still feeling slightly out-of-body, I'm glad to let my two protectors handle things. I'm jarred out my daze by a voice I never thought I'd have to hear in this house again.

"Where is everyone? Hello?"
"I'm in here," I call from the couch.
Richard enters the room, dripping wet, giving me a crazed look.
"What?" I ask, uncurling from my comfortable spot and plunking down my tea cup on the table.
"A *towel* would be nice, Grace."
"Really, Richard? You know where they are - help yourself."
He stalks off mumbling under his breath and on cue, there's Sal watching Richard go off in a huff.
"Did he just ask you for a towel?"
"Yep," I snap.
"He didn't ask what happened or how you are? Just a towel?"

"Yep," I reply again. So frustrated, I'm not all that sure I'm capable of much more in terms of answers, but I'd better get myself together.

Drying himself off and looking all kinds of annoyed, Richard re-enters the room.

"Well, what happened Grace?" he barks.

I take a deep breath. *Here we go...* I give him the short version.

"I came home the doorknob was broken and the door was ajar, whoever it was went right to the study, no where else. They busted the cabinet that holds the safe."

"Was the alarm set, Grace? I know how scatterbrained you can be – you used to always forget." I sigh. But, something's shifted in me. His comment doesn't bait me. "Yes Richard, the alarm was set. Someone knew the damn code."

"Did you give it to someone? One of your leech friends, maybe?" he snarls.

Okay, I'm done being pushed around by this dick. "What? Richard have you lost your mind? Why would I give any of my friends the alarm code?"

"Who knows what you do Grace or why? You trust everyone. Do the police have anything yet?"

"I don't know. They are just getting finished."

"Do you know anything at all, Grace?"

His sarcasm is obnoxious and I don't want to talk to him any more. I really want him out of the house. I look at him and then glance at Sal who's standing there with fists clenched. I don't need another scene, though, either. My anxiety issues are already on overload.

"Well?" Richard asks me again as if I'm two years old.

Sal takes a step towards Richard. "She's told you what she knows. The police are looking forward to questioning you. It's good you stopped by, though I wonder why you did. Oh, and Gracie is fine by the way. She was a little terrified but we calmed her down. Thanks for asking."

"I didn't ask, *Romeo*, I can see she is fine."

Richard turns and stalks off to go talk with the police. As he's walking away I flip him my middle finger. Sal blinks his big brown eyes in disbelief and then bursts into laughter.

"Do you believe him?" I say, shaking my head. *What did I ever see in him?*

Sal gets his laughter under control to answer me. "No," he says, "but I know his type though. Controlling, everyone is wrong except him, his way or no way–how am I doing?"

I confirm his assessment with a grin. We don't have much quiet time, though.

"Grace," Richard yells from the foyer.

I look at Sal. "I truly hate when he calls my name. It literally makes my skin crawl."

Sal reaches out a hand to help me off the couch. "Let's go see what his problem is. I just hope I don't have to hit him."

Putting my arm around Sal, I smile. "Get in line," I joke.

Richard and Officer Dan are in the foyer. "We didn't get any prints from the safe itself, or, curiously, the doorjamb or the desk. I suspect they used gloves and it looks like someone wiped down the area, too. No prints at all – not even yours," he says to me. "Are your fingerprints on file?" he asks, almost as an afterthought.

"Sure. I had to be fingerprinted before I could take Toby to the children's hospital."

Richard is tapping on the alarm panel.

"The code last used was mine? How the hell did someone get *my* code?"

Officer Dan watched as Richard hit more buttons on the keypad. "Good question, I'd say. Mr. Boumont, did you give your code to anyone who would want to get in here and steal anything? Where were you at today?"

Richard looks over at Officer Dan and if looks could kill, the cop would have dropped right there. "Are you seriously thinking I would have something to with this?" The tone of his voice dripping in attitude

Officer Dan shook his head. "My job is to gather information, sir. I'm not accusing you of anything. But maybe accidentally you did–you could have given your code to—"

Richard's rage is visible and I step just behind Sal. My breathing is an indication that I'm not as calm and collected as I thought I was.

"I DON'T ACCIDENTALLY DO ANYTHING! Unlike Grace, I watch every word and move I make. I have been telling her for years that when you have this kind of status you must take extra precautions. She never understood that."

Richard's words, as always, were starting to slowly unravel me. I forced a breath and cleared my throat. Sal bends his head a little to look in my face. "Gracie, you alright?"

"No, I'm not..." The room is beginning to move around me. Never a good sign.

"Richard," Sal snaps, "why don't you just back off now? Gracie is upset and you're making it worse. I think everyone needs to go. Now. You all have what you need."

Richard puts his hands on his hips. "Leave? You all seem to forget this is my house and I am allowing Grace to stay here until the divorce is final."

"How generous of you," Sal shoots back sarcastically.

"Yes, it *is* generous," Richard snips at Sal. "The least she can do is be more careful. "You'll see, you just wait, she'll wear you down too." Richard glanced in my direction.

"She never cared about anything I did for her, did you Grace? I move her to a beach with a big house and she complained about *all* of it. Did you tell him that Grace?"

I can feel hot tears burning in my eyes and a lump choking my throat.

"I said that's enough for today!" Sal yells, putting his six feet-two inch frame in front of Richard's slighter five feet seven inches.

"Did you ever ask her if that's what she wanted or if she was happy?! You come in here like a bull practically accusing Gracie for getting robbed! You don't even show the courtesy of asking how she is, or if she was hurt, or.."

Antonio yells something in Italian, cutting Sal off mid sentence; Sal backs off, but just a little. Officer Dan steps in between the two men.

"You should leave Mr. Boumont, before a simple break-in turns into domestic violence. If Mrs. Boumont has the court's permission to be in the house during divorce procedures, then it really doesn't matter if you own it. Her rights come first. She is very upset, and I think we did all we can do today. I have enough info to work with, thank you, Mrs. Boumont. We will do all we can. We'll be in touch. I'm sure with Antonio and Sal near, you will be safe and secure. Try to relax."

I thank him – and all of them – for their help and ask them to call me as soon as they have any new information.

Richard takes out a business card and hands it to Officer Dan. "You'd be better to call me," he says with a sneer.

The officer takes the card and cocks an eyebrow at Richard. "Oh don't worry, Mr. Boumont, you can count on it."

After the police escorted Richard to his car, the three of us returned to the parlor.

Sal looks over at his father and speaks again in fluent Italian. Antonio answers him. Back and forth they go, their voices getting louder and hotter by the moment.

"ENOUGH!" I scream. "Stop! I don't understand what you're saying and you're arguing. I have had enough!"

Antonio's expression is part surprise, part shame. He nods that lovely silver head that I love. "Caro, we see things different. My son is ready to go on a mission half cocked over this–I tell him to just wait. The police are-a-my friends. I want to see what they come up with then we can go from-a-there."

Sal takes my hands in his, "Gracie, I know people. I want to make some calls, phone in a few favors. I can probably get answers a little faster then the cops."

I look over at Antonio. "Is that such a bad thing, Tony?"

"Look you two, let's not step on-a-toes in the county. Some-a-times some of the cops are on-a-the take but Danny is clean, he's a good cop, I knew his father. He and I agree this was not a random burglary like what I encountered years ago, let him poke around, when he finds some-a-thing, then, only then we call in the favors. Please, Gracie, Salvatore, trust me. I know what-a-to do."

I look back at Sal, his face twisted in a smirk, his chocolate velvet eyes piercing mine, hands on his hips, looking like a little boy who just got punked. He's adorable.

I cock an eyebrow at him. "I say we give the old guy a shot, what could it hurt?"

Sal drops his hands and laughs, shaking his head. "Okay fine, but as soon as we know something, it's my turn."

* * *

The thunderstorm raged the rest of the afternoon. Sal returned before dark, shower-fresh and wearing a tee shirt, sweats and slippers. He had some 2x4's under one arm, a bag of nails and a hammer. In the other hand, a small box that said, *PHOTOS* in black marker. He drops the supplies on the floor in the foyer.

"Wanna help? Come hold the front door steady for me so I can nail these boards to it and keep it secure. The locksmith will be here in the morning."

"Thanks. It's been open so long today, I forgot about it not locking," I say. "Thought I'd make some homemade chicken soup for dinner, are you hungry?

"Sure, that sounds great. I'll help you."

Once the door is good and secure, Sal and I venture to the kitchen. I hand him a bottle of wine and the corkscrew, then I take out onions, celery, and carrots from the fridge.

Sal pours us each some wine, we clink our glasses and take a sip. With wine still on his lips, he leans in and kisses me, slow and long. I taste the wine, feel the heat, feel my own heat building deep inside.

I feel his hands in my hair, then he moves them down my back...he presses me into him. His kiss got deeper. This breathlessness is to die for and I feel as though I'm melting from the inside out. Sal's Kisses always feel like his life depended on it. I squeeze my fingers in his hard muscled arms and surrender to it. It terrifies me and yet it feels right.

When he lets me go, we stand there in each other's arms, foreheads together and out of breath.

"Gracie." His whisper is thick. I put my hands on his chest and back away, just a little.

I clear my throat. *Whew!* "What do you say we start that soup?"

His crooked smile touches my heart. "Give me a knife," he says. "I'll chop."

"You like to cook?" I ask.

"Yeah, I know my way around a kitchen."

"I can see that," I say, "and other things as well." He flashed me a big smile then shook his head.

"So tell me Sal, what else were you and your father fighting about earlier? I may not have understood all the words but anyone could tell there was more going on than you guys are sharing with me."

"I figured you might have caught that," he said, as he put some olive oil in a pre-heated pot with chopped garlic and tossed in the rest of the ingredients.

"Pop wanted me to back off Richard. He was afraid I was going to hit him and make things worse." He put the knife and cutting board in the sink.

"I go to counseling to work on controlling my anger. I know I haven't told you everything, yet." He took a deep breath and exhaled. "Okay, here goes. I've seen a lot of crap. The military programs you like a machine; to fight, to kill. Quantico programs you in other countless ways. For lack of a better term, now that I'm out, I'm being deprogrammed. And, I'm making progress. But, when I see how Richard treats you, or when I think anything is going to harm you, I tend to loose it a little."

He turns back to the pot and stirs at the mixture. I bring over the boxes of broth and some chopped chicken and dump it in. He continues to stir for a few minutes, then lowers the heat and puts the lid on.

I take out a loaf of Italian bread and began slicing it. Sal comes up behind me, puts his hands at my waist and turns me around.

"You're quiet. What's wrong?" He lifts my chin to look in my eyes.

"You could have told me this from the beginning," I say. "I thought all your doctor visits were about physical therapy for your shoulder. Your father did mention there was some kind of counseling but I guess I really didn't understand."

"My shoulder is nothing. That heals, but my mind never turns off. I didn't want to tell you a lot of this because I didn't want to scare you away. And it's not easy to talk about."

I look right into his brown eyes. "That wouldn't have scared me, but hiding stuff about yourself does."

"I'm sorry. My bad–you forgive me? I promise I will tell you everything in time when I can. I told you, you can trust me, Gracie."

A five letter word that changes so much. *Trust*.

Part of me did trust him. Part of me wondered about this mysterious man who was falling for me. My spy guy - who speaks ten different languages, has killed for the government, has a gun, has lived all over the world.

I can't imagine what he sees in me.

* * *

"Come sit here next to me–I brought something to show you," he said, patting the couch cushion next to him. He picked up the small box marked PHOTOS and handed it to me. "Open it up."

I lifted the lid and picked up all kinds of pictures. Some of Sal, and some with his mom. Sal with his brother Joe; "Look here," he pointed, "that's me at high school graduation.

"That's you?" I laughed. "Look at your hair, you look like a Bon Jovi wanna be! Were you in a hair band?"

"Okaaayyy," he said laughing, "I bet you got some big hair pictures yourself."

"Oh I do, and I think I was a blonde in one or two of them."

He showed me his Marine picture and pictures of his buddies when they were stationed over seas.

"Your father has pictures up in the house of your brother and your mom, but I only saw one of you as a young boy. He didn't really ever talk about you, Sal. What happened? What went wrong with you two?"

Sal felt his smile melt away and he watched Gracie tense up. She was so fragile in a way....

"I'm sorry, you don't have to tell me..I didn't mean to..."

"No no it's okay," he cut in. If he got this out now, his worst nightmare would begin to heal. Would the truth cost him her heart? He took the box from her hands.

"My father doesn't know, that, umm—around the time that mom got sick, I was in Bosnia. It was supposed to be a routine job, I was with the C.I.A by then. The mission was to get in, get our guys, blow up the base, get out." Sal hesitated for a moment, glanced at Gracie. Took another breath.

"We were ambushed from behind. Our people on the inside gave us false information. These were people we thought we could trust. They pulled the rug out from under us. I led my team right into a pile of shit. I lost some really good men. Me and two others were captured. We got thrown in a prison. I was in that hell for a year. That's why I didn't make it home. It took a year to get us rescued, even then, they didn't know if we were alive or dead. I spent another year back in DC getting medical and psychological treatment. I didn't want my father to know while mom was sick, then dying. To tell them I was MIA, I couldn't do it to them. He thinks I took an assignment because I couldn't handle my mom dying. I would have been with her the whole time if I could. But I would rather him think what he thinks than for him to know I was captured and tortured."

"Oh my god Sal," I whispered. "I think you need to tell him. Your mom is gone now I think

Antonio should know this. I can't even begin to imagine what you have seen or been through. You are so lucky to be alive."

He knew that now, though for many months he cursed every breath. "One night," he said, "I was beaten within an inch of my life. I knew I had a concussion, maybe even a skull fracture. They threw me back in my cell and I passed out. Later, I dreamt of my mother; she begged me to hang on; said she was watching over me and everything would be okay. I swear that's when I knew she must have passed on. I believe she was really there and she got me through. A few months later we were rescued."

Sal looked at the pain on Gracie's face and had to look away. He wasn't a hero, he was just a survivor. But since meeting Gracie, he'd never been to glad that he did. She reached over to touch his arm.

"Hey, I'm not sure I know what to say. But I'm glad you told me—it must be hard to talk about."

He leaned over Gracie and pulled her down beside him on the couch. He had to hold her. Needed to feel her arms around him.

"It's getting easier now that you are part of my life, Gracie. You're helping me in so many ways you don't even know."

"I think I understand, Sal. You are helping me too."

They lay on the couch for a moment curled in each other's arms, Sal's chin resting on the top of her head. She reached up and touched his shoulder, feeling the little scar.

"Sal, can I ask you one more thing?"

"You're going to ask me how I got shot."

"I was, but if you can't, or maybe if it's too much?"

Sal's body vibrated as he quietly chuckled. "It's fine, Princess, it's really kind of stupid actually. We had a mission in Egypt—you might have seen it on the news—they had an uprising of sorts. Anyway, we get there to help protect our embassy. The rebels there started firing guns at each other in the streets. We were getting one of our ambassadors in a car to get him to a secure location, and that's when I saw this insurgent come around firing his weapon. I jumped him and got hit by a stray bullet that actually bounced off the car and grazed my shoulder. The adrenaline at the time was so high I didn't know I was hit until we finally got in the car and one of the other agents told me." She sucked in her breath and he held her just a little tighter.

"Are you kidding me? Dear god, Sal! How do you go through all you have been through and you're basically functioning everyday? No wonder you can't sleep!"

"It's getting better, Gracie," he said. "And talking with you about it seems easier."

She gently rubbed his chest. "So, what happened after you got shot?"

"They bandaged me up, sent me back to Quantico for evaluation. They know I'm good, but they think I've seen and done enough. They want me to retire. They will give me just about anything I want—its not much mind you—but I will be comfortable. It's just a hard adjustment."

Without words, she tightened her arms around him in response. He could feel something loosening inside. It's her, he realized. She calms me deep inside.

Was she the healing he wanted so desperately?

CHAPTER 10

"What time is it?" I ask. Sal got up and helped me off the couch. "It's about 9:30 or so he said, you should go up to bed, I'll be right here."
 "Sal you don't have to stay on the couch.."
 "Gracie. He cut in. It's all right. I want to be down here to watch the house. Whoever broke in knows too much, and they know you live alone. I'll stay down here with Toby if he will stay with me. And you know I don't sleep so well."
 "Okay fine. I..I just thought, umm- meant, there are other bedrooms and,..or,.. you could stay with me we don't have to..."
  Sal pulls me to him and gives me a slow deep kiss. When he pulled away he searched my face. "I'm staying down here,"
 "Sal, we are adults, I meant just sleep." He smiles and raises an eyebrow at me. He slowly lifted my chin and put his lips on mine. Our kiss is fire. I feel it burn all the way to my core. Sal's hands explore my body. I start to tremble nervously as he kisses down the side of my jaw to my neck and collarbone. He could feel me quiver in his touch. When his lips and tongue made the slow journey back to my ear, he whispers, "You're not ready."

* * *

With Sal tucked in on the couch as my protector on the first floor, and Toby on the foot of my bed to keep me safe upstairs, I'm laying here thinking about everything that's happened today. Who the hell broke in here and what are they looking for?

I can't help but smile at the wonder that Sal and Antonio are to me. A few short weeks ago, I was so flat lined about my life I couldn't see from one day to the next. But these two special men have made such a difference for me.

One is like a father to me, helping and guiding me with so much. And then there's Sal, this wonderful handsome man who I'm falling for, who is taking his time with my heart and wants nothing but my trust. A man strong on the outside but so tortured on the inside.

I battle more tears as I consider his revelations this evening. I can't begin to imagine what else he endured in that God forsaking prison. The thought wrecks me. I hope he can tell Antonio the truth soon about where he was and what happened to him. I think Antonio would want to know.

It's amazing how close Sal and I are and how easy it is to talk to him. He's so familiar to me that I still feel like I've known him all my life. Not for one minute did I experience anything like this with Richard....

Soon, the heavy pull of sleep enters my eyes, and the sound I hear is the rain beating on the house.

* * *

Looking out a window I see rain, I feel overwhelmingly sad. I have been crying. A door opens and closes. I look up. It's Sal, but it doesn't look like him, his hair is very short. And he has a mustache. He is wearing some kind of uniform, forest green jacket, narrowed leg trousers and copper tack buttons on his suspenders.

"Come, it's time", he says, the bus is set to arrive shortly. "Dry your eyes, my love. You know there is nothing I can do, it's my duty. I will be back before you know it."

"Where are they stationing you? Did they tell you?" I ask.

He leans over to pick up his hat off the bed, a U.S. military campaign hat with a light tan hat cord around the top.

"Yes, I'm being sent to the port of Saint Nazaire in France. I will be with the Sixteenth Infantry."

I stand and put my arms around him. "I'm so scared. What will I do if I lose you?"

"All will be fine. Now be my strong, little Princess and see me off. I promise my love, I will come back to you."

The familiar, suffocating feeling of sadness is over taking me. My vision gets so murky I can't see.

I'm in complete darkness. Suddenly, I'm so cold. A biting cold wind blows dry autumn leaves around my high-button shoes and around my long skirt. I bundle my long overcoat tighter to keep the chill off.

Looking around, I'm on a busy city street. I hear a boy yelling, "PAPER, GET YOUR PAPER!" I hear people talking, something about bad news overseas.

"What's happening? I cry out. A man with a handle bar mustache turns in my direction.

"Terrible news," he states., "Seems the Germans raided the trenches on November the second. We lost most of the Sixteenth Infantry."

I felt like I was electrocuted! I started to run as fast as the long skirt would allow, the tears running down my face.

"No! Dear God, No!" I cried as I ran. I couldn't see where I was going, running in the biting cold wind.

I knew he was gone. The man I loved would not be coming home. Running, screaming, someone is trying to stop me.

"Let go!" I snarl, struggling to free myself.

"Gracie." Someone has my arms and they won't let me go. I want to run.

"LET ME GO!" I shriek.

"Gracie, wake up!"

"Sal?" I say, dry mouthed and out of breath.

"Shhh. You're safe. You were having a nightmare–sit up."

He reaches over to my lamp and turns it on. The light hurts my eyes for a second and then I realize the tears are real.

"Oh God, Sal, I had an *awful* dream."

"No kidding. You scared the shit out of me, Princess. I was checking around downstairs with Toby and we heard you scream. I thought someone broke in again. I heard you yelling *no* over and over. You want to tell me about it?"

"No, not really," I whispered. "I mean, it makes me sad." As I say the words I start to cry, big hot tears.

"Gracie, what the hell did you dream? You must have had a bad nightmare. Shhh.. You're safe. It's okay," he said, strong hands smoothing my hair away from my face. "Let me get you some water."

While I wait I look down at Toby who's wagging his tail and whining softly.

Sal is back in a minute with a glass of ice water with him.

"Here, drink this," he says, handing me the glass.

I chug it down. It's soothing on my slightly sore throat.

"You going to tell me what you were dreaming about that was causing you scream like that?" he asks as he sits on the bed next to me. Toby jumps up to join in on the conversation and rests his big furry head in my lap.

"Okay," I huff. "I dreamt you went off to war and then I got news you weren't coming back. But everything was so real. I saw and felt everything as if I was there!"

"I'm sorry, sweetheart. You know I fought in Iraq and Afghanistan, Gracie. But here I am - I came back! No more stories for you, they give you nightmares."

"No, Sal, you don't understand. It wasn't now, it was World War I. I saw it. I saw your uniform and a..a.. date! I have a date! November second. You were with the Sixteenth Infantry."

"That's pretty specific Gracie," Sal says cocking his head and frowning in confusion. "You are a vivid dreamer, but it was just a bad dream. Probably due to all of the things I told you earlier."

I shake my head and clutch his hand. I need to make him understand that it's more than a dream – but I don't understand it myself.

"Sal, this isn't the first one I had. I had a dream shortly after we met, and again you went off to fight in a war, and in that dream you were on a horse in blue coat."

"What, like The Revolutionary War?"

"That's the one!"

"Gracie, you knew I was military from the start. I'm sure you're just having random dreams. They'll probably go away in time."

"These dreams freak me out. I truly feel as though I'm there - it feels so real. I have had regular dreams, these are more then dreams."

"Because they're nightmares," he says, "they mess with your mind." He gets a tissue, wipes at my face and takes the empty glass from my hand.

"Gracie, you're shaking. Hey, look at me." I shift my gaze to his. He gives me a smile. "Breathe, Gracie. Keep your eyes on mine. Take a deep breath and let it out, now breathe. Again with me–that's it Gracie, innn...ooout. Keep it steady, breathe...."

In a few minutes I stop shaking and my heart doesn't feel like it's going to leap out of my chest. The tears are about done, too. *He is so good for me...*

"Thank you, Sal. You always know how to pull me out of the panic."

"Well, you are so welcome, Princess. I am at your service." He bows playfully. "Now go back to bed."

I can't bear the idea that the dream will come back. "Sal? Do you mind staying until I fall back to sleep?"

"I can, but only if Toby doesn't mind."

Sal walks around to the other side of the bed, plops himself on top of the blanket and fixes the pillows behind him. I hand him the T.V. remote and get comfortable. Toby scoots up higher and closer to me so he's lying between us.

Sal looks at Toby, then at me and shakes his head. "Okay, I get the hint, buddy."

I giggle and turn off the light. I snuggle with Toby and feel the smile on my face linger a little longer. Sal reaches over, gives Toby a scratch, then takes my hand and holds it. I close my eyes.

I feel good. I feel safe. I feel happy.

* * *

The sun is up when I wake and I hurry through my morning routine, anxious to find out where Sal and Toby have gotten to.

I can smell bacon and coffee as I make my way down the stairs. Since Toby doesn't cook, I know it's got to be Sal and before I get to the kitchen, I'm wearing a grin that hurts.

I stop just a ways back to peek at Sal cooking in my kitchen. Except for my grumbling stomach, I stand in silence watching him fry bacon and slice fruit and cheeses. He's shirtless and his black sweat pants are slung low on his narrow hips. The muscles in his arms and chest are well defined and from here I can see scars across his back and my stomach knots.

As he slices he's tossing a piece of cheese at Toby every now and again and when Toby snags it, Sal says, *touch down, good boy.* I have to put my hand over my mouth to muffle my laughter.

"Good morning, Princess. You going to stand there and stare at me or you gonna come here and kiss me hello? Coffee is ready, come get some. He points with the busy spatula at the coffee maker.

"How did you know I was standing there? I was quiet and behind a wall. Is that a spy thing?" I ask as I shuffle into the kitchen.

He laughs and I realize how I love that sound. "Let's just say I am very observant of my surroundings, especially when they are as beautiful as you." He kisses me, two quick ones on the mouth.

"I over slept," I mutter as I reach for a coffee mug. "I have to take Toby for his walk."

"Nope," Sal says, "I already did that. And I borrowed your car—we went up to the grocery and got a few extra things for breakfast—hope you're hungry. I didn't want to wake you, you were out cold. You needed to sleep."

"*We* went to the grocery?" I ask as I fix my coffee.

"Toby and I." He turns to flash me a smile.

"Toby went in the car with you?" *Wow.* "*Really?*"

"Yeah, I guess he's coming around to me. Maybe he trusts me now."

"You took my car?"

"Yeah, that was okay right? I hope. I didn't think Toby would like the Beast much. I found your keys in your closet next to your purse. I put air in your tires by the way–you're going to need new ones in the front–they're a little bald. And I checked your oil–needs a change, so I'll do that after breakfast.

I stand there holding my mug of coffee, just totally amazed. *Whose life did I wake up in? Because mine doesn't look like this!*

Sal laughs. "Earth to Gracie – you okay? Come back, look at me."

I move my eyes in his direction.

"Ah good, she's back. You kind of went away there on me. You okay?"

I nod. "Umm, yeah, I'm just---speechless! You did a lot already wow."

"It's a nice day out," he says, "go outside and sit at the table with your coffee. Pop is out there waiting for you to get up."

While I'm not sure yet that I'm awake and in the real world, I pad my way out to the lanai where I find Antonio with coffee and the newspaper. I stop short when I see the table is set with dishes, flatware and glasses filled with juice.

"Good morning, mio caro. I hear you sleep-a-well?"

"Morning, Tony," I say, still trying to wrap my head around the wonderful things going on in my house.

"You feel okay today? I hear you had a nightmare last-a-night."

I nod. "I did, but, Sal helped me through it. Did I get elves visit here last night?" I ask as I motion with my hand at the wonder of the set breakfast table.

"No caro,", says Antonio with a laugh. My Marie taught-a-the boys well and how to take care of their woman. You like?"

"Oh, I like." *I really, really like.*

Antonio lifts a finger and winks. "Real men Gracie, take care of-a-the one they love. Capisce?"

I nod in agreement. *Does Sal love me already?* Just as that thought sends me spinning, Sal appears with a tray of food.

"Here we go; we got bacon, scrambled eggs, fruit, cheese, and some whole wheat toast. Gracie? What do you want?" he asks grinning ear to ear.

"I want it all Sal," I say as I stand up from my chair, wrap my arms around him and gave him a big hug.

"You know, I think I'm going to make you breakfast more often!" He kisses the top of my head.

When we are almost done eating, Sal's cell phone chirps.

"The locksmith is here. I'm gonna go let him in." I start to get up and Sal tells me to finish eating—he'll handle it. I have to admit, I'm not used to being pampered, but holy hell, I sure could get used to it.

I look over at Antonio. "What do you think happened here yesterday while we were out?" I asked him.

"I don't know caro, but I have-a-some ideas."

"Like?" I ask, waving my hands for him to continue.

"Okay, first," he begins, "they didn't have a key or did they? The doorknob is busted but-a-the way it is broken, seems like it was an afterthought to make it look like they broke in. Some of the grooves that-a-don't make sense to me, they are on-a-the inside of the door."

"Oh, really? I would have never realized that."

Antonio nods. All his years of security work are paying off for me, too. "Yes, and-a-they knew the house, or at least they knew where to go. They knew where the safe was too, right to that cabinet, nothing else in-a-the house was disturbed."

"That's true. I just wish I knew what they thought they were gonna find."

"When did Richard take-a-the stuff out of the safe?" he asked.

"Shortly after his mom died. He said he put it all in safety deposit boxes."

"Does he have all of it there?" Antonio asked.

"Well, everything that was his. His mother left me one of her diamond necklaces. It's a simple necklace, but, the diamonds are pristine. She lent it to me on our wedding day–when I gave it back to her, she told me that since I loved it so much, one day I would have it. It was really very sweet."

"Gracie, where is that necklace now?

"I keep it in a safety deposit box at the bank. I got one just for that necklace. I don't really have expensive jewelry lying around since it's not really my thing anyway, but, that necklace is worth at least $5,000. And it has special meaning for me so I wanted to keep it safe.

"Who else but-a-you or Richard would know these things?"

"That's a good question, Tony. Back then we had help in the house. And Rich brought home the clients for dinner parties that he and Camille were trying to win over."

I can see Tony's mental wheels spinning.

"Alright, Gracie, I'm-a-gonna think about what-a-you say, maybe something click."

I get up to start clearing the table. As I enter the kitchen, Sal is standing there talking with a man who's holding a clipboard. I can hear the buzz of a drill and some banging coming from the foyer.

"Gracie, this is Pete from the Alarm Company. He is going to change your alarm system and upgrade it. Give you a new code–one that no has, including Richard."

"Wait, is that going to be more money? Maybe we should tell Rich..."

"Not at all, ma'am," Pete says. "The upgrade has been over due and it's in your contract, so there will be no extra charge."

"Oh, okay! Great! Carry on." I tell him with a chuckle.

I walk over to the front door and spot a short stocky man with black hair and glasses working on my new doorknob and lock. He has tattoos up and down his arms, and the way he is talking to a young boy who is helping him, I hear a distinct New York accent. I smile and say hello.

"How ya doin." he replies in a deep voice.

Sal comes up from behind me and puts his hands on my shoulders. "Gracie, this is Louie Locks. Louie, this is my girlfriend, Gracie."

Hearing Sal introduce me as his girlfriend sends a butterfly brigade through my body. "I hear you had some trouble yesterday," Lou says. Don't worry 'bout a 'ting Gracie, were gonna hook ya up real good. Those bastards won't be able tah get in here again, I can god dam guarantee ya that!"

"That's good to know, Lou. Thanks for your help."

Don't mention it. Me and Sal here, we go way back. I would do anything for him."

"Great! Well, I leave you to it. Nice to meet you!"

Sal and I walk back out on the lanai and I elbow him in the side. "Why do I get the feeling the door isn't going to cost me anything either?"

"Because it's not. I've known Lou a long time. He's a good guy. Believe him when he says no one is breaking in that lock again."

"Sal, I don't know what to say. Seriously, I'm overwhelmed with emotion right now. How can I ever re pay you for all this?"

"Gracie, I don't know what kind of friends you have, but there is no pay back. He furrows his eyebrows at me. You're part of my life now. I'm falling in love with you–in case you need me to tell you that. You will never have to pay me back or have to fight for a spot in my life because I want you there. I need you in it. Do you understand?" He wraps those strong arms around me and pulls me into a hug. With my head pressed against his bare chest, a sigh of relief leaves my gut.

I glance at Antonio who is still sitting at the table with his little black book and cell phone. He looks at us with a smile and a wink.

*   *   *

The next day, after Toby, Sal and I, had our morning walk and breakfast. Sal left on his motorcycle to his therapy appointment. I went home to do some cleaning, pay some bills on the computer, and do some laundry.

I also decided I should call Celine and Maggie and fill them in on the good and bad news going on around here.

Maggie was pleased to hear that I am all right and no one got hurt. She told me to keep her posted and she is thrilled Sal and I are making progress with our relationship. "Write down those dreams Gracie, she said. I'm with you, I believe there is something giving you a sign of some sort. Oh and I'm still waiting for a picture of Sal."

"Don't hold your breath Mags."

"Seriously? What's the big secret? Just send me a picture, he can't be that ugly!"

"Shut up Mags, I'm hanging up, love you!"

Laughing, she says "ditto! Chat soon girly."

Celine's take on the break in was more angry, she was ready to line people up, shoot first, and ask questions later.

"Baby Girl, I hate to say it but I think Richard that dick, is involved some how, weather it's directly or indirectly, it's going to stem from him. I know it. Feel it in my bones."

She also was pleased to hear about how Sal and I are moving along falling in love.

"Oh Gracie that's great darlin! I bet the sex blew your mind am I right?"

"Well, Celine, here's the thing."

"There's a thing? Don't want there to be a thing Gracie."

"Celine, listen, we, well he, is taking it real slow with me. I believe he knows I may not be entirely ready at this time for that step in our relationship."

"Step? It's not a step. It's sex. Say the word Gracie sex sex sex, it's not gonna hurt you, for god sakes your both grown adults?"

"Yes Celine, I know, but it's just not sex for me. I don't think it is for him either. He knows I have trust issues and I'm a bit broken. I think he is waiting for me to be self assured and healed before he, we, get there. That fact he is willing to wait is such a turn on!"

"Wow that takes some big balls for a guy, Blue to be exact!"

"Oh, Celine I yelled, and laughed, you're terrible. I think it's sweet, and I think it's honorable. He is a total gentleman, I'm telling you it's a turn on."

"I think your both nuts! But, listen, joking aside, baby girl, I am very happy for you. You deserve someone who treats you like a, Princess. I hope it all works out and he sweeps you up and away into a happy ever after. Oh and, those dreams you told me about, that's some freaky shit. I would try and find a psychic, see if they can give you some insight on that. It may be nothin' but it wouldn't hurt to check it out?"

"A psychic? Where the hell would I find a psychic? It's not really a bad idea Celine, you think it's true they can see stuff or you think it's a bunch of mind tricks?"

Maybe she said, but what could it hurt, I'll keep my eyes and ears peeled for ya. Now don't forget, we have that meetin' tomorrow."

"Oh how can I forget all those lovely ladies at the southern woman society."

"Sarcasm fits you darlin', I like it."

"Thanks, I do like the cause we are doing, I was up at the hospital visiting those kids, they need a happy Christmas."

"Yes they do, bless their hearts. Okay baby girl I'll see tomorrow 11am bring your Jersey attitude."

"I always try to Celine, by."

* * *

After dinner was done at my house that night, Antonio excused himself to head home. I suspect he was still puzzling over the best suspect for the break in. I hoped it wouldn't keep him up – he needed his rest, too.

"Night, Pop, see ya later." Sal got up and opened the screen door for his Dad, then came back to sit with me.

"I've got something for you," he says.

"Oh, I hope you didn't buy me anything, Sal."

"Nooo..but even if I did? You shouldn't feel uncomfortable accepting my gifts. That would hurt my feelings."

"This is going to take me some time to get used to, okay? I will do my best to accept things from you graciously." I grinned at him and put out my hand, palm up. "What did you get me?"

He handed me a business card that had a dog and cat silhouette on it. In bold letters it said:

Beach side veterinarian clinic - Dr. Veronica L. Torcan Vet.

"What's this?" He just smiles. "Come on, tell me!" I insist.

"You have a job interview there if you want it. She's a new vet in town. She's on the beach so it's not far, you can have part time or whatever, and you can bring Toby to work with you, if you want. It's up to you.

"Are you serious! How did you find this? Oh my god, Sal!" I can't even stand still, I'm so elated.

He laughs at my excitement.

"I was cruising back home the other day and I passed this small Victorian house that had a sign out front announcing a new veterinarian clinic in two weeks. So I pulled up and knocked on the door. Long story short, I told her about you and she said for me to tell you to stop by anytime. I think she knew Pop when he was on the force in Jacksonville. She said my last name sounded familiar. She's worked on some of the K-9 dogs every now and then."

"I don't know what to say. This would be perfect for me. I have an SWS meeting tomorrow, but maybe Saturday I'll go over there and introduce myself."

"Good, I'm glad this makes you happy.", he said as he cocks his head and looks at me. "Gracie, what's SWS?"

I rolled my eyes. "It stands for the Southern Women's Society. My mother-in-law got me involved years ago. I don't get too involved with them, but, around the holidays I like to do the fundraisers for the sick kids at the hospital. We have a big formal holiday party, raise money and give a nice Christmas for the children."

"See? This is why I'm falling deeply in love with you. You have got a heart of gold, you give more then you take. But, you need to stop feeling guilty about receiving. I think that's something Richard might have done to you. I intend to fix it."

"What do you mean Richard did it?"

"You wanted him around more right?"

I nod.

"You wanted his approval, and his affections, he didn't give it and made you feel bad for asking. How am I doing so far?"

I just sit there, staring at Sal as the tears well up in my eyes.

"Oh...Gracie, don't cry...Shit, I didn't mean to make you cry." He comes over to hold me in his arms. "I'm so sorry, Gracie, I never want to say or do anything that makes you cry."

"Sal, you didn't upset me. I'm ashamed that I let Richard walk all over me. But my tears are really because you notice me–you notice everything about me–and it makes me happy."

I can feel my soul healing.

CHAPTER 11

The sunrise on the beach this morning was a magnificent sight. The sky had cast's of peach and yellow hues, reminding me of a mai tai cocktail. The weather had a brisk feel to it, which was a welcome change to the warm muggy humidity we tolerate all summer. Fall was finally making its way down south.

"Cold out this morning." Sal speculated as we sat watching the sky turn to daylight.

"Yeah I love it, feels good" I answer as a gust of wind rushed through us and I caught a little chill.

"Come here," he says sitting down patting a sandy spot in between his legs. I climb in and sit down. Sal wraps his arms and legs gently around me, and I lean in, my back to his chest. He felt warm and I could feel the steady thumps of his heart.

* * *

On our way back from the beach, we go up to the deck and Antonio mentions he's got fresh, hot coffee. "Sounds great," I say with a wink. "One cup though. I can't stay too long–I have a SWS meeting today."

"Ahh...yes, those-a poor kid's. Let-a-me know when that dinner is. I want to go."

"I figured you would Tony. I'll get you the information as soon as I know the details."

Entering the house expecting to see Sal, I hear the bathroom door shut and then the spray of the shower.

I grab a mug and pour myself some coffee. After a few sips I meander down the hall to Sal's bedroom. Pretty tidy for a guy, but since it was Antonio's spare room there wasn't much to it, really. It had a desk under a window with two dressers on one side of the room, and pocket door closets on the other with shelves.

There was a brown recliner and a medium size flat screen mounted to the wall. "New additions." There was a queen- size bed and a side night table.

Noticing the bed was messed with the blankets and pillows thrown about, I figure I'll go in and fix it up while Sal is showering.

I place my coffee mug on the side table and see a small metal suitcase on the bed. I go to move it and notice the top is ajar. Next thing I know, the lid opens hydraulically on it's own making a slight hiss sound. To my surprise it looks like some high tech custom-made lap top computer built right into it and the thing lit up like a Christmas tree. Just then I hear the door close.

"Graaacieee?" Sal says my name like I'm being reprimanded for steeling a cookie out of a cookie jar.

"I'm sorry," I say with a red face. "I wasn't spying on you or being nosey, I was going to make your bed and the case opened on it's own when I tried to move it." I pointed at the colorful box. "What the hell is this, Sal? Looks very hi-tech."

"That is my computer," he says with a laugh. "Just a lap top, but you're correct when you say high tech. It was issued to me at the CIA. I will probably have to return it, but for now, I'm still using it. You're fine, Gracie—you did nothing wrong." He pads his partially-clad self over in his bare feet, shuts it down, locks it up and shoves it under the bed.

He tosses the towel he used to dry his hair to the recliner, then pulls me into his arms. He's only got on his faded jeans, his eyes smoldering into mine, he kisses me and backs us towards the bed. Putting my hands on his chest I push away, breaking our kiss.

"I really have to go," I pant, though it's the last thing I want to say at the moment. "I have that meeting, and I have to get ready to go."

Sal, ignoring me the whole time I'm talking keeps kissing my face and neck and proceeds to gently place me on the bed. As our kisses continue, we fall back into his unmade sheets and blankets.

He smells as good as he feels. When his tongue trails up my throat and back to my mouth I take his bottom lip in my teeth and gently suck on it. My legs are wrapped around him, holding him tightly on top of me. I can feel he's hard and our hips automatically move in rhythm. I break the kiss again.

"I really have to go," I hiss through clenched teeth. I'm aching for him like I've never hurt for anyone. Both our bodies are tight and vibrating with anticipation, our breathing heavy.

"Gracie," he whispers, his breath hitched.

"Sal," I whisper back. "Oh my god, I *really* have to go."

* * *

I arrive at the little restaurant where we have our SWS meetings, on time. Celine is already there and chatting with our president and all around snobby busy body, Barbara Dalton. I wave to get her attention and she makes a beeline straight towards me.

"Hey baby girl, good to see you." She gives me a hug. "Do I sense a bit of a flush about you?"

Despite a quick cold shower, I know I'm still steaming from this morning's near-miss with Sal. I shake my head and wrinkle my nose to throw her off track. "Hi, Celine. How's everyone's mood today?"

"Oh, the usual," she says as she points around the room. "Barb's got a bug up her ass the size of Texas. Mimi's nervous eating habit has returned and she keeps poppin' cookies in her mouth and thinks no one is noticing. Chloe keeps running to the ladies room to barf. Says she has a stomach bug of some kind, and the rest of them are just zombies following whatever Barb the Dictator tells them to do."

"Oh god," I moaned, making a face. "Lets just get this done and over with."

Celine and I take seats at a table with a couple of the other gals. We eat brunch and talk over all options and discuss who can get or give the biggest donations. Also, where to have the event and who should decide the menu.

After a few long hours, the meeting is winding down when Barbara Dalton's inquisitive nasal voice pierces the room.

"Grace, we have heard your divorce will be final soon. I do hope you will still be able to help with the up coming events we have scheduled. The Boumonts have always been a force of prominence to us and to the community. Do you think Richard will still send his usual generous donation to our cause?"

All twelve women shimmy in their chairs to face me. I feel Celine put her hand on my knee under the table, a signal to stay cool and calm. Clearing my throat and putting my shoulder's back I find my voice.

"I'm so glad to hear you know more then I do about my divorce. I'm very excited to learn it's coming to and end soon. While hoping that is true, I believe Richard will give the donations you seek. I'm sure he wants his mother's good work to continue. In the eyes of the community it makes him appear to be the good guy and it's good business so he would never pass that opportunity by. I also believe I should have no problems helping with the benefit. I love this charity for the children and it is a pleasure to do, but that is the only one I will devote my time to this year." The women nod in happy agreement to my reply and Barbara actually thanks me.

But I am on a roll. "Oh, one more thought I had, ladies. When I am no longer a Boumont, I'm pretty sure a new one will take my place. I know for a fact she would love to be involved with all your events. So sure in fact, that she will probably want to run for president of the SWS. Richard I heard, is basically engaged to Camille James. You all *know* her right? I'm sure she will be a new force in your lives. I hope you treat her just as warmly as you have treated me. You may even get bigger donations."

I take a sip of water. The room is so still you can hear the ice melting in the tea glasses. All eyes circle back to Barbara who appears as though she is about to explode. She stands up and points a bony finger down at the table and in a voice similar to the wicked witch from Oz, she threatens, "Over my dead body!"

* * *

Celine, Mimi, and I decide to stay at the bar and have one afternoon cocktail. We take a booth and decompress with a martini.

"I never really liked martini's," says Mimi. "I was never much for alcohol."

"That's why I ordered you a green apple martini," Celine mentions, "it's sweet–you'll like it. I'm sure it will mix well with the two dozen cookies you ate."

"Oh, you saw that?" Mimi answers shyly.

"Yes, we all saw that."

" I didn't notice, Mimi," I say. "If you want to eat cookies then you should eat cookies, knock yourself out. But, if you are eating because something is bothering you, then you need to address it and fix it."

Mimi gives me a little nod then sips her drink.

"Speaking of bothering–hot and bothered that is–how's Mr. Sexy spy guy? Did you guys do the deed?"

"Celine, you truly have a way with words," I sigh. "No we didn't. Taking it slow, remember?"

"Y'all are killin' me," Celine says in a huff. "How can you stand the tension?"

"It *is* getting difficult, I will tell you that. Before I came out here today, Sal and I had a moment. A *very* close moment."

"Ooh, what happened baby girl? Details now! Don't leave anything out."

"Celine, your sex life is way more active then mine. Really, there is nothing to tell you except, that this damned meeting interrupted a *very* heated moment."

Celine spits her martini in Mimi's direction and coughs. "You stopped *a heated moment* because you had this idiotic meetin'? My god darlin', you could have been late–no one would have gave two shits. Hell, you could have sent me a text, told me you were getting your spy game on and I would have sent you the cliff note version!"

Poor Mimi. I hand her some napkins along with an apologetic look.

"Shhh.. keep it down, will you? I don't want the whole bar knowing about my intimacies. I like that he is taking it slow, I told you, he's being a gentlemen. Plus when that time comes, I don't want it to be just casual and then get up and leave. I want to make *love,* Celine. I can't do what you and a lot of others can do. It's just not me."

"Good for Gracie," Mimi cheers without putting down her drink.

"Alright," Celine says with her hands up in surrender. It's your love life, but when that day comes darlin' don't worry bout just the bar. All of north Florida is probably going to hear your intimacies, I'll goddam guarantee ya that!"

Celine and Mimi roar with laughter while I just roll my eyes and shake my head. *Friends. Geezz.*

"Honestly, what am I gonna do with you?" I giggle.

After some more girl chit-chat, I look at Mimi who has a funny look on her face.

"What's wrong, Mimi? I ask, "you look as green as your martini. Don't you like it?"

"I don't know," she says, putting her forehead in her hand. I feel sick all of a sudden. I think I'm gonna go, ladies. I'll see you soon."

Celine and I both wish her well and we all walk out together to the parking lot.

"I'll call ya in a few days, darlin'. Good luck with your spy guy. I really am happy for you."

"Thanks Celine, be good," I tell her as she's walking towards her car. She turns with a big smile,

"Sugah, I'm *always* good."

* * *

On the drive home my cell phone whistled. I know it's a text from Sal. Only his text whistled, he programmed my phone to do that. When I got to a red light I check what he sent.

Hi! where r u? I miss u ☺

I smile and feel butterflies. I hit the call button and on the first ring he answers.

"Hi, Princess, where are you?"

"I'm almost home where are you?"

"Home, I just got back a few minutes ago and noticed you weren't home yet, how was the meeting?"

"Interesting as always, I mentioned a few facts that I thought they would want to know, the gossip is gonna be hot tonight."

"Oh, so you didn't play nice this afternoon, Princess?"

"No, and you know what Sal, It was long over due for that."

"How about I take you to a nice dinner and you can tell me all about it. Maybe some dancing afterward at the Rafters, I hear they have a pretty good DJ on the weekends."

"Sounds wonderful, I'm almost home."

"I missed you today Gracie, I thought about you all day."

"I missed you too Sal." I hear him smile even though we were on the phone. "Drive safe see you soon."

As I get ready, I feel the twinge of a headache shoot through my temples. I grab some Tylenol and curse Celine for that martini. I feed Toby and five minutes later I hear the thundering roar of the beast. Sal pulls up and greets me with open arms and a smile. He is so handsome I thought to myself, I feel this longing ache in the pit of my stomach every time I see him.

"You look beautiful, Gracie. He gives me a tender kiss hello. I really did miss you today."

Soon we arrive at the Mardi Gras Café. This place is a New Orleans theme restaurant. The décor was all purples and gold's. Thrown beads of all colors hung on everything, and party mask's covered the walls. The place is packed and loud with Friday night party people eating gumbo and drinking cocktails. We were lucky we only waited fifteen minutes for a table for two.

Sal pulls out my chair for me and shoves me in, as he takes his seat I open my menu, I'm not really hungry and my headache seems to pound along with the music being pumped into the restaurants sound system.

I feel eyes on me and glance across the table at Sal, his menu is still closed and there is a look of concern on his handsome face.

"Something wrong Sal?"

"You don't look so well, are you feeling alright your face is very flush. You passed on a glass of wine while we were waiting for the table, and you're quieter then normal moving a bit slow."

"I'm fine just a headache, it started earlier, I thought it was the martini I had with Celine after the meeting. But it's getting worse."

"Why didn't you tell me you were not feeling good, we could have stayed in."

"No, I'll be fine, I just need some food in me."

"You sure you're fine? Squinting his eyes at me, We can go."

After the food arrived I just pushed it around on my plate. "Don't you like what you ordered? He asks, I've never seen you not eat, it's one of the many things that intrigue me about you."

That made me smile. "My food is great, I just don't have an appetite, my headache is turning into a migraine." Sal got up from his chair and took a step towards me, he put his hand on the side of my face.

"Gracie you're burning up, I think you have a fever."

"A fever? No way, it's just a migraine I'll have to sleep it off, I'll be right as rain tomorrow." Sal looks at me suspiciously. "Come on, he says, were leaving."

The ride home was torture on my head, the sound of the motor and vibration of the viper rattled my brain, and my stomach was staring to turn. Sal held my hand the whole time. I just sat with my eyes closed trying to concentrate on not throwing up in the car.

We got to my front door in record time.

"Go to bed, he orders, your starting to look pale, I'll stay the night in case you need me."

Feeling the way I do, I don't want him to stay. I didn't want to barf or god knows what else while he was here.

"Thanks, but you really don't have to stay, I'm not that far, and I really just need to sleep this off I promise I'll call you if I need you, thank you for dinner, I wish I felt better, I'm sorry I ruined our date."

"Hey.. Sal put a finger to my lips. Never be sorry, Princess, you're not well, get some rest, my phone will be next to me all night incase you need me." He hugs me and kisses my forehead.

By the time I get up to my bedroom, threw my purse in the closet and strip out of my clothes I am feeling like death. The room began to spin and my head hurt. I grab a bottle of cold water and put it to my forehead. All at once the pain in my head rolled my stomach into a knot, my throat thickening, I run to the toilet and heave. Oh how I hate to barf.

I sat there for a few minutes and placed the cold water bottle on the back of my neck. Toby padded in to see the sight of me and gave me a curious sniff.

When the dizzy pounding in my head slowed down a little I took a sip of water, but my stomach groans in protest. I still feel clammy and sweat is just dripping from my pours. I need some air. I open the door to the balcony, when the cool air passes over me, I feel such relief I stand there just breathing it in and cooling me down. Toby prances out too, sniffing the cool night breeze, and decides he wants to stay out there for a while.

"Okay, fine, I tell him. I'm leaving the door open anyway." Sleeping with the fresh air coming in would feel good.

I crawled into my bed all my muscles were getting soar and I had a stiff neck. Sleep would be the best thing I could do now.

* * *

Antonio got two mugs of coffee and brought it out to his deck and hands one to his son. The sun is up and it's a clear cool morning. Sal stands legs shoulder width a part, arms folded across his chest watching Gracie's house for any signs of her.

"Nothing?" Antonio says as he hands the mug to Sal.

"No, I called her four times, it's going right to voice mail. She hasn't called me back and she hasn't come out and walked Toby, I'm getting concerned."

Antonio looks at his son, nods towards Gracie's house, "Go, go over there and check." As soon as he said it Toby comes out on the balcony and spots them. He barks and runs in and out of the open door.

"Pop, something is wrong!" Antonio watches as Sal runs off toward Gracie's house.

He gets threw the screen door and to the French doors in seconds, they are locked. "Shit!" Toby is still barking. I kick at the doorknob and the seam of the doors, they shatter and I get in.

"GRACIE!" no answer. I race up the stairs and down the hall to her bedroom, she is in her bed not moving.

"Gracie, Gracie, wake up!" I call out as I approach her. I reach out and grab her, gently lifting her dead weight, she is breathing and mumbling but not responsive.

She is burning hot with fever and dehydrated. "Gracie can you hear me!"

CHAPTER 12

I'm thinking that I'm just glad to be alive. Following that damned SWS meeting, where I apparently contracted the flu, I almost died. If it hadn't been for Sal breaking down the French doors and hauling me off to the hospital, I probably would have. That was five days ago. Since then, he's taken care of me. I have no idea why I'm so lucky, but I'm happy that I am.

I sit at my kitchen table watching Sal and Antonio preparing food. They place a bowl of chicken soup in front of me and encourage me to eat. I pick up the spoon which takes a monumental effort, lift some to my lips, but my stomach swirls and I drop the spoon back in the bowl. Everything still nauseates me.

"You look better, Princess," Sal comments. "Do feel any better?"

"Well, my head doesn't hurt as much, but, I have some pains in my legs and feet."

"You got to get more fluids in you, Gracie, please just try. Sip slowly at the soup."

I do as he asks, the best I can. I still feel like I've been run over by a steam roller.

Sal watched me play with the soup. "Okay, Princess, enough," he sighs. "Back to bed."

I nod carefully. "Not going to argue. I feel crappy." After he tucks me in, he retrieves my medicine and I remember the job interview at the vet.

Sal raises his hand to hush me. "I took care of it. I called her, told her what happened. She said to tell you when you feel better her door is open anytime."

"Really? Good, because I'm very interested in the job."

"Here," he says handing me a pill. I swallow it down and lay back already worn out from just going down to the kitchen. Sal climbs up on the bed and I curl up next to him.

"Aren't you afraid you're going to catch this flu?"

"No, I won't catch it."

"How can you be so sure?"

"Gracie, for years I traveled to all different countries. The CIA treated me with a series of injections for all kinds of infections. I should be good for a few more years."

"Really," I say. "When was the last time you got sick?"

He raises his eyebrows and his lips at the corner's come down as he thinks about it. "I can't remember. I might get a little cold every now and then, but I haven't had the flu or something that bad for many years.

"That must be nice," I say. "But, when will I ever take care of you?"

"You already do, Princess. Almost since the first day I met you, you have taken care of me."

My eyes are getting heavy again. "How?" I mumble.

He gives a small laugh. " You ground me. Umm.. let me see, the way you look at me. Your smile and the way you laugh, all medicine for my soul. Just being near you keeps me sane, that's the only way I can explain it."

I lower my head down in the crook of his arm and he cradled me as I fall asleep.

"I love you," he whispers in my ear.

*   *   *

I woke up that morning alone in my bed. I knew Sal was not far. I sit up and do a quick diagnostic of how I'm feeling, much better to my relief. I got out of bed, brushed my teeth, and thought a hot shower later would feel great. I pulled my hair back in a ponytail then climbed back into bed. The first one to enter my room is Toby, he stuck only his head in first as if to peek.

"Hi big boy let me see you" I chime. He was so happy to see me he jumped right up on the bed licking me, his tail swinging fast.

"There she is, Sal says as he enters the room holding a tray. You look better Gracie, how do you feel?"

"I'm feeling much better thank you. My body still has some aches but what ever is on that tray smells good."

"I cooked you some scrambled eggs and some toast. Do you think you can get it down? There's some tea too."

He placed the tray over my legs and sits down. The two of them watch me, as if I have never eaten.

"Looks good," I say. I pick up the fork and shovel in the first bite, then the second.

He smiles, "I think your appetite has returned."

"You did it. You nursed me back to health.

He put his hand up. "It was my pleasure."

Sal glanced at my plate and noticed it was clean. His eyes widened with pride.

"Good god Gracie, you ate it all. I thought you would take a few bites but you cleaned your plate, do you want more?"

I thought about it for a second. " No I better not push it, but... I would love a hot shower."

Sal got up and took the tray away. "Alright, he agreed. But you should soak in a bath, it'll be better for your muscles."

"Stay right here. He said. I'll get it ready for you."

I sit there waiting. I heard the water in my tub go on and some cabinets opening and closing. After a few moments he comes to help me out of bed. When I reached the tub there were bubbles to the rim, and fluffy towels piled on one side. Sal gestured to the tub, "Get in."

I give him a bashful glance.

"Gracie who do you think put clothes on you to go to the hospital."

"Yeah but I wasn't completely naked and I was kind of unconscious, and you were worried. It's not the same thing. I'm just a little shy."

He smiles, "Okay, I'll be right out side the door. Let me know when you get in.

I climb in the tub and slowly lay back. The hot bubbly water feels so good on my sore weak body I almost melt. I am covered with bubbles when I tell Sal I'm in the tub.

He approaches me, stands gazing at me with his warm brown eyes and a small smile.

"How's it feel?" He asks.

"Wonderful, this was a good idea."

Sal sits down on the edge of the tub by my feet. He picks up a wash cloth and soaks it in the bubbly water. He gently snatches my foot brings it up and washes it, then does the same with the other.

"Come, sit up over here He says beckoning me with his hand.

With my back to him I sit in the middle of the tub with my knees bent up to my chest. Sal pours more soap gel onto his palms, massaging it into my back with his strong hands. He went around my neck, under each arm and down my ribs. I giggle.

When he was done he helped me wash my hair, slowly massaging the tension away. How did I get so blessed with a man who actually cared. I don't remember a time when Richard was even remotely this caring.

When he was done rinsing me off he stood up with one of my big fluffy towels and held it up over his face so he couldn't see me. I stood and stepped into it. He wrapped the towel and his arms around me patting me dry.

He brought me my robe and turned away as I put it on. How did I get this lucky I thought again, was it fate, did all the stars and planets align? I know he is the one I'm supposed to be with now. I love him, and was ready to be loved.

*   *   *

After a few days I'm finally feeling better, but then with the care Sal's been giving me, who wouldn't? Hot baths, shampoos, foot rubs to ease the pain are only some of the special treatment I'm getting. If I'd had any doubts about him loving me before I got sick, I didn't have any now.

Celine had called while I was recuperating to tell me that nearly everyone at the SWS meeting that day got the stomach flu from Chloe and everyone was pissed at her.

When I felt up to it, I sent a text message to Maggie:

I'm sick, stomach flu, and Sal is taking such good care of me that I'm in absolute heaven. I am not used to being spoiled... he is gentle and tender with me!

A moment later she replied:

Get better soon my friend and get used to it. that's how someone treats you when they really love you!

As if surviving the damn flu and being spoiled rotten by Sal weren't enough, the next call I received was from my lawyer, Leonard Burnes. He called to tell me that my divorce should be final as soon as Richard's bank accounts were thoroughly checked.

"It seems money has slowly been missing here and there," he says.

"Missing?" I say, not sure I understand. "How could that be? Richard is so particular with his business. I can't imagine this happening under his nose."

"Well," Mr. Burnes continues, "we're calling in a forensic accountant to straighten it out. Seems someone is embezzling. For now most of the accounts are frozen until further notice. Good news is when you are feeling up to it, come by the office. I have the final papers for you to sign.

"And then I'm divorced?" I ask, unable to keep the joy from my voice. *Thank you, thank you, thank you.*

"You will be one paper away from finalizing it, but, yes for all purpose and circumstance you will basically be divorced. The final paper is about your share of the monies, but like I said, Richard's accounts are frozen due to a big red flag, but don't worry Gracie, it'll get squared away."

I hang up feeling kind of giddy but also confused about the red flag on Richard's financial status. *Embezzlement?* Mr. *Perfect apparently isn't so perfect, is he?* The whole situation did not sit well with me at all and I hoped it was all just a mistake.

* * *

My new job at the vet clinic is just what I needed. My first week is fun and productive and the bonus is that Toby gets to go to work with me. Veronica is a sweet lady and we hit it off right from the beginning.

Veronica told me all about the big animal hospital in Jacksonville she worked at for many years and the high stress she was under all the time.

"This is why," Veronica explains when I go for my interview, "I wanted a nice quiet place to keep my hands busy, working with animals at my own pace. I was getting burned out at the big city practice. Too much stress."

I understand what stress can do to a person. "I'm so happy you opened a clinic so close to my home. For years everything I looked at for jobs was just too far. And I love to work with the animals. Toby is such a blessing to me and everyone we meet."

"Speaking of that," Veronica says, "I knew your boyfriend's dad a long time ago–Antonio Petroni. What a great guy and a great officer too. He was a K-9 cop and his partner was a German Shepard named Enzo. Enzo was so smart and he never left Antonio's side–they were a great team. He would bring Enzo in for check ups and vaccines. It was so sad when Enzo had to be put to sleep because of a gunshot wound. It broke Antonio's heart. I think that's what drove him into early retirement."

"What?" I ask, snapping my head in her direction. "What are you telling me? I've known Antonio for years and we got very close in the last few. He never mentioned any of this! Wait a minute–, K-9 officer? Oh my god.. TOBY!"

Veronica looks at me with wide eyes. "You didn't know?"

I stand there, quiet, having an epiphany as I mentally review certain conversations in my memories. "I found Toby on the beach, I always thought that was strange but I thought maybe someone dumped him there. Antonio told me I should keep him–it was right before Richard and I split."

Veronica bursts into laughter. "That is something Antonio would do. How old is Toby now?"

"He's about six, why?"

She gives me a shy smile. "Just about five or six years ago, Antonio came down to the shelter where they train the K-9's. This one pup was just a little too soft to be an officer, but he would make a great protector and pet. I heard through the grapevine that Antonio took him. I assumed he took him because his wife had passed on a while back and he wanted a companion. But to let you find that dog is something he would do. Antonio must think very highly of you. I can tell Toby loves and protects you. Gracie, couldn't you tell the dog had some training in him?"

"Well, yes," I say, rolling my eyes and turning red. "Now I feel like a total idiot, thank you very much."

As I'm getting ready to leave for the day I peek my head into Veronica's office.

"Wait till I get home," I say, "I'm going to have a nice chat with Antonio."

"Oh don't get me in trouble," Veronica says with a laugh.

"You're not the one in trouble," I reply with a wave of my hand Toby is at my side.

Veronica shakes her head, still laughing. "You better let me know about the look on his face when you bust him!"

"Oh, don't worry. I might take a picture and send it to you!"

* * *

As Sal worked in the kitchen on dinner, I ask Tony to join me in the living room. When I tell him I know about Toby, his color goes pale instead of red.

"Caro, please forgive me! You know you would-a-never took a dog as a gift from me. You needed-a-something to take care of and-a-love. You love Toby now and he love's you. I didn't want you to be alone. I used to hear you cry at night, it made me sad. Finding Toby helped a little? No?"

"Yes, Tony, but Why didn't you tell me you were K-9. If you told me there was a dog that needed a home I probably would have taken him."

I'm-a-sorry. I really didn't keep it from you, I just didn't mention it.

I look up from Antonio and glance over at Sal. "What's with the smug smile?"

Sal shakes his head. "I told him he was going to get busted one day."

Raising my eyebrow I pace slowly over to the kitchen. We are on opposite sides of the counter and I lean in a little. "So you knew, too?"

He leaned toward me and our lips are only inches apart. "I knew the moment you told me you found a Germen Shepard on the beach, Princess. I know my dad. Don't be mad–he did it with good intentions." Sal leans all the way over and plants a very sweet kiss on my lips.

"I'm not mad I think I'm just shocked at the way I found this out. No more secrets deal?"

"Deal, mio caro," Tony says softly.

Sal motioned for me to come into the kitchen. I did and he handed me a glass of wine, a nice woodsy Chardonnay.

"Mmm it smells great Sal."

"Hungry?"

"Always," I say with a smile and sip at my wine. I watch Sal move about the kitchen. I could watch him all day long.

"What's the matter Princess?"

"Do you know how sexy it is to watch a man cook dinner for you?"

144

"No..not a clue. I'm not really into men..."

I made my way over to him and put my arms around him—he pulled me in tight. I sealed my mouth over his, the kiss is long and hard with purpose. His hands trailed up my back and into my hair. I'm lost in the rush of heat between us until Antonio clears his throat. We both jump apart.

"Don't burn dinner, Casanova I'm-a-hungry too. You two need to go get mushy on-a-your own time and not in front of me. Capisce?"

I feel my cheeks turn red and I bury my face in Sal's chest and laugh.

"Pop, go to the table. It's done. We're gonna eat now."

* * *

After dinner Sal helps Gracie clean up, as he dries some pots, he turns to her. "Gracie, Halloween is this Saturday. What do you say we take the Beast and drive into St. Augustine for the weekend? I'll bet Pop will take care of Toby for you."

"That sounds like fun," she croons. It's a beautiful old city. I haven't been there in years!"

"Good. We'll leave about mid morning—it should take about two hours to drive there. I'll go online and see about a hotel, okay? Searching her face he knows what he's looking for and she gives him a shy smile and a tiny nod. He exhales.

"You're all right, then? You're ready?" He asks as he reaches for her and takes her in his arms. "I love you Gracie, with all my heart and soul."

His kiss tells every cell in her body that he's telling the truth.

"I love you too, Sal. I am more than all right–, and I am *very* ready."

CHAPTER 13

I can't help but marvel at the glorious clear blue sky, even if the temperatures have dipped into the high 60's. The perfect day for a drive along the A1A coast highway to St. Augustine.

The Beast gives a rough, but fun ride with the sun and air in my face and hair. Watching Sal's strong hands on the steering wheel, I shiver. Those same hands make me feel special and safe and loved with every touch.

Once we wind our way past the Castillo de San Marco with it's Spanish flags flying in the bay breeze, we're only blocks from our destination.

We arrive at the Casa Monica Hotel and Sal pulls into the underground valet parking driveway.

The young attendant is looking at the car with wide eyes and I wonder if he's going to blurt out "voluptuous" and I keep my laugh to myself.

"Wow," he says to Sal with reverence in his eyes, "is that a Viper?" Without waiting for Sal's reply, he continues on. "I've heard about these cars but I've never actually seen one!"

Sal gets out and hands him the keys. "Well, now you get to drive one. Keep her safe for me."

"Yes sir, not a problem." He hands Sal the claim check, waits while I remove our duffle bag from the back, and carefully drives away.

We enter the hotel through the valet side of the lobby and we're transported to the days when hotels were rich and elegant. The huge, dark mahogany registration desk is off to the right and all around us are high-ceilinged walls displaying oil paintings that are taller than Sal is.

As Sal checks us in, I look around, still thinking I should pinch myself at the change my life has taken. To the left is an old-time bar and elegant restaurant.

Key in hand, Sal collects me from my wandering and we ride the elevator to our room which is as luxurious as the lobby. A suite with a king size bed, and a Jacuzzi tub off to the side, we've got a balcony view of the bay and the Bridge of Lions. He puts the duffel bag on the luggage stand and turns to me.

"What would you like to do first, Princess?"

I spin around in a circle, arms spread wide. When I stop, I give him a grin. "I'm hungry! Let's go out and walk St. George Street and take in the sites–get some lunch or maybe do a food crawl!"

He shakes his head and chuckles. "Hungry", he mumbles, looking up at the ceiling and rolling his eyes. "She's always hungry. Okay, lets get you some food." His big sigh makes me laugh even more.

As we walk hand in hand along St. George Street, we look into some of the shop windows, though I resist the fudge shop which smells insanely good.

Being a famous "ghost" city, and this being Halloween weekend, it's fun to watch all the people in costumes walking about as though it's nothing special. The shops with all sorts of decorations are festive, too. We decide on an early dinner at a restaurant called The Columbia House.

"Now what, Princess?" Sal asks as we come out of the cool alcove of the restaurant. I point to a booth on the corner opposite where we're standing.

"How about we get in on that walking ghost tour? Should be fun!"

He nods, gives me slight bow, and I take his arm as we walk across Hypolito Street. We make our reservation for the eight o'clock tour, but it's only seven, so we spot a bench on the opposite corner and deposit ourselves there.

Sal spots a sign in a shop announcing they serve gelato and he points at it "Would you like a Gelatto?" I look at him as though he'd lost his mind. "Of *course* I would," I say with a giggle.

"Yeah, what was I thinking? Any particular flavor?"

I tilt my head and gaze into his eyes which are sparkling with fun. "Surprise me."

Sal disappears to place our order. While I'm sitting there I notice a group of people sitting at small tables. Some are dressed in Gypsy costumes, some are in everyday clothes. The sign above them says, PSYCHIC READINGS.

I get up from the bench and look in the window of the ice cream pallor–Sal is fourth in line. I glance again at the psychics and see a young girl just sitting quietly. She smiles at me and I smile back. She waves me over so I walk over to her.

We shake hands. "Hi," she says, "my name is Yvette. Would you like your cards read?"

I hesitate for a second, but then something felt so right about her that I plunked down in the chair. "I'm Gracie. Nice to meet you. Okay, let's do this."

She hands me a deck of cards with funny pictures on them and tells me to shuffle them good. I follow the directions and hand them back to her. She proceeds to spread them out on the table.

"These are tarot cards," she points out, "have you ever done this before?"

I nod with a slight smile. "Once. But, it was a long time ago at a party. I don't think the girl was very good–she could not get a true reading on me and she didn't know why."

Yvette keeps placing the cards on the table. She stares at the cards for a minute or two, cocking her head from side to side, her brows knitted in a frown. She looks steadily at me. "You have been here before."

Well, that was a lucky guess... "Yes, but it has been a few years," I tell her. "I *love* St. Augustine."

"No," she chuckles, "your *Soul* has been here before, many times as a matter of fact. You keep coming back. You're what is called an *old soul*."

I look at her and wrinkle my nose. "What, like I have past lives?"

Her laugh is soft. "Yes, your cards are amazing. It takes someone really experienced to read these. Will you excuse me for a moment? I'd like to get my grandmother, she can read these *and* you better then I can. This is something really special. I'll be right back."

Yvette leaves me at her little table and I stare at the tarot cards wondering what the fuss is all about. Sal walks over to me and hands me a cup with my gelato.

"Hey, what's going here?" he asks around a mouthful of cold delight.

"Well, I saw these psychics doing readings and I thought what the hell. Yvette went to get her grandmother to help her read my cards. She said I'm special." I smile and raise my eyebrows up and down.

"You *are* special," he replies with a wink. "Try your gelato, it's a seasonal flavor."

"Ohh, it's pumpkin!" I moan in surprise. This is great! It taste's just like pumpkin pie!"

He executes his signature bow. "I knew you would like it."

Just then, Yvette returns with her grandmother. The old woman is a little shorter than Yvette, has wavy salt and pepper hair and looks to be seventy-five to eighty years old. Her striking emerald-green eyes are piercing. She comes to me and gently takes my hand. "I'm Amina and I'm seventy eight."

I gasp. "How did you know what I was thinking?"

She cuts me off with a wave of her hand and laughs. "Just a little psychic joke, honey. When you're old everyone wonders about age. That wasn't mind reading, that's just knowing people, but it gets them every time."

"Whoa! That was freaky." I look at Sal and we both laugh.

"So, my granddaughter here says you're an old soul and you have amazing cards. She asked me for some help reading you. Is this agreeable with you?"

I nod and place my folded hands on the table.

She takes a seat and studies the cards, then asks me to pick them up, shuffle again and hand them back to her.

With a slight smile on her mouth, she stares at me and then Sal, as I do as she asked. I hand her the deck and once again my cards are spread out on the little table. She studies them again for what seemed to be a long time.

She lets out a long breath, then taps the table with her long fingers. "Okay Gracie. My granddaughter is correct. You are an old soul and you have been here many times. Something in your past lives has gone terribly wrong and you keep coming back. In one of your lives, you took your own life–you were that distraught. Also, you were once murdered. Tell me," she says, pointing to Sal. "Is he your husband?"

For a minute or two I'm frozen by her words Suicide...murder? Unable to speak, I shake my head. Finally I stammer, "N-n-no he's my boyfriend."

She reaches over and takes my hand, then offers her other hand to Sal. Sal looks at her like she's a little crazy.

She gives him a warm smile. "Humor me, please?"

Sal complies and the old woman closes her eyes and takes a deep breath.

We sit like that for a long moment. "The both of you are old souls. You have been in love with each other many times. You are *soul mates*. But something always tears you apart. You have found each other again, in this life, and believe me it's no accident–you are destined to be together.

"Now, just because bad things have happened in your past lives does not mean they will happen again. You can change your future, but be aware of some forces around you that can–and will–try to pull you apart."

Sal lets go of her hand like it's too hot to hold. He looks at the old woman with concern. "Please forgive me, but this is a little too crazy. Gracie," he turns to me, "I don't think you should listen to this. It might give you more nightmares."

The woman's eyes focus on me. Her tone is sharp like this is something I have to get. "Have you had dreams of your past lives Gracie?"

"Well, I didn't know that's what they were, but I'd say yes. On and off since I first met Sal."

The old woman give me a tiny nod. "He triggered them for you. You are probably a little psychic as well, but you've never developed it. So, only when you sleep, the subconscious mind comes awake and shows you."

Sal takes my hand from Amina. "I was with her one night when she had one. It totally wrecked her. She was hyperventilating and shaking in fear. I'm begging you both, *please* stop talking about this."

I turn to Sal and put my hand on his face. "I need to know this. I think it will help. I sensed those dreams were not just dreams, and I knew from the first moment our eyes met there was something familiar about you. You said the same about me. If I understand this, maybe the dreams will stop. Please let her finish."

He looks at me, searches my face for something he must see. He leans over and kisses my forehead before he sits down again.

I look at Amina. "Please continue."

"Very well. Listen, both of you. Souls find one another through each life, most of the time it's the same people we know now. Some are new and come and go. Be aware of some surrounding you–they can cause you harm. Your future is not a fixed or definitive outcome–there are no endings or absolutes. We all can change things. That's why we keep coming back. You two are in love and that emotion is one of the strongest–as are revenge and pain. Gracie, don't be afraid of your past lives. When and if you dream again, try to remember it is a vision and cannot hurt you. Awaken your deep connection to your spirit and soul–it will guide you. The both of you are together now so stay that way. It *is* your destiny. You have been together for centuries and there was much heartbreak and sadness. Try not to repeat the past. Stay together always."

I thank her for her help and Sal pays her for her time. As we get up and start to leave, Amina stops us.

"Wait! Good luck, both of you. True love is hard to find and you have found it." She comes and gives me a hug and hands me a card with her number on it. "He will always protect you, it is in his nature". She reaches a hand to my shoulder and with her concerned green eyes tells me to call her anytime if I have any questions.

"God Bless you both."

Shaken, but committed, Sal and I cross back to the booth to join up with our ghost walk. They parade us up and down the streets of St. Augustine and through two cemeteries. The story of the star-crossed lovers that still haunt the sea wall touches me in a special way.

The entertaining guide, dressed in eighteenth century garb, tells story after story about ghosts woven into the history of the old city. What a terrific way to spend Halloween.

On our way back to our hotel we pass a candle shop with an open door. The scent of the candles wafts out to the sidewalk. I peek in and there is an older gentleman making thin tapers by hand. He waves at us and I wave back. Sal points in the air. "He's listening to one of Pop's favorites."

"Sure is. Andrea Bocelli. This song is one of *my* favorites as well. *A Time to Say Goodbye.*"

We hang out there on the sidewalk listening for a moment. "This song is hauntingly beautiful," I whisper, standing there with my eyes closed, feeling the music.

Sal wraps his arms around me and we look into each other's eyes. Time seems to slow as he kisses me tenderly and whispers, *"You're* hauntingly beautiful."

*   *   *

Back in our room, I send Sal into the bathroom to shower, first. I plop down on a wing-back chair by the window and gaze out over the old town, now lit with gaslight reproductions that cast a soft, yellowish light.

I think about Amina's reading and what she told us. I don't know how much Sal believes, but to me a lot of things are making more sense.

When she spoke of the warning–*be aware some who surround you can cause you harm*–freaks me out along with the notion that I've already committed suicide and been murdered. I find it really bizarre that these things happened to me, but it does explain the sadness I feel when I have those dreams. *Even the realization of past lives doesn't feel all that strange, which in itself, is strange.* I laugh in the quiet.

The bathroom door opens and Sal comes out with a towel wrapped around his waist. I'm startled out of my thoughts, but the view is pretty great here, too. "All yours, Princess."

I look at him, unable to completely shake my thoughts clear.

"You alright, Gracie? Is something wrong?"

"Wrong? No, nothing wrong. I was just thinking about Amina and the reading. About you and me."

"I hope you don't have a nightmare tonight because of what that old woman said to you," he says quietly.

I get up from the chair and face Sal. "Do you believe what she told us?"

He scratches at his head and wrinkles his nose. "Well truthfully? I guess I do to some degree, but I wouldn't let it rule our lives. Don't waste too much time on this Gracie, I don't want it stressing you. This weekend is about us."

I step into his arms and he hugs me tight. Somehow, I'm going to let him know I have never been better.

"I am having a *very* nice time Sal. Thanks for getting us away. I promise, I'm not going to stress about it–I kind of enjoyed it. You have to admit it was interesting information."

Sal nods. "Yes, I think it freaked me out more then you, but then I'm not the slightly psychic one." He kisses my forehead and gives me a light tap on my butt. "Go take a nice hot shower. It'll relax you"

I step into the shower. The water is soothingly hot and feels good on my achy feet after a day and night sight seeing. Then it registers in my mind that tonight is the night that Sal is finally going to make love to me. My stomach jumps at the thought. Then I feel the rest of my body responding to the idea. A small smile is on my lips, I am ready. I dry myself with what must be the world's softest and largest towel, put on some pretty panties, and a Victoria's Secret nightshirt that buttons down the front. I blow dry my hair so I'm not dripping wet and scrunch it a bit. I opened the door and turn off the bathroom light. I step into a very dark room.

"Gracie, What's wrong?" Sal asks from somewhere in the darkness.

"Nothing, it was so bright in the bathroom, my eyes are adjusting to the dark."

Suddenly a pair of arms encircle me. Finding my face with his hands, he kisses me long and slow. I put my arms around his neck, then trail down his back with my fingernails until I land on his bare ass.

Oh god, Sal is naked. As I get lost in the heat and depth of his kiss, I feel his erection hard against my stomach. I reach for him and hold him firmly in my hand. Sal's soft hiss is my reward and the kiss gets even hotter.

Sal's hands are everywhere, then trail back to my face. He pulls away just enough to look into my eyes. The darkness isn't so dark now and I focus on his expression. Love. Desire. Passion. My breath catches in my throat. I can't remember a more perfect moment – ever.

"Gracie," he whispers against my lips, "I love you. Let me love you. Do you trust me?"

I nod – words won't describe what I'm feeling. He gives a little chuckle and we take a short stroll over to the bed. He reaches up under my night shirt and slides my panties down my legs, tapping each foot to lift them. My panties get tossed to the floor somewhere and he proceeds to unbutton my nightshirt, but I still his hands, grab it by the hem and yank it over my head. No longer shy, I'm naked and unafraid.

Wrapped in each other's arms, we fall onto the bed. Sal is on top of me, my legs dangling off the side. He trails wet, exploring kisses on every inch of my body to the waist. I can barely breath but if he stops, I'll disappear.

Then down a thigh as he parts my legs and finds my soft core with his mouth. I clutch the bed sheet wanting to scream, my hips moved in rhythm with his tongue. When he works a finger slowly inside me, I'm lost. I moan in pleasure.

"Gracie," his voice is husky. "You are so ready for me."

Sal lifts my hips in his strong hands and gently pushes me back to the middle of the bed, then settles between my legs. He pauses a moment and looks deep into my eyes. He's asking permission and I gladly give it as I touch his face. "I love you Sal and I trust you. Make love to me."

Slowly, he slides inside me and then lays still. Gently he begins a rhythm that steadily builds as our breath gets shorter and our bodies tighten with passion. I wrap my legs around him and he puts his hands under my back and lifts my hips to get as deep as he can. I'm filled with him, with my love for him.

He brings me to the edge and I blow apart, digging my fingers into his back as I cry out his name. His release exploded deep within me.

We lie there for moments, out of breath and spent. Sal gently reaches up and brushes a strand of hair out of my face.

"Gracie, you feel so good I could lay here with you forever. Are you okay?"

I sigh. "That was amazing. You're a tender lover."

He smiles and kisses me again like it is his last day on earth.

"You're mine, Princess. I want you to be mine."

My body shudders with his whispered words. My emotions choke off every attempt to speak. I finally manage to whisper, " Don't ever leave me. Don't ever lie to me. Don't ever hurt me and I will be yours."

Sal stops his flurry of kisses and looks me square in the face, his warm chocolate eyes slightly misty.

"I love you Gracie, with all my might and soul. I don't think I can survive without you, now. You are my peace, you are what calms my mind and helps me sleep from all the evil and dark I have witnessed. I promise I will never lie, leave or hurt you. I need you."

* * *

In the morning I wake to a thunderstorm rumbling about outside. Sal and I are in bed tangled around each other. I'm a little sore from yesterday's trekking around the city and our all night lovemaking. Sal took me to the edge three more times before we collapsed and fell into a deep sleep. I start to get up slowly so I won't disturb him, but a strong arm pulls me back into his embrace.

"Where you going, Princess?" he mumbles.

"Just to the bathroom," I whisper.

"What do you want to do today?" he asks, letting me loose from his grip.

He looks almost like a little boy with his face all smushed in the pillow.

I find my nightshirt on the floor and slip it over my head since the room is cool. "Well, it sounds like November first brought in one wicked thunderstorm so I don't know, we *could* stay in bed all day." I playfully mention.

Sal lifts his head just enough to hear the storm. He shoots me half a smile and raises one of his eyebrows over a puffy eye.

"Hurry back."

      *   *   *

Camille James sat in her home office tapping her French manicured nails on her desk staring at her cell phone. "Come on, where *are* you?" she spit through clenched teeth.

Finally her cell buzzed. She read the text.

House being watched. No sign of them around and I can't get close enough. Have to wait for a new plan.

Camille put her hand on her face, shook her head, and sent a response:

FINE! Talk with you later

Idiot. Taking a deep breath, she thought about the forensic accountant going through their personal banking records, sweat started to form on her upper lip and her stomach caved in.

"If she isn't stopped, Gracie is going to ruin everything I have worked for!"

      *   *   *

Curled up in Sal's arms I look at him curiously.

"What is it, Gracie?" he asks softly.

"I was wondering what happens now. You know, when we go home. Everything's changed. I don't want to sleep without you but what will Antonio say? Your dad is old school Italian just like my father was. The idea of 'shacking up' is not going to go over well. And, I don't want him to lose respect for me."

Sal kisses the top of my head and I feel the vibration of his chuckle in his chest. "The only thing I really heard was you don't want to sleep without me!"

I poke him with my hand. "Hey, I'm serious. How should we handle this?"

"I know you're serious, Princess. Pop will be fine with me living over at your place for many reasons. First, we're not children and he really has no say about it. Also, I know for a fact Pop would *kill* me if, after this weekend, we were casual about our relationship. He knows why I took you away. He once told me if I was going to pursue you that I better be serious and not break your heart, so, I think if I didn't move in with you he would kill me."

"Wait," I put my hands up. "You and Tony talked about our relationship?"

Sal rolls his head and his eyes and lets out a big breath. "No, more like Pop told *me* about our relationship. Gracie, you know how Pop feels about you. He thought I should stay away from you. Then, when I told him I couldn't, and he saw how you make me feel, he approved. But, he gave me fair warning."

I laugh because I can just picture Tony going after Sal about this. "Just thinking about Tony giving you the third degree on us is priceless!"

"Oh, so glad that's amusing to you."

"I'm sorry," I say. Having people in my life who care about me makes me giddy. I'm realizing that I'm not just lucky – I'm blessed.

"So, Princess, would you like to get dressed and go downstairs for dinner? I know you must be starved."

"Yes! That restaurant down in the lobby looked fabulous, and if it's anything like the room service it's going to be delicious!"

We get dressed and head down to the lobby that housed an exquisite Restaurant. We enjoy a wonderful dinner in the very busy 95 Cordova restaurant, then we sit at the bar sipping an after dinner cocktail while listening to a little piano music.

We come back to the room and settled in for our last night. I'm sad that our trip has to end, but I know this man who mended my heart and made me smile and trust again will be with me always. I can feel his love for me in every kiss, in every touch. I can see how he feels about me in his eyes whenever he looks at me. I've heard eyes are the mirrors to the soul, and Sal saw deep into mine.

After we make love again, I say a silent prayer before falling asleep – something I haven't done a lot of recently. I pray that Sal is my true soul mate. I pray that our love is strong enough that nothing can break us apart.

Right now, life seems so great, but there's my intuition nagging at me. Something is wrong. I can't put a finger on what is troubling me. So, I pray that whatever difficulty I feel is coming for me; I'll be strong to fight it—with Sal by my side.

CHAPTER 14

When we arrive home in the late morning, Antonio and Toby seem very happy to see us. But I'm still nervous about how Tony's going to take all this. He loves us both and I know that so I take a deep breath.

Still, I feel my face blush when Antonio asks me how the weekend went–and follows it with a wink.

"It was very nice. I love St. Augustine."

"That's-a-nice, Gracie' I missed you both. It was–a-too quiet around here."

Toby won't be ignored any more and jumps up on me so he can get lots of my attention. I pat and scratch at his fur, and in return, I get licks and whined at.

Sal comes in from outside and that father-son look passes between them.

"*Okay*, I say firmly. "I'm getting to recognize these glances you two give each other. What's going on?"

Sal looks a little guilty and shuffles his feet. "While we were away I had Louie keep an eye on the house. He and Pop saw some guy in a Dodge Ram pick-up drive around and stop in front of your house. Louie approached him, asked what he wanted and the guy said he was lost and drove away.

"Louie saw him the next day in a dark van but couldn't get close enough to talk to him again. He might have been the one who broke in last month."

My fairytale weekend is truly over. I feel light-headed and sit down. *Is this what's been nagging at me?* I clear my throat. I'm not wimping out about this. "Did he get a plate number? Can we do a check?"

Antonio puts a hand up. "We did–it's all fake. I called Danny at the police station. They put more patrol cars in the area but really that's about all they can-a-do unless we catch them red handed."

I take a deep breath and Sal sits beside me. "That's kind of scary. Who is he? What is he looking for?"

Sal hugs me. "We'll find out and no one will hurt you. I can keep you safe. I didn't want you to know any of this–I don't want you to worry. Gracie, anyone comes close to you I will kill them, you understand?" He puts a hand under my chin to look into my eyes and I hear him but the feeling of impending disaster remains. "Capisce?" he asks, sounding just like his father.

I can't do anything but believe him, so I smile and nod. My reward is a quick kiss on the nose.

* * *

Sal, Toby and I walk up the pathway to the mansion. From the outside everything looked fine. I was beginning to appreciate that old saying about looks being deceiving.

"I'm gonna go upstairs and open up some windows," I tell Sal who was busy going from room to room downstairs. "What are you doing?"

"Just checking things out," he answers. "I'm gonna talk to Pop about me moving in here with you. I'll be right back with some of my things."

I give him a seriously nervous look and he smiles from ear to ear. "It's alright. Pop knows. He's not blind–it will be fine."

"Okay," I sigh, hoping he's right. "I trust your judgment. But it still feels awkward."

Sal laughs and rattles his head, "I love you Gracie. Just always know that–and so does Pop."

*   *   *

I can't wait any longer to call Celine and tell her about my weekend–hell, tell her about my life–so I grab my cellphone and hit the call button.

"Hey, baby girl! How's things with Mr. Hottie?"

"Could not be any better. I will only tell you that we are a perfect fit. And, I mean a *perfect fit!*"

"Oh, thank god!" Celine shouts. "I'm so happy for you!" She drops her voice to just above a whisper. "So tell me, is he hung well?"

I almost drop the phone and my face is so hot it hurts. "Oh my god, Celine–I can't believe you just asked that! No, no, I take it back. I totally should have seen that coming. I'm just saying, he is beautiful! Everything was great. Just thinking it is making me flush!"

Celine is all giggles. "Where? When?"

So, I tell her about our drive in the Viper, our days in the Ancient City and our nights at the Casa Monica.

"Good, baby. That's the way it's supposed be. Hey, I was thinkin' 'bout you and your dreams. Have you had any more?"

"No, I haven't, but while we were in St. Augustine, I got my tarot cards read. To make a long story short, the psychic told Sal and me that we are old souls and have always been in love. We keep finding each other but there is always something getting in our way to tear us apart, so we keep coming back to get it right."

"Holy crap on a cracker! Gracie! That's incredibly deep. What do you think? You believe it? I think it makes sense, baby."

"I know it sounds crazy, but I think there is something to it–those dreams I had are not just normal dreams. I felt like at least I wasn't nuts. It's an answer to these dreams and why they give me strong emotional trauma. Sal wasn't very happy, though. He's worried it will trigger more dreams."

"Wow, Gracie, murder, suicide? Are you sure you're not upset with all this? That's a lot to take in. I might have to agree with Sal on this one."

"No Celine, really I'm okay. I just hope nothing bad happens to us. I keep feeling something is wrong and I just don't know what."

"Gracie, what could possibly be wrong? Don't get your panties all twisted–I know your gut has never let you down before but maybe it's just all the stuff the psychic told you."

I fill her in on my divorce settlement and she promises me a martini celebration. Then I tell her about Tony and Louie's discovery of the house being watched.

"But, Sal is moving in here today, so I'm not so worried about being in the house alone. Between him and Toby, I'll be okay."

"Good! Don't let this get to ya. I gotta gun. You should let Sal teach ya how to use one, too."

"I've thought about it only recently. I never thought I needed one before now."

"Something to think about. Talk to Sal about it, baby. Now listen, you take care, I gotta go. I will see you soon. The SWS has picked the first Saturday in December for the children's Christmas benefit. I believe it's the seventh."

"Okay. I'll write it down on the calendar. Antonio and Sal are going with me. That date is familiar..."

"It's Pearl Harbor Day," Celine says.

"Oh yeah, that's it. I'll tell the guys the date and make sure Sal gets a tux."

Celine made a yummy noise. "Mmmmm, Sal in a tux. Can't wait!"

"Oh go cool yourself off," I say with a giggle. Call me later in the week for that celebration!"

"You got it, baby girl. So happy for you! Truly I can breathe and worry less about you."

We say our good-bye's and I hear Sal enter the house. I start to make my way out of my room when I he calls me.

"Gracie, you still upstairs?"

I head for the stairs, talking as I go. "Yeah, I was on the phone with Celine. Everything go alright with your dad?"

At the top of the staircase, I look down. There he stands a duffel bag in one hand and his silver metal briefcase laptop in the other—with Antonio by his side, who reaches a hand out to me and his smile warm as always. I walk down the stairs feeling a bit like a fool.

"Come here, mio caro." he motions to me. He takes my hand in his. "Ah my Gracie, I hear you are a little upset over how I would feel if-a- my son moved in with you. You are a good and- respectful gal, I know all this is true or else it would not bother you how I feel. Your parents, God Bless them, have-a- raised you right. Life has thrown you some disappointments. You deserve to be happy and you also make-a-my son very happy. Don't worry mio caro, I give you both-a-my blessing. I think you two were meant to be." He pulls my hand to his lips and puts a gentle kiss on my knuckles, then puts it to his cheek. He gazes up at me with his dark eyes.

"I was-a-not blessed with a daughter, but you are just-a-like one to me. I tell-a-my son to treat you right. I will kill him if he breaks your heart."

I burst into laughter and tears at the same time. Sal puts down his stuff and comes to my side putting his arm around my waist.

"Pop, I won't break her heart. It took too much to mend it."

Antonio nodded, then put up his hands to suggest surrender.

"Enough with the mushy," he grunts playfully. "You two get-a-settled and then come over later for dinner. I'll make-a-something nice and-a-we eat like a family, yes?"

"Sounds great, Pop. See you later and thanks for that."

"I love her too, son. Your momma would have-a-loved to see this."

I gave them both a curious look. "I'd like to believe she can," I offer.

Antonio wipes his eyes and quickly moves his wheelchair to the door. "See you both later," he says after clearing his throat. "I got-a-cooking to do."

I raise an eyebrow at Sal. "What did you tell him?"

"I might have mentioned that you feel uncomfortable living together in front of him. So he decided he would talk to you, make you feel better...did it work?"

Smiling, I shrug. "Yeah, I think it did."

* * *

While we eat, I mentioned to the guys about the SWS benefit on December seventh and mention that they'll need tuxedos.

Sal and I also tell Antonio all about what the psychic had told me about the dreams.

"She said you *both* were old souls?" Antonio asks.

I nod. "She says we have been in love before—many times, in past lives. I'm pretty sure that's what I'm dreaming about."

"Caro, when you say dream, what exactly are-a-you *dreaming* about?"

I explain about the wars; the uniforms, the smell of leather, and horses and the smoke from the train. I tell him about the leaves and the wind and the noise and confusion. And, the heartbreaking sorrow I wake with.

Sal picks up the bottle of wine and pours more into all our glasses. "Tell Pop about the newspaper."

"What newspaper?" Antonio asks.

"The one in my dream. It read, *The Germans raided the trenches on November 2nd and we lost the 16th Infantry*. That's where Sal in the dream was going and I knew he'd been killed. Sal woke me up that night because I was screaming like a banshee. It felt so real!"

Antonio is still, staring into space like he's deep in thought.

"Pop, you alright?" Sal asks, leaning toward his father.

"Tony? What happened?" I'm ready to get out of my chair. He doesn't look good at all.

Antonio looks back in our direction. He looks as if he's seen a ghost. "Gracie, have you looked up that date or anything about World War One?"

"No, why?"

"Because I believe that's what really happened. I was trying to remember my history."

Sal jumps up from the table. "Give me five minutes to get my computer. Be right back!"

Tony leans forward and takes my hand. "Does this frighten you, caro?

I pat his hand and smile. "I'm not sure. If it's true, and if the gypsy is right, maybe this time we can have a happy ending. I'm not sure I'm psychic, no matter what she says. Or, if I want to do anything about it."

I let go of his hand and reached for my wine. Tony picked up his glass and raised it to me. "I am-a-hoping for a happy ending, mia caro."

Sal returns, out of breath, toting his hi-tech laptop. He drops into the couch and starts tapping at the keys like a mad man. I just sit there stunned and a little nervous at what he might find.

"Here... Right here!" Sal shouts, pointing to his screen. I get up from the table and go to read what he's found. There, lit up for all to see, a piece of American history.

"My dream really happened. Holy shit!" I say with surprise. "I didn't believe it!"

Sal rubs his hand over his face. He's lost some of his color. "That's incredible!" he whispers.

I got back to the table were Tony is still sitting like he's in a trance. Then I realize his dark eyes are starring at me. Maybe it's *me* he can't believe.

I gulp down the last of my wine, because god knows I need it right now. "My dreams are from past lives–maybe the psychic was really right. Well, I'm officially freaked the hell out!" I drop into my chair and rest my chin in my hand and I catch Tony's gaze.

Sal comes back to the table looking back and forth between his father and me. "I'm at a loss for words here," he says, putting up his hands. "I didn't really put much stock into all this. I *still* don't think we should live by what the psychic said; old souls, past lives. Sounds like a sci-fi plot. Can this really be happening?"

Antonio looks at us and whispers, "*Anima Gemella*.

I look to Sal for a translation.

"Soul mates," Sal says.

"Soul mates never die." Antonio speaks again. "It is true. That explains so much. You really *are* soul mates."

* * *

Richard Boumont was just getting out of a late meeting when his secretary sent him a text.

Children Xmas benefit 12-7 @ Sawgrass Marriot 7pm. Should I send the usual donation?

Richard thought for a split second then responded:

Not yet, must talk with accountant. I will let you know.

When he arrived back at his penthouse Camille was waiting with martini's.
"How did it go? Are our accounts still frozen?"
Richard grabbed the martini from her and took a big gulp. "Our private accounts are fine, now. The business accounts are still being looked over. Someone is very slowly stealing from us, making it look like mistakes here and there. There is a little over fifty grand gone and the number is rising. I hope they catch the son-of-a-bitch."
Camille tossed back her drink. "Do they have any idea who it is yet?"
"No. Whoever it is was very smart, left no trail. Probably had this in the works for a long time. I'm sure they will figure it out. In the meantime, I can give Gracie what she wants, cut her loose and then that's one less thing on my plate. The Children's Christmas benefit is on December 7th and I've got to get a nice donation together– don't want to give less then I normally do. I don't want people finding out the company has a money situation–that's bad publicity for potential clients. I usually give five thousand–I might have to borrow some money from you from your private account if you don't mind. It would

be in the company's best interest—eventually I'll pay you back. Now I am so exhausted, I really must go to bed. Are you coming or are you staying up a while longer?"

"Go on ahead, darling. I'm going to do some work. I'll be in momentarily."

After Richard went to bed, Camille poured another martini. She went into her office and turned on the computer. She sat staring at her bank accounts, heart pounding so hard she heard it in her ears. She'd been raised so poor that there would never be enough to take away all the fear – not really. The idea of loaning Richard money to give away to some kids who didn't earn it made her skin crawl.

She was so close to her goal. She tapped on the keys: *First Caribbean International Bank. Grand Cayman Island*, and put in her password. Up came her statement: 2.5million. She guessed that would have to be enough to get out of here and buy that high rise condo on the beach she had her eye on.

There'd also be enough left over to get her mother out of that dirty mental institution and into a better facility so she would be set for life. "No one ever helped me or my mom at Christmas or any other time," She said aloud to herself. "I worked for assholes and stole, begged and borrowed for all I have."

I just have to bide my time–a few more thousand and I can disappear. Gracie, where are you hiding that damned necklace?

* * *

We spent the month of November forming our own routines in the mansion. Sal's easy, constant love and affection, not to mention his cooking, made the old place warmer and comfortable. Now that I'd have to find a new place, the house I loathed to be in had become a home.

We didn't have a hard time living together. I thought at first we'd bump heads and have to get used to each other's habits. But like everything I encountered with Sal it was easy and we fit perfectly like pieces in a puzzle. Even Antonio mentioned to us that we were adjusting like we were always meant to be.

Sal still got up sometimes in the middle of the night but it wasn't as intense. I encouraged him to tell his father about the imprisonment, knowing that the truth really was freeing, but it wasn't my story to tell. I had to wait and hope that he'd find his way.

My dreams calmed down, but apparently my notion that I could turn off my psychic ability was naive. I began getting fuzzy images of things I couldn't figure out–but all of it felt *very* familiar.

* * *

A week before Thanksgiving I come home from work to find Sal and Antonio in my kitchen. I can tell they're excited about something – it's in the air. Toby bumps up against me, wanting to be petted and stroked and I reach down to do that.

"Something smells very good! I can smell it from outside!" Sal comes around the island and wraps me in a hug. "Welcome home, Princess. How was your day?" "Not bad. What's going on around here?"

The two men look at each other. "Gracie", Antonio speaks up. "Leonard Burns called. Richard is going to sign off and give you the last of the money you asked for. The divorce will be final."

Not exactly sure of what I'm hearing, I stand there still wrapped in Sal's embrace feeling confused.

"Hey, Gracie?" Sal shakes me gently, then turns to his dad, "I think she's in shock."

"What?" I nearly shout. "WHEN? WHO? How did this happen? I've got to sit down—give me some wine."

Antonio wheels himself in my direction. "Caro, yes, he is-a-willing to end it. He has bigger problems at-a-the company. He's a-gonna cut you loose so they can figure out who is stealing from them." Looking satisfied with this report, he nods at me. "And, the police, and us too, suspect the burglary is tied in with the business—so, Richard was advised to finalize the divorce. Hopefully it should keep you out of the loop."

"When?" I ask as eager as a kid the week before Christmas.

"Either next week or the first week of December," Sal answers me while handing me a glass of wine.

Uh oh. "Wait, what about the house? Do I have to move out by then? That will really suck."

Antonio laughs, clapping his hands. "No, no Gracie that-a Leonard worked a deal for you. You have six months to find a new place you can afford, or Richard will provide you one of his apartments until you do—rent-a-free."

"Really?" I squeak. "When did Richard all of a sudden become so generous—especially toward me?"

Sal turns, tongs in hand. "It's probably a recent change of heart now that his accounts are frozen and being examined under a microscope."

"Yeah, how about that!" I take a long full sip of a nice cold Chardonnay with crispy oak tones. "So what's for dinner?"

"Nothing," Sal answers. "Pop just roasted some chestnuts to have with the wine. I made reservations—we are all going out to celebrate!"

It was a perfect ending for a perfect night. Sal made love to me so tenderly, he always handled me as if I could break. Things are good, divorce final, money, a job. The dust seemed to be clearing. Before drifting off I said a silent prayer of thanks. Still, in the back of my head a feeling of sadness still clung to me, some days it was not so strong other days it was all I thought about.

* * *

Bright and early the next morning Sal, Toby and I walk the beach, watch the sun come up and chase Toby up and down the water's edge, then Sal chases me all the way back to Antonio's house with Toby barking playfully right beside us. My four-legged protector it seems is quite happy to let Sal chase me anywhere he pleases. Toby and Sal have finally become good friends.

Over our laughter we hear Antonio calling us from his deck. He has the phone to his ear with one hand and is waving us to come to him, with the other.

When we arrive still laughing and out of breath, he hands the phone to Sal. "Here, say hi to your brother."

Sal puts the phone to his ear. "Joe? Hey brother! Yeah, good... we're good." Sal goes into the house with the phone. I hang back and stay on the deck with Tony.

"How are Joey and Mary?" I ask. "Are they okay? You look funny. What's wrong?"

Tony laughs. "Oh, no no... they are-a-fine, they want to know if we want to go out there for Christmas and visit."

"Really? Don't you want to go?"

"I would," he says, "but, its hard-a-to fly when I'm like this." He motions at his wheelchair and for the first time that I've ever seen, he looks sad about his handicap.

"We can help you, Tony. It's not impossible. We have time to figure it out. Let's plan what days we want to go and Sal and I will call the airlines and see what's available."

Sal sticks his head out the door. "I have to make a phone call. I'll be right back."

"Wait," I nearly shout before he turns to go back in. "Your brother wants us all to go visit them for Christmas, but Tony is feeling like it would be too hard for him."

Antonio grabs my hand. "Caro, could you please call-a-me Pop now? You are like-a-one of my own. Please call me Pop."

Sal's smile was brighter than the sun. I bend down and hug Antonio tight and kiss his cheek. "I love you, Pop!"

Sal interrupts. "I'm going to call a good friend of mine who happens to be a pilot and has his own private jet—so the flight to California will be comfortable for Pop. Free of charge, and we can bring Toby. Just let me call him and see what two days he can take us and pick us up."

"Are you serious, Sal?!" I screech.

"No joke, Princess. Let me call him. Be right back." And this time he disappears. I'm still reeling at the idea that Sal – my Sal – has the kind of friends who own private jets. *Holy shit!!*

I look over at Antonio, my eye's bugging out of their sockets. "He's serious!"

"Oh yes, Caro. Sal's got lots of buddies from the service and CIA. I'm-a-sure he can make it happen."

"Do you feel better now about going?"

"Yes Caro, much better. You know, when-a-Mary is ready to give birth I would-a-love to be there to see my only grandson arrive."

"I absolutely agree. You should be there. When the time arrives we will get you there."

Sal sticks his head out of the door. " We are going to Napa for Christmas!"

"When do we leave? What's the plan?" I ask, and for the second time in two days, I'm thinking about Christmas.

We go December twenty-second and come back on the twenty-seventh. Is that good with you guys?"

"Perfect, son. Where do we meet him?"

"Jacksonville airport. He'll leave us in San Francisco. Then we'll rent a van and drive into Napa. Joe has a cottage we can stay in on his property. I've never been there, but you went Pop, didn't you?"

"Yes, right after your momma died. I went out there for a month—it's-a- beautiful. You guys are-a-gonna love it."

"Wow, Christmas in Napa Valley, California!" I look up at Sal, then over to Pop. "Thank you both for making me a part of your lives and your family."

Sal puts his hands on my waist, pulls me to his lips and kisses me. With our foreheads still touching, he whispers, "Thank *you*—for loving me."

CHAPTER 15

Thanksgiving morning, my kitchen is noisy. Antonio is in charge of the turkey and stuffing, I'm doing both the sweet potato and the green bean casseroles and Sal is stuffing mushrooms and slicing rolls. And Toby... well, Toby is drooling all over the floor and us.

"Toby, you poor-a-thing. The smell of-a-the turkey cooking is making him crazy." Antonio makes tisking noises and shakes his head at the dog.

"Don't worry, he will get plenty," I comment, laughing.

Sal throws a piece of cheese at him and he catches it like a pro. "So spoiled,"I mutter.

After a while, with not much else to do and everything cooking or on simmer, I go inside and turn the television on to watch the Macy's parade. Sal peeks in after a little while. "Do you need anything?"

"No thanks, I'm fine. I just love to watch this parade–kind of a nice traditional memory from my childhood."

He gives me a loving smile. "Best seat is at home. Did you ever go to the parade?"

"Once. My father took us. It was brutally cold and there were just way too many people. You are right about the best seat is being home on your couch."

* * *

I wake to loud voices coming from the kitchen. I open my eyes and try to get my bearings. Glancing at the parade, it's almost time for the big guy in the red suit to make his grand entrance, when I hear Sal and Antonio arguing.

"I *couldn't* get back. Let it go, Pop, will you just let it *go*?"

"Your mother asked for-a-you on her death bed. You missed *all* the last holidays of-a-her life."

"ENOUGH POP! Please!" Sal's pleading.

I get up quickly and bolt into the kitchen. I see Sal and Antonio staring each other down. They look like two angry bulls. *Uh-oh. This is not going to be pretty.*

"No more Pop, I can't. Please, I don't want to talk about it."

"YOU *COULD* HAVE BEEN HERE! NO MORE LIES!"

I can feel my body trembling, but I'm not willing to watch the two men I love most in the world, hurt each other.

"What the hell is going on in here?" I demand.

Sal turns away from his father. "He's starting with me about where I was when Mom was sick."

I glance at Antonio whose eyes are blood red. He also appears to be getting short of breath. I slowly step to his side. "Pop, are you alright? Can you breathe? Sal, get him some water."

Sal brings a glass of water over to his father but Antonio won't take it. I give Sal a very serious look of disappointment. I take the water glass and hand it to Tony. With shaky hands he sips but won't glance in my direction.

"I should go, caro. Please forgive me, Holiday's are hard

I step back to get a good look at both of them. "Stop this!" I scolded. "YOU TWO ARE NOT

GOING TO FIGHT AND RUIN THIS HOLIDAY! THIS HAS GONE FAR ENOUGH!"

The two of them glare at me in shock. I'm sure neither one has ever heard me yell at anyone.

"Gracie, it's okay, calm down," Sal says, pain etched into his handsome face.

"NO, SAL. I will not. You have got to tell him where you were and what happened to you. It's time. Right now–or I will!"

Sal knows he is defeated because I'm standing my ground. I know this will help him – and Antonio.

"What is she talking about, Sal? What happened? Where were you? Talk to me, son."

"Why don't you guys go out to the lanai and talk. Leave Toby in here with me."

As Antonio starts for the door, I turn to Sal and he pulls me into a fierce hug. I feel him trembling and I understand how hard this is.

In a low voice he whispers, "I'm sorry. Gracie. I didn't want it to come out this way. I was going to tell him, I swear I was."

I put my hands on his face and look into his eyes. "I believe that, Sal. But now's your chance. I think it will help you and I *know* he is going to understand. He loves you very much."

He follows his dad out to the pool deck.

How does a son tell his father about prison and torture? About the fears and long days and nights of wishing he was home with his mother. Knowing he would probably never see her again....

A few times I walk by and peek in on them. I see Antonio crying, I see Sal furiously wiping his own eyes. I hear them get loud again–but it turned into laughter.

When they return to the kitchen, Antonio seems better and Sal seems lighter, as though a huge burden has been lifted. The rest of the day is happy, calm. Maybe now that we all know the truth, now that another ghost is banished, we're closer than before.

When we sit down to have our Thanksgiving dinner, Antonio says a prayer of thanks and blessings. I've heard it many times before, but today, behind his words, being thankful has more of a heart-felt meaning.

I'm thankful for them both. Sal by some miracle survived that prison and found me. Some people say there are no accidents in life. Maybe miracles *do* happen.

* * *

I wake up to feather light kisses on the back of my neck that trail down to my shoulder.

"Wake up, Princess," Sal whispers in muffled tones. "Hey sleepy head, wake up."

I open my eyes and see Sal's handsome face smiling.

"What's going on? What time is it?"

"It's about five. Sun won't be up for hours. But you were mumbling in your sleep."

"I was? What was I saying?"

Still exploring my body with kisses, his voice is muffled. "If I knew, I would tell you."

"And when I mumble in my sleep you wake me with kisses?"

"Yes," he continues between kisses. "You were starting to panic and I wanted to wake you up calmly. Is it working?"

"Emm hmmm."

"Good."

Sal rolls me on my back and keeps me secure. He kisses my throat, then my breasts, lightly sucking, first the left one, then the right. I'm about ready to scream with the delightful pain of anticipation. He lets his hand slide down between my legs and slips fingers inside me.

"Sal," I moan, thrusting my hips upward.

"Gracie, you're so warm." His breath on my skin makes me tremble. "I need to be in you, now," he whispers as he thrusts inside and holds me still.

"Don't move," he groans, "I just want to be inside you." His dark eyes focus on mine. "I love you, Gracianna D'Anella."

I just about come undone right then. Lying naked with the man I love buried inside me, eyes piercing into my soul, using my full, given name to proclaim his love is mind blowing.

"I can stay like this with you, forever."

I can't reply. I'm going to come whether he moves or not. Slowly we move, finding our rhythm. He rolls us over and I'm straddling him, his hands securely on my hips keeping me in place. And I am over the cliff. When Sal follows me into ecstasy, an orgasm vibrates me again. I collapse on top of him. I'm panting so hard, I can barely speak.

"Is this how you are going to wake me every morning?"

"It's a possibility" he says with a smile, as he playfully pats my ass.

I kiss him. "I love you too, Salvetore Anthony Petroni.". We rest for a while, our bodies still entwined, until my stomach growled. Sal puts his hand on my belly.

"You're hungry, Princess. Let me get your breakfast. What time are you going into work today?"

"Around ten," I mutter into my pillow.

* * *

We go for our morning walk on the beach, a chilly day but beautiful. Sal and I walk hand in hand while Toby searches the beach for treasures.

"Gracie, would you do something for me?"

I stop walking and turn to Sal. He places his hands one on each of my arms. "What's wrong?" I ask, searching his face.

"I was thinking about your dreams. On some nights you mumble and appear to be struggling. Maybe you could go talk to a doctor."

"Doctor?" I echo. "You mean a psychiatrist?"

He nods. "Yeah. You could go see the one I was going to. I'm just concerned about you."

Now I know he doesn't understand. *Does he think I'm crazy after all?* I look down at our sneakers in the sand. Sal coaxes my chin up with his fingers. "It's just a suggestion. Gracie, sometimes talking about stuff helps bring it to the surface and then you can purge it. It helped me. You know that."

"I do know... I just don't know about it for me. Can I think about it? Maybe after the holidays."

"Gracie, do this for me. Sometimes one or two sessions is all you need. I'll call Dr. Brooks today and see about an appointment."

I gaze into Sal's deep brown eyes. He looks truly worried and for that reason alone I tell him to go ahead and make the call. Might even help this psychic thing.

* * *

"Holy mother of god!" I say as I look at the tree in my living room that certainly rivals the one in Rockefeller Center. Every time I come into the room I'm in awe of the largest tree I've ever had.

We had a blast picking it out and Sal only dropped it twice after we got the netting cut free and into the stand.

Sal battles with the lights while I went off to find my ornaments. When we are finished it really looks beautiful and the smell of fresh fir takes over the room, Pop is worn out by the time we've got the ornaments on, so he leaves Sal and me to finish the last touches. Sal hits the switch and we are basking in the glow of a million twinkling red, white and green lights.

"It's beautiful, Sal, I love it. Thank you for this" Sal comes over to my side to get a better look.

"No need to thank me, Gracie-It's ours together. I love you."

We both take a seat on the couch to admire our work and snuggle. Sal takes my hand. "I called Dr. Brooks for you. They got you in on Monday afternoon 3pm." I tense a little. I know I agreed to go, but I'm not feeling happy about it. He gives me a little squeeze. "It'll be fine. Just talk to him" Feeling nervous I quickly change the subject.

"You all ready for the benefit tomorrow? Tuxedo and all?" He smiles big maybe understanding my apprehension. "Yesssss, I'm looking forward to a fancy evening with you on my arm."

"Richard will be there too," I remind him.

"I know," he answers with a smile that reminds me of a cat that's eaten a canary. "I can't wait."

CHAPTER 16

The night of the children's Christmas benefit arrives and it's a beautiful night—not too warm, not too cold.

Earlier in the day I'd made a trip to my bank so I could retrieve my diamond necklace from the safety deposit box. Now standing in my closet with my hair in rollers trying to decide on the strapless black velvet gown with the slit up the side to my mid thigh or the shimmery maroon gown with the sweetheart neckline that shows off my cleavage. I take both dresses out and hold them against me in front of the mirror.

"The maroon one," Sal says in a soft voice. "I like the way it shimmers and lights up your face. It's festive." I glance over my shoulder Sal is half dressed and apparently spying on me.

"Funny, I was thinking the maroon one, too. I'll save the black one for New Year's Eve."

Sal raises his eyebrows. "New Year's? What are we doing for New Year's?"

I turn and toss the dresses on the bed and pad my way over to him, reaching my arms around his muscular frame.

"Celine and her husband throw a big party at the club every year. It's fantastic. She gets a D.J. and the best caterer in Jacksonville. Every year she comes up with something special at midnight—

last year it was a fire works display. I go every year. Your father was my *plus one* last year."

"Was he?" he says with a smile.

"Yes. I'm glad he didn't stay home like an old fart—we had a ball!"

"Well, I guess you will have two Petroni men escorting you to the New Year's bash this year." He bent his head a little so he could gently brush his lips with mine.

I deepen the kiss and he pulls me in closer. Through his trousers I can feel his arousal, my body responds to him and I'm almost gasping for air. He pulls his lips from mine and gives me a searing gaze.

"Princess," he growls, "I guess were gonna be a little late."

*   *   *

I'm just putting the finishing touches on my make-up when Sal calls from down stairs.

"Gracie, you ready to go? Pop's here and we're running late."

Grabbing my purse and slipping on my shoes, I check the mirror one last time. I'm happy with how I look and my face has a warm glow that has nothing to do with my make-up.

I start to make my way down the staircase and Antonio whistles. "Momma mia! Gracie, you look-a-like an angel!"

Sal walks over to the bottom of the stairs staring at me with an open mouth. "You look amazing. Like a Princess—you are absolutely beautiful."

I take in the sight of Sal in his black tuxedo. He's gelled back his hair and tied it in a small ponytail at the nape of his neck. The square of his jaw line and his broad shoulders make my stomach quiver.

"And you, are devastatingly handsome," I whisper, touching his face.

"Okay, you two love birds, lets go. Si?"

"Oh Pop, one more thing before we go. Take my cell phone and get a quick picture of me and Sal right here on the stairs. I want to send it to my best friend, Maggie."

Sal puts his arm around me and we pose, all smiles. I check the picture–it's a good one. I scroll to Maggie's name in my contacts and send her the picture.

When I get outside, there is an SUV limo waiting in my driveway. I stand in awe of the massive vehicle. "Which one of you ordered the limo?"

Sal and Pop point to each other. "We thought this would be a nice surprise." Sal motions with his hand.

"Oh is it ever! You guys are amazing."

The driver opens the car door for me and I slide in. Sal follows right behind and sits next to me in the back. The driver then helps Pop get in the front and secures his wheel chair in a special place designed just for that.

On the way to the Marriot, my cell buzzes and I glance to see who's texting me.

Where you at baby girl? Oh I hope you're late because you guys are doing the dance with no pants!! ☺

I burst out laughing.

"What's so funny? Sal asks.

"Celine just sent me a text."

"Annnnnd...?"

"And here. Read it!"

Sal takes my phone and reads the message. He chuckles, too. "Are you going to answer her?"

"She'll know the answer when she sees me."

Sal taps like crazy at the phone.

"Huh?" I gasp. "Wait! What are you doing? What are you saying?"

185

He hands my cell back with a devilish smile playing across his face. "Read it."

Can't wait to meet you. You are right, but it was more of a tango than a dance. Almost there and your girlfriend looks beautiful. Don't know how much longer I can control myself. We might not get out of the limo! ;-) Sal.

"Oh my god! Sal!" I'm laughing and gasping at the same time and can barely get the words out. My cell buzzes again.
Excellent!! I hope you made her toes curl and I hope she made you take the lord's name in vain! See ya soon!
"OH GOD!!" I shout, 'I'm so mortified!" But I can't stop laughing. My make-up is going to be a mess.
I show Sal what Celine sent back and we both roar with laughter until I've got tears streaming down my face.
"She sounds like a trip."
"Oh, she's a trip alright. Don't be too shocked if she makes a pass at you. Remember I told you, she's a big flirt, and a bit of a cougar, but, harmless. She's like an older sister to me."
Sal's still smiling, then nods. "Duly noted."
We finally arrive and locate our table number. The decorations are stunning just like most of the people attending and a D.J is playing some Christmas carols softly in the back round.
Celine spots us and bolts across the room like she's been shot out of a cannon.
"Hey, you made it!" Looking me over she hugs me and whispers in my ear, "Oh baby girl you got that *I just got properly fucked* glow! She's bouncing on her Manolo Blahniks' heels.
"Yesss, I do. Thanks for noticing. Celine, this is Sal. Sal, my great friend and partner-in-crime, Celine."

"Well hello, handsome!" Sal puts his hand out to shake hers and Celine pushes it away.

"Oh, you're gonna give me a hug now, no formal handshake for me—no, sir. Now let me get a look at ya. Oh, you a handsome devil, no wonder Gracie was late. Probably can't keep her hands off you."

Sal smiles and reaches for me, putting his arm around me. "Correction, Celine. I'm the one who can't keep my hands off of *her*."

We excuse ourselves to walk and mingle around. I introduce Sal to some of the ladies of the SWS. Mimi gives me a thumbs up. Sal spots Dr. Brooks and introduces us.

"Oh, Sal. Hey, how are you? This must be Gracie? Pleasure to meet you," he says, shaking my hand.

"Hi, Dr. Brooks. I guess I'll see you on Monday."

"Oh yes, looking forward to it. You two have a good time, tonight."

"You do the same," I say back. I turn to Sal and whisper, "He seems very nice."

He gives my hand a little squeeze. "He is. Don't worry—you'll like him—easy to talk to."

Just then I spot Celine waving me over. Sal tells me to go ahead and promises to meet me back at the table.

"What's up, Celine?" I say softly. The room is filling up with rich guests and I don't want to be overheard. With Celine, there's no telling what's going on.

"Richard and the gold diggin' whore just arrived."

"Wonderful. It's a party now," I drawl sarcastically. I stand my ground and keep on eye out for Sal. It would be great if he's standing next to me when Richard and Camille make their entrance.

The long table up front is where the SWS has their door prizes for the fifty/fifty raffle. Celine,

Mimi and I are helping the rest of the members sell tickets. Barbra Dalton is schmoozing her way around the room and poor Chloe is following right behind her like a lost puppy.

As I stand at the table selling tickets, I see Camille and Richard making their way through the crowded area.

I spot Richard first, of course. He's walked way ahead of Camille instead of beside her. He used to do that to me too, and never looked back to see where I was. I guess some things never change. From the looks of it she isn't happy with that behavior, either.

Camille's dress is a white sparkly high-collared gown. She has too much glitter around her eyes and looks like an evil snow queen from a Disney movie.

Richard approaches the table and Mimi stutters asking him if he wants to buy a chance.

"Yes, I would, thank you. Hello, Grace. You're looking well."

I give him a tight smile, trying to calm the chill that comes over me because he's spoken my name.

"Darling!" Camille calls coming up behind him, "there you are. Oh, hello, Gracie."

I give a quick glance in her direction. "Camille."

Out of nowhere an arm snakes around my waist. "Princess, how's it going? Do you need some help?"

"How do you always know when I need you?" I whisper, leaning toward him.

"We're soul mates, remember? I always have my eyes on you."

Camille looks at us and smiles. " I see you guys are still together."

I ignore her but Sal looks at me and says, "I adore her."

Richard ignores us both and Camille keeps smiling as they walk away to find their table.

After a wonderful meal, the D.J plays all kinds of music and people hit the dance floor with vigor. Sal gets up from the table and takes my hand.

"Shall we dance, Princess?"

I let him lead me to the dance floor and I can feel all eyes are upon us.

"Everyone is watching," I whisper. I realize that for the first time in months I'm self-conscious of the attention.

Sal winks and shrugs and I laugh. I relax.

"Let them watch. Know how to tango?" he whispers as he puts his right hip against mine.

I nod and place my weight on my left toe so I'm ready for our first turn.

The D.J is playing "Save the Last Dance for Me, and Sal tangoes me all over the floor, twirling me out and into his side, leaning me down into dips. At one point I hear a little applause coming from the crowd and I chuckle. It wasn't perfect but Sal is a good leader and we are having fun. We're making quite a spectacle of ourselves and I can imagine Celine's delighted reaction.

When the song stops, Sal spins me so that I end up cradled in his arms looking up into his eyes.

Everyone claps and cheers. I glance over at our table and Pop is all smiles while Celine's hands cupped at her mouth, screams "BRAVO!!"

Laughing and breathless, we hold hands and take a bow. "Well, Mr. Petroni, you never told me you could *really* tango," I whisper out the side of my smile.

"You never asked, Princess." Then he gives me a quick kiss.

Overwhelmed and panting, I need air and point to the balcony doors. Sal escorts me out into a star lit sky where a cool ocean breeze is blowing in from the north.

He stands behind me and wraps his arms around my waist. I look over my shoulder at him.

"You never cease to amaze me."

"I'm amazed by *you*," he says, kissing the tip of my nose.

"Whew! My legs are a little shaky but that was fun. I haven't danced like that in years! You dance like a pro–did you learn that or does it come naturally for you?"

Sal made a wagging motion with his hand. "A little of both, I suppose. Mom loved to dance, so she showed Joey and me some moves here and there when we were growing up."

I shiver a little and Sal pulls me tighter against him and moves my hair over so he can nibble my neck. The music inside changes to a slower pace and the first few notes of Andrea Bocelli's, "A Time to Say Goodbye" comes floating out of the ballroom.

I peek up at Sal. "They are playing our song."

He turns me in his arms, lifts my chin, stealing a kiss " Mmm, yes I hear it."

We sway to our song under the moon lit sky. He caresses my face.

"Gracie, you look so beautiful tonight and everyone knows it, too. I've been watching. I notice things–I've heard some people say how happy you seem."

"It's because of you, Sal. You make me happy. You made me whole again–your love surrounds me."

"You're my everything, Gracie. I feel such desire when were together–and a longing when we're not. He chuckles a little. "You've turned me upside down. Believe me when I tell you, you are all I think about."

Our kiss is way too hot for being in public and he pulls back just a little.

"I can't wait to get you home."

I give him a shy smile. "Its almost over, maybe thirty more minutes–an hour tops."

He gets a playful look on his face and takes my hand, leading me back to the doors. "Lets get you back inside before I do something we both regret."

We get back to the table and I excuse myself to go to the ladies room. I leave my little purse on the chair and ask Celine if she wants to take the trip, too.

"Mmm, no thanks, baby. I'm going to see if I can get your boyfriend here to dance with me, next."

Sal being a gentleman, holds his hand out for her. "How can I refuse and invitation like that?"

Celine takes his hand. "You can't," she drawls. As they start their way to the dance floor, Celine turns to me and winks. "I might not give him back to ya–look out now."

I wander down the corridor to where the rest rooms are and there's timid Mimi sitting on a chair holding some Advil's.

"Hey, Mimi, how you doing? Can I get something for you?"

"No, I'll be alright, thanks Gracie. Sometimes champagne just gives me a little headache."

Since she's okay, I make my way over to a stall and go in, careful not to drop my dress in the water. When I come back out, Mimi's still there sipping her water.

"Gee Gracie, you and Sal look so great together, and wow, what a dancer. I'm so happy for you. Pay no attention to the other women in the club–believe me, underneath their snobbyness they are happy for you too–and if some are not, well then they are green with envy. That's a win-win if you ask me!"

I look around the rest room searching to see if anyone is listening. Mimi waves her hand.

"No one's here but us, I already checked. I've been in here a while, hiding out I suppose," she titters. "I guess I should try to pee."

I giggle in reply. Mimi is very down to earth and not uppity like the rest of the ladies. She gets up and goes into a stall while I finish washing my hands. We can walk back together, so I plan to wait until she's ready.

All at once, a man dressed all in black with a ski mask covering his face explodes through the door and points a gun in my face. He backs up a step and I'm looking at a metal barrel that looks awfully big around. I suck in a breath as my brain tries to register what's happening.

"The necklace bitch! Get it off! Lets go!" he snarls.

I'm frozen in my tracks, to frightened to move. My heart is beating so hard it'll either give out or jump out of my chest. *Oh god, Sal....*

"Please," I squeak as tears choke my throat, "please don't shoot me." My knees are buckling and my eyesight begins to flash.

"Give me the fucking necklace now and I won't *have* to shoot you. Hurry up!"

I put my hands up slowly to get to the latch, but I'm trembling so much I can't get it undone. Staring at the gun, I can't breath. The first wave of panic is consuming me, the room begins to spin and I feel myself going down.

The man grabs my arm. " Bitch, don't play with me, what are you doing? Oh shit, you're *not* gonna pass out!" Using his forearm, he pins me up against the wall and holds me up from under my chin. The gun is now up against the side of my head.

"Listen bitch, its really simple. Just get the necklace off and I won't have to hurt you." He's pressing under my chin so hard I begin to choke.

Just before everything goes black, I hear a thunderous rumble and the man lets go as I crumble to the tile floor.

* * *

"Celine, thank you for the dance," I said as I offered her my arm and we headed back to our table.

"No, thank you. And Gracie looks great by the way. Whatever you're doing, keep it up."

"I intend to," I told her, pulling out the chair for her. She fumbled with her cell phone, then grabbed at my arm. Her eyes were wide as she held the phone up to my face. I read the text:

HELP-in bathroom man with gun at Gracie!

* * *

"So, Sal," the deputy started again. "I need to take your statement. Let's get this done. Then you can see to your lady."

Sal bit back a growl and stuffed his hands in the pockets of his trousers.

"I raced out of the ballroom, down a corridor, found the ladies room and kicked in the door. When I spotted the little piece of shit standing over Gracie, I didn't think–there was no time–my combat instincts took over. I grabbed him by his neck and bent the arm with the gun back. He struggled with me and managed to cock the gun.

He said, 'I'll shoot her man let me go, I'll shoot her!'" Sal ran a hand through his hair that had lost it's tie a while ago, probably during the attack.

"I knew I had him in a good sleeper hold but he let one shot out and it hit the wall above the sinks. I glanced at Gracie who was sprawled on the floor but I didn't know if she was hurt or dead or what. I saw red fury and hauled him back with me and slammed his head to the porcelain sink. Heard a snap. Then I got over to Gracie."

"Ever see this guy before?" the deputy asked.

Sal shook his head. "Mimi said he wanted her necklace."

"Okay, so he's dead, what happened next?"

"I went over to Gracie and checked her over. Then I realized she fainted. She gets severe anxiety attacks sometimes and I'll bet this one was awful."

The cop nodded.

"I brought her around and sat her in the chair in that little alcove and then Mimi came out of the stall, shaking and stuttering so bad, I thought she'd faint, too. She handed me her bottle of water. Next thing I know, you guys are here."

"Okay, sir. I've got what I need for tonight. You can go. If we need anything more, we'll be in touch."

Sal turns away and jogs over to the ambulance where the lights are still flashing red and white beams all around the country club front lawn.

She looks at him, her eyes still too wide, too dark. He knows what she's seeing in her mind. He reaches out to take her hand and Mimi gives him a little smile.

"You doing okay, Mimi?" he asks as he squeezes Gracie's hand.

"Ss..sal?...is..is he dead?" she asks, pointing at the front door of the building.

He lets out a big sigh and looks back to Gracie. "Yeah," he said quietly, "he's dead.

* * *

In upstate New York in a quaint little Norman Rockwell town, Maggie spent a nice quiet winter's eve safe and warm with her husband and girls in their old but cozy Victorian home. Before retiring to bed she searched for her cell phone, tracing her steps and coming up empty.

"Jess, I can't find my cell—did you see it?"

"No Mom, did you try calling it with Dad's phone?"

"AH! See? This is why we keep you kids around."

"HONEY!" Maggie called to her husband. "I need to use your phone to find mine."

"Oh here, I'll call it for you," he said.

Maggie stood still, waiting to hear the Marvin Gaye ring tone, "Let's Get It On."

"It's ringing," he shouted, "do you hear it?"

"I think I do. Keep it going!" Maggie raced up the stairs and realized it was coming from her art studio on the third floor.

"OKAY, thanks I got it!" She entered her studio and flipped the light switch on. There it sat on her desk. "Yep, right where I left it," she commented to herself. She hit the button and saw a text from Gracie–about three hours earlier. She tapped her message icon and up popped a picture.

"Oooh... oh how beautiful they look." She stared at the photo for a bit, then a little longer. *Hmm how strange. This photo seems familiar, like I have seen it before.*

She sent the picture to her computer. Within seconds she clicked on the big screen and there they were, larger, so she could get a better look.

"Oh my, Gracie". She said to herself. "You really do have a handsome devil there."

"Hey hon," her husband called from the hall. "Ready to go to bed? The girls are tucked in."

"Huh? Oh yeah, yeah. Hey Mike, come up here a minute."

He stands in the doorway. "Yeah, sure, what's up?"

"Look at this photo. It's Gracie and her new boyfriend. I talked to her earlier–she sounds head over heels happy."

"Wow! She looks great!" Mike commented. "Hey, he looks like he stepped out of GQ or something. Good for her!"

"Yeah, yeah besides that–this picture, does it remind you of anything?"

Mike took a longer look. "No, why? Should it?"

"I'm not sure, but for some reason it looks familiar to me. It's giving me like a deja vu feeling."

Mike chuckled at his wife. "Should I get the tin foil hats out or the Ouija board?"

"Hey, really, no jokes." Maggie turned towards her husband. He saw her face was serious which meant the wheels in her brain were going full throttle.

"I'll call Gracie in the morning," she said. "See how the party went."

"Okay you do that. Now will you come to bed?"

Maggie turned back to the picture on the computer screen. "Yeah, I'll be there in a minute." Her husband kissed the top of her head and started for the door.

As he was leaving the studio he muttered, "Truly it's not that surprising–you and Gracie have been friends a long time. You two have always had some kind of mental connection."

Maggie sat for a minute longer or so staring at the picture. She just couldn't shake the weird feeling she got when she looked at it. She smiled in spite of herself. "They look so regal," she thought out loud. "Wait till Gracie hears all this, she'll think I'm crazy."

From down the hall her husband called out, "You *are* crazy. Now come to bed!"

CHAPTER 17

Sitting in an ambulance outside in the Marriott's parking lot, the EMT examines me. He shines his bright little light in my eyes and has a blood pressure cuff on my arm.

"I think you'll be okay miss, but maybe you should come to the hospital anyway. You've had quite a scare and you're still a bit shaky."

"No, please, I just want to go home." I crane my neck and spot Sal, Pop and Mimi talking with the police. I let out a long sigh and the EMT adjusts the blanket he's wrapped around my shoulders now that the BP cuff is gone.

"Finally!" I hear Celine yell as she comes over to the ambulance. "They wouldn't let me near you. My god, Gracie, I think I've had my first heart attack!"

I smile at her. "I'm fine Celine, really. If you've had a heart attack, maybe we should trade places and let this EMT look at you, too."

She swats at me with her lovely hands, but I can see by her color that she's had a fright, too. I try to smile, but I don't think it really works. She clutches her fist to her chest. "If it wasn't for Mimi hiding in that stall sending texts, I don't know what would have happened."

"Celine," I whisper, "Sal killed that man. He *killed* that man." *What if this triggers something awful in Sal? Because of me...* I feel the familiar burn of tears in my eyes my body keeps shuddering in nervous spasms. *I will not cry...*

"He had a gun, Gracie. You don't know what that shit stain could have done. I'm thankful Sal was here. Mimi said she saw the whole thing from the stall." Celine chuckles. "She's tellin' the cops he was like some kind of superhero."

"Sal told me he would kill anyone who got close enough to harm me. I'm just glad I didn't actually *see* it. I know Sal is strong. I know he's killed before because he had to, but, I know the tender, loving Sal, the one who touches me like I might break–those same gentle hands took a life." I drop my heavy head into my hands. What if *his* dreams come back?

Celine reaches for my hands and gently pulls them away from my face. "Hey, you..." she says in a motherly tone. "Don't you *dare* make Sal feel guilty about what he's done." She points a scarlet fingernail at me. "That guy loves the shit out of you! He is the same guy. He fought for our country and I'm sure he's seen things no human should ever see. But I'm also sure he has taken out bigger and more important problems than some dick weasel with a gun!"

She's right and I know it, but I can't stop the fear that threatens to choke me. How many men and women serving this country can't handle the guilt? How many lost their battle with those ugly memories?

"I know Celine, it's not that. The past couple of years have been a long road for Sal - to get back to normal. I'm just scared this might set him back. He was finally finding some peace."

"Yeah, baby girl." She smiles and pats my leg. "He found *you*."

This time I can give her a smile. Hasn't Sal told me that same thing more than once? I nod and she relaxes.

Sal strides over to the ambulance and as I watch him approach us, my heart skips a beat. Celine hugs me and then hugs Sal.

"Let me get the old man home. I'll talk to you both tomorrow—make sure she gets some sleep tonight, Sal. I think it be best if you skipped the hokey pokey tonight."

Sal's smile is weary, but genuine. "Yes, I'll take care of her. Thanks, Celine."

She winks, points her manicured finger at me one more time and races off.

"How are you feeling?" he asks as he tightens the blanket that was given to me.

"I'm fine." I search his eyes. I see fatigue, but nothing else. "How about you?"

He chucks my chin with his index finger. "I'm good."

"I know you're *physically* good". I reach my hand to his cheek and then place it over his heart. How are you *here*?"

He takes my hand and kisses it. His voice is quiet but urgent as he looks at me. "I was scared, Gracie—really scared. I saw you on the floor and I thought he hurt you. He was scared himself—he would of shot us *all* out of fear. I know that look."

Just then the EMT comes back. We've all been checked out and they are ready to get going.

"Ma'am are you sure you don't want to get checked out at the hospital?"

Sal cuts in before I can answer. "I'm taking her home. Thank you for your help."

"No problem, sir. If she starts to feel shaky or light headed don't hesitate to get her to the hospital."

* * *

Camille had enjoyed their evening, but was delighted to be headed home. She was expecting some good news shortly.

On their way home from the benefit Richard's cell phone rang.

"Yes, Jessica," Richard answered. "WHAT? When? We were just there."

Camille managed to convey just the right amount of concern. "What's happened Richard?"

Richard, still on the phone waved at her so he could hear more information. When he disconnected the call he turned the Escalade around.

"Richard, what in god's name is going on?" she asked, unable to control the rising concern.

"Someone attacked Gracie at the benefit. Tried to steal her necklace–at gunpoint."

Camille started to sweat, took a breath. "Do they know anything? Why are we going back? I don't think going back there is going to help anything, Darling."

"I want to check on her–see if I can help. Jessica said the man who attacked her is dead, but doesn't know anything more."

"Dead?" Camille shrieked. *Had little Gracie killed that idiot? Had he told anyone anything before he died?* Her dinner was beginning to churn in her stomach.

When they arrived back at the Marriott the parking lot was full of police and ambulances. Richard jammed the car into park, opened the door and literally sprinted toward the flashing lights. Camille wondered if he'd ever move that fast for her...

She stayed behind in the car almost holding her breath as she tried to battle the panic back. Finally the car door opened and Richard jumped back in.

"Well?" Camille asked, not bothering to hide her concern. Let him think it was for *poor* Gracie.

He recapped what he'd learned, then took a breath. "Sal apparently crashed into the ladies room and there was a struggle, but he cracked the guy's head open, broke his neck!"

"And Gracie is fine?"

"Yes everyone I hear is fine, I just couldn't get close enough to talk to anyone, I'll try calling her in the morning."

"Richard?" Camille willed herself to stay cool. "Do they have any leads? Do they think there's any connection to the burglary?"

Richard shrugged. "No idea." He shook his head. "What the hell is going on? Poor Gracie..."

Camille wanted to scream, but she stayed calm. She reached over and touched his face. "I hope you don't feel guilty, Richard. None of this is your fault–don't make yourself feel bad about it."

He brushed her hand away from his face and put the car into Drive.

"Jesus Christ, Camille. I know it's not my fault, but what's been happening to Gracie is not *her* fault either. We may have fallen apart, but she was once my wife. I don't want to see anything bad happen to her."

They drove the rest of the way home in silence. Camille had not only calmed herself, but she was feeling a bit relieved. What was that saying? Dead men told no tales?

* * *

"I'm never going to fall asleep tonight," I announce as we walk through the door. Toby approaches us with caution, sensing something is off.

"It's okay, Toby, come here, boy," I call. He comes toward us and I pat his fur and kiss his head. He calms down a bit and Antonio takes him outside. Sal gently tugs my arm.

"Hey, you're going to get into bed. This is all over for tonight. You need to rest."

I cock my head and raise an eyebrow. "Just like Toby knows something's off, I know there is something on your mind. We need to talk."

He shakes his head as he opens the top button on the tux shirt. "Princess, it can wait till tomorrow. I'm concerned about you. I want you in bed resting."

"Ha! Like *that's* going happen."

Antonio came back in with Toby. I stand in place, hands on my hips, my eyes darting back and forth at them both.

"Was it the guy who was snooping around here a month ago when we went to St. Augustine?" I demand to know.

Sal and his father exchange that look of theirs. Sal takes his hand and wipes at his face, taking a deep breath. "Yes."

I raise my eyebrows. "Do we know who he was or why he came after me?"

Antonio puts up a hand as if to slow me down. "Caro, he was a petty thief, he had many aliases. He is some-a-one who would be paid to do a job or a hit. Now they have a face to identify- they find he has record a mile long."

Sal swipes at his face again and drags his fingers through his hair. "He was a piece of shit someone hired to steal your necklace. He had a gun. He was a threat—kept saying he was going to shoot you and I took him out. But, now we can't question him. We have no idea who hired him."

I can see, hell—*feel* his frustration. The staccato report-like phrases. The expressionless face that I hardly recognize. Like he was talking about a military operation. I wonder if *he* can handle what he's done...

"Son, you did what-a you had to do. No charges—it was self defense." Pop turns his head back to me and points a finger. "Your friend Mimi, she witnessed the whole-a-thing. He was caught in the act with a weapon."

Sal scratches his head. "I'd like to know who hired him, that's all. I don't get it. And until we know that, she's not safe. Guys like that are all over the place."

"I saw Officer Dan there tonight. What did he have to say?" I ask with one eye on Sal.

Pop just lifts a shoulder. "He thinks it could be random, but they have-a-no leads yet. He had a throw away cell phone, wiped clean."

"RANDOM!" Sal's voice lifts in fury. "They think it could be random? Holy shit! Are they stupid, Pop? She had someone break in. The suspect did a drive-by twice, Lou put that on record. Then the same guy shows up at the benefit and knew to go in the bathroom. He's been watching. Nothing random about any of this."

"Okay son, calm-a-down. What else can we do for now?"

Sal shakes his head. "I'm making some phone calls."

I just stand there, listening. The look on my face must be pretty bad because I feel like puking. It's not over...

Sal registers my look and steps into my arms. "Don't worry, I'm making assumptions. But, the threat still worries me. Did someone hire him? Gracie think, do you know of anyone who would want to hurt you? Has anyone threatened you in the past year?"

"No," I squeak. "I can't imagine anyone, not even Richard."

"Son," Antonio says evenly. "Maybe it was random. He could have-a-been watching from before the break in. Knowing she was alone here."

"I don't know, Pop. How'd he know the code?"

"Thieves know how to figure out codes, nothing is impossible. Now, this old man is-a-going home. Good benefit, Gracie! The kids will do well–at least that turned out good, si?"

I bend down and give Antonio a big hug. "Yes, that's a good thing. And, both Mimi and I are fine, too. Thank you for coming with us, Pop."

We walk him to the back door and Sal watches as Tony wheels himself the short distance to his house, then enters. We see the kitchen light switch on.

Sal turns in my direction. "Off to bed, Princess. Let's go. Are you feeling any better?"

"I'm freaked out but I'll be alright. I thank god you were there–you saved my life. How do I ever..."

Sal puts a finger to my lips. "Don't you dare say *re-pay*. This isn't about keeping score. I thought I lost you tonight. That would have ended me in ways you can not imagine–and I can't explain." He takes my hand in his and we walk toward the stairs.

"Now, I want you to get into bed and don't worry about any of this. I'm going to do my own checking and make some calls. It should be quiet for awhile. If someone is out for you or this necklace, after tonight, they will lay low."

"How can you be so sure?"

"It's my job to know. Trust me, Princess."

We enter the bedroom and what I really want is a hot shower. Maybe I can scrub some of the terror out of my body. And maybe I'll feel clean enough to get to sleep.

Sal assures me he'll be in the study while I shower, but not to worry. After I'm in the shower long enough that I begin to wrinkle, I quickly dry off, put on some warm P.J's and crawl into bed. Sal peeks in to check on me.

"You okay now?"

"Yes, but..." I wrinkle my nose at him. "Would you be opposed to me taking a Xanax tonight?"

He takes a long deep breath and exhales. "No, I guess not." He goes into the bathroom and comes out with a little pill and a glass of water.

"I thought you got rid of those, Gracie."

"I promised not to take them-and I haven't needed one in months."

"Alright, lay back, relax and try to fall asleep. I'll be in soon. He nestles me under the covers and bends down to touch his lips to mine. He pulls away but stays close, brushing the back of his hand to my cheek. Looking deep into my eyes, "I love you Gracie, he whispers. More than you'll ever know."

He kisses me again, slow and lingering a little longer. Then he kisses my forehead, straightens and clicks off the light.

I take his hand before he turns away. "I love you too, Sal."

* * *

"I ship out at the crack of dawn."

Sal is so tall and proud in his Marine dress blues; White belt, and hat that he calls a cover. He appears a little different but I can tell it's Sal.

I raise my chin to him and pout, "I wish you didn't have to go. I'll be doing wedding plans by myself."

Placing his thumb and forefinger on my chin he chuckled. "You've got your mom to help. I'll be back before you know it. It's just six months more. Hey, look on the bright side. I'm stationed here in the states."

I reach my arms around my handsome marine and hug him close. "Yeah, but, clear across the country in Hawaii. Doesn't feel like the states to me."

"It won't be a vacation. I'll be on the USS Oklahoma and when I get back we'll get married. I promise-you'll see. Hell, maybe I can send for you to come to Hawaii in six months time. We'll get married there. That would be swell, right?"

"What–you mean like ELOPE?" I say with surprise. "What would my parents think?"

"You're nineteen, Princess and you're already wearing my ring–you're practically mine. What could they think?"

He kisses me hard, and I giggle.

"Now, you ready to go? Get your sweater it's cold out. Don't want you getting sick."

I reach for my sweater and steal a last minute glance in the mirror. That's not my face–but, it's me. I start to feel very strange and begin to panic. Suddenly to my right is a woman at a table with cards, No–wait–that's Amina.

She's speaking to me and I'm back in St. Augustine. "Gracie, don't be afraid of your past lives... nothing can hurt you. Your soul will guide you."

Amina vanishes and I am back in the mirror putting a comb to my page boy styled hair. We're so very young....

Next thing I know we're at a dance, a USO dance. There are many soldiers around and big band swing music fills the huge room. It was all so familiar. I waved to other girls that I knew. Most of us were happy because our boys were stateside for the rest of their tours. Some like Sal would be stationed in Pearl Harbor, Hawaii. The night was full of laughter and war stories...and hope.

Then, I'm home...not my home but familiar and I'm in the kitchen making toast. I look out the window at a snowy cold morning.

"Ah you started the coffee. Thank you."

"You're welcome, Mom. No problem."

"What's happening with that toast, baby? It smells like it's burning."

I blink in my mother's direction–she reminds me of Celine–but I know she is my mom.

"No, it's alright–you want a piece?" I ask.

"Sure, with jelly," she answers.

"How 'bout a little morning music?" She pushes a button on the dark brown radio. At first there is static. She tunes it in and it's the news. A reporter is yelling something about the Japanese have just bombed Pearl Harbor.

I drop the jelly jar and it crashes to the floor. My mom has her hands to her mouth and is screaming DEAR GOD NO! She holds out an arm to me and motions to me.

"Come here baby, it'll be alright...he's all right"

I'm too shocked to cry, but tears wash down my face that I did not feel.

"He's not dead, mom," I say, my body violently shaking. "I know it. He will come home to me—he promised."

"Shhh, shhh...my baby girl, yes I know." She tries soothing me the only way a mother can, both of us sitting on the floor next to broken glass and jelly rocking back and forth.

Overwhelming sadness fills my head like a fog and my stomach is so rancid it feels as though I've been poisoned. Standing there in a cemetery, so close to Christmas, I watch other Marines fold a flag and hand it to me. I feel nothing but pure rage. I don't hear people talking to me. I don't feel their hands holding me.

The rope hangs firm and I'm balancing on a chair in front of it up in the attic. It's so cold up here I can see my breath coming out in puffs of smoke. I put the dog tags I was given around my neck. Soon I will be with him—I know he is waiting for me. I kick out the chair from beneath me.

I can't breathe and my body begins to twitch. Some how calmly I accept the fate of what I have done.

"BREATHE...GRACIE!"

I awake to Sal holding me by my arms. I focus and take a deep breath and exhale.

"Gracie, you were coughing–you stopped breathing. What happened?"

Still taking in gulps of air I put my hands up. "I'm fine, I'm okay...a vision. Oh my god, Sal, it was so real–I know it was."

"Shh, okay, shh...just keep breathing. Calm down, I want to make sure you're fine." He loosened his grip on my arms and lightly rubbed them instead. His voice is shaky. "Again, you have scared the shit out of me."

"I'm sorry," I said, getting out of bed on wobbly legs.

"Hey, hey..where you going?" he shouts, "be careful."

Before I can reply, he's out of bed and at my side, propping me up.

"Sal listen, I need to get on the computer. I dreamt you were stationed at Pearl Harbor in the 1940's. That's how you died. I want to look some things up while it's still fresh in my mind."

"Gracie," he says my name like he's speaking to a small child, "It might upset you even more. Don't you think you had enough trauma for one night?"

Stepping away from him in quick paces I pull him by the arm. "Come on. I'm fine, really. Remember Amina the psychic?"

He rolls his eyes but nods.

"Well for some reason, she was in my dream, my mind went over what she told me to do the next time I have a dream like this, to stay clam, it's just a vision. It can't hurt me, to follow my soul to guide me. Remember?"

"Jesus, Gracie, you're scaring me–and you know I've seen a lot of shit!"

I look at him and see the fear – and worry – on his face, but I know this is what I have to do. He follows close behind me as I make my way into the study. I move the mouse to fire up the computer and I search for WWII the USS Oklahoma.

Sal gives me a questioning shrug.

"In my dream this time, you were stationed in Pearl Harbor on that ship."

I hit the search button and we both read about the horrible fate of the sailor's and Marines who lost their lives when the Oklahoma was hit and sunk by several bombs and torpedoes. It capsized in battleship row. Many were trapped inside and below the water line. Though the trapped men banged on the hull, they could not be rescued. The few survivors never forgot how horrible it was to hear the banging and how much worse it was when it stopped.

"Jesus Christ, Gracie. Did you dream that?"

"No, thank god," I whisper, wiping the tears that drizzle down my face. "I just wanted to know what happened to that ship. In my dream, we were making wedding plans, so happy because you were stateside." I smile at the memory.

Sal leans against the desk facing me and crosses his arms over his chest. His expression urging me to go on.

"You only had six months more of duty and you thought maybe you send for me and we would get married in Hawaii. You had on your dress blues, we went to a USO dance." I said, with half a smile, still wiping my eyes and nose.

"That's pretty detailed Gracie. But you were choking–you stopped breathing!"

"Oh that, well..." I hesitate for a moment and compose myself. "I was completely wrecked Sal– I hung myself."

"You did what?" he snaps.

"In my dream I could not live without you so I went to be with you."

He drops his arms, hitting the desk. "This is not happening," he says, shaking his head.

I sniff back more tears. "I think it did."

He cocks his head to the side and scrunches his eyebrows together. "Are you getting any names that we could research?"

I shake my head. "No, I never hear any names, but you did call me, Princess. Now whether that's just past lives mixing with new I don't know. Oh and Celine was there—she was my mother. She called me *baby* like she does now. Isn't that funny?"

Sal reaches over and hits the home button with the mouse to shut the computer down. "That's enough. My brain is gonna explode. Let's go back to bed." Reaching and lifting me up out of the chair, he adds, "You're going to tell Dr. Brooks all about this on Monday. He'll get to the bottom of this."

As we lay in bed spooning, I think about what Dr. Brooks might say about this—or do? What if he gives me medicine to take the dreams away? Or what if he wants to hypnotize me and it makes me forget? *I don't want to forget.*

Some how those dreams or visions are a part of me, a part of Sal—and intertwined in us—they make me feel such a deep connection to him. I have never felt this kind of love. There is a deep ache in my chest that pulls me to him and him to me. I don't want to lose that feeling. I understand why my past-life soul took her life. I would rather call Amina than go see the shrink.

I hear Sal's breathing slow and steady. I feel puffs of air on my shoulder. His legs are wrapped around mine and his arms have me in a secure embrace.

At last, I'm peaceful.

CHAPTER 18

I wake up in the morning to bright sunlight and Toby, walking on Sal, then me. It would seem we've slept in after our big night.

"Alright, Toby. I'm getting up," I say with a yawn.

With a bark, he hops off the bed and trots to the bedroom door, pacing in circles.

"I know how he feels," Sal says, "I got to go, too."

I run down the stairs with Toby so I can put him out. When I open the back entrance I see Antonio making his way over to us. Toby gets a morning pat and goes about his business.

Giving him a little smile, I wave to him. "Morning, Pop."

"Good morning, Caro. Are you feeling any better since last night?"

"To tell you the truth Pop, I'm not sure *what* I feel. What would have happened if Sal wasn't in my life? Or if something had happened to him?" I shudder at the thoughts.

I move aside so he can wheel himself inside, Toby following after. I suddenly feel two arms come around me from behind.

"Morning Pop–and good morning, Princess." Sal plants a chaste kiss to my lips. "What about your life?" he asks.

"Just reflecting on last night and our good fortune. Last night could have gone quite differently..."

Sal shrugs with a bit of a frown. "I'd like to believe you would have passed out and he would have just ripped the necklace off your neck. But I have witnessed things go bad real quick–and, to be honest, when I saw the text, I didn't think. Some asshole was holding a gun on you. I just reacted with my training." He cupped my chin with his hand. "No one will ever hurt you, Gracie."

Tears sting my eyes. Only my own father would have protected me as desperately. I'm still in awe. In the vastness of the universe this man collided into my life. I focus on his gaze. "How did I get so blessed?"

"I am the one who's blessed, Gracie." Kissing me again then patting me on the bottom he says, "Go get dressed. Pop and I will start breakfast."

* * *

"I tried-a-last night not to get her too upset. I didn't want to worry her," Antonio said to his son.

"I know, Pop. She'll be okay–she's tougher then she thinks."

"That perp last night, we all-a-know he was hired but I just don't know why. I didn't want to confirm too much in front of-a-her."

Sal handed his father a mug of coffee and started cracking eggs in a bowl. "How different is the break in she had here compared to the one her in-laws had when you got hurt?"

"Totally different. They were-a-two stupid young boys trying to get an initiation into a gang. They came to this part of town to burglarize and shoot someone whether they killed them or not. Gracie's incident however, seems like a personal thing."

Sal nodded his head. "That's what I was thinking too, Pop. Vengeance? But from who and why? That's what's not adding up here." Sal stopped prepping breakfast for a moment. "You have been around here and knew the family a long time, You can't think of anyone who wants revenge for anything?"

"Not really, but-a the Boumont's have passed on, why not go after Richard? Why Gracie? And she's almost divorced. I can't make a connection."

* * *

I grab my towel and wrap it around me. The steam from my shower fills the bathroom and soothes my nerves. I hear my cell phone ring and see it's Richard.

"Great," I mutter under my breath, "just what I need." I touch the button, suck in a deep breath and answer the call.

"Hello, Richard," I say as flatly as I can, surprisingly, my heart isn't racing and my breath isn't short.

"Grace, for Christ-sake, what happened last night?"

"I'm fine, thanks for asking," I say with a grin. I think I'm finally free of my reactions to him and that makes me very happy.

"Okay, really, Grace." He sighs. "Look, I know you're fine I came back last night to see if I could help but the police wouldn't let me near you. I'm not a monster Grace–I am sorry I come off that way to you. I really am happy that you weren't hurt. I heard Antonio's son killed the son of a bitch."

"Yes, he did but, I ah...I had a panic attack and passed out so I really don't know much. Thank god for Mimi—if she had left the bathroom five minutes earlier I don't know what could have been."

"Yes, Mimi mentioned all this to me last night. He wanted mom's necklace?"

"Your mother gave that to me Rich, it's *my* necklace."

"Grace stop. You know what I mean—"

I'm going to set this straight right now. "No, I never know what you mean–that's the problem, Richard. I always feel defensive around you. You've never let me in and you've never really recognized me as your family. I never once felt truly wanted."

"Grace, honestly, I didn't mean that the way it came out. Just let me expla…."

"Richard, I'm running late for breakfast and I don't really want to have this conversation. I'm doing fine. In fact, I'm better then fine. Sal and Antonio love me and care for me, something you never did. Or, knew how to do."

"That's not true…"

"Richard please, Soon I'll sign the final divorce paper–thank you. I'm sorry I was such a burden to you when we were married–I don't think we were ever meant to be–I know that now. I don't know if the break in and last night's attack are connected or not, but my guys and the police are working on it. There's no need to be concerned but thanks for calling, Richard. Goodbye."

* * *

Sal was cooking bacon and glanced at his father. "Hey, ahh…Gracie," he started. "She ahh… she had an other dream last night"

"She did? What was-a-this one about?" Antonio's asked carefully.

The bacon sizzled as Sal turned it in the pan. "Pop, it's all so crazy–when she comes down why don't you ask her? She believes all these dreams are visions and really happened. I'm just hoping she isn't losing her mind with everything that's been going on."

Antonio put down his coffee mug and looked curiously at his son. "You don't believe? You said-a-to me not so long ago how you fell so quickly for her, how you feel a connection to her, and how strongly the need to protect her is. Come on son, you have had your fun with plenty-a-women—you never felt this way before."

Sal leaned over the counter propping himself on his elbows, shook his head and chuckled in surrender.

Antonio clapped his hands together and laughed uproariously. "AH HA!" He pointed at his son. "Because you are meant to be–things happen, son. Don't question–miracles happen some-a-times."

"So you believe, then?"

"Son, I'm an old man. I have seen many things I can not understand. The fact that you are here now and in love is a miracle."

* * *

During breakfast we talk about the events of the night prior, Sal and pop tell me not to worry but I do. I catch a glimpse of sadness in Antonio's features when I tell him about my latest dream. As I tell my story Sal comes closer to me and holds my hand, coaxing me to sit on his lap.

When I'm done pop went home and Sal and I decided to brave the cooler breezy weather and take a stroll on the beach with Toby.

I talked to Sal about my phone call with Richard.

"You know, he sounded genuinely concerned."

Sal's eyebrows shot up. "Really? When did the Tin Man get his heart?"

"I don't know. But, I basically blew him off and cut the conversation short. I feel a little bad now. I think he was calling to see how I was. I'm just so used to him yelling and making everything my fault, I'm not going to give him that opportunity." Sal takes me in an embrace and gives me a wide grin.

"What are you smiling at?"

"You," he says. "You're stronger now than when I met you. Everyday I watch a light come back to your eyes. The real you was trampled down. Now you're resurfacing. You laugh more and you're more confident in yourself."

Smiling back at him, I poke him in the ribs. "It's because of you, Sal. I feel loved."

Sal runs his fingers through my hair, cupping the nape of my neck. "Yes, Princess, but you are learning to love yourself–that's where you get your strength from–then no one can break you down, ever again."

* * *

That night in bed I'm thumbing through my new issue of Entertainment weekly while Sal is in the study on the computer. Checking the buzz I hear on my cell, I smile when I spot it's a text from Maggie.

Hey...you up?

YES!

Within a second my phone chimes. "Hey Mags, did you get the picture?" I ask.

"Yes I did! How was the benefit?"

"Well it all started like a fairy tale then turned into a very scary nightmare. I was mugged in the bathroom at the Marriott!"

"ARE YOU SERIOUS?"

I get to tell what little I know about the entire event. I hear Maggie catching her breath from time to time, but she doesn't interrupt. Finally, I stop talking, afraid to say the words.

"What, Gracie? WHAT?!" she hisses at me.

"Well..." my voice catches. I whisper, "Sal killed him."

I hear Maggie suck in air. "He did? Oh my god, Gracie, is Sal all right?"

"Yes, he's doing fine. I just keep feeling sick when I think about how this could of turned out...what if he was killed trying to help me. How would I live with that?"

"Don't do that, honey. If everyone is all right, you have to focus on that. I can't believe this has happened to you of all people, but I'm so glad Sal and Mimi were there for you."

"Yes, so am I." Some tears slip down my cheeks at the thought of the alternatives and I wipe at them. Toby comes closer and tries to lick at my face.

"I swear your going to give me heart failure one day Gracie. Where is Sal now?"

"He's on the computer, he still keeps up with his work, plus I think he is doing a little detective work surrounding what's been going on around here."

"Wow, Gracie, unbelievable!" So, she says, jesting, "check you out sleeping with the Secret Service. Just like that movie, The Bodyguard!"

We both break up with laughter. "Mags, I can always count on you for comic relief."

"Glad to be of service," she says on a chuckle. "Oh yeah, Gracie, before I forget, the picture you sent? You looked stunning as always, and, Sal is a very handsome guy. Mike even said Sal looks like he stepped out of GQ! I have to tell you though, the way you're dressed and posed in this picture with Sal, I don't know why...but, it just seems like I've seen this picture somewhere before."

"What are you talking about, Mags? You mean like a deja vu?"

"Yeah, it just kind of hit a chord somewhere in my gut. Don't get me wrong now, I love the picture. I don't feel bad vibes, I feel really *good* ones. You look very happy. I just get a familiar feeling when I look at the both of you in this picture. You both look like royalty, or something."

I chuckle at my best friend's comment. I inform her of my latest dream and my appointment to see his psychiatrist.

"Gotta tell ya Gracie, go for it. They know about stuff like past life regression–and if we mix in what the psychic told you, how can we not believe? You're not crazy–I feel it too, every time I look at this picture. Keep me in the loop, okay? We'll chat soon, my friend."

"Thanks, Mags, I will. I'm glad you called–I always feel better after a chat with you."

"Yep, me too, Gracie. Good night!"

* * *

The next morning Sal brought me coffee in bed.

"Good morning, Princess, I noticed you slept well last night."

"I did, no dreams, did you sleep good?" I ask.

He nods once, "I did too."

I take a sip and look at him, I have the appointment with Dr. Brooks later. I'm a little nervous about it."

Sal stood and leans over to kiss me on my nose. "You'll do fine, Dr. Brooks helped me." Sal took his thumb and rubs at the crease between my eyebrows. "Don't worry, nothing to be concerned about, then he seals his lips to mine.

* * *

I left the veterinary clinic just early enough to get to Dr. Brooks' office ten minutes before my scheduled appointment.

I walk into the small waiting area, surprised to see how simple and quiet it is with only a couple of chairs and magazines. There's no receptionist, just another door with a smoky glass window. I'm just about to take a seat when the door opens and Dr. Brooks pops his head out.

"Gracie," he says, smiling, "come on in."

"I'm early Dr. Brooks. I didn't know if I was supposed to knock or.."

Dr. Brooks shakes my hand, his eyes kind, his manner friendly. He's my kind of person in jeans and a button down shirt, no tie, and a pair of loafers.

"No," he says, "you're just fine! I spread out my appointments so clients don't usually overlap."

I follow him into the interior office. "Have a seat," he gestures to a pale blue wingback chair.

I sit but feel my hands perspire and my feet want to tap. He takes a seat in front of me and laughs softly.

"It's perfectly fine to be nervous, Gracie. Everyone is at first. Why don't we start with Sal? Tell me how and where you met."

I fill the Doctor in on the particulars of how Sal and I became a couple. I tell him about Richard and our tumultuous marriage. Then, I tell him about the dreams. He's taking notes and looking pensive. Dr. Brooks puts the end of the pen in his mouth and raises his eyebrows. "And when did you say these dreams or visions started?"

I could feel my face begin to warm. "Right after I met Sal. I believe it was the first night we kissed."

He smiles. "Okay, now, so you both went on a trip. A romantic weekend. You sat with a psychic who told you about old souls and soul mates. Did you dream that night?"

"No, but Sal thought I would. He wasn't too thrilled about the whole thing."

"And what about you, Gracie? How do you feel about what she told you?"

I tilt my head to look up at the ceiling while taking a deep breath, then I look back at the doctor. "Well...at first I was a bit shocked, but not scared. I rolled it around in my head for a while. Now it makes sense to me." I need to be honest with him. "Dr. Brooks, these dreams or visions I have are a part of me and Sal. Please don't hypnotize or medicate them away – that would scare me more."

Dr. Brooks sits back in his chair and puts both his hands up. "We will not do anything you don't want to do Gracie, but, I will tell you this: hypnosis is not harmful and maybe we can get more details if I put you under. Would you like to try? I promise you, this won't impact the dreams."

I agree to let him try.

After several attempts, and no matter how many ways he tries to persuade me to relax, I won't go under.

At one point I giggle. "Sorry, Dr. Brooks. I guess I'm broken..."

"On the contrary. You're will is very strong and protective. Not everyone can be put under, but that's all right Gracie, we will figure all this out."

He grabs his schedule book and flips through. "Now tell me...would it be at all possible to get you and Sal in here together say, Friday afternoon?"

I shoot him a cocked eyebrow. "Together? Yes, I suppose we can, but why?"

He sits behind his desk and smiles into space for a bit. Then his gaze meets mine. "I want you both here to discuss some things. Now nothing at all to be alarmed about but, I want to talk to both of you about past life regression."

"Is that what I'm experiencing Dr. Brooks?"

"I'll see you both on Friday—we'll talk about it then. Have a nice week Gracie and don't worry. You're fine."

*   *   *

Richard paced the floor of Leonard Burnes' office as they waited for Gracie. The last divorce paper was awaiting signature on the big oak desk and he knew from their conversation that she was aware of it. Where the hell was she? Did something else happen?

"Mr. Boumont, why don't you have a seat? I'm sure she will be here momentarily."

Richard peered at the old lawyer, sitting there looking so smug. "She's early for *everything*. Why can't she be early today? That was one of the good things I did love about her."

"Why don't you just have a seat, Mr. Boumont. She'll be here.

Richard checked is watch for the third time in as many minutes. Burnes was staring at his gold-lettered law books on the shelf, but in two minutes, Richard was leaving. Grace could just set up another appointment that met with her busy life.

"So Mr. Boumont, everything going okay at the offices?" Richard gave him a sarcastic grin. The man had obviously never been audited and been caught short. "Oh sure. Things are just fantastic, thank you."

"Hey, don't get pissy with me. If not for us, you would have never known you were being embezzled. It could have been too late before you found out."

"Yes that was a fortunate accident."

"Any word yet?" Burnes asked.

"No, it has seemed to appear that whoever was stealing has ceased. But everything is locked and or frozen until further notice."

"Ahumm, I see, and how's Ms. James feeling about that?"

"How do you think she feels, she's pissed off! She's worked hard to grow the company and now this...."

Both men snapped their heads to the door as Gracie breezed in.

"Hello, Mr. Burnes," she said, stopping short just inside the office doorway. "What's he doing here? I thought he signed already."

Mr. Burnes stood and handed her a pen. "This paper gets signed together, with a witness—me."

While she read the document and bent to sign it, Richard looked at her and pondered for a moment how really confident and radiant she seemed to be. He wondered if the ghost she had turned into during their marriage had been his doing. He'd known she was miserable but just didn't know how to help her. Perhaps she was right and they were just not meant to be.

"There—done."

Richard took the pen from Burnes and scribbled his name on the line.

Mr. Burnes picked up the paper and shot them both a satisfied smile. "So, now it's done. Your marriage has been dissolved. Gracie is to be rewarded half a million up front and on the first of every month residuals from the company until she remarries or God forbid, dies—as per the deal instead of alimony, correct?"

Both Richard and Gracie nodded in agreement.

As they were leaving the attorney's office, Richard turned to Gracie, taking her by the arm. "How are you? Any news on the thief who cornered you?"

"I'm fine, really. And I haven't heard anything new about the whole thing. Sal is with me all the time and so is Pop, so I'm sure I'm safe."

"POP?" Richard looked at her with raised eyebrows.

"Yes, Antonio...ahh... Tony wants me to call him Pop now that Sal and I are together."

They both got onto the elevator.

"Well Grace, I must say, you have been looking wonderful. I guess having Sal around makes you happy."

She touched the sleeve of his jacket lightly. "Yes, Richard, having anyone you love around you all the time should make you happy. Aren't you happy with Camille?"

"You *love* Sal? Already?" *How long had they really known each other?*

"Yes, I do." She swallowed and he thought he might have seen tears, but she continued. "He mended my heart Richard, something you don't know anything about. Why are you so cold? Was it the money? The power? Maybe it's just in your gene pool–your dad was cold, too. I used to feel sorry for your mother sometimes."

The elevator doors opened and they walked into the lobby.

He fought the urge to shake her. Was she out of her mind? "Feel sorry for her? For my mother? My mother had everything she ever wanted; cars, a beautiful home, maids. She wanted for nothing– my father gave her everything!"

He was talking to her back, but she stopped and turned, giving him what seemed to be sympathetic eyes.

"Not *everything*, Richard. Your father forgot to give her the one thing she wanted, and what most women want.... Love."

He watched her waltz through the doors and had a sense that he'd lost something very special.

* * *

I arrive home to find Sal in the driveway cleaning his motorcycle. He flashes me that big wide smile of his and comes to open my door.

"My Princess," he bows. "How was your visit with Dr. Brooks?"

"Really interesting."

Sal scrunches his eyebrows and twitches a crooked smile. "Interesting? That's a different reply..." I lean in to hug him. "Umm... he wants to see us *both* on Friday afternoon. Is that alright with you?"

"Yes, of course, but about what? Did he explain anything for you?"

"He mentioned past life regression, he also tried to hypnotize me, but, I wouldn't go under."

"He has put me under a few times to relax me. I don't remember much, he just says I talk about some of my missions, when I was held prisoner, and some other stuff he was never quite sure about. But it helped some with the night terrors."

"Really? You never told me you've been hypnotized."

"Yeah. I didn't think I could be put under, but he was able to."

Raising my eyebrows, I'm wondering. "Huh....How does the CIA or your special tactical people feel about knowing one of their special agents can get hypnotized?"

Sal gives me a narrow-eyed look. "Well..." he hesitates as though searching for words. "It's kind of what I went through years ago. To be programmed to become good soldiers they drill stuff into your head. I chose Dr. Brooks for just that reason—he needed to de-program me. He can't take it all away, but I learned coping mechanisms, and, then...there was you." He reaches out, pulling me into him for a kiss. I lean away from him.

"Me?"

"You," he answers. "I told you when we first met. Talking to you, being around you, was like snapping back to reality from a bad fog. You calmed my thoughts—you calmed me."

I put my hand to his stubbled cheek. "You have the kindest heart."

Sal ducks in for another passion-filled kiss. When he backs away from me, he's got a wicked grin spreading across his face.

I grab at his dimpled chin. "What are you thinking?"

He tosses a glance at his bike then back at me with a raised eyebrow. "Want to go for a ride, Princess?"

Reluctantly I agree. Sal helps me put on a purple helmet he purchased for me a while back. He lowers the dark face shield and taps me on the helmet.

"I'll get on, then you swing your leg over and climb up behind me, okay?"

All I can do is nod. I'm partly terrified, partly excited.

He straddles the Harley, hits the start button and points at me. I climb on board, wrap my arms tightly around him and he pats my leg.

"Ready?" he yells over the throb of the engine.

"Ready," I shout back.

Sal takes off nice and easy until he feels me relax against him. As the feeling in my fingers returns because I'm no longer terrified, he speeds up and we follow the winding road easily. I feel as though I'm flying as I hang on against the steady rush of wind. When we stopped at a traffic light, he checks to see if I'm okay.

"I am. I trust you, Sal."

"Good to know, Princess. Good to know."

We rode up and down the coast taking in the sights and in a matter of an hour or so, I can understand why he loves to ride the bike and why I'll be right behind him again soon.

I love my life-my free, stable and secure life. I love this man. There is no doubt in my mind we are kindred spirits.

CHAPTER 19

Friday afternoon Gracie and Sal arrived at Dr. Brooks' office hand and hand.

The doctor sat behind his desk this time and told them to have a seat.

"How are you both this afternoon?" he asked.

"Good," we answered in unison.

"How 'bout you, Sal?" he continued, "any more night terrors, or fatigue?"

"No," Sal answered, "I'm calmer." Squeezing her hand a little tighter he and Gracie gave each other a knowing smile. Dr. Brooks nodded.

"Yes, I can see. Well then, let me get on it, then." He pulled a file from his desk and opened it. "Sal," he said, "this is your file. After I had my chat with Gracie I went back and went over some things. Would you care if I shared what happened on some of our sessions?"

Sal's eyebrows bunched as he lifted his chin. "No, if you think it'll help."

"There were times when I put you under hypnosis and you talked about many things, but, it wasn't until my appointment with Gracie that I realized you both mentioned some of the same things.

"If I may, for instance, Gracie told me about her dreams. Now during one in particular, she mentions you in a revolutionary uniform taking off on a horse. In one of our sessions, while you were under, you mentioned a horse and leaving behind a fiancée. Then you mentioned a freezing winter, and you were enfeebled with hunger, a word used in 1700's. When I asked you what you were doing, you replied, 'Fighting for what's right.' I asked you who you were fighting and you indicated the British. Then you jumped to a battle you were fighting in–British troops attacked in a frontal assault–you were shot and stabbed by a bayonet. I made you come to because you were in pain."

Sal shook his head. *None of this makes sense...* "Wait a minute. Are you telling me I spoke about a past life? Why didn't you tell me any of this before?"

Dr. Brooks scratched at his head. "To tell you the truth Sal, I didn't think that it was anything other then mixing what you been through into something like a nightmare. That's usually how our minds cope with traumatic situations and it's quite common."

Sal glanced at Gracie and then looked back at the doctor, but remained quiet.

"Dr. Brooks, tell us please, is there more?" Gracie asked softly.

Scratching his head some more, he responded almost excitedly. "Yes, a few more things. Sal, one time you muttered on about Germans raiding trenches and then it just went dark. Gracie had a dream about WWI and that was the puzzle piece for me right there. And her latest dream of WWII...." Dr. Brooks smiled and shook his head in amazement.

"I've got to tell you, she mentioned Pearl Harbor and the USS Oklahoma. Now Sal, in a session we had a few months ago, I wrote here that you were mumbling on, but, I managed to hear the mention of a fiancée again, and *Hawaii*. You also went into a bit of a trauma about explosions, fire and being trapped on a ship. Again I thought it was your mind compensating.

It wasn't until Monday during Gracie's visit that I started to come to conclusions. Never did I put much belief in the theory of past lives, but I have been reading up since Gracie came in. I have to be honest with you both- I am stunned and almost speechless over these comparisons."

Lifting her hand, Gracie approached the subject of the psychic. "Dr. Brooks, going back to Amina, the psychic. She told us about being old souls and soul mates. We were *always* together and a trauma has always separated us".

"Yes, I remember you mentioning that. I don't usually put stock into that sort of thing either, but it looks like I am getting enlightened. I suppose all of this is plausible."

Sal sat forward in his seat. "Did I ever mention names?"

"Ah," the doctor lifted a finger, "not really. Every time I asked you about who you were, your response was vague or you would say you were a soldier. I have asked on occasion who your fiancé is, but you always say *Gracie*. Hence my thinking you're just mixing things up since she is a constant in your life as of now."

Sal and Gracie sat holding hands tight, listening to the doctor go on.

"Let me tell you what I have found. Sal, you and Gracie both have told me about how you met. Now, both stories are a little different but you both have said the attraction was magnetic, and familiar.

"Past life regression is a reincarnation of our souls. We may have lived multiple lives and we keep finding each other or should I say the heart recognizes each other even when our appearance isn't what we are now. They say the souls know. There is a sudden feeling of familiarity, and perhaps a feeling of safety. For Gracie, meeting you was her jolt of recognition, and hence she has dreams. This can also happen with family members or best friends. Our souls seem to seek out each other over and over. It's not always a romantic thing.

"Sal, you were repressing memories from Iraq, Bosnia and a few other missions. Under hypnosis, past life regression came out, but it didn't surface until after you met Gracie. I wrote down what you told me that day before I put you under."

Doc, I met a princess named, Gracie. I don't know what it is, but I have to be near her. It's like I have been missing her my whole life. Something about her calms the crazy in my head.

For you Sal, that was *your* awakening."

Sal put a hand up to his scruffy chin and scratched. "I got to wrap my head around this. It's all so unbelievable and hard to rationalize." He took Gracie's hand and brought it to his lips, giving it a peck. "Gracie, what are you thinking?"

She took a deep breath and exhaled. He was almost afraid of what she had to say...

"I am very pleased with what Dr. Brooks has surmised. "I knew this," she said, eyes sparkling. "I knew, I felt it in my heart. Those dreams were very real. I could smell things and feel things. Emotionally I was affected by it. Normal dreams don't do that. I believe it, Sal. The day I met you I looked into your eyes and it was a shock. Like Dr. Brooks said, a jolt of recognition. I just *knew.*"

They left Dr. Brooks' office with a tentative appointment for January. He wished them a wonderful Christmas and a great trip to Napa and sent them off with a short list of books that might be useful to their quest for answers.

* * *

Later that evening as I was getting into bed, Sal was deeply engrossed in the book we'd stopped to buy on the way home.

"Any good?" I ask.

He looks up from the book, his serious expression relaxing as I climb in and snuggle under his arm.

"Yeah, it's . . . just so hard to comprehend. I need time to wrap my head around it and let it soak in."

"Why is it so hard to believe? Your dad believes it and so do my friends."

"Maybe I could believe it more if I had dreams like you do. When I'm hypnotized I don't remember anything. When Dr. Brooks tells me I said these things, it's not real to me." He closed the book and wrapped an arm around me. "I do know without a doubt, I love you and we are meant to be together."

Sal gazes at me with sleepy eyes, then he smothers my mouth in a searing kiss and his tongue searches out mine. His hands move up and down my body, setting little fires all over me.

As he rolls on top of me, I feel his hardness press against me. He pauses for a moment to look at me as if he is waiting for permission.

I arch my back, coaxing him on. His mouth once again seals on mine. I hear a thump as the book falls to the floor... along with my panties.

* * *

Christmas is fast approaching as I send cards, bake cookies, wrap presents and get some shipped. An unexpected call from my brother Steve is a delightful gift.

He tells me he will be celebrating Christmas in Haiti at the mission post along with the other missionaries, but he's going to have a few days off right after Christmas and he wants to come see me for New Years.

I'm thrilled, of course and I tell him all I can about Sal and the abbreviated version of everything else.

"I'm spending Christmas in Napa with Sal and his family," I conclude with giggles. "We will be home on the twenty-seventh.

"Perfect," my brother says. "I can be in by the twenty-eighth, then I leave on the second of January. I'll see ya then, sister dear. Have fun and Merry Christmas!"

* * *

The morning of the twenty second of December I'm getting ready to leave for the airport and going over things in my mind. I've shipped presents to Napa ahead of us and made a fresh batch of cookies to bring to Mary and Joe. That is if they make it... maybe I'll hide them in a suitcase to be sure.

I pull out a long black jersey knit cotton skirt that feels like sweat pants. It has a slit to my knee and a drawstring waist with a matching hoodie that zips up the front with pockets. I slide on my chunky sandals knowing I can take them off and put my feet up on the plane.

"You ready to go, Gracie?" Sal shouts as he hauls suitcases out of the house and into Pop's van.

"Yes, Toby is out back and I just want to check all the doors before we go."

I call for Toby, then do a sweep of all the doors making sure they are locked up good. Sal joins me in the process and does a double check upstairs.

"I told Lou to come and drive around a few times to check on things. He'll keep a watch out but I'm sure it's going to be fine," Sal reassures me.

We set the house alarm, pile in the van and head to Jacksonville Airport.

We arrive, park and make our way to the terminal that services the private planes. We are through security in a flash. Sal sees his friend and waves.

A tall thin man with short-cropped brown hair and ice blue eyes strides over to us. "Sal! Merry Christmas, mate!" They hug like two drunken sailors and I can't hide my grin.

"Good to see you, man," Sal says to his buddy. "Hey thanks for helping us out. I appreciate it."

"Oh, no worries then. Always a pleasure to be in the company of a true mate."

Turning and pulling me by the hand Sal introduces us. "Nick, this is the love of my life, Gracie, and my father, Antonio."

"Pleasure to meet you both. Ah and who do we have here?" Nick squats down and lets Toby have a sniff.

"That would be Toby," I answer. "It will be his first time to fly."

"Oh, he is a handsome boy. No cargo hold for you on this flight boy. You get to sit with your mum in the human section."

"Are you from the U.K, Nick?" I love the accent.

"No, I'm an Aussie, but everyone gets it confused."

"Have you been a pilot for a while?"

"Twenty years! I am in the air more than on the ground. Have no fear, it's a good day to fly."

He gives me a wink and a smile. "Right, if the inquisition is over, why don't we make our way out? After you." He gestures with his hand and bows to the glass doors that slide open with motion detection.

|

We walk on the tarmac and up a flight of stairs that enter the plane. Toby is the first to trail his way in. I look up at the jet, a silver exterior with a red metallic stripe running along the body.

I make my way inside and stand in awe of the elegant interior. My face must tell it all because when Sal turns to see where I am, he chuckles.

Pop gets a ride up in a special chair lift and we help him settle into one of the white leather recliner's.

"Isn't it something?" Sal says. "Come, let me show you around. This jet is a 2010 Bombardier global XRS. Nick bought it last year. It's his baby."

As I make my way through the fourteen-passenger jet, I take in the white leather recliner seats on the right and a long white couch on the left with black and red throw pillows. A black plush carpet covers the floor. In the back is a black mirrored wall with a door. I walk through it and can't believe there's a galley kitchen equipped with microwave and coffee maker and black granite counter tops.

Behind the galley is a room with four white leather club chairs, a shiny black conference table and wifi hook ups. In the corner is a door that is marked: LAVATORY.

Does the plane meet your standards then?" a voice asks.

I turn to see Nick with his hands at his hips, his smile proud and friendly. Sal is right behind him.

"Yes, it's spectacular. I've only flown commercial, so I'm a bit speechless!"

"I'm glad you like her. Alrighty then, everyone take your seats and let's get this baby up, shall we? Sal, how would you like to join me as first mate and get her up?"

Sal nods and rubs his hands together. "I'd love to. Sounds great."

"Wait a minute," I stop them, holding up a finger, "if I may cut into this bro-mance, Sal, you can fly a plane?"

He frowns, then smiles. "I can make my way around a cockpit. I'm not a seasoned pilot like Nick, but, I can fly a plane."

"SHUT UP!" I exclaim.

Sal laughs and tugs me toward him so I slam up against him. "I'm special agent secret spy guy, remember?"

He looks at me with a little smile playing on his lips as he places his arms around me and squeezes my ass with both his hands.

"Did I tell you how cute you look today? He kisses me hard and quick. "Princess," he growls in my ear, "when I'm done getting this plane up, I'd like to see you in the back room on that conference table."

"On...tthe...con.. c..conference table?" I stutter and my breath hitches in my throat.

Sal puts a finger under my chin and coaxes me to look him in his eyes. "You're so adorable, and you would look even more adorable laid out on that table. If I don't make love to you soon I'm going to explode."

I'm stunned into silence and find the use of my brain malfunctioning and it's impossible to speak. I realize my mouth is hanging open when Sal gently closes it with the tip of his finger. He kisses my nose and pulls back quickly. "You alright?"

"What?" I barely manage.

Sal shakes his head. "Okay, Princess, get to your seat and buckle up."

I take a seat across from Pop. Toby is already at home on the couch with his head on top of a pillow. I buckle myself in and smile excitedly.

"Here we go! You excited, Pop?"

"Si, this-a-gonna be a good trip, we all together for Christmas."

We hear the screech of the engines come to life. Then Nick's voice comes over the intercom telling us we are ready to take off and what time we should land in San Francisco. *The temperature is a mild fifty-eight degrees, the skies ahead are clear, so relax and enjoy the flight.*

In the cockpit Sal sat in the co-pilot's chair so the co-pilot takes a seat just outside the door and buckles himself in. He smiles and nods at me. "Ma'am." I smile back.

Soon we are speeding down the runway and rising into the blue sky. I feel the lift off in my stomach and as we climb to altitude, Toby whines and cocks his head, not entirely happy.

Antonio calls for him and on shaky paws, Toby slowly moves to sit on the floor between us. Reaching for him, I pet the scruff of his neck, noting his body is shaking a little.

After about twenty minutes, we level off, our ears pop back to normal and Toby is back on the couch falling asleep. Sal appears out of the cockpit and the co-pilot goes back in with Nick to resume his station.

"Good job! We're alive!" I say, laughing.

"Really, it was all Nick," Sal says. "But it was all familiar–once I got in the seat–a lot of my training came back."

"Did you have to fly much at your job?" I ask.

He takes the seat next to me and reaches for my hand. "Very little. When I was Marine in special ops, I flew helicopters a few times, but mostly I was jumping off the copters and planes."

He changes the subject. "Nick tells me there are snacks and champagne for us in the galley. You hungry now or should we wait? We have about a six-hour flight."

"Maybe wait a little longer. I'm not that hungry yet."

"Really? That's a first–you're always hungry. Are you feeling okay? You're not air sick, are you?"

"No Sal, I'm fine," I laugh. "I love flying–it's peaceful. Toby had a moment when we took off, but he's calmed down now and getting sleepy."

Sal taps me on my leg and points to Pop, "Looks like someone else is sleeping."

Sal got up and finds a blanket and drapes it over Pop. "Would you like one, too?"

"I'm fine for now, maybe later, I might need a nap after my initiation into the Mile High Club," I whisper.

I pull out a magazine to thumb through then glance back at Sal. Now he's the one stunned, a devilish smile playing shyly across his lips.

He sits down and again takes my hand. He kisses it and reclines in his seat, laughing.

* * *

After a few hours I get up and use the lavatory. On my way back through the galley, Sal is pouring us some Champagne.

"One for you and one for me." He hands me a glass. We clink our glasses together then sip. The Champagne is nice and chilled and the carbonation dances all the way down my throat with a nice fruity after taste. "Oh that's good," I purr.

He picks up the bottle to read the label. "Mumms," he says. "They're in Napa–Nick got it for us."

"Nice!" I drink some more. "Remind me to thank him later."

Sal takes me by the hand and leads me back to the room with the conference table. We look out the tiny round windows and watch as the landscape sweeps by below us.

"We're just about to change into the Mountain Time zone," Sal comments. "So, I guess a few more hours to go."

I finish my champagne. Sal brings the bottle and pours a little more into my glass. He picks up his glass and tosses back the remaining liquid.

I take a few more gulps of my champagne, my eyes on him the whole time. Slowly he reaches for my glass, placing it beside his. Cupping my face in his hands he comes in swift for a kiss, parting my lips with his and I taste the sweet Champagne on our tongues. He draws me in close, our bodies press together. I tangle my fingers in his wavy hair.

"Gracie," he groans. Still frantically kissing me. I....I... love you and.....I... want to ask you to...

"What, Sal? Ask me to....?"

I'm so hot I can barely breath. I feel my need for him in every part of my body as I grab at him.

He picks me up and I wrap my legs around him. I can feel his arousal about to bust through his jeans as his hands clasp me tight against him.

He places me on that big black table and unzips his pants. Yanking my skirt up higher, I lie back. He tugs at my panties and I feel them slide off past my bare feet. Sal grabs my legs one in each hand and slides me to the edge of that table. As he trails kisses down my throat, I grind my hips against him, urging him on. He enters in one swift move. My breath catches in my chest.

"Gracie." Sal hisses my name. He's not as gentle as normal, a blinding passion drives his thrusts. "Oh Gracie," he moans. "Oh my god, I had to be inside you." He pushes and pumps. His whisper is raw. "I'm not hurting you, am I?"

"No.." I beg him, "don't... stop." A moan escapes my throat. He spreads my thighs farther apart and I perched up on my elbows, feeling the orgasm rise as he pounds into me. "Sal, I'm gonna...!!"

"Me too!" he growls.

Trembling with pleasure and exhaustion, I collapse back on the table, my arms giving out. Sal lifts the bottom of my hoodie and places some kisses all over my belly. When our breathing slows he helps me down. Dizzy with shaky legs, I have to find my balance. Sal holds onto me until I do.

"That was hot," I laugh shakily.

Sal is smiling. "Hell yeah it was–you should have seen how sexy you were on that table. I couldn't help myself. Was I too rough with you? I don't ever want to make you..."

I shut him up with a kiss. I break away and stare at him. In a breathy voice I repeat, "It. Was. Hot!" I push away from him to go into the bathroom to clean up, scooping up my panties in the process. Sal tugs my arm, stopping me.

"Gracie, wait please. I want you to know I always make love to you. I don't ever want you to feel as if you've been fucked or used. You mean too much to me—I love and respect you with all my heart. I...I..want you to be......"

"Sal, nooo..." I cut him off. "I don't think that! Not ever! I know you do. Our passion and love for each other is growing stronger. I know you love me. I love you. So much I swear it hurts."

He embraces me again, giving me the softest kiss. He lightly brushes his lips with mine as his tongue darts inside. When he pulls back, I see his eyes are the slightest bit damp.

He smiles and puts his forefinger and thumb to my chin. "I love you so damned much."

* * *

Hours later we are on the ground at San Francisco International Airport. Nick comes out of the cockpit smiling and sends a questioning look at Sal. Where upon Sal answers with no words—just a slight frown and a shake of his head.

"Chicken shit. Alrighty then, moving on," Nick says, how was the flight? Was it as good for you as it was for me?"

My eyes dart between Sal and Nick. I shrug guessing it is some inside secret service joke.

"Yes," I answer with a smile. "Very smooth flight, thank you".

"Well, I hope everything was satisfactory and that you and Salvatore had a most memorable conference."

"Nick!" Sal scolds.

I feel my face blush, but a giggle escapes my throat despite my embarrassment.

"All in good fun, mates! Enjoy your holiday. See you back here in five days."

CHAPTER 20

Taking in the surrounding scenery as we drove through Napa and Sonoma, I feel as though I've left the country. Row after row of vineyards spread out along the hillsides. I point out some famous wineries: Robert Mondavi, Francis Ford Coppola. I point at Mumms when we drive by. I smile at Sal and he winks back.

Turning off the main road, we arrive at a gate and Sal taps in the code Joe gave him at the intercom station. The gates pop open. I spot a huge sign that has a wreath with a big wine-colored bow attached to it. *AMICI Winery of Napa Valley.*

I point–"Friends?" I ask.

"Very good, caro. Si. Joe and a friend of-a-his bought the place years ago. It was in shambles–they got it for a steal. They re-built and learned the business. They do alright."

As we drive through I see all the vines are bare, the harvest is done. There are only a few hands cleaning up the fields. We pull around a huge horseshoe driveway and stop in front of the main house, which appears to be somewhat Victorian with a big, wide, front door.

"It's beautiful," I squeal. "I can't wait to see what it looks like inside!"

Sal honks the horn and Joe comes flying out the front door. Sal gets out and the brothers hug.

Joe is the same height as Sal, just not as muscular. His hair is dark and cropped really short. I get out of the SUV and Joe eyes me.

With the same big smile as Sal's, he yells, "Gracie! Finally, a face behind the voice on the phone!" He gives me a big hug that lifts me off my feet. "Welcome! Mary can't wait to meet you!"

The brothers help their father out of the SUV and Joe gives Antonio a hug.

"Miss you, Pop. It's been too long." He pauses a minute, taking in the sight of us all, smiling as he does. I noticed all three men had the same chocolate brown eyes and big smile, Joe didn't have a cleft chin, but he had the Patroni Roman nose.

Toby runs ahead of us towards the door. "Toby! I yell but he keeps going. "I'm sorry, he's usually a good dog." I say to Joe.

"Oh no he's fine. Besides, he's had a long day, right? And he probably senses Bridget."

"Bridget?" I ask.

"Our golden doodle. Come in, come in! Mary is waiting."

We enter through the door and we're standing in a huge parlor with a fireplace. Cathedral ceilings house a bridge from the stairway that must lead to bedrooms. A huge Christmas tree stands in a corner and almost touches that bridge.

"I see the love of huge Christmas trees runs in the family," I say to Sal with a grin. This one is even bigger than ours.

"Yes–it's *stupid* big! A voice bellows from behind me. I turn around.

"Gracie!"

A tall slender blonde with a little bump in her tummy marches over to me with open arms. "So nice to finally meet you! I have heard so much about you. And, I'm so happy to hear you and Sal are together."

"Thank you for inviting me," I tell her, returning the hug. Mary is taller than I am and has long blonde hair, dark blue eyes and a few freckles across her button nose.

She turns and gives Pop a hug. "It has been too long! I am *so* happy you're here! Everyone come in. I just pulled sour dough bread out of the oven." She turns to her husband and gestures with her hands. "Joe, open some wine for them."

She puts her arm through mine and ushers me toward the kitchen. The smell of slightly sour, yeasty bread makes my stomach growl.

In keeping with its wholesome and warm mistress, the brick walls, huge, worn wooden table and light oak cabinets all work together to make a very welcoming space.

On the way through the house, I notice gingerbread-scented candles spread out and lit all through the rooms. Plush green laurels with tiny white lights entwined hang in the doorways and electric candles reflect in the windows.

"Your home is gorgeous! So warm and friendly," I tell her.

"Thanks. I hear *you* live in a plantation-style mansion on the beach. Wow! That must be beautiful!"

I smile. "It is, but it's too big for me and now that my divorce is final I'll be moving."

She hands me a glass of red wine and motions to the long table. The guys are hovering at one end of the kitchen island having a laugh. Mary and I take our seats. I sip at the wine and she drinks from a bottle of water. Joe comes over holding a small plate of bread and cubes of sharp cheese and places it on the table for us.

"How do you like that wine, Gracie? It's our own Cabernet. What do you think?"

"It's delicious!" I reply. "Very smooth."

"Tell me," he says, "what other flavors can you detect in it?"

I laugh. "Oh boy! I'm no wine expert, Joe, I don't—"

"You can do it," he says. "Here, hold the glass all the way up to your nose, like this." He demonstrates. "Take in the aroma."

I smell the dark red liquid. It's bold.

He nods. "Give it a good swirl around the glass. Now, take a sip and hold it on your tongue for just a second. Good swallow–well? What do you taste?"

"Hey, that really does do something, doesn't it? I taste a little cocoa?" He smiles and nods again.

"Umm, oak?"

"Yes, good. Keep going."

"I wanna say cherry?"

He laughs. "Very close. You're tasting a hint of plum."

"Really? Wow!"

Sal comes over and sits next to me.

"Hey," I say, patting his knee. "Did you see what I did there with the wine? I want to try that again!"

"You have time," Joe says. Then he looks at Sal. "Take her around to some of the wineries, do a little sight seeing. Tonight though, I have a treat with dinner. A different wine with each course. I'll show you how to recognize other aromas and flavors."

After a bit more family talk, including Tony's stories about Toby and me, I lose the battle with a yawn. Mary looks at Joe and gets to her feet.

"How about we show you where you'll be staying? You can rest and get settled if you like."

We grab our suitcases and follow them out the kitchen door. Outside is a circular garden courtyard. Teak patio furniture occupies the center, a matching table with place settings for eight is on the far end, closer to the outside kitchen and fireplace. A few trees adorned with tiny white lights surround the area making the lovely courtyard seem like it could be in the hills of France. We follow the walkway to a smaller house that also faces the courtyard.

"This was a detached garage at one time," Mary noted. "We remodeled and converted it into a guesthouse. I hope you love it."

We swing open the door and step inside. The living area has a couch and two wing-backed chairs and a coffee table. To the right, the fireplace is already lit and Joe points to a doorway beside it.

"The bedroom is through there. The fireplace is double-sided."

"Romantic," Mary whispers, poking me in my side with her elbow. I smile and agree.

"The kitchen area is straight back." Mary gestures and I follow her. "A little dinette table for two and a full kitchen, microwave, coffee maker and fridge."

This kitchen too is warm and cozy. Light oak cabinets against honey golden walls match the wood floors. Sage green and dusty rose accents were used throughout. Pillows and quilts tie it all together. I turn back to Mary. "What's not to love? This is adorable!"

"Oh, I'm so glad. I want you guys to be comfy while you're here."

"I'm sure we will be, don't worry."

"Oh," she says, holding up her index finger. "There is a half bath off the kitchen here," she points to a door. "And, the full size bath is adjacent to the bedroom."

"Great," I gush. Mary, this is wonderful. Tell me, what can I help you with while I'm here?"

She pats my hand. "Not much. Joe and I prepped a lot of stuff ahead of time, and truly, he is the cook for the holidays."

"Well, you just say the word and I'll be happy to help out!"

Joe and Sal return from dropping our suitcases in the bedroom.

"Hon," Joe says to Mary, taking her hand. "Let's leave them to settle in. Dinner at eight, okay? Lets go see if Pop needs anything."

"Where did you put Pop?" Sal asks Joe.

"In the house," Joe answers. "The spare room is down stairs and he has a bathroom to himself–it's big enough for the wheelchair. I remodeled it that way on purpose in case he needed to come live with us. This cottage also is wheelchair accessible for him."

Just then we hear barking and two rambunctious big dogs come flying through the door.

"Toby! Hey, calm down!" I shout. He sniffs around and around while Bridget watches her new friend take in his new surroundings.

Toby finally circles and plops down on the round rug in front of the fireplace looking completely exhausted. Bridget joins him in a yawn. They look as content as I feel. As tired, too.

* * *

I awake with a gasp! I look around and focus. Forgetting where I am for a second, I sit at the edge of the bed, remembering I'd taken a shower and felt worn out from the day's travels, so Sal told me to rest before dinner.

The fire is still burning warm and it's darker out. I call for Sal but don't get an answer. No Toby, either.

I get up and stalk around the room until I hear voices outside. I peek out the window and see Sal and Joe cooking on the grill while Mary sets the table in the courtyard.

Watching the two brother's catch up makes me smile. Side by side, they look much alike, and yet the differences are easy for me to see, even at a distance. Sal's posture is alert, never quite completely relaxed, while Joe, about the same build, stands more casually, like a man comfortable in his surroundings.

I decide to change and freshen up for dinner and join them in a little bit.

* * *

"What do you mean you couldn't get the words out?"

I roll my eyes and give my brother Joe a smirk. "We were right in the middle of a... moment"

"Okay, and after *the*...moment?" Joe hesitates.

I glance back an forth between my brother and sister-in-law, "I just want it be special, she deserves that."

"I agree." Mary smiles, and whispers. "I have an idea Sal, but I'll tell you later, she's coming out."

* * *

I walk out onto the patio and Sal, Joe and Mary all stopped their soft chatter.

"Sorry, did I interrupt a family conversation?" I ask, moving to Sal's side. He slips his arm around my back and kisses me on my cheek.

"Not at all. And dinner is just about ready," Mary says with a smile. "Are you hungry?"

"I'm starved!" I reply. Sal and Joe burst out laughing and it feels good to be in a safe and happy place.

Dinner is delightful, as promised. Joe's five course dinner, paired with five different wines teaches me a lot about both the reds and the whites.

I learn that Merlot's and Cabernet's are blended with cocoa and ripe cherries or plums, and a Pinot Grigio or Chardonnay can have almond blossom, apple and pear tones, or even tropical fruits. As I'm helping Mary clear the table, Joe asks me what my favorite wine is.

"Well, I've always favored Chianti's or a Sangiovise."

Joe smiles. "I'll see what I can do."

I find as I chat with Mary that I really like her-she's comfortable, gentle and strong. She fills me in a little on Sal and Joe's mother, Marie-and how Antonio mourned her passing.

"Pop was so sad," Mary says quietly, even though the men are outside and can't hear us. "I thought he'd never get over it and then he got shot-and Sal was gone. I don't know how you did it, getting them back in good graces." She laughs and puts a hand over her mouth. "I guess your name fits you"

"Truly I didn't do much. When Pop learned the truth about why Sal couldn't be home for his mom, all the old barriers came down."

"Oh I know, I'm just glad that somehow Joe persuaded his brother to go home. I think you being around helped a lot. Things happen for a reason, I always say. It was meant to be. Look, you and Sal found each other. He loves you, Gracie. He seems different-better, thanks to you."

I smile at Mary. "Thank you, he seems to think the same thing."

Mary looks at me closely. "Do you love him, Gracie?"

"More then words can describe," I say, feeling just a little choked up. "It's insane how much I ache for him."

"Good, because I know he feels the same way. I'm *so* happy for both of you."

Mary reaches over and gives me a hug. I feel comfortable with her, so I decide to share everything about the dreams, the psychic, and what Dr. Brooks told us about past life regression.

"Oh my god! See? Things DO happen for a reason. There's always a plan, Gracie; sometimes we don't always see it, but its there."

I exhale. "Oh good, you don't think I'm crazy then."

Mary looks at me, her eye's wide. "Crazy? It's crazy *not* to believe it. How incredibly mind blowing. Tell me, what does Pop think?"

"Pop believes. Sal..." I squint, then continue,. "is having a harder time with it. He is still trying to let it soak in, I think. Hell, even Dr. Brooks is a believer after talking with us."

"A real miracle, Gracie... Oh hell, I'm gonna cry."

"Oh, please don't cry–you'll make *me* cry!" I say, chuckling as I feel tears sting my eyes.

"Yes, but I'm pregnant now," she says in between her sniffs, "and EVERYTHING makes me cry! It's so annoying!"

* * *

Later that night in bed, with the remnants of a fire slowly going out, the two dogs are asleep on the floor snoring. Sal and I are cuddling, waiting for sleep to come.

"Hey, you still awake?" I ask softly.

"Yeah," he answers as he rubs my arm and places a kiss on my shoulder.

"I dreamt something this afternoon and it woke me up with a jolt."

"What was it?"

"Water. I was in water. And it was so cold. I couldn't see anything–it was dark and I was drowning, I think."

"Was there anyone with you? Was I there?"

"No, ah, I don't know–like I said, it was dark. I didn't feel afraid though, like other times. I felt like I didn't have the strength to swim or help myself–totally exhausted. I think it was the ocean. I think I heard the waves, but it was very fuzzy this time and out of focus."

Sal splays his hand across my belly and draws me tighter to him. "Do you think it was a past life dream or a random one?"

"I'm gonna say random, mostly because I knew somehow it was me–in the present. The dream just startled me awake and I gasped for air. It didn't give me any lingering feelings of sadness or being frightened. I forgot where I was when I woke up," I say with a little chuckle, "then I remembered."

"That's happened to me also," Sal whispers into my neck. "I think you were exhausted from the trip. That confusion is scary stuff. The first few times we slept together, before we made love, it scared me to think I might have one of those dreams were I was back in the military – and I might have hurt you thinking you were the enemy."

I roll on my back and he cradles me in his arms. "You haven't done it yet," I remind him.

"Yeah, thank god. I would kill myself if I hurt you," he growls.

I can't help but shiver. "Are you still afraid of this happening?"

"Not so much anymore," he whispers. "It's less of a worry now that we make love. Just in the very beginning of our relationship, I had concerns. It's better but it always plays in the back of my mind."

I put my hand to his cheek. "I believe that you could never hurt me, Sal."

"I love you, Gracie."

His lips find mine and as it always does, the passion drives our lovemaking, until completely exhausted, we sleep.

CHAPTER 21

I get up early the next morning and let both dogs out back. I supervise for a minute and watch as they sniff around and do their thing.

The sun is barely up and it's chilly. Toby follows Bridget around through the courtyard, up the ramp, and through a doggie door that I just realize is there.

I laugh in spite of myself, shaking my head. I see Mary at the door and I wave.

She waves her hand, shooing me back to the cottage. "Go back to bed, sleep in. Toby is fine–really, go."

I smile and give her a nod. " Okay, see ya later."

We sleep until eleven. Sal goes over to the main house and comes back with a coffee for me.

"Rise and shine, Princess." He hands me the steamy mug and sits on the bed in front of me.

"You spoil me, you know that, don't you?"

"Yes," he answers. "I live to spoil you. He smiles, You spoil me too."

"How is that even possible." I say with a shrug. "You have done so much, and you take such good care of me! "

"Gracie, you spoil me with your love, and your body."

We sit there quietly, eyes locked. "As for taking care of you properly, that's my job as a man. Now, drink your coffee, then get dressed. We're spending the day together, just us."

"Just us? Where are we going? Where is everyone?"

Sal gets up from the bed laughing. "So many questions. You'll see–it'll be fun."

*   *   *

Within an hour, we are both showered and dressed. We walk out of our little cottage and see Joe, Mary and Pop in the courtyard. Joe's holding a big picnic basket and a blanket.

"Here ya go", Joe motions to the basket. It's ready to go."

"Sal, where are we going?" I ask again.

"I told you, we're spending the day alone. Joe and Mary told me about a beautiful place we shouldn't miss seeing while we're here. Trust me!"

I'm still confused, but everyone else is all smiles. Joe hands Sal the basket and I took the blanket.

"Just follow the trail," Joe points, "through the vineyard–you'll see the hill shortly. Have fun you guys! We'll see ya later."

"Have-a-good time, caro. I look after–a-Toby," Antonio says, smiling from ear to ear.

As we walk along, I wonder why everyone seems just a little bit strange, this morning. "What's up with them?"" I ask Sal.

He glances back over his shoulder, then down at me. He laughs. " Nothing, they're fine."

We discover the trail and follow it along through the open field and out past the vineyard. It's a bright, beautiful day and not too cool.

I take in the hilly and plush green landscape stretched out before us. It's truly breathtaking and nothing like what I'm used to on the east coast. Because the vines are bare and cut back for the season, the winery employees are all gone, so it's very quiet–I can hear a few birds and an occasional wind gust rattles past us.

We walk about fifteen minutes when we spot the hill with the big tree that Joe told us about. It isn't very steep so it's easy to reach the top. We set down the blanket and basket and look out at the scenery surrounding us. Hills roll into hills. Row after row of crops. And an endless blue sky.

"I said it before, I'll say it again. I feel like we left the country. The land here is beautiful! And that funny sense of impending doom isn't as strong here, either."

Sal comes up from behind me and hugs me, then kisses the top of my head. "It is beautiful out here–and so peaceful. Don't worry, Whatever's coming, we'll handle it, together."

"I agree with him. "So, tell me... why did you want to spend the day together alone? We're here visiting with your family–tomorrow's Christmas Eve. We should be with *them*."

He turns me around to face him. "Gracie, it's all good. Actually, this was their idea. Come over here."

I shrug. Obviously, something's up, but I choose to relax. We spread out the blanket and sit down. Sal opens the basket and pulls out a bottle of wine and some container's of food. He opens the wine–a bottle of Chianti–one of my favorites! "My brother came through!" Sal chuckles.

We have an array of cheese and fruit, and one huge sandwich layered with meats that we cut up into sections. There are also a couple of napoleon pastries for dessert.

A while after we eat, I feel Sal's eyes all over me.

"Why are you staring at me? Do I have food on my face?"

He laughs and it's a sound I'll never get tired of.

"No, Princess, I'm just watching you. You seem calmer. Being away agrees with you. You like it here?"

I smile and look around us. "Yes, I love it here. It's nice being away–home seems a million miles away."

Sal runs a hand through his wavy hair. "It is miles away–around two-thousand two-hundred and eighty six –give or take."

I give him a sarcastic look. He winks back.

"No, I mean, home seems like a distant memory since we arrived here."

"I'm glad you're relaxed. I want this to be a happy time for you. Come here." He holds his arm out to me and I snuggle in closer.

We sit like that for a while, then open the other bottle of wine. We share kisses and conversation. We watch as the sun starts to drop and the sky changes from blue to golden orange with purple hues.

"It's getting late, should we go back?" I ask.

He takes my face in both his hands and gazes into my eyes then slowly he kisses me. I feel that kiss all the way down to my toes. When he stops, I grab at his shirt fisting the material, pulling him back to my lips.

He puts a hand on the back of my head securing me, deepening the kiss. I let go of his shirt and twist my fingers in his hair, breaking the kiss and panting. "Maybe we should go," I say again.

He leans me back on the blanket and settles on top of me, kissing my lips and trailing down my throat. "I want you Gracie... Now. Right here."

When he says the words, fire heats my stomach, I nip at his bottom lip and we start to undress each other. Laying on the blanket I feel the cool air rush around my naked body when Sal gets up to shrug off his jeans. Slowly he makes his way back to me, kissing me from my instep to my belly and breasts, till he is completely smothering me again with his body. He raises up on his elbows so he can look into my face–his eyes pierce mine.

"Gracie," he whispers, his voice thick with emotion, I want you to know…god, I love you so much–more than I know how to say." He blinks, then swallows.

"From the moment I met you, I knew it. You knew it. We are made for each other. Until you, I was lost. No one has ever captivated me so deep. You own my heart. I'm not living without you"

He takes my left hand and I feel something cool slide down my ring finger…. He whispers, "Marry me."

My heart skips a beat. Tears well up and drop from my eyes. I can't speak.

"Shhh, don't cry, Gracie." He kisses me tenderly.

My entire body trembles with emotion. I try to respond, to speak, but I'm paralyzed with joy.

"Gracie," Sal smiles, wiping at my cheeks. "Can you nod your head or something?" He laughs, nervously.

"Yes…" I squeak out on a breath. It comes out so faint I almost can't hear it myself. I put my hands on Sal face and take a deep breath. "YES! Sal, yes!"

I look at the gold band with a marquee cut diamond in the center and smaller diamonds surrounding it.

"It's beautiful, Sal. I love you, too."

Sal kisses me hard. I return his passion. "I love you," he whispers over and over.

I open myself wide to receive him and he buries himself deep into my core. He rocks his hips giving all of himself to me and I meet his every thrust.

I arch my back and a moan escapes from my throat as I begin to feel my release coil within.

Sal hisses and we both climax so violently our bodies shake with tremors for long moments afterward.

The cool night air on our naked, perspired bodies makes me shiver, and Sal wraps us up in the blanket. We lay still, intertwined in one other. Sal reaches up and brushes some hair out of my eyes and seals his lips once more over mine.

"You have made me so happy Gracie, and I swear to God, I will take care of you until the last breath I take...I promise."

* * *

Christmas Eve ushers in happy and welcome cheers of good luck and joy for the Petroni family.

Pop is as proud as a peacock. He has a grandchild on the way from his eldest son Joseph and his wife Mary, and intended future nuptials for his second son, Salvatore.

"This is a wonderful, wonderful Christmas." Antonio is beaming. "It's just what-a-this family needs–happy, good things. My Mary, full with a bambino, and-a-mio caro Gracie, my heart is about to-a-burst with much happiness."

That night we eat a traditional Italian-American Christmas Eve dinner consisting mostly of seafood. And, as is another tradition, we eat until we can't move–and then go back for more.

We nestle around the Christmas tree and talk of baby names and wedding dates.

"I really don't want a big wedding," I say. "I did that already, but, Sal's never been married–what do you want to do, Sal?"

Sal shrugs and urges me up on his lap. "I think a nice small ceremony with friends and family would be just fine. I would rather spend the money taking you on a tour of Europe for....let's see, two, maybe three months?" He tosses me his best toothy smile.

"OH MY GOD! Are you serious?" I scream.

Sal laughs, along with the rest of the family.

"Very serious, Princess. You've never been–I thought you might like that. I was thinking Italy, of course–and Pop, if you want to go with us on that part–you're welcome to do that." I nod in agreement.

"Then, England, France, Monaco, to name a few. You can choose. We'll sit some night and map it all out–sound good?"

Shaking my head in awe, I whisper, "Perfect." Then I seal the idea with a kiss.

* * *

As magical as the days before it were, Christmas Day comes and goes like a blur. All morning we open presents, drink coffee and eat delectable pastries. The horrible loss that has marked my past six Christmases is completely gone. Once more surrounded by a loving family, I feel more complete than I can ever remember.

After the paper and mess is cleaned up, we get ready to resume the holiday regiment of feasting–and we do it well into the evening. By the time we crawl into bed Christmas night, I'm asleep when my head hits the pillow, blissfully wrapped in Sal's arms.

When I wake the day after Christmas and step on the bathroom scale, I want to just vomit. I put my hands to my mouth and whisper, "oh holy crap" to myself.

"You're beautiful," Sal says from the doorway of the bathroom.

"How long have you been standing there?"

"Not long, he laughs. What's got you so worried, Princess?"

I look at the scale again and cringe.

Sal takes a few steps in my direction as I get off the scale.

"Gracie, you have a woman's body. I happen to be very turned on by your curves" He takes me in his arms. "And it's mine."

"I just don't want to get too curvy."" I mumble.

"You won't.–besides, wait till you see all the Renaissance paintings in Europe–you know the woman in those paintings are chubby–you might have been considered too thin to be painted back then."

"I'm still gonna watch it though," I grumble.

"Fine," he says. "But don't worry so much– You enjoyed yourself and I loved every minute watching you do so. Now get dressed." He pats my behind. "Joey and Mary are taking us all out for a little sightseeing around Napa."

"Oh good I want to see more of the area– though that probably means more eating and drinking."

"Last day, Princess," he kisses my nose. "You're beautiful–stop worrying so much."

We all pile into the rented Chevy Tahoe SUV and get a tour of Napa. We visit other wineries and participate in wine pairings, then we shop in some local gift shops and have lunch at the cutest little bistro.

As we're leaving the bistro, Mary suggests one more place we have to see. We travel up the North St. Helena Highway into the heart of Napa.

There stands the Castello di Amorosa winery.

"How cool!" I shriek. "It looks like a medieval style Tuscany Castle!"

We pull up and take the tour, which was magnificent. Again I experience the sense that it's somehow familiar.

I spend some time taking photos of the castle from various places on the grounds when Mary holds out her hands and points at my phone.

"I'll take a picture of you and Sal with the castle behind you. Smile!"

Sal and I pose together, arms wrapped around each other's waist. We smile at Mary.

I look at the picture and break into a grin. "Good shot!" I tell her. Taking another peek at it, I think about Maggie. *She'll get a real kick out of this picture.* I send it off to her with a text.

Merry Xmas Mags!
Guess what? He asked. I said yes!
Napa is beautiful–they even have a castle.
It made me think of you!
Talk soon!

After a few more stops, we head back to Joey and Mary's. I'm not looking forward to packing, and the thought of it makes me sad. It's been such a magical time, surrounded by family. And, free from that relentless sense of disaster that annoys me from day to day...

* * *

Nick was very pleased to see that Sal had popped the question. Only then did Gracie realize why Nick had called him "chicken shit" on the flight out.

Upon safe arrival back into Jacksonville, Nick gave Sal a wide grin. "Let me know about the honeymoon plans, mate. I'll help you work out a schedule for Europe."

"Thanks, Nick, Sal said, giving him a hug and a pat on the back. "I'll let you know the minute we work out some details."

"Have you heard from the Department?" Nick asked, his voice low.

"No, why?" asked Sal, glancing over his shoulder.

"The director has called some of the team. Some mission is going down—class C, I think. Anyway, I know you keep in touch with them. They haven't sent you an alert?"

"No," Sal shrugged, "but I'm done. They said I could walk, so I did. I'm finished."

Nick laughed at his statement. "Yes done, but *never* finished."

Sal chose to ignore his old friend. He *was* finished with that life. "Hey, listen man, thanks for taking care of us. Happy New Year! We'll be talking to you soon, Nick. Take care, brother."

"Yes, same to you, and congratulations again," Nick said as he hugged all of them including Toby, and they departed the plane.

On the way home from the airport Gracie asked Sal what Nick was talking about.

"You heard that, huh?" Sal asked with a lightheartedness he didn't feel.

"Yeah, I heard it," she said, her brow furrowed, the sparkle in her eyes gone. "What's class C and the team?"

Sal grinned and glanced at her, then returned his eyes to the road. "Now, you know you're not supposed to know *any* of those terms. Nick really should not have said anything in front of you or Pop. There's obviously a mission going down—class C is a code yellow—not real dangerous. Sounds like they have assembled some of the team—my old team. But I haven't gotten any word."

Pop said something in Italian from the back seat, and Sal looked at him coldly in the rear view mirror.

Sal felt his jaw muscle tighten. *Damn it..*

Pop said it again, but louder.

"NO! Sal shouted. "No.. and they haven't called me anyway, so now, can we drop it?" Sal took Gracie's hand in his.

"They haven't called you... not *yet*," Pop muttered.

Gracie glanced at her hand in Sal's. He rubbed the back of her hand with his thumb, then toyed with the ring he had put on her finger just days ago. Finally he lifted her hand to his lips and kissed it. Giving her a sideways glance, he whispered, "I love you."

CHAPTER 22

Maggie was cleaning up wrapping paper and empty boxes that cluttered her living room when she heard her phone beep. She grabbed for it and tapped the icon. Up popped Gracie's photo and message.

"OH MY GOD!" Maggie shouted, scaring her husband out of his Christmas nap. "Holy Shit!"

"What, what..Maggie? What's the matter?" Mike said, trying to focus.

"Mike, Gracie's engaged! And look-look at this picture!" Shoving the phone in her husband's face, she babbled on. "Look how happy they are."

"Yeah? Good for Gracie! What a Merry Christmas for her. Where are they?"

"They went to Napa-Sal's brother and wife live there. Huh, that's is so peculiar," Maggie said as she gazed at the picture some more.

"What's peculiar?" Mike asked.

"Oh nothing, just, the Castle behind them. It's funny because I told her, the last picture she sent they looked like royalty, so she took this one as a joke. But, I'm getting that shiver up my spine again."

Mike just gave his wife a caring look. "Bad or good shiver?" he asked.

"Humm, I'm not sure. Not real bad, just weird."

Maggie tapped at the keys on her phone:

Congratulations!!!!! Holy shit!!! I am over the moon happy for you! Love you!

She finished cleaning up and her husband Mike resumed his horizontal position on the couch. Maggie went up to her studio, and downloaded the photo on her big screen computer. She glanced back and forth between the two photos then eyed a blank canvas that sat patiently on an easel.

She stood, grabbed a smock and a paintbrush, and went to work.

* * *

On December twenty-eighth as promised, my brother Steve shows up with a few fun presents from all of the places his ministry has taken him. A nice bottle of rum from one of the islands and a silver necklace with white onyx stones in between the links were among my favorites.

Sal and my brother seem to hit it off. Steve is a little concerned with the speed of our engagement but happy for me just the same.

"Now don't get me wrong, guys," Steve cautions. "I'm thrilled you're getting married, but *you* just got divorced," he points in my direction. "Maybe you should just go slower. Make sure."

Sal gives Steve a sympathetic look. "We're in no hurry. We haven't set a date yet. I understand your trepidations for Gracie's future, but, even though she is just recently divorced, she was separated from Rich a long time. I love your sister. I promised I'd love her forever and I will."

Steve seems relieved to hear we're not rushing to the altar. I give him a shove. "Will you walk me down the aisle?"

"Sure, if you give me enough warning ahead of time. Just keep me in the loop."

That evening Pop joins us and we all have dinner together. I tell my brother about the New Year's bash.

"You might want to get a dress shirt and tie" I suggest and he wrinkles his nose.

Sal laughs. "I got some you can borrow."

"I'm just not used to wearing confining clothes," my brother mentions.

"Yeah, not one of my favorite things either," Sal agrees. It would seem they are simpatico on the topic.

"All three of you will look so handsome at Celine's party," I brag. "It should be fun—they always are!"

Pop looks up from his plate. "Yes, last-a-year I went, we had a nice time. Did-a-you tell Celine about your news yet?"

"No Pop, I was going to surprise her with it on New Year's. She's going to die! I told Mag's, though—she's very happy for me."

*   *   *

The next day is a blur. Still on an emotional high from being in Napa and getting engaged, I struggle to quickly fall back into my routine. When I get into the office, I can't wait to tell Veronica my happy news.

"Oh, that's just the best news I have heard in months," she says, her happiness showing in her eyes. "I bet Antonio's very happy."

"Very happy, I would say. He didn't think Sal would ever settle down and he worried about me and my future, too. Now he seems content."

"Good. Hey, your brother is here for a few days, right?"

"Yes, why?"

She taps me on the shoulder. "Go ahead home and don't come in till he's gone. You hardly see him. Go home and be with your family. Things will keep around here."

"Really? Oh my god! Thank you! I guess I'll see you after New Year's then."

"Happy New Year, Gracie. Now go on and get out of here!"

I give her a big hug. "Happy New Year, Veronica!"

*   *   *

I wake up at two in the morning on December 30th, to an empty bed. Oddly enough, not even Toby is here.

I go to the bedroom door and peek down the hall and notice the dim light of the study is on. Quietly, I pad my way down the hall. When I get to the door, Sal is behind the desk staring out into space, deep in thought, the light from the computer screen glowing on his face.

As quiet as I am, Toby whines when he sees me and Sal turns toward me.

"Gracie? What's wrong? Why aren't you sleeping?"

"I could ask you the same question? I answer, moving closer to the desk. Somehow I know something is wrong. "I woke up to an empty bed. I don't like that. What's the matter? I know you well enough to know you're far away in thought."

Sal takes a deep breath, then holds out his hand for me to come sit on his lap.

"Gracie, I have something to tell you and you must promise me you won't get upset."

I feel that feeling–that dreaded sense of foreboding that makes the hairs on my neck stand up. Slowly, I asked around the lump in my throat and the knot in my stomach, I grind out a question. "You need to go, don't you?"

For a moment, he's quiet, softly caressing my bare arms. Then I feel him sigh. "I got a call, yes. My team has been reassembled for a call of duty. I've been asked to come and supervise the mission for the captain acting in my place."

"I don't understand, Sal." I groan, trying not to unravel. "I thought you were done? You said they let you go because you have been through so much." I looked out the window as a horrible thought came to mind. "You didn't lie to me, did you?"

"Oh, god no, Gracie. I've never lied to you. He turns my face back to his. Won't ever lie to you. But, they feel my skills are needed." He pauses rubbing my back. "Those men–the agents–they are my brother's, Gracie. We've worked together a long time–some of us have been to hell and back– in some cases, more than once."

My mind screams for me to get up, leave him in the dark, go back to bed and find it's all another horrible dream. But I've learned not to run anymore. Sal's taught me that I'm strong and capable, so I sit still in his lap and concentrate on his touch. I speak softly because he deserves that from me.

"My point exactly. You've been to hell enough. How can they ask? Is it mandatory? Or is this your choice?"

"That depends on me," he says. I pitch my eyebrow at him and he continues. "I'll fly to Quantico, sit in on the meetings, get the orders, and see how much I'm needed. I may be able to just handle the situation from there." He drops his hands from my back and puts them in my lap. "Gracie, those are my men. I have to help if I can."

I pull away from him and get to my feet. "NO! No, you are *not* going," I command. Sal reaches for my hands and I pull away from him. I'm so angry I can't even think. Why doesn't he understand he can't do this?

"Gracie, calm down," he whispers. "I have to go."

I spin on my heel and get right in close to his face. "How long will you be gone? Where the hell will you be? Will I even *know* where you'll be? We, we....won't be able to communicate!"

I feel tears burn my eyes and my stomach pitches. As I clutch my hands over my mouth, my anger is transformed into a fear so large I can't breath. Something bad is coming and not even Sal can talk me out of knowing this.

He stands from his seat and clasps me firmly at my shoulders. "Gracie, stop! Stop...shhhh.. it's all right! Everything is going to be all right. I won't be gone long. It's just a supervising mission. It'll be done before you know it and I'll do all I can to try to keep contact with you."

The tears are running down my face and I can't stop them. I look at him with my red eyes and runny nose. "You don't get it, Sal. This is where it all goes to hell. You leave me...and...and...you don't come back. I can feel it–just like in my dreams! Something's wrong. You can't leave–not this time. Not now–now that we've found each other. The psychic, she..she told us not to separate! You can't go!"

My heart is pounding all the way up into my ears. My chest is tightening and my head is swimming. Sal scoops me up and carries me to the bedroom and places me on the bed.

Sitting next to me, he looks into my face. "Gracie, breathe. Come on, nice and slow–in....out...look at me, Gracie. Don't take your eyes off me. Breathe, deep, breathe, good, that's my girl. Relax. Shhh.. don't get upset, please, don't get upset."

He sits me up and encircles me with himself. "Gracie, you're shaking. Please calm down, it's all going to be fine." He coaxes my chin up, looks at me.

"It's all good. Nothing is going to happen to me. I told you not to listen to that crazy psychic."

"But Dr. Brooks believes it, too," I cry. "Sal please, for me, don't leave on this mission."

"I'll fly up there and see what the details are. I told you, that might be it and then I'll be home."

"And what if you decide to go?" I whisper. "You can't tell me anything. I'm in the dark. You know how scary this is for me?"

"That's for your protection, Gracie. Please understand. I will come back to you, I promise.

His words sent a shiver up my spine and knocked the wind out of my lungs. The look on my face scares Sal into getting to his feet.

"Gracie, what is it? Are you ill? You look like you've seen a ghost."

I can't speak for several minutes. How many lifetimes have we had together? How many times have we lost each other? Sal stands before me, clenching and unclenching his fists, but waits for me to collect myself.

"Every dream, Sal," I whisper. He kneels at the side of the bed so he can hear my words. "In every dream, this is what happens. You tell me you have to leave and you promise me you will come back to me. Those are the last words I ever hear from you, time and time again. You can't keep that promise. You *always* promise me you will come back, but you never do. Don't you see? Our history is going to repeat itself. We can change it—we have the free will to change our path. Don't go! How about you promise me you won't go?"

* * *

I wake up late after a fitful sleep. Again Sal is not beside me. The sun is high in the sky and my clock informs me it's almost noon.

I get up and shuffle about but even Toby is gone. I'm sure he's outside with Sal. I feel beat up, like I've been punched in my gut. And then the tears start again. Sal is not changing his mind, and shortly I am going to be out of mine.

I get dressed quickly and head downstairs, spotting my brother sitting by the pool, reading the paper. Toby is laying by his feet. He cocks one doggy-eyebrow at me, expectantly.

"Hey," I say as I come out of the house, "what's going on?"

"Oh hey," he answers with a grin. Sleep much, it's noon?"

"I had a rough night."

"You need to talk about it?" he asks.

I look at my older brother and manage a smile. "Not yet."

"Well, something's up." He points to Antonio's house. Those two have been arguing for at least two hours."

I follow his finger with my eyes and out on Antonio's deck, father and son are yelling at each other.

I can't make out every word, but the knot in my stomach knows exactly what they are fighting about—I don't need to hear it. I sit down hard on one of my patio chairs as if someone's dropped me into it.

"Everything okay Gracie? What the hell is going on?"

"Did Sal mention to you what he does—or did—for a living?" I narrow my eyes as I ask.

"He told me he was in the military. Why?"

"Yes, he was in the military, then Special Forces. And lastly, he told me he retired from the CIA as a special agent."

My brother's eyebrows shot up with excitement. "Wow, no shit? Makes even more sense to me now how easily he killed that mugger! Okay, so what's the problem, Sis?"

"He got called in for one more mission. I don't want him to go and I'm guessing from the sounds of it, Pop's not happy either."

My brother sat back in his chair and gave me a sympathetic smile. "Gracie, he has to go. Unless—he has a choice. Can he choose his missions?"

"Yeah, he can," I answer. "He feels it's very necessary for him to go on this last mission because it's his team, his men. He knows each of them, their personalities, how they work, who's right for what job. That's why they want him on this detail, so he can train the new captain."

"And this is why you're upset and he's fighting with his dad?" I nod.

"Okay, so he chooses to go. He'll be back-how long could it take? The man is serving his country. He's not going on the front line of combat. he'll be fine Sis."

I start to cry, again. "You don't understand, Steve. If I tell you something, swear to me you won't think I'm crazy... please, on mommy and daddy's graves."

My brother leans over the table and rests on his elbows. "All right, tell me."

I tell Steve about it all. The dreams, the sense I've known Sal forever, the gypsy, the psychiatrist. The promises. He sits very still and quiet through the whole story. Then he rubs at his eyes and shakes his head.

"I have been all over this world Gracie," he says. "I have seen way too many unexplainable things. Every culture has their own take on all kinds of spiritual beliefs. The words *soul mate* are used all over. Every culture have various representations of it, like angel or guardian, even protector. In Haiti it's called *Konpayon nanm*. In Hindi, *Sathina*. But it all comes down to the same thing. All believe we have them. I know you Gracie, and I don't think you are crazy. I believe, just knowing how strongly you're feeling about it.

"What your doctor and the psychic told you seems right to me. I also have read a little on past life regression. Like I said, I have seen a lot of unexplainable things in my travels. Who's to say it's not true?"

I swipe my arm across my face. My eyes are burning with tears and lack of rest. "Now you know. That's why I don't want him to leave. This is just like one of my dreams, Steve. He might not come back."

"I can understand how you must feel." My brother sighs. "I do see how much you both love each other. I just don't know what to tell you guys." He pauses. "Maybe this time, it really *will* be okay."

The shouting gets louder, but it's in Italian. My brother and I both look over at Antonio's.

"Should you go over there?" my brother asks.

"No, I think I'm gonna let Pop help me out on his own on this one."

I was so grateful my older brother came for a visit. His love of travel and helping the less fortunate around the world made him stronger and wiser then his years. I was glad I filled him in and he understood.

* * *

Sal sat down on a chair on his father's deck staring at him. "Pop, I'm going to come back, I swear it, I would never leave Gracie."

"I told you from-a-the beginning! Don't you hurt that girl, she can't take no more. You love her–a-son, what are you doing this for?"

"Pop please, I have a job to do, just please keep an eye on her. I'll have Lou come by, too. Listen, I know you and Gracie are upset because of her dreams, but I've got a duty to do. Would you leave your partner or other police officer's hanging? No you wouldn't! Just please, understand. I will come home and I will marry the love of my life!"

"The thing is son, what if you don't? I'm-a-so afraid of-a- what she might do. She loves you so much–why you gotta tempt fate? You almost died once in-a-that prison. What if some thing goes wrong again?"

*   *   *

The rest of the day was a quiet one. Gracie stayed up in her room. Sal did his best to get her to help take down their first, glorious tree, but she refused, explaining she wasn't feeling up to it. So, he and Steve spent the afternoon packing ornaments and lights and hauling the tree out of the house.

When it was time for dinner, Sal again approached her. "Gracie, your brother and I would like to know what you would like for dinner? Or we could go out..."

"I'm not hungry," she answered. "Why don't you guys go out? I have no appetite."

"Gracie, you have to eat. You've been up here all day and I'm not going to leave you alone. We have a few days left..."

"A FEW DAYS?" she shrieked, cutting him off. "When do you have to leave?"

Sal looked down to the floor and hesitated. "I leave on the second."

She looked away from him, and tears started to flood her eyes again. Sal rushed to her side to hold her.

She put up her hand to keep him away. "Don't. Just don't. Please, just leave me alone."

Sal slowly bent down to try to make eye contact. "Understand this," he growled. "I will never leave you alone. NEVER!"

She put her hand to his chest and looked up at him. "But you are leaving me," she said in a small voice.

His heart was breaking. If he didn't go, he'd never be able to look himself in the mirror again. And if he did go, it just might kill the woman he loved.

"Gracie," he whispered, kneeling in front of her and putting his head in her lap. "You are my life. Please understand when I tell you I will be back. Class C, remember? Nothing should go wrong. It's all I can tell you for now. Please come down and eat. Spend the last few days at my side. Tomorrow is New Year's Eve and I want to bring in the New Year with the woman I am going to spend the rest of life with. Please don't shut me out."

CHAPTER 23

Though I'm no good at pretending, I manage to join Sal and Steve and we ordered a pizza. I barely got one slice down my throat. Sal watches me struggle to eat it. My brother on the other hand took a different approach, he just made sure my wine glass wasn't empty.

Later that night in bed, Sal holds me while I cry silently into my pillow. He doesn't know what to say or do anymore. He rolls me over to face him so I'm on my side, my head resting on his bare chest. He caresses my hair and rubs my back. I finally start to relax.

"Sal," I whimper, "I understand why you have to do this, but I'm so scared of what might happen–and I'm going to stay scared until you come home."

"I will come home, Gracie. But I'm worried you're going to make yourself sick in the meantime. You won't eat and I *know* you won't sleep. I wish your brother was going to stay longer, but he leaves the same day as me. Please promise me you'll take care of yourself. I understand why you're scared, but *please* don't make yourself sick about it."

Soon the wine and the tears catch up to me and I drift off to the sound of Sal's heartbeat.

* * *

I wake before daybreak with a pounding migraine. I stumble to the bathroom to take some aspirin while Sal sleeps peacefully. I search for Toby who is sleeping on the floor. Making kissy noises, I get him to follow me down the stairs. Air—I need fresh air and a walk on the beach with some time to think, by myself.

It's cool but not freezing and it feels so good on my swollen face. I can tell my eyes are puffy from all the crying and I'm sure I'll look like hell for the New Year's Eve party. Celine would know something's wrong she has seen these eyes before she'll be insane when she sees them again.

Just a day ago I was so excited to show her my ring, tell her our plans. And now, I feel like I've died and it's all over.

As I walk on the beach the tears start again. Toby stays very close to me this morning, looking up at me every now and then.

I decide to go sit at the edge of the little pier that jets out over the water. I watch the sunrise in the purple, winter sky. I pray for Sal—and I pray for us. I shed a few more tears.

I sit very still, so still I can feel my heart beat with the pain in my head. I take slow, deep breaths with Toby lying right at my side.

When the sun is just about up, my headache is finally subsiding. I hear Toby's tail thump on the wooden pier, I open my eyes and find Sal standing there. He doesn't speak. He sits behind me and holds me in his arms as I lean back into him.

We don't need to talk, we just need to be right there with each other.

* * *

Like I'm running on autopilot, I get ready for Celine's big party. To keep the tears from starting, I have to subdue all emotion. My ring glitters in the mirror and I cringe.

I decide to wear my hair pinned up. I slither into my strapless black velvet gown with the slit to my thigh, matching it with a pair of sparkly black pumps. My diamond necklace and earrings finish the look. Simple yet classic.

I make my way towards the stairs. Sal is waiting as I come down. He smiles when he sees me. "Gracie, you are so damn beautiful."

I smile, but I know it doesn't reach my eyes. My eyes are still so sore from crying that they ache to close.

He lifts my chin, forcing me to look at him. "Beautiful... even when you're sad," he says as he leans in to kiss me tenderly on the lips.

My brother Steve shuffles in from outside and clears his throat, interrupting our kiss.

"The limo's here, guys. Antonio's already getting settled," he says as he watches Sal and me descend the stairs. "Gracie, you look great!"

I answer him with a tight smile and a nod of my head. It is the best I can do.

We arrive at Celine's party a little after eight. Though I hadn't talked with her all week, I still battle the emotional war raging inside me. Would this be the last New Year's with Sal in this lifetime?

Walking into the club with Sal on my arm, I can't help but notice the decorations. As usual, Celine's done an amazing job. Black table clothes on top of longer white ones cover the tables. The centerpieces are silver and gold Mylar balloons and each place is set with black, silver, and gold hats, favors and noisemakers to match. The D.J is playing popular current hits, and the dance floor is alive with excitement.

I spot Celine and manage a proper smile. I wave to her and she bolts toward us.

"BABYGIRL!" She yells, grabbing me into a hug. "I missed you like crazy. How was the trip?"

I take a deep breath and hold my left hand up to my face, exposing the ring and I wiggle my finger.

"AHHH!" She squeals in delight. "Are you shittin' me? Oh my god–lemme see it!" She tugs my hand closer to her face. "You done good, Sal, You done real good."

I can't help the tears that develop in my eyes and my smile contorts into a pain-filled mask. Sal squeezes his arm around my shoulders. "Gracie, please don't," he whispers.

"I'm trying," I hiss.

Celine takes a step back, her eyes darting between Sal and me. "Okay, cut the bullshit, you two. What's wrong?" She raises an eyebrow at Sal.

"Looks like you ladies need some girl chat," Sal notes.

Celine takes me by my arm. "We sure do, I'll bring her right back, Sal. Go to the bar and get yourself a drink or two."

Celine rushes me out of the club and we head for the ladies room. On the way, she grabs two flutes of champagne off of a waiter's tray.

"Here," she says as she shoves one at me. "Drink." I take the glass but it reminds me of the champagne on the plane and more tears burn at my eyes.

"Jesus, Gracie, what the hell is wrong, baby?"

"He's leaving," I say in between deep breaths. "He's going to leave on a mission." Clutching my hand over my heart as I continue to sob, I try to explain. "Bad feelings....I have a bad feeling."

I do my best to calm down and tell Celine the whole story. Finally, I'm out of steam. "He's sure he'll return-that he'll be safe."

"Do you believe him baby?" Celine says, tilting her head.

"A part of me wants to. But it's being overshadowed by this overwhelming feeling of dread and sadness. I had it months before I knew any of this, but I couldn't put my finger on it. Why Celine, why would fate do this? Why would God let this happen? What have I done to deserve so much pain?"

"Oh no you don't, Gracie," Celine says with a firm shake of her head. "Oh no, you just didn't say that to me. You have done *nothing* wrong. It's gonna be all right. Maybe Sal's right and you should believe him. Look at me. You're gonna be fine," she says as she grabs my shoulders, giving me a shake.

She takes a tissue and dabs my eyes. I knew your eyes looked puffy to me. I couldn't imagine you'd be crying that much about your engagement. Now I get it. This sucks! It just plain out sucks!"

"I'm sorry Celine, I don't want to be a party pooper..."

"Now Gracie cut the crap. We are going to fix your make-up. You're going to tell everyone you're engaged. And you are going to dance with your sexy man. Next week we will get to the bottom of this—we'll call that Dr. Brooks or hell maybe we should call the psychic—you still have her number? She might have a little insight to all this that might make you feel better."

I nod, then gulp the rest of my champagne down. "I'm going to need another one of these," I say, handing her the empty glass. "I like your idea Celine, but let's keep that to ourselves."

Celine nods in agreement and helps fix my make-up. She looks at me in the mirror as she asks, "So when does he leave?"

"Day after tomorrow," I whisper as though by not saying it too loud will keep it from happening.

"Alright then, I'll be over the day after that." Then she hugs me.

I make it back to the party and find my three men stuffing their faces with shrimp at the seafood bar. They are a handsome trio in their suits. Sal's in his tux again so he can match my black dress. He spots me instantly and holds up a small plate that consists of shrimp and some other appetizers. I take the plate and just stare at the food.

"You will eat tonight, Princess, if I have to feed you myself." he warns. "You and Celine have a nice talk?"

"Yep," I reply, still looking at the food.

"Is everything all right?"

I look up at him, his beautiful soft brown eyes so kind and warm searching mine for an answer. "I hope it will be."

Dinner is served and I manage a few nibbles here and there. I tried to listen to the conversations around the table, but the chatter was almost incoherent. The entire time Sal has me in his touch. My arm, my hand, even a squeeze on my leg under the table now and then.

Celine dances with my brother and flirts with him. It's all in good fun and my brother played right along with her. I can't help but to laugh and it's a welcome relief.

About a half an hour before midnight, Celine announces for everyone to go outside into the courtyard. There we are each given a sky lantern.

"Has everyone received their lanterns?" Celine asks using a microphone. "Everyone also should have received an index card. This is what we're gonna do. Write down on your cards the name of a loved one who's passed, or send up a message for good luck and hope. Or, maybe you need to make a little wish, or you have to say goodbye..." Celine glances in my direction. She puts her hand to her mouth to catch her emotions.

"Okay everyone," she continues and then clears her throat. "Let's get started! We launch them at midnight!"

Sal, my brother Steve, Antonio and I each have a sky lantern and an index card. The lanterns are made of some sort of tissue paper-like material with a bamboo frame. A small wax fuel cell is suspended in the middle.

We each write something on our cards and stick them in the lantern. Steve asks me to join him on a little prayer for our parents, and Sal and Pop write something for Marie.

When it comes time for me to write my note, my stomach twists in a knot. Through watery eyes I write out my New Year's wish.

Salvatore, my protector, You healed my heart and made me believe in love again. For what I feel, love is not a strong enough word. You have awoken my soul. May you come back to me unharmed. Until then, I will pray on your promise.

My eternal soul mate.

Sal hands me his card, speaking softly. "Here," he says, "I want you to read it."

I take the card from him and hand him mine.

Gracianna, my, Princess. My heart missed you before I knew you existed, I found you broken, and you let me in. In my darkness you gave my life back its light. My love for you is as big as the universe and beyond. I will always protect and cherish you. I am forever by your side, a promise that I won't break.

My love, my soul mate.

Time seems to freeze while we read our cards. Sal smiles and pulls me into his embrace. We kiss and our emotions swirl around us.

"It's all going to be fine, Princess," he whispers in my ear. "It's all going to be fine."

On the stroke of midnight, everyone lights their lanterns and lets them go. Sal and I watch as ours rise up into the night sky. I cling to Sal's arm as though he might fly away, too.

People clap and cheer and blow their noisemakers to ring in the New Year. I give New Year's hugs and kisses to family and friends. We sing along to "Auld Lang Syne" and when it's over and the lanterns are far away from sight, Sal takes my hand and escorts me back into the club. That's when I hear it... *our song.*

"A Time to Say Goodbye." The haunting melody stops me cold, paralyzing me and breaking me in two. Sal holds me tighter as if knowing I will crumble if he doesn't. He puts a hand under my chin and gives me a reassuring look. "Dance with me, Princess. They're playing our song."

He leads me to the dance floor and holds me tight. We slowly sway to the music and he wipes away a stray tear and kisses me gently as we dance.

Most of the guests stare and smile at us in celebration of our engagement. Our close friends and family gaze upon us with mixed emotions, knowing our situation.

Sal has to leave me and I'm petrified I'll loose him forever...

* * *

We get home shortly after one o'clock in the morning. An exhausted Antonio bids us goodnight and my brother heads to his room, as well.

Sal takes my hand and we stroll down the hall and into our room. He shuts the door and proceeds to get undressed. As he does he never removes his eyes from me.

I take my jewelry off, then my shoes. Sal tosses his shirt onto the floor and kicks his shoes off to the side. He comes over to me and turns me away from him so he can pull out the pins supporting my hair, letting it fall around my shoulders. Then he unzips my gown. I hold it so it won't fall, leaving me exposed. Sal steps in front of me.

"Let me see you," he pleads.

I let the gown fall to the floor and all I have on is lacy, little black panties. Sal kneels and slides them down my legs. Tapping at each foot for me to lift. He stands back up and flings them away. His eyes sear into me the whole time.

"Make love with me, Gracie," he says, pulling me towards him. His kiss is so deep, so urgent, the sensation makes him hard. Putting my hands on his chest, I try to push away, but he has me tight in his strong grip.

"Don't," he says firmly. "Don't push me away. I need you. We need this. I want to make love to you all night and into the morning."

"I'm afraid," I whisper to him. "What if it's the last time?" And then I realize that if it is the last time, do I want to miss it? Do I want to regret my last hours with him?

Without a word, he picks me up, and I wrap my legs around him. He places me on the bed and turns out the light. I hear the swoosh of his pants and he is on me.

"I'm here, always," he whispers as he kisses my throat and between my breasts. "I will always be right here." And he kisses over my heart.

Licking his way down my belly he settles on my sweet spot, gently dipping his tongue at my core. I run my fingers through his wavy hair as he works me. My blood runs hot and my heart is pounding.

I'm close, so close, when he stops and kneels on the bed between my legs. He gathers me up in an embrace and my legs encompass him as he gently sets me in place. I bury him deep inside me as he sits back, gripping my hips. We move, pumping with the beat of our hearts. My body quivers at the feeling of Sal's hard body beneath me and inside me—my hands are splayed on his chest and I can feel his heart thumping as fast as mine. Rocking back and forth, the passion is rising.

"Look at me," Sal orders. "Tell me when. Don't look away from me."

All my muscles contracted as my orgasm began. "NOW!" I cry out in pleasure. Our gaze locked and together we soared into ecstasy on moans of satisfaction.

Sal guides my hips until he is drained, and I collapse on his chest, the hair tickling my nose.

Wrapping his arms around my back and holding me securely in place, he whispers, "Don't move." His voice is raw, "I want to be inside of you forever. I want to remember how you feel inside and out while I'm away from you."

I stay perfectly still, as he caresses my back and legs. He strokes my hair and traces my face with his fingertips. I listen as his heart rate slows and his breathing evens out.

Not a word is spoken, we just cling to each other, softly touching then kissing, he rolls me on my back. Passion rising to high oblivion, we love again and again till we are debilitated and sleep consumes us.

* * *

We sleep late into the morning of the New Year. The sun is creeping in the windows casting a golden-yellow glow around the room.

Steve knocks on the door. "Hey, you guys up and or decent? I need to talk to you."

"Just a minute, Steve." Sal calls out. He gets up and quickly throws on a pair of sweats. He grabs my fuzzy robe and swings it over to me. When I'm covered, Sal opens the door.

"Hey guys, listen. I checked some flights and was able to get one that leaves in about three hours. I'm headed out today instead of tomorrow.

I think you both should have a quiet day alone. I've got a cab on the way."

He reaches over to Sal and shakes his hand. "Stay well, bro, and come home to my sister! And good luck!"

They lean in for a manly hug and a slap on the back. "Thanks, Steve," Sal says. "I'm glad I got to meet you. I'll come home, don't you worry. I love your sister too much to stay away."

I stand there with a small smile, arms folded at my chest because I'm beginning to feel empty again. My bother looks at me with his worldly eyes.

"You gonna hug me or what?" he jokes.

I close the space between us and give him a big hug around the middle like I used to when we were kids. My big brother, sometimes took the place of our dad for me.

"You don't have to leave you know. I barely see you as it is," I murmur into his chest.

"Yes, I do," he says, patting me on the back. "It's almost noon and I could tell you guys were not rushing to get up anytime soon. You both need this day together and you don't need me hanging around. It'll be all right, Gracie, be strong. You've got my cell, so call me anytime-and keep me posted about wedding plans. I'm there for ya, just say the word."

We walk him to the door just as the cab pulls up. Steve tosses his bags in the trunk. Before he gets in he puts his hand on top of my head and tousles my hair, which is already messed.

He and Sal give each other nods and one more handshake.

"Okay, talk to ya both soon," he says as he gets in the cab.

I wait till it's out of sight. And then he was gone.

CHAPTER 24

We stay in each other's arms till the sun fades out and shadows of the evening move across the bedroom.

"Pop didn't call today. Should we have checked in on him?" I ask.

Sal snorts a laugh. "No, I'm pretty sure your brother and Pop planned this together last night so we'd have this day alone. I have a little time in the morning to go see him."

"I don't think I can take this," I whisper. "I feel sick–like I'm gonna die without you."

Sal holds me tighter, squeezing his arms around me. "I know the feeling. And I'm so sorry. Will you promise me something? Please, *please*, take care of yourself. I'm not even gone yet and you're not eating normally–and I know you won't sleep. The thought of you out on the balcony in the middle of the night crying or worrying is killing me. I need you to be strong, Princess. We've got plans when I get back, right? Trust me, I'm coming back."

"I'll try," I say, knowing courage isn't exactly my strongest quality. "But I can't help what I'm feeling–something terrible is going to happen."

"Shhh... I love you, Gracie." He cradles and caresses me, touching my whole body as if to memorize me inch by inch.

* * *

A cold rainy gray morning dawns, and as soon as my eyes are open, my stomach clenches and a lump forms in my throat. Sal is leaving this morning.

The all too familiar anxiety attack builds and I sit up as though urged by a cattle prod. As I'm gasping for breath, Sal wakes and grabs my arms.

"Gracie, what's wrong? What is it? Did you dream?"

"No…" I choke. "Panic… can't.. breathe…"

"Shhh…okay, okay," Sal says in a soothing voice. "Look at me," he begs, taking my face in his hands. "Look at me, Gracie. Breathe." We inhale and exhale together, eyes connected.

"Again, breathe… Good…." He kisses my forehead. "Better?"

I shake my head and will the tears back. This is hard enough on him and at this rate I won't even be able to see him off. I clear my throat and force a smile. "I'm going to be okay. It's just this fear is suffocating sometimes. I don't want you to leave, God knows I don't, but I know why you have to go. I'll have to learn to deal with this."

He sits down in front of me wiping at his own eyes with the palms of his hands. "Gracie, It's hard to leave you especially knowing how these dreams of yours have got you scared. I don't know what to say or do to ease your mind."

He raises his voice to make a point and grips my shoulders. "I PROMISE YOU I'M COMING BACK!"

* * *

After Sal got back from talking to Pop, he went to the garage and put a tarp over the Beast and one over his motorcycle. He met Gracie in the foyer and handed the keys to her.

"If I'm not back in less then a month, just start up the Viper every now and then and gently rev the engine. I know you don't drive a stick—I'll teach you when I return.

He gave her a smile. Her sadness was so deep, so consuming that he thought his heart might break and for a moment, he wondered if Pop hadn't been right. Maybe he should never have fallen for Gracie...but then, like now, it was never a choice. It was the path he was on and he had no regrets. He could only pray that Gracie didn't regret it once he was out of sight.

He cleared his throat. "I left Lou's number for you—he is at your beck and call for anything you need. You understand? Capisci?"

She nodded with a small smile.

"Maybe he can take the beast out for a spin and keep her warm for me. He'll be close by. I'm gonna go grab my stuff. Be right back."

Sal went up the stairs. He took a good look around the bedroom. Smelled the air – the scent that was Gracie. He looked at the bed where they'd made love so often just in the past twenty-four hours. His clothes, hanging in her closet. That view through the French doors to the balcony.

He grabbed his duffle bag, went back downstairs and placed it by the front door.

"The cab should be here soon. Come here." He held his arms out for her and they stood in the doorway in each other's arms, kissing goodbye.

Silent tears streamed down her cheeks as she clutched the wool of his sweater in her fists. The cab pulled up and honked. Toby barked and went out the door.

"This is my ride, Princess," Sal whispered. "Be a good girl for me, take care of Toby and Pop. I love you."

He walked out and gave Toby a good scratching. "Take care of her for me, buddy. I'll see you soon." He opened the cab door and looked back at her, gave her a nod and got in the car.

As the taxi slowly pulled away, Sal mouthed the words, *I love you* and he watched her struggle to give him a brave smile. Toby stood close by her side. As they turned the bend in the drive, he faced forward and put on his game face.

He was soldier first, a man second. But by the grace of God, this time he'd keep that promise to Gracie. He'd do his part to make sure of it.

*   *   *

After Sal leaves, I got back in the house, I slam and lock the door and collapse on the floor in a pool of tears. I'm not sure that I won't die of this ache in my heart. Toby wraps himself around me and I hold him, soaking his fur. After a moment I decide to go back to bed.

I wake to the sound of my cell ringing. I check the clock–I had a four hour nap. Reaching for my phone, my heart skips.

"Sal?" I squeak, my throat horribly dry.

"Hey, Princess. What are you doing? I miss you already."

"Sal," I begin to cry and then stop. I will try to be brave for at least 2 minutes. I'll have myself a big ole pity party later, as Celine would say.

"Gracie, I'm sorry." He sighs. "I just wanted to hear your voice. I landed a little while ago and in a few minutes I go right into briefing so, I won't have any contact with you or anyone for a while."

Well, that reality is my undoing. "Oh god, Sal. Please stay alive. Come home to me," I wail.

"Please don't cry, Gracie...I promise you it's gonna be all right. I gotta go now, Princess–they're calling me up. Try to relax, babe. I love you."

"I love you too," I sniff. "I'm going to be okay. Just come home as soon as you can."

"I will...Love you." And the line went dead.

I sit there in bed staring out at nothing, my mind working over time. Have I ever loved anyone this much? It takes a nanosecond to realize the answer is no. What Sal and I have is a firestorm that has been ignited through time and will never burn out.

*   *   *

"Agent Petroni! Nice to have you back. You're looking well."

"Thank you, sir. I'm feeling well," Sal answered his supervisor. They shook hands and Sal took a seat at the briefing table among the other agents assigned for the mission.

"Retirement suits you–or is it a woman? His supervisor chuckled. "We heard you went and finally got yourself engaged. Congratulations! When's the big day?"

"We a...We haven't set a date yet. I'm sure she's waiting till I get home to make a decision." Sal gave him a small smile.

"I verified you to the police and got you cleared of the situation in Jacksonville."

"Yes, thank you sir." Sal says. "The police there know some of my back round so they didn't question me much, but I knew they would have to follow through. They seemed pleased I took out one of their local scumbags. It would have been nice to question him though."

"He was a threat, You had to do what had to be done. Okay, Shall we begin gentlemen? Let's get down to business."

He tried to get comfortable in the cold, stark conference room as the supervisor, Carl, talked about options and passed out files. Concentration was hard because his heart was back in Florida.

The night before, he'd barely slept. He hated that he'd had to remove his civilian clothes and take a shower, because Gracie's scent lingered on his skin, on his sweater. He could still feel her soft smooth lips and the taste of her. He felt her body in his arms like a phantom.

When the meeting finished and he returned to his hotel room, he tried to get his head into work but all he could think about was Gracie.

Getting up to stretch, he eyed the sweater he'd had on the day before. He grabbed it and held it to his face, inhaling her in.

He'd never loved anyone as much or as completely as he did her. He'd come back this time—or as many times as it took, to give her a lifetime of happiness.

* * *

"GOOD LORD, GRACIE! Have you been in this bed for three days? You called in sick at work. And seriously, when was the last time you showered, for heaven's sake? I do hope you got my messages, though now I suspect you didn't."

"Yes, you said you'd be here as soon as you could. I don't need anything. Leave me alone, Celine," I moan. "I just need some time. I feel sick."

"Well, you *are* sick. No food, dehydrated, and baby, you smell. So..." She snaps her fingers at me. "Come on, get up. You don't want to go to work fine, but you *will* take a shower, even if I have to hose you down myself."

I get up against my will, and head for the bathroom. I hear Celine fumbling with the bed.

"DON'T TOUCH THE SHEETS!" I yell and she jumps.

"Jesus, Gracie, what the hell is wrong with you? You just about gave me a heart attack!"

"Don't change my sheets," I repeat more calmly. "I'll do it when I'm ready to do it."

"Why? Let me help you," she insists. "You can't sleep on these anymore...."

"I smell him," I say, cutting her off.

"You what?" Celine looks puzzled.

"I can still smell him, don't take it away...don't take it...." I crack as my tears begin again. "He's on the pillow, on the sheets...I can smell him. I don't want to forget..."

Celine's eyes grow wide. She puts down the blanket and calmly comes over to me. "Baby girl," she breathes out, "oh my poor, baby girl."

She holds me as I cry, my eyes now so swollen it hurts to blink them.

"Gracie, listen to me, you can't continue this behavior darlin'. It's not healthy. Listen to me now," she demands. "You are going to march in that shower and I am going to change your bed sheets. Then you are going to call Dr. Brooks and go find that psychic's number. Taking some action is going to make you feel better about all this."

I protest but Celine wins the laundry detail. She does agree to leave Sal's pillow alone, but, for only one more week.

I shower and call Dr. Brooks. After hearing what's happened since our last visit, he wants me to come right down—he has the afternoon open. Celine volunteers to drive me, and within the hour I'm in his office.

"Gracie," Dr. Brooks greets me. "Come in, come in."

If my appearance shocks him, he doesn't let it show, but I know I'm not looking anything like a human being. That's okay because I don't feel very human, either.

I turn to Celine, then back to the Doctor. "Can she come in with me?"

He smiles. "I don't mind if you don't. Support is always good to have."

We follow Dr. Brooks into his little office and sit across from him in front of his desk.

"So Gracie, how were the holidays for you and Sal?"

"They were wonderful, Dr. Brooks. We got engaged," I say, holding up my left hand.

"Yes, that's great news indeed," he says, smiling. "I knew he was going to ask you I just didn't know when." His smile fades a bit. "So, Sal is away again, on a mission? Correct?"

I bow my head and nod.

"You said on the phone you're having bad feelings. Have you dreamt anything? Or is it more like a premonition?"

"More like a premonition," I answer. "I haven't really been sleeping sound enough to dream, but I did dream once of water or the ocean–it was cold–and I couldn't swim–I was tired or something–it was all very fuzzy."

"When did you have this dream?"

"While we were in Napa at Christmas."

Dr. Brooks cocks his head. "So what was that, about three weeks ago, you would say? And nothing since?"

"No nothing since, but, like I said, I'm not sleeping soundly. I have feelings of terror. You know, like what I've dreamt about. I fear for Sal's life. How can I not? In every life, he always leaves me, promises he will come back, but it always ends tragically."

"Okay, Gracie, I comprehend why this is so emotional for you– believe me, I really do. The situation is very complicated and unique. I understand your feelings of fear, because of the past lives. But that being said, the things that are put in place now, may cause the future to change. In other words, Sal and you are, in a way, more aware of the circumstances surrounding your bonds to each other. So both of you might change decisions subconsciously, thus creating a different outcome."

I look at Dr. Brooks and scrunch my eyebrows. "So you think there's a chance Sal might make a choice because he is more aware of a danger and not put himself in its way?"

Dr. Brooks nods. "Yes, or, you Gracie, for instance. You might do something or choose to do something that changes the outcome, good or bad. I can see how upset you are, and probably fatigued from lack of sleep. Dehydration and malnutrition will cause hallucinations as well. You will make yourself seriously sick, Gracie. I know it's hard, but you have *got* to relax. Let me check your blood pressure."

Dr. Brooks gets up and snatches the cuff off his desk and wraps it around my arm. He pumps up the valve and waits to see the results.

"It's a little on the high side, but, you are very upset—as upset as someone who is bereft and grieving. Here's what I recommend. I'm going to give you a prescription for a sleep aid and something for your nerves."

"No, I protest. "I have some, but Sal doesn't like me to take them. I used them to control my panic attacks."

"Gracie, I'm afraid I am going to have to disagree on this. The way you're going, you will end up in the hospital if you can't calm down, and that will be worse. These prescriptions I'm giving to you are mild, but I want you to start them immediately. If anything, you need restful sleep. How are you eating?"

Before I can answer Celine opens her mouth. "She's not. I know her—my friend has a good appetite normally, and I can tell you she's not eaten properly for days."

"Well, the Valium should calm your stomach and lower the adrenaline so your appetite can come back. Get some liquid protein in your system till it does, or else you'll end up very sick." He looks at me a long moment. "Sal could be back in a week or so, right? If he returns to find you in a bad way because he had to leave, he will never forgive himself. He's got enough guilt issues, Gracie. If you can't take care of yourself for you, then do it for him, okay?"

I nod and for the first time all day, feel an easy smile. "Thank you, Doctor," I say, exhaling loudly. "I'll try."

As we get up to go, Celine grabs the papers with the prescriptions. She looks at Dr. Brooks. "I'm gonna make sure these get filled while we have an early supper."

"Gracie, I'd like to see you in about ten days, but if you feel you need me before then, please don't hesitate to call. I'm here for you."

We get the prescriptions filled, then drive to our local sports bar on the beach. We go in, get seated and Celine orders herself a salad and me a bacon cheeseburger and sweet potato fries.

When the burger arrives it looks and smells delicious. I pick it up and take a small bite. I chew but I find it's still hard to swallow, so I wait a minute before trying again.

"You're going to eat at least half of that. The doctor is right. How do you think Sal would feel if he found out you ended up in the hospital? He killed a man to protect you and then you go and take yourself out? Think about that."

"I'm not gonna take myself out Celine, and he wouldn't know it if I did," I state, the reality hitting home. "He's off the grid. And he chose to go off the grid. If he wasn't going to go on the mission, he'd be home by now. He said it could be months, Celine. For months, I won't know if he's alive or dead. Maybe I'll never know."

"Okay, baby, I can see you're hurt and scared. And before you met Sal, you couldn't stand on your own very well. But you're stronger than that. If anything happens to you, it will kill him, Gracie. You know it. I know it."

"He shouldn't have left. Maybe that was the choice right there, Celine. He shouldn't have gone!" I yell, slamming my hand on the table.

"I get it, I really do, baby, I know you're scared. Truth be told, I'm scared with ya. But let's pray for the better–think positive! Being the guest of honor at this old pity party isn't doing anything for you, Gracie."

I sigh and drink my iced tea, then take another bite of the burger.

"So, what are you thinking about for your wedding colors? You two are so stunning together, it won't really matter, but I'd love to help. I was thinking..."

Celine chatters on, trying to cheer me up with talk of wedding plans and color schemes. On occasion, I offer her a smile or take another bite of food.

The waitress comes by and asks if I want a box. "No thank you," I tell her.

But Celine cuts in. "Yes, she does. Wrap it up she'll take it to go.

I was never so relived to get home from an outing, I was tired and drained, I felt a headache coming on too.

CHAPTER 25

"Come on baby," Celine demands when we get home. "Take these."

"Fine," I sigh. "Maybe they'll make me sleep for a month."

"Ooh, sarcasm," she replies with a grin. "That's a good sign!"

I swallow the pills and open my mouth, making a joke to prove I took them.

"Good girl," Celine chuckles. "By the way, how's Antonio?"

"I haven't seen him." I shrug. "I just...aahh.... I think it's going to be very emotional. He hasn't called or come over to me, either. I think we feel the same way."

"Well, someone's got to break the ice. I think it should be you."

"Yeah, I will," I agree. "Just not right now. I think I need it all to settle. Doc is right–it does feel like I'm grieving."

"Well, you remember our plan? Where's that psychic's phone number? Tell her your dilemma–she told you to call her. Maybe she can give you something positive to cling to."

"I have it in the desk drawer in the study." I yawned. "I put it there for safekeeping. Her name is Amina."

"Those pills are kicking in Gracie. Go to bed baby, get some rest. I'm spending the night, so

I'll be here if you need anything and I'll take care of Toby. Tomorrow we can call Amina."

Even though it's only six o'clock in the evening, I climb into bed and reach for Sal's pillow. I curl myself around it as though it is him. I breathe in deep, the scent of him is almost faded, but enough to fill my soul.

I'm so glad for Celine and her friendship. And Antonio's love, too. Soon I feel as though I'm floating—my body relaxes and I can't keep my swollen eyelids open any longer.

* * *

I'm in water—the ocean. It's dark. It's freezing and rough. I can't move—I'm so tired. The waves roll me under—the salty liquid in my mouth, up my nose—it's burning. I hear bells—I can't breathe......

Startled and gasping for air, I wake and sit straight up in my bed. Semi confused, it takes a moment to get focused. I'm home. My room. My bed. Sal's been gone for 4 days.

Catching my breath, I hear my cell phone "bells" as a text comes in. I eye the time: 11:45 pm. I reach for my cell and tap the screen. "Maggie! I sigh with a smile.

11:38pm. *R U Up?...* then,

11:42pm. *Hello??*

I tap her name on the phone and the call goes through.

"Gracie!" she answers. "I haven't heard from you but you are on my mind—something's wrong, isn't it?"

"Oh God, Mags.. yes something is really wrong." And I proceed to tell her all about Sal's assignment and my fears.

"When is he coming home?"

"If he comes home at all, it could be a month or more. I don't know."

"I thought he was retired?"

"He is or that's what he told me. He couldn't tell me much except it was important that he help his team. But what if he gets hurt? What if he gets killed?"

"Gracie, you poor thing! I know you–you're a mess aren't you? I knew it! I knew something was wrong–I kept getting bad feelings about you!"

"I totally understand that, Mags. I have been feeling like something terrible has been coming for months and now I know what it is–Sal's not coming back, I know it. I finally meet my soul mate and start to get truly happy, and again history repeats, like in my dreams."

"Okay Gracie calm down, take a deep breath. I don't know Sal, but I guess I'm picking up on your anguish."

"Maggie, if something happens to him, I will be shattered, knowing he could have prevented it."

"How's his father taking all this?" she asks.

"Poor Pop, I think he is as devastated as I am. I haven't heard from him since Sal left. He was not happy either, I can tell ya that."

"Gracie, listen–you hang in there. I'm still very worried, mostly about you. Don't get me wrong, I pray Sal comes home safe and sound, but, watch *yourself*–don't get sick, I just feel I need to tell you to be careful."

"I'll try Maggie, but really don't worry. Despite how bad I feel, how terrified I am, I probably can't cry myself to death, right?"

"No, but you can make yourself awfully sick in the meantime. Toby needs you and so does Sal's father. I love you, too. I couldn't bear it if you let this take you down." I hear her sniff and then blow her nose.

"Don't be scared, Gracie. I believe you have met your destiny, and I believe it will be different. He'll come home, I know it. You need to take care of yourself so you're there when he does!"

"Thanks Mags, you always know how to cheer me up, –even if it's just for a minute."

"Go back to sleep, Gracie. We'll talk soon–it's all gonna work out."

"Okay," I whisper. "Goodnight Mags–love ya!"

"Love ya, too! Sweet dreams."

But I don't have sweet dreams or any other kind because I can't go back to sleep, and I don't want another pill. I'd rather be miserable than too numb to think about Sal.

On the balcony, the air is crisp and the sky is clear. I hear a little squeak and look toward Antonio's house. I step to the railing so he can see me if he looks this way – and he does. I wave and he waves back, then puts his hand over his heart and blows me a kiss.

I put my hands over my mouth and whisper, "Pop."

I retreat back to bed but tears are all I have. Finally, I get up and take the Zanax and let the calm roll over me in waves. Anything is better than the constant flood of tears.

* * *

Toby pulls me out of slumber, with a bark. I bolt upright and my room is freezing. I hear him bark again.

Looking around I notice I left the balcony door open, which accounts for the cold air. Toby is out on the balcony barking. Grabbing my fluffy robe I go to check it out.

"Toby," I bellow, "whatcha looking at, boy?"

He pads over to me, then trots back to the railing and jumps up with his front paws, keeping his hind legs planted. He yawns and lets out a whine.

I shuffle over and see Pop making his way over to my back screen door. Toby dashes inside, through the bedroom, and down the stairs with excitement. *Poor dog's missed his buddy–and I have, too.*

I follow Toby downstairs to greet Pop. On the way, I eye Celine, talking on her cell phone with a mug of coffee in her hand. I breeze by her to open the door for Pop.

Toby just about jumps halfway onto his lap. Antonio returns the love with scratches and pats. It makes me smile. Toby runs off into the yard and Pop rolls in.

"You want some coffee, Pop? I ask.

"No, caro, I'm-a-fine.

"You want some breakfast?"

"No, caro, come-a- here, sit with me."

I let Toby back in, then follow Pop back into the house. I glance over at Celine who's still on her cell, but watching us wide eyed.

"Everything okay, Pop? I ask hoping this will not turn me into a weeping wreck.

"Mio caro," he starts. "I know your-a scared and sad, it's breaking my heart. Sal told me before he left how much it hurts him to leave you. I told him not to leave then–I told him that if you were right and he got himself killed it would destroy you. 'Stay here,' I told him. But he would not change-a-his decision.

"Gracie..." he quietly goes on. "The Sal I thought I knew, the one I thought-a-was avoiding his mother in her last days was a selfish boy who was incapable of loving anyone except himself. I now know how wrong I was. My son turned out to be a man; a strong-a-man with honor. A man me and-a-his momma can be proud of." Pop wipes at his moist eyes, then continues.

"I never seen him love anyone the way he loves you Gracie. Watching him with you opened my heart. My eyes see him differently than before. He was dark and distant until you. I told-a-my son that I will trust his word, when he says he will come home. He needs you to believe it to. He told me the mission should be a secure one, no danger. Caro, he loves you, he won't put himself in danger now like he did before. He won't take-a-that risk."

"I know, Pop. But my mind won't stop thinking of things that could go wrong–'its driving me crazy!"

"I know what you have-a dreamt, and all the promises... Caro, he's going to come-a-home this time. Have-a some faith."

"I want to Pop. I will try." I can see how my pain adds to his and I take a good breath and smile. I'm so sick of crying. So sick of the nauseating fear.

He looks at me and winks like the old days. "Now, give this old man a hug." He stretches his arms out wide.

I gave him a hug and he pats my back just like any dad would do. "It's going to be all right Caro, its-a-gonna be all right."

I help Pop out the door, keeping an eye on him as he makes his way back to his deck and disappears into the house. Then I head to the sofa. The pills make me groggy like I was out drinking all night. Celine follows and sits next to me, handing me a coffee.

"Thanks," I say without looking in her direction. I just sit still waiting for my head to explode. That must be what happens when you lose your mind...

"You okay?" Celine asks, tugging on my robe.

"Yeah, I guess. Talked to Maggie last night. She gets 'feelings' too. She had one about me. She thinks Sal will be okay. She's more worried about me." I take a sip of coffee and stare out the lanai doors. I shake my head in confusion.

"Well, I'm worried about you, too. We've got to get you back on your feet, baby."

We sit quiet for a while not talking, just drinking our coffee. Finally I look over at Celine. "I really need to talk to Amina."

* * *

After I shower, dress and pull my bed together, I go into the study and rummage around the desk drawer to find the card with Amina's number on it.

"I found it! I yell to Celine.

"Oh good," she hollers back. "Call her!"

We sit down in the parlor, making our selves comfy on the couch. I pick up my cell phone and hit the numbers Amina had scribbled on the back of the card, remembering she told me to call her anytime if I had more questions. Well, holy hell did I ever! As it rings I put the phone on speaker so Celine can hear her, too.

"Hello?" A young female voice answers.

"Hello. Umm, I'm calling for Amina," I say. "I had a reading a while back and she told me I could call her if I had any questions."

"Oh? Who is this please?"

"My name is Gracie. I met Amina in St. Augustine at the psychic fair back in October. She read me and my boyfriend–well, now he's my fiancé."

"Oh, hi, Gracie! I remember you. This is Yvette, Amina's granddaughter."

"Yes! I remember you, too! I don't think I will ever forget that Halloween as long as I live. How are you?"

"I am fine, but grandma passed on about a month or so ago. She died peacefully, in her sleep.

Celine and I look at each other in horror. "Oh my god, Yvette! I am so sorry!" I wail.

"Thank you. But it's all right," she replied. "She was old and had some health complications."

"Yvette, I will never forget her. Even though I met her once, she touched me so deeply and told me things that blew me away! I had a dream one night and she was there. I saw her so vividly!"

"Yeah, she was something. She touched a lot of people's hearts. Hey, tell me something?" Yvette paused for a second. "How did you get my private number?"

"This is *your* number?" I repeat. "Amina gave it to me. She wrote it on the back of her card and told me to call her if I needed anything. I just assumed it was *her* number."

"Gracie, when did you have the dream that you saw her?"

"About a month or so... maybe... Oh, I remember. It was the night of the benefit—December seventh."

"Gracie, Grandma died on the fourth. She must have come to you—and I just bet she gave you my number on purpose. Grandma had a very special and powerful gift and she didn't share that with many people. I'm positive she knew what she was doing. So, tell me, why did you call? Is there something wrong? I am picking up some mixed emotions from you—sadness for one—can I help?"

Celine's blue eyes grow wider as I shoot her a glance.

"Well, maybe you can," I answer. "I *am* sad but I'm also frightened. Amina mentioned to Sal and me that we should never separate now that we'd found each other. Just recently Sal had to leave me for a while, I'm not sure for how long and I can't contact him. He's military, so he's on a job, I'm nervous for his safety. Giving her the quick version of my visions. "I guess I wanted to ask your grandmother if she could help, maybe see something that would help me to believe this time will be different."

Yvette blows out a breath. "Ooh.. Gracie, I'm not as talented as Grandma was, but, I can sense something is wrong. Around you. Did you get hurt or have you been sick recently?'

"No... well, the night of the benefit I was mugged, but Sal saved me. I didn't really get hurt..."

She is quiet for a few seconds. "Do you have friends or family with you now that Sal's away? Or are you alone most of the time?"

"I have some friends around, but I'm mostly alone, why?" I ask.

"I'm not picking up any danger around Sal. I can feel he deeply loves you–he killed that man who attacked you, didn't he?"

"Yes! I shout. Celine's mouth flies open in surprise and playfully slaps my leg.

"Okay, so he's not a danger to you anymore... But something is...hmmm... I am sensing something, but it's foggy like if I was under water–it's just not very clear. I just feel I need to tell you to be careful while you're alone. Try to surround yourself with friends. And, you might feel better if you do. Take care of yourself Gracie. Right now, I feel that's very important for you to know."

Wasn't that what Maggie said last night? I look at Celine, then back to the phone. "Can you see Sal at all? Is he safe?

I hear her take a deep breath and blow it out. Then I hear a friendly chuckle.

"I don't have a crystal ball, Gracie. And honestly, I don't see danger around Sal – I see it around you. Our futures can always switch lanes. I see you right now at a crossroads. It's just so scrambled I can't say for sure what I'm really seeing and I think sometimes your past lives interfere with my ability. That's what happened when I first tried reading you. I'm sorry I'm not as good as my grandmother was. But I hope I helped you a little."

"I'm sorry I'm difficult to read," I say with a little laugh.

"Don't be sorry!" she says, sounding like she's smiling. "You have a very old and strong soul—you've had many lives—it shows me too much at once and that makes it hard for me to tune into."

"Okay, I can understand that," I say, surprised that it does make some sense.

"I have learned a lot from my grandmother," Yvette confides, "I can tell you souls don't die, even if there is a suicide—it always comes back to learn something, realizing that wasn't the answer. Gracie, I can feel you are sensing a danger coming. Be careful, as I said. Use your ability of strong intuition to help you."

"Okay, I will try to stay alert and be positive about Sal. I do have one question I wanted to ask Amina, but maybe you can answer it. Sal *is* my soul mate, I have no doubts. But, why didn't we meet earlier?"

"Destiny," she blurts. "Destiny helps us out." Maybe it knew your chances were better at this point in both your lives."

Celine and I both look up at each other. Celine mouths, "WOW." I shrug and nod my head.

"Okay, Yvette," I say, "I will take all this in—thank you. I think Amina would be proud. How can I pay you for your time?"

"Oh, don't worry about it. Grandma gave you my private number for a reason—it's my gift to you. I hope it helped. *Please* take care of yourself, I can't stress that enough. Oh - watch what you eat or drink - and get rest. Maybe we'll chat again soon!"

"Thank you so much Yvette! I so appreciate your time. You did help. Bye, and take care."

"Bye, Gracie. God bless."

I tap the *end* button on my phone and put it down between Celine and me. "Well, that was interesting," I murmur.

Celine tilts her head at me., "You're not feeling any better, I can see it."

"She can't read me, so, yeah.. not so much." I sigh.

"Well, she's got a point – you knew she didn't have a crystal ball. But I do like what she said to you about taking care of yourself and paying attention to your gut feelings."

"Celine, my *gut* is telling me Sal's gonna get killed! If she saw that she wasn't going to tell me!" I shout in frustration. Damn it, why did the one person who could help me have to die, just weeks ago?

"Actually, she said she didn't see danger around Sal. She wasn't so sure about you, though. Maybe you're confused about what your intuition is saying to you? I think it's also a positive that destiny has stepped in. The answer she gave you about why you and Sal met now instead of years ago. That sounds like there's a damn good possibility the ending will be different this time."

"I don't know," I say, tossing up my hands. "If I met Sal instead of Richard, maybe Sal wouldn't have gone on this job– maybe I could have prevented it–what if our destiny just keeps repeating itself?"

Celine smiles wickedly, waving her empty coffee mug in the air. "What if, destiny made you marry Richard who brought you here, to meet Antonio, which led you to Sal. Like she said, it knew your chances were better now. When Sal was younger, he was full- blown military, right? It would have never worked out. It makes perfect sense to me Gracie!"

"Okay, I chuckle, you have a point," I admit, feeling just a bit lighter. "He was everywhere and he did survive being a prisoner in Bosnia. But my intuition is still telling me something terrible is going to happen. Do you think I'm just confused"?

"Baby girl," Celine says with a motherly tone. "I think you're in love, and you're missing your man, and it's making you very sad and a bit crazy. Maybe your mind is playing tricks on you."

"I hope so, Celine, I just don't know anymore. I just feel it—everyday it gets stronger."

Celine takes my hand in hers and looks me in the eyes. "You can choose to mourn something that probably will not happen, or you can be very careful, take good care of yourself, and go on with your plans for a lovely wedding and a happily-ever-after life. It's up to you, baby."

Celine leaves a few hours later, after we eat a light supper of salmon and salad. As I watch her pull away, the emptiness in my chest feels deeper. I return inside the house and look around. The cold lonely silence of the mansion is back as though it's mocking me. But this time around it's worse.

Now that Sal's gone the loneliness feels colder and darker.

CHAPTER 26

The tears have slowed down some. Not enough sleep and still no appetite I decide to go with Sal's method and stay away from the pills. But, I'm not sleeping more than a few hours at a time and the constant sense that tragedy is just around the corner is wearing me down.

Two days after Celine left, I call Veronica and tell her I'll be coming back to work—if I still have a job, that is. She laughs and tells me my job is not at risk.

On one particular day I get to work at the animal clinic ten minutes late. Veronica is standing right by the door as Toby and I blaze through it. I'm almost breathless.

"AH, you made it!" Veronica chimes. "I was getting worried."

"I'm sorry. My head is just not where it should be, I guess. I was in deep thought and drove right past the office," I confess with some embarrassment. "By the time I realized what I did, I was a good five minutes up the road. I had to turn around."

"We've got a full morning, Gracie," Veronica says, eyeing me with concern. "Are you here now? All of you? I mean mind and body?"

I give her scrunched up eyebrows and a salute. "Yes, I'm all here."

"Good!" she says. "Because the past couple of weeks you have been an absolute freak show. You're physically here, but mentally you're far away. I kind of miss you."

I sigh, knowing she's right. If I were the boss, I'd have fired me by now. I give her a little smile. "I'm so sorry. I just have a lot on my mind."

"Yeah, no doubt. With Sal away I'm sure you're missing him and I know it's making you nervous that you can't talk with him or know where he is." Veronica ushered them inside the office.

"Just be thankful this is the last one, I don't think you'd be able to handle it if he wasn't retired from this line of work. And to top it off, planning a wedding without him," she shakes her head. "It's a lot, but you need to relax sweetie–you don't look good."

I nod my head. She's right and I know it, but I just don't seem to have what it takes to overcome the dread that accompanies me day and night. It's not just that I miss Sal so much, there is something else going on, but I don't understand it. Even my visits with Dr. Brooks give me little relief.

I battle to stay focused on each case and maybe for the first time in weeks, Veronica thanks me for my help.

On my lunch break I go out on the front porch of the clinic and gag down a half a yogurt while I'm mindlessly gazing into the ocean. The sun reflects off of the water and shimmers across the surface like gems. The cool ocean breeze whips around but I don't feel it.

"Gracie?" Veronica calls. "Oh, there you are. I thought maybe we'd eat our lunch together and I couldn't find you. It's freezing out here–how can you stand it!" She wraps her arms around herself to keep from shivering.

"Huh? Oh, I'm fine," I tell her. I hold up my yogurt cup. "I just had my lunch, but thanks for the thought."

Veronica stands there for a minute, then goes inside. When she returns, she's got a blanket and drapes it over me. Taking the chair next to me, she puts her hand on me.

"Gracie, is there something wrong? Did I do something to offend you? Or maybe you don't like your job anymore?"

"Oh, no–no... I love it here!" I assure her. "And you're a *wonderful* boss. I'm so sorry I've been acting so crazy. I'm not sleeping well because I don't want to keep taking pills, so that's most of it, I guess. I'll get through it."

"Is there something you need to talk to me about? I can listen, maybe help?"

I toss Veronica a little smile and consider telling her the whole maddening story, but decide not to. "Mostly, I'm just scared all the time. I keep getting the feeling something bad is going to happen to Sal, you know, like intuition."

Veronica nods and pats my hand. "I suppose that's normal. Police wives and firemen's wives feel like this most of the time. I imagine you're feeling what a military wife or girlfriend would feel. But, at least he's not gone off to war and fighting on enemy grounds Hell, for all you know he might still be in this country doing what needs to be done. It's the not knowing that's killing you. You need to think positive, Gracie. Sal will be home before you know it, I'm sure."

"I hope so Veronica. Thanks for understanding."

"Well, it's too damned cold out here for me" she says, getting to her feet. "I think you'd better get inside too. You don't look good to me. You're making yourself sick over this. You need to snap out of it. Sal loves you, he'll come home safe and sound – but what will he do if you're in the hospital – or worse?"

"That's what Antonio says, too," I tell her and smile a brighter smile.

"Come inside, Gracie," she says, pulling me to my feet. "Just another hour or so, then the surgeries are done and you can go home. Try to relax."

Two dogs and an old cat later, I clean up, call Toby and we head for home. The only problem is, I don't want to go home to the cold, dark mansion. Maybe I'll go see Antonio, but then again, I think that every day and never do.

When Toby and I get home, I feed him and curl up on the couch. I glance at the mail–there's nothing too important and I toss it on the coffee table.

I think about my conversation with Veronica, wondering what she would say if she knew the whole story. But then Dr. Brooks and Celine know the whole story and keep telling me I'm worrying for nothing.

I wish I could figure out how to do that.

* * *

Camille James was happy today. The bank accounts had been back on track for a while and Richard was headed out of town in a few days for a business trip.

As soon as he left she would make a final transfer of money into her secret Cayman bank account. Pack her bags. Grab her mom out of the mental home and fly them to the penthouse condo that she put a deposit on.

She couldn't wait to get out of this town that had branded her with a crappy reputation–and start over new and fresh. Before she would leave though, there was someone she needed to pay a special visit to.

* * *

January turned into February and my days and nights melded into each other.

It's almost two months since Sal left. Every morning I wake up nauseous with fear. I battle day to day to eat, to sleep, to keep going to work. I know it's important. I know it's what Sal wants. But the dread is winning. I thank God for Toby who keeps me moving.

Celine sends me a text that she's stopping by. I don't answer it. I stay in bed till I hear her knock on the door.

"Ho-ly Shit!" Celine says, giving me a look of disdain. I move aside allowing her to enter the house. I shut the door and she just stands there staring at me.

"Gracie you look like shit! Jesus have mercy, you look like something on one of those zombie shows! Oh, no, no, no...I'm taking you to the hospital. This ain't right." She waves a hand at me. "You're not well!"

"Celine, please," I huff. "I am not going to a hospital. I'll be fine."

"You don't look fine, Gracie! Have you looked at yourself in a mirror lately? What happened to those warnings about taking care of yourself? About being aware of what's going on?"

I walk away from her to make myself a cup of tea. "I don't need this right now, Celine. My nerves are shot. But I feel it... it's closer now. Something terrible is coming and I don't think I can stop it!"

"Gracie, you need to calm down," Celine scolded. "Look what you've done to yourself! Have you seen Antonio? Has he seen what you look like?"

"I wave to him from a distance and at night when I can't sleep, I see him out on his deck. I know he's keeping an eye on me. But being with Tony is too painful a reminder that Sal is gone."

"Have you been anywhere, recently?"

"I've been to work!" I snap. "And, I've seen Dr. Brooks. I went to the store for dog food..."

She slashes the air with her hand. "Okay, that's what–a few hours a week? I came here to take you out. Mimi and some of the girls from SWS want to know how you are. They know Sal is away on duty– they thought maybe a girl's night out would cheer you up!"

I sigh. "All the girls know Sal's away?"

"The whole *town* knows it, baby. Everyone is truly concerned about you. Come out with us for a little bit, get some air, walk among the living!"

"I can't, Celine," I really want to, but just not up to it yet.. "I just can't. I'm grateful for your friendship, but please, I need to be alone."

"Remember what the psychic said". She points one of her red fingernails at me. "She told you not to be alone and to take care of yourself. Not join the zombie apocalypse!" I actually laugh at her remark.

"I know, I know...just give me some time."

"It's been two months, Gracie. And by the looks of you, you are out of time. But fine," she hissed, her eyes boring into me. "I'm telling you now, baby girl, I'm giving you a week. If I don't like what I see, I'm getting Antonio and we are taking your crazy ass to the hospital! I don't care if I have to Baker Act you to do it. We clear?"

I sarcastically salute her, walk her to the door, and watch her drive away.

I sit and drink my tea. Toby comes and puts his big head on my lap. He snuggles up with me while I watch the T.V. which is nonstop coverage about the nasty winter weather headed our way for the next few days.

A little while later, I feed Toby and go outside with him in the yard. Antonio comes out and waves.

"Hello, caro, How are you doing?" he calls from his deck.

"I'm doing a little better, Pops," I lie. "Don't worry about me. How about you?"

He looks at me and I see the shock in his eyes. "I miss you caro." He says."

I nod and blow him a kiss. I call after Toby and retreat back inside. Glancing back over at Pop, I see him swipe a hand across his eyes.

I get into bed but I don't have any tears left. I don't have anything left. Slowly but surely the tiny pill eases my raw nerves and I wander off to sleep.

* * *

"Nice work, Agent Petroni. The team is in place and targets are locked."

"Good", Sal said, nodding his head once at Carl. I'll wait for their return back at the embassy and suit up. I'm going in with them."

"No you won't, Sal." Carl said flatly. "End of the line for you, agent. You were called in for consulting only. Your work is done here. The team will get the job done just fine, thanks to you."

"Sir, they are on my strategic plans. I should be helping the new commander!" Sal countered.

"Agent Petroni," Carl shouted, putting a hand up. "Sal," he said in a calmer voice. "Your duties to your country went far beyond any man's expectations. You've been through too much. You were an exceptional soldier and one of the best agent's I've known. The service is in your debt. I called you in for help on this case for your expertise. As usual, you did not let us down."

"Thank you, Carl, I appreciate that. But, I feel I need to see this through—"

"Agent!" Carl cut him off. "I've known you most of my life. I know how you work–you're not all here–you're distracted now. Your eyes used to be cold, emotionless, fearless; you've changed. You have something to live for now."

A small smile spread across Sal's mouth. Carl was right, Sal had been distracted and he wasn't going to risk his life again. Gracie was home waiting for him, convinced something was going to end his life and it petrified her. He wouldn't do this to her–to them.

He nodded at his supervisor. "You're right, Carl. I have to go home–it's wear my heart is. I made her a promise."

"I'm happy for you, Sal." Carl smiles back. "You deserve a real life. Go home, get married, live your life–you more than earned it."

* * *

Within a few hours he was on a jet headed back to the states. The entire flight, his thoughts were about Gracie and how happy she'd be when he got home.

The whole time he was away, he couldn't shake the haunting image of how sad and terrified she looked the day he left. Even her brave face had frightened him. It was killing him to be away from her at all, let alone for months.

He glanced at the time on his watch. It would be over twenty-four hours by the time he touched down in D.C. and another twenty-four for debriefing. Then he'd call her.

He couldn't wait to get her in his arms again. He missed her–everything about her. That laugh and smile, her appetite, the way she'd glowed when he proposed; the softness of her skin and how incredibly warm she was deep inside; the desires he saw in her eyes when they made love; every little sound and moan of pleasure. He missed her scent. He missed all of it–all of her.

* * *

I jolt and gasp for air. It snaps me awake from a pill-induced slumber and my stomach rolls. I stumble to the bathroom and purge mostly bile. My head swims in and out of dizzy waves until I breathe calmer and steady myself. I'm getting pretty good at calming myself down, now.

Toby watches me, then comes to my side. "Good boy, Toby," I say as I pet his thick scruff. "You are such a good boy."

I decide to take him for his morning walk on the beach since we can both use some fresh air. I can hear the weather changing. The wind is picking up and howling around the mansion, just as the weather stations had predicted.

As we venture out I see the clouds building in the distance and the wind is starting to have an icy feel to it. The waves in the ocean rumble like thunder, churning over and slamming into the sand.

"I guess the Weather Channel was right, Toby. A nor'easter is coming our way, bringing in a cold front."

Toby runs all over the beach taking a sniff here and there. The strong winds are blowing us around. I stroll down our little wooden pier while Toby views me from a distance because the loud crashing of the waves hitting the pilings makes him nervous. I stand remembering the morning Sal and I sat here quiet and he held me for hours. *Oh god how I miss him.*

Walking back from the beach, I see Pop. He waves. "Hello caro. Come sit with me for a while." I hesitate for a moment but I go. "Just a little while pop, my stomach isn't too good today. We chat for a minute about the weather and Toby. He tells me he has missed me, and when the conversation turns to Sal, Antonio gazes at me with dark, sad eyes. Before I break into a blubbering fool I leave and give him a quick kiss on his cheek. As I head home I turn to wave at him. Pop puts his hand over his heart and blows me a kiss.

I'm not exactly lying. Almost everything I try to eat turns my stomach—even coffee isn't good. I've lost at least twenty pounds and even Dr. Brooks is making sounds about me going into the hospital for tests and care.

I make some ginger tea and manage to get down some saltines with jelly until my stomach revolts. Breathing in a deep sigh, I pick up the keys to the Beast and with damp eyes, I go to the garage. I stared at the tarp that covers it, then hit the garage door button. The door opens and a rush of cold, salty air filters in, giving me the chills. I go to the car and pull at the tarp exposing just enough of the shiny silver gray Viper so I can climb in.

The vehicle smell reminds me of Sal—I spot his baseball cap lying in the passenger seat. I pick it up and hold it to my face. His scent is there and I feel closer to him. I put the key in the ignition and start it up. It roars to life and the vibration makes me smile for a moment. I rev the gas like Sal told me to do and I just let her purr for a few minutes.

As I hang there listening to the car hum, thoughts of our trip and my first ride in this car flood my memories. I'm no longer sure that Sal is not coming back, but bad vibes surround me. They are so strong today it has me jumpy and fatigued. Every sound I hear makes my heart race and my nerves rattle.

After I shut the car off I stare at the Viper one more minute before putting the tarp back in place. Clutching Sal's ball cap, I close up the garage and go back inside. The tightness in my chest is so strong that I can barely breathe. I take a pill, crawl into bed and switch the TV on.

News of severe weather bombards every channel and breaks into every show. Freeze warnings, high winds and sleet are expected for the next twelve hours.

I hear my cell phone chime and glance at the texts. Celine and Maggie, over and over. I know they want to help, but they can't. And I know they don't understand. I'm mad, scared, and helpless. I shut down my phone for the remainder of the weekend. I just want to rest my head for now. I'll call everyone back on Monday.

*　　*　　*

Maggie got up from her chair and eyed the painting. She smiled.. *I need to get this to Gracie.* "Mike, come have a look at the painting I did of Sal and Gracie."

He appeared in the doorway. "That's beautiful, hon," he said. "Where did you get the idea to make the painting as though it were a Renaissance?"

"The pictures she sent me. This one here, especially," she said, pointing to the one at the winery that looked like a castle. "I swear it's just how I see them. I painted this portrait from my mind's eye, as though it were a memory I've had. Crazy right?"

"Maggie," he sighed. "In all our years together I've learned one thing–crazy you are not, but, you are creatively blessed. Your talent is a gift." He laughed and kissed the top of her head. "Speaking of gifts, what are you gonna do with it? You gonna send it to her?"

She stood and starred quietly at the painting her uneasiness growing. "Mike," she snapped, "I have to go see her–I'll bring it to her."

"You're going to fly down to Florida with the painting? Why don't you wait till spring break–I'll take the week off, we'll all go, I'll drive us down and—"

"Mike, something's wrong," she told him. "As nice as that sounds, I need to go like, now!"

"What is it, hon? What's wrong?" Questioning her with a look of concern, he knew his wife–and he knew Gracie and Maggie shared a strong bond.

"I'm not sure, Mike, but I just got a bad feeling. Gracie's alone right now and she's been very depressed about Sal being away. She hasn't returned my text or calls. Something is wrong. I need to get on a plane!"

He looked at her and nodded. He knew better than to argue. "Okay, I'll call the airlines about a flight, but the weather is bad up and down the East Coast. It might be a day or two before you can fly."

"Okay, make the call. I want to go as soon as possible!"

* * *

Sal thought he'd lose his mind before debriefing was over. He'd never experienced such impatience with the process before, but he was desperate to get back to Gracie.

Wasting no time, he got the first flight he could get. Bad weather was coming in and he was lucky to get out of D.C., thanks to the Agency. But he couldn't reach Gracie or Pop.

Before the flight he called her cell but it kept going to voice mail–and now the cells were not working on the flight.

With the heavy winds, the pilot's weren't sure if they'd land in Jacksonville or Atlanta. While Sal waits for word on which it will be, it feels like torture.

* * *

I wake abruptly out of a dream–coughing. I feel a burning in my throat and stomach. I gasp for air and I am drenched in sweat. I remember seeing Mother Boumont in my dream–she looked panic stricken. I have never dreamt of her before.

The dream makes me extremely tense and a bad vibe crawls up my spine. "Please God, don't let me have a panic attack!" I pray aloud. I get out of bed to get a hold of myself. I go into the bathroom and splash water on my face. I'm shaky and my breaths are shallow.

After a few minutes, the feeling subsides and I'm breathing easier. I decide to take a hot bath and try to relax. I fill the tub with eucalyptus and vanilla-scented bubbles. Submerging myself, the water is hot to my sensitive skin at first, but I quickly get used to it.

I soak in the steamy water till my fingers wrinkle. Getting out, I grab a big towel and go to find the warmest pajama's I own.

The weather is really nasty. I can hear the tapping of rain or sleet against the windows as the wind drives it sideways. I venture out on the balcony to look at the ocean—it's just starting to get dark out and it's freezing; I can see my breath in puffs. Toby wants no part of the stormy conditions and is hiding in my closet.

I watch as angry waves pound the shoreline and the wind howls like it's screaming. Every so often the wind switches directions pelting my face with icy rain.

I go back into the house and turn on the heat. I try to coax Toby out from the closet, but fail. "You big chicken," I tease him. "It's all right, big boy," I try to soothe him, but he stays put.

Still a little rattled from the dream, I'm getting chills up my back and I go take a Valium. It's the last one, but I know my other prescriptions are downstairs on the kitchen counter where Celine left them.

Deciding something hot to drink will help with the chills, I make my way downstairs. Halfway there, the power goes out. I freeze in place holding the railing, waiting for my eyes to adjust.

"Just great!" I mutter to the dark, empty house. Carefully navigating the stairs, I go to the kitchen. Instead of the microwave, I'm going to have to put water on the gas stove to boil. While I wait, I light the fireplace and some candles. I find a flashlight in one of the kitchen drawers—to my surprise it actually works.

I eye my medications and think that a sleeping pill combined with the Valium I took should get me through this wretched night.

I gulp the pill down, then return to the stove and pour the boiling water into a mug containing a ginger spice tea bag.

The fragrance is wonderful. I sip my tea by the fire listening to the howling storm. The warmth of the fire and tea just don't take away the chill that keeps tingling up my spine.

A loud knock at the front door paralyzes me. *Who the hell would be here? Who would come out in this weather?*

My stomach rolls and more chills race up my body along with a panicky sweat. *This can't be anything good.*

More knocking.

A hundred things go through my head at once, making it hard to concentrate. Slowly I make my way to the door. I hear Toby growling from somewhere up above me.

Knock. Knock. Knock....

I hold my breath. *Dear God, please don't let it bad news about Sal.* I glance through the little glass but it is too dark to see who is there.

I grab the handle and slowly pull open the door.

CHAPTER 27

He was relieved when the pilot landed in Jacksonville airport. All he could think of was getting home to Gracie. He called for a cab and was on his way–an hour or so and he'd be holding her in his arms.

He was a man of action, but not one who didn't understand instinct. How often had it helped save him–or one of his team–on a mission? Try as he did, his instinct was screaming that something was wrong at home. What if Gracie's premonition was about her, instead of him? He would die if anything happened to her...

"This is one wicked storm!" The cab driver mentioned to Sal, pulling him out of his darkening thoughts. "The power's been out for a while–the northern part of the state is really getting hit!"

"Yes," Sal agreed. "I was up in the plane and almost couldn't land." He tapped at his cell to call Gracie – *shit* right to voice mail. He tried Pop–*he's not answering either?* Sal left a message:

Pop, it's Sal. I'm home. I just landed. I'm in a taxi headed home. Where is Gracie? Where are you?

He hit the end button and glanced out the window at the storm. His uneasiness was growing. Lord, if Gracie was dealing with anything like this, no wonder she was scared out of her mind. He could barely sit still.

"Hey buddy! He nearly shouts to the driver, "I know the conditions are bad, but can you hurry?"

"I'll do what I can —we've had some sleet—the roads are slick."

"Yeah, you're right." He thought better of it. "I just want to get home— just be careful."

"I don't blame ya, you're worried 'bout the family. I'll get ya there—the good news is, not many people out tonight so the roads are kinda bare."

"Thanks, I…uh..I've been away… two months, for work. I can't get in touch with anyone."

"Well then it'll be a nice surprise for them. I'm sure they're fine, just the storm messin' with the signals."

Sal sat back and tried to relax. *I hope he is right about the storm.* He told himself Gracie and Pop were fine. But it felt like a lie. *Please, God….*

* * *

"Well you gonna just stand there? Let me in!"

I stand there staring at Camille James in my doorway. "Camille? What are you doing here?" I ask flatly. Of course I'm relieved it isn't some big Marine with bad news, but I'm so damned tired.

She saunters in as if she owns the place. I almost laugh—she just about does. She eyes me up and down.

"What's the matter Gracie? Are you sick? You don't look so good," she says with a tight smile.

"What do you want, Camille?" I ask, exhausted by her already. "I'm in no mood for company or your shit."

"I wanted to drop by to have a little girl talk."

We both hear growling from the top of the stairs and Camille follows the sound with her eyes.

"Where's that mutt of yours?"

"Upstairs–he doesn't like storms, *or* you. So....why are you here?" I snap.

"Girl talk. I heard Sal's away on some adventure and you are completely heart broken. Close to a complete nervous breakdown if the rumors are to be believed."

Bitch. "He's on a mission, Camille. Sal's with the military. Why are you really here? Where's Richard?" I question, furrowing my eyebrows.

"Richard's away too, on business. Boston, I believe this time. I thought I'd stop by and talk about some things."

"What could we have to talk about?" I shrug my shoulders turning to go back by the fire where it's warm. I pick up my tea which is now cold and walk back to the kitchen to reheat some water. I place my cold mug on the counter and Camille takes a seat.

"Would you like some tea, Camille?"

"Okay," she answers.

I retrieve the pot, fill it with more water and return it to the stove. Grabbing a clean mug for Camille, I toss in a tea bag. As I wait in my candle-lit kitchen for the water to boil, I can feel Camille's eyes on me, searing the back of my head. I'm getting annoyed.

In a few minutes the water is ready and I fill her mug, and place it and some sugar in front of her. Then poured what was left of the hot, bubbly water into my mug to re-heat it.

I take little sips at first, blowing the steam. Camille's watching me. "So..? I huff, looking at her with my eyebrows raised.

She eyes my pill bottles. "What's all this?"

"None of your business," I say politely, moving them to another space. She sips her tea and looks at me with her head cocked. "You miss him that much you have trouble sleeping?"

"If you must know–yes. I miss him that much."

"Valium too, I see. Your just having a bad time, aren't you Gracie? Bless your heart.."

I drink my tea in bigger gulps, wishing it was wine. I take a deep breath and blow it out. "Camille, what do you want?"

"I came to tell you a little story, Gracie. A story that no one knows–not even Richard."

"Really? How did I luck out for story time with Camille?" I ask sarcastically.

"Well...first, let me tell you about a young girl who used to clean houses for a living. She was a single mom, trying to make ends meet. One day she got a job cleaning a huge house–the money was almost three times what she charged for an average house. And she got to bring her daughter with her while she cleaned.

Her little girl loved to go–she would play and pretend she was the princess of the big house. The owners that lived there liked her so much they let her do almost anything she wanted, and the lady of the house gave her clothes to play in and sometimes played with her.

One day the lady of the house saw the little girl looking at some pictures of a young man. "Who is that?" the young girl asked.

"Oh, that's my son," she answered. "He is away at boarding school."

"Is he the prince?" the child asked.

"Yes sweetie, you could say that. He's the prince of the house." They giggled together.

"Some day," the girl said, "he will come and take me away!"

"Oh?" the lady said, "yes I suppose the prince will someday need a princess."

Listening to Camille's weird story, the effects of the medication start to kick in. I yawn. It figures, I'm finally tired enough to really sleep and Camille the storyteller is here.

"Camille," I interrupt her. "I truly don't know what you're talking about. I'm very tired and I haven't been feeling good. I really need you to go so I can go to sleep."

She waits a minute and sips her tea. I've finished mine and put the empty mug down on the coffee table.

"But I've not finished my tea, Gracie, and I really need you to hear the rest of my story."

I bunch my eyebrows together and sit back. "Fine," I say on an exhale.

Camille stands up. "Let me speed ahead a little bit for you. Months later, the little girl hears the lady of the house arguing with her husband. She hears words like *whore* and *slut, white trash.*

Not sure what was going on, she just knew the lady of the house didn't want to play and was very upset. The little girl's mother was very nervous and fidgety and kept telling her to go outside and mind her business. So she did.

About a week after that, the man of the house came by the child and mother's little trailer. He gave the woman an envelope with some money. A long black car came and took them to a doctor's office. The little girl never seen a car like that let alone been in one. She was excited for the ride, but her momma was crying and she didn't know why?

The big long car dropped off her mother and she was told to wait with the driver and be a good girl. She did what was asked. She shyly looked at the big man behind the steering wheel.

"It's all right," he said, "I'm a policeman too. You're safe with me. Don't worry, you momma is fine. We'll *come-a-back and-a-pick her up in few hours, si?"*

Camille's last sentence stops me in mid yawn. I look at her–she's getting fuzzy. "Are you trying to talk with an Italian accent? I slur.

She smiled an evil smirk. "Yes, the driver told me his name was Tony. I believe that's short for Antonio."

Suddenly, all that dread makes sense. I feel panic but the sleeping pill and valium are masking it. I know this is really bad–and I don't have the strength to do anything about it. I try to stand but my legs are like rubber. Shit, I thought the doctor said the pills were mild...

"Camille–what are you talking about? Tony? *My* Antonio? Sal's father?"

"That's the one, Gracie. Let me get to the point before you pass out. When I was a little girl, my mother was the cleaning lady for the Boumont's. Mr. Boumont and my mother had an affair and she got pregnant. Mrs. Boumont found out and was not pleased. My mother thought that for sure he was going to leave his wife and marry her. But he showed up at our door with money and a ride to a clinic. Antonio was new to the family as the Boumont's driver and security."

I try again to stand, but fail.

"What's the matter, Gracie? Someone dope your tea?"

I point at her and it takes a lot of energy. "You...you put something in my tea! Why?"

"Oh Gracie, I'm not done with my story."

I have no way to throw her out. I sit like a lump, listening to her story unfold like a nightmare.

"Now, let me see where was I... Oh, yes, Mr. Boumont, err, Jonathan gave my mother money to abort the pregnancy. Luann, Mrs. Boumont of course, found out and was livid – fired my mother.

When mom was done at the clinic, Antonio picked her up and drove us back home. My mother slept and cried for days She tried to call Jonathan but he avoided her.

One day Antonio pulled up to our little trailer, and presented my mother with a gift box. She asked him what it was—but Tony didn't know—he was handed the little gift to bring to her. Momma took the gift and thanked Tony for bringing it by. There was a note attached. My mother cried, then opened the box. Inside was a diamond necklace. The one *you* now have! I want it back, Gracie and I am returning it to my mother."

"My necklace? Why would?.. Luann gave that to me. How... Camille, please... I don't understand what's going on."

"Gracie, I don't know how, but Luann found out about the diamonds. She was very intelligent and strong willed—she came by about a month or two after my mother received her gift. She told my mother she knew Jonathan gave her a necklace and he had no right to do so. She came to get it back and if she didn't hand it over, she would call child welfare services on us.

"My mother could not compete with Luann Boumont and tearfully gave her the necklace. That necklace may not have cost very much, but it was something nice—something from *him*. Momma didn't have anything.

"After a year or so and we were forgotten in the Boumont's life—my mother went scitzo. I blamed the Boumonts for her health. So Gracie, long story short, that drove me to get all the help and education I could. They were going to pay for hurting us. I felt some relief when they both passed away. Even poor Tony got himself shot in an accident. Seriously, how lucky was I? The Boumonts were gone!"

She sips at her tea and then looks at me as though we're the best of friends. *The dread...the warnings...*

"Then Richard inherited it all, but, he came back with you, and *you* had my mother's necklace. Things were so easy, you and Richard grew apart. Truly, I think the Boumont men just can't keep their dicks in their pants. Meanwhile, I maneuvered my way into the business, then into

Richard's life. You know? I will agree on one thing with you—he *is* an asshole."

"You're the one," I say panting, slurring my words. "You...embezzled the money!" I suck in air in surprise. "And you... broke into my house? Did you hire that guy with the gun? You're just as insane as your mother!"

"It was all going so easy, Gracie. Then, Tony's son shows up, like a knight in shining armor, for Christ sakes. Loads you down with security, takes out the guy I hired to get the necklace..."

"That guy was a killer Camille! He would have shot up the place and killed me! Or anyone! What the fuck is wrong with you?"

As though I'd said nothing, she puts down her mug and looks at me. "Where's the necklace Gracie." Her eyes are dark and cold.

"I'm not giving you anything...." I stammer. I use all my might to stand. "YOU CRAZY BITCH! GET OUT!" I yell, but stumble forward. Camille grabs my arm. I try to yell for Toby, but she slaps a hand across my mouth.

"I think you need some air, Gracie. You took too many sleeping pills—a nice walk down at the beach is exactly what you need."

I try to fight her, but I can't control my limbs. I feel like a puppet with no strings...she's got my arm in a death grip.

"Don't fight me, Gracie, and don't call that mutt of yours! I have a gun and I'd be delighted to shoot him. Come on—easy does it—lets go get some air."

She opens the door and the stormy wind yanks it out of her hand, slamming it against the house. She drags me out through the screen and over to the wooden bridge, the whole time asking me where I keep the necklace.

I don't tell her a thing—I'm dead, and maybe Toby too, whether I tell her or not. With me and Toby gone, she'd have all the time in the world to ransack the house, looking for it. .

Passing by Pop's house, I try to scream but she grabs me by the throat and I almost go to my knees.

The wind is roaring and the ocean is dark, mean, choppy. Big waves smash on to the beach– it's so cold my teeth are chattering. Or maybe that's fear.

"Poor, poor, Gracie. So sad she couldn't go on," Camille mutters.

* * *

Opening his eyes, Tony realized he'd fallen asleep when the power went out. The sound of the T.V. woke him up, along with that annoying buzz from his cell phone.

He tapped at the cell and it lit up: three missed calls and a message from Sal! He touched the screen and called him back.

"POP?!"

"Yes! Son, Where are you?"

"Pop, I'm in a taxi–I'm almost home. I've been trying to call Gracie–she's not answering– something's wrong. I can't get through!"

"Son, calm-a-down. The power just came back on. When was the last time you tried?"

"A few minutes ago– it goes right to voice mail. I think her cell might be dead–I don't understand."

"Son, I need to warn you. Gracie has been very depressed since you left. I have barely seen her. Celine called and told me it's not good–she wants to take her to the hospital. She's been that distraught."

Whoof, whoof.

"Son, hold on a minute. I think Toby is at my door barking – he's scratching like crazy."

"What? Pop? Hello?"

Tony wheeled over to the door, opened it and there was Toby, barking and jumping, running in a circle.

"POP TALK TO ME!" Sal yelled.

Tony glanced over at Gracie's—the door was open and banging against the house.

"Yeah son, Gracie's back door is open. Toby got out and came here—he's barking and wanting me to follow. I think something is-a-wrong! How far away are you?"

"NOT FAR—ALMOST THERE! CAN YOU SEE HER?" Sal's voice was filled with panic.

"No, the house is dark. Toby wants me to go on the beach—I can't go on the beach, son, not in my wheelchair. Hurry, Sal! I'm gonna call-a-the police to be safe."

Tony hung up with Sal and strained to see something, anything, but it was too dark and the wind was blowing sand into his face. Toby took off on his own towards the beach.

Tony touched the screen to his cell and called the police station.

* * *

"Keep moving Gracie," Camille snarls through her teeth. "Just to the edge of the pier, looks like you're going to have an accident or some might even say you committed suicide. I bet even Richard would believe that—he always says how weak-minded you are."

I've got a fistful of Camille's coat. If I'm going in, she is too. "Don't!... Just leave me alone, Camille... not weak" I puff. But I am weak. And so tired...

"Let go, Gracie!" Camille shouts.

I try hard to hold on and to help myself. My pajamas are soaked and I'm freezing. And so weak from the pills. I can't believe this is happening—Yvette was right. The threat was about me. It would be Sal's turn to live without me...

They say your life flashes before your eyes when you die. As Camille pushes me into the enraged ocean, I see so many memories—good and bad—racing through my mind like lightening.

I hit the water and the coldness is like being electrocuted. Struggling, trying to swim with the waves twirling me, lifting me up, then sucking me under. I hold my breath till it hurts.

The sea slams me up against one of the pilings, I try to hold on but my arms are as strong as wet noodles.

Some where I hear Toby barking—then I hear a gunshot. I try to look around, but wave after ferocious wave keeps slamming me into the wood. I try to hold on as the undertow pulls at me—it's impossible.

Water fills my throat and goes up my nose, burning like fire every time. I gasp for air. I can't feel my hands and feet anymore. I'm exhausted and so tired... I finally just let go.

* * *

"GRACIE!! I yell, as my feet hit the sand.

I spot a figure of a woman running up the beach to the access road. "GRACIE!" I call out, but she kept running.

I bolt up the beach, fighting the winds and the sand nicking at my face. TOBY! I see Toby lying on the sand. I kneel beside him and run my hands over his wet fur, I came away with blood all over my hands. He was shot, but alive and whimpering.

"Oh no Toby." I moan. I strip out of my coat and laid it over him. *Shit, where the hell is Gracie?*

I look around—search the beach, the ocean—and there in the waves I see her! I run down to the water—I see Gracie holding on to the piling under the pier.

A huge wave encases the top of her, dragging her out. I dive into the churning sea, the cold waves slapping at me. I swim as hard as I could in her direction—fighting the current and pounding the water like I'm boxing.

I spot her briefly and dive under. Blinded by the dark water I reach out to her but come up empty. I make it to the same piling I'd seen her holding onto. I focus on the choppy ocean trying to center myself when I spot her again—she's caught in a wave.

I dive after her and her body slams into mine. I held onto her and headed back to the shore. A strong wave helped push us to land. I carry her body, limp as a rag doll out of the water. The cold wind slices us, zapping the rest of my energy. I set her down gently.

"Gracie...Gracie..." I give her CPR. "BREATHE, GRACIE, BREATHE!" I scream. I breathe some more air into her and finally some bubbles come out on a choke. She coughs. "GRACIE.. COME ON! OH, NO PLEASE!! BREATHE!" I scream again.

"SAL! Hey SAL!"

I focus on two police officers running up the beach towards us yelling my name. "CALL 911!" I yell to them.

"We did—they're on their way! Hang on!"

They toss me a blanket and I wrap it around her. I hold her tight and kiss her head. They wrap Toby up too. He let out a soft growl.

I call over to him. "Easy, buddy. Easy."

"Did you see the woman?" I ask them, still panting for my breath. She was headed up to the access road. A blonde, I think."

"Yes, the other officer's in the patrol car apprehended a woman running to a black Escalade. She was armed. They're taking her in."

The one officer knelt down beside me. "Sal—it's Mr. Boumont's fiancée, Camille James."

CHAPTER 28

In the emergency room I wait in a private area for the doctor. Pop arrived a few minutes after I did and we watched the medical staff as they hooked Gracie to monitors, and tubes, then wheeled her down a hall for tests. Her hands and arms where bloody and cut from the barnacles on the wood pilings of the pier. I shudder thinking about how close I was to losing her.

"Son, she is alive, she will pull through..." Pop says softly.

"She hasn't opened her eyes. She's out cold."

"Sal, you saved her–she's a strong girl–she'll pull through."

A nurse dressed in yellow scrubs heads toward us, her eyes are warm, friendly. She nods at me.

"Mr. Petroni? I'm Julie–I'm going to clean up your cuts for you. Can you step over to the table for me please?"

I glance down at my arms and notice that I have a few open cuts - I didn't even know they were there. I go over to the table and let her fix me up.

"Your fiancée was lucky you showed up when you did. The nurse tells me you saved her life!"

"How is she? Did she wake up?"

"Her vitals are stable, but, let the doctor fill you in. I don't get all the details. I'm sure he'll be just another few moments."

She continues cleaning my arms and wraps them in gauze. "You were lucky too–the cuts aren't real deep, but we'll start you on an antibiotic anyway. Just wait here–the doctor will be in shortly."

When the nurse leaves the room, I look over at Pop. "Where's Toby?" I ask.

"Veronica picked him up–the paramedics helped him till she came. She'll call me as soon as she's done getting the bullet out."

"Pop, what the hell happened?" I say, shaking my head. "Why was Camille there with a gun?"

Before Pop can answer, the doctor walks in. "Salvatore Petroni?" He asks, holding out his hand to me. "I'm Doctor Rosaro. I've been taking care of Gracie. I understand you're the next of kin?"

"I am. How is she? Can I see her?"

"She's...doing pretty well. She got pretty banged up: she has a concussion from a blow to the back of her head, causing trauma; she's lost some blood; and we also found a mix of barbiturates in her system."

"Barbiturates?" I question, "like what?"

"A mix of the commonly used ones for sleeping. Some Xanax, Valium that kind of stuff. Did you know if she took these regularly?"

"She used to. She sees Dr. Brooks on occasion. I'll check with him when I can. She took them for her anxiety attacks but for the most part she's gotten over them. I've been away on business for a while. When I left, she'd stopped–she didn't need them anymore." I tilt my head toward the doctor.

"When you say a *mix*, you're not thinking she overdosed, are you? Gracie would never do that!"

"Well, that's what we're trying to figure out. It wasn't enough to kill her, but enough to knock her out, put her in a weakened state. Sometimes, people taking sedatives don't realize they've mixed meds or they get confused. At any rate, we've cleaned her system but, with the head injury and all, she's in a coma."

I catch my breath and stifle the desire to scream. "A coma?" I whisper instead.

The doctor puts his hand on my arm, then glances at Pop. His smile is gentle. "The good news is she is breathing on her own—we just have to wait for the swelling to the brain go down. I'm pretty confident she'll wake up—I just can't say when. We have to give it time."

I swallow around the huge lump in my throat and battle back tears. *Princess, Have I done this to you?* I look at the doctor. "Can I see her now?"

"Yes, of course. Follow me."

Pop and I follow the doctor down a hall into the ICU. We walk into the room and there's my Gracie sleeping and hooked up to an EKG. The sound of steady bleeps tells me her heart is pumping. She has an IV drip along with an arterial line measuring her blood pressure.

Bandages cover her arms from above her elbows down to her hands—just her fingertips are showing.

My heart on the other hand, is beating loud and erratically. I want to rage against all this, turn back time and sweep her into my arms. Make love to her. Hear her laugh. See that smile that's just for me. I kept my promise and came home safe, didn't I? I swallow again and get my feet to move.

I go to her side—touch her—she's cold. I start to tuck the sheet around her. "She's cold—she feels cold! Get her a blanket!" I demand.

Doctor Rosaro echoes my request to the nurses standing near. One of them returns with a warmed blanket on her arm. I put my hand out to stop her from covering Gracie. "Let me do it...please? And, thank you. I didn't mean to snap."

"It's all right, sir," she says, handing me the blanket.

I tuck the blanket around her and kiss her forehead, then her lips. I gently put my head on her chest, listening to her heart, her lungs taking in breaths.

"You should talk to her," one of the nurses suggests. "Let her know you're here–tell her you're waiting for her. She'll hear you."

I slowly pull myself away from Gracie's heart and warm tears slide down my face. I wipe at them as I turn to the nurse standing in the doorway who smiles before exiting the room. I look over at Pop and he nods. "Go ahead, son", he says. "Talk-a-to her–she loves you, her heart–her soul–will hear you."

I bend down close to her beautiful face. "Gracie," I say softly. "I'm here. I came home. I promised you I would." My breath catches in my throat as more tears flood my eyes.

"I'm not going anywhere–I promised you I'd never leave you. I'm staying right here till you wake up, I love you. I'm never going to leave you again. Please Gracie,... baby, come back to me."

After a few minutes, I kiss her. I pull up a chair next to her bedside. I look over at Pop–he's drying his eyes with a handkerchief. I inhale a deep breath and let it out, lean back in the chair, and turn my eyes back to her.

"Where are you, Gracie?"

*   *   *

Sun is shining through a small window and it wakes me. I'm warm and comfortable in my strange bed. I lay very still, listening to the chirps of the birds outside my colored glass window. I hear a commotion and the big wooden door bursts open.

"Sophia! Get up!" a voice calls and I feel a thump as someone jumps on my bed.

Today's the day!" she says with such excitement. I open my eyes wide and rub them.

The young girl sitting next to me is smiling, dressed in a long billowy dress with long sleeves and corset. Brown curls try to escape from a clip on top of her head. I know her—she's my sister—and my heart recognizes her as Maggie.

"What are you going on about sister?" I ask.

"Today is the day—Uncle Sabastion's ceremony! For the Knights Templar, remember? We are to have a feast this afternoon!"

I sit up quickly. "Yes!" I squeal. "Of course I remember—Marsilio comes home today!"

"That's right," she answers. "And mother is promising your hand to him! Now get up—we must prepare for the day's events."

As my feet hit a cold stony floor, some women come in with hot buckets of water and fill a small tub.

"My Lady," they say as they cursy upon entering my sleeping chambers. "We'll leave you to bathe, My Lady."

I slip into the little tub and soak. My sister comes and sits in a big wooden chair next to me. Her glee is radiating from her like heat off the stove in the kitchen chambers.

"Everyone has arrived! You can see ships at the harbor. When do you think you will marry Sir Marsilio?" she asks.

"Picking up a cloth, I rub it over my belly. "As soon as possible, Anne. I think I am with child from my last meeting with my handsome knight." I giggle, despite the fact that our mother, the Queen, might want to kill me for not waiting.

"SISTER! Are you sure? How long since?"

"Three fortnights, I believe."

"You have not bled?"

"No sister, I have not. And my breasts feel tender."

She skips and claps around the room happily laughing. "Anne...ANNE," I shout and she halts in place, still grinning at me, her light eyes twinkling.

"You must promise me, not a word to mother or to our half-sister Caterina. No one must know—do you understand?"

"Yes of course sister, you can trust me.. You will tell Marsilio, won't you?" she asks, her smile replaced by a frown.

"Yes, after the feast when I am properly betrothed to him. We may be able to steal a moment of privacy. Then and only then will I share my news with my beloved."

"Good enough, sister," she says, making a cross across her chest with two fingers. "If you don't need my help to dress, I will see you out on the castle yard. Mother is already at court waiting our arrival."

* * *

While Gracie sleeps, Pop and I sit vigil, praying, hoping, and looking for any sign that she knows we're here. And, while Pop kept watch, I showered the salt and sand off and redressed in stiff jeans and sweater.

The next afternoon I'm still by Gracie's bedside. Every half-hour, I tell her we're still waiting for her—that I still love her and I'll wait no matter how long it takes. The nurses come in every two hours and check on us. They're monitoring Gracie from the desk as well, so they know as well as I do that there's been no change. Once a shift, they come and draw more blood. I wonder if she's got enough to spare. She's lost a lot of weight in the weeks I've been gone and the dark circles beneath her eyes tell me the whole story.

The evening tech comes in and draws the blood they need for more tests. "Any changes," she asks. "Sometimes they can be subtle, but you'll see them.

I shake my head. "No, she's the same."

"Well, it's only been twenty-four hours," the tech says. "It takes time. I've seen coma patients wake after two days or sometimes it may take two months. Depends how much rest their brain and body needs. Only time will tell."

"Two months?" I groan.. "Oh, please god... no."

Just as the tech is putting away the vials and labels, the floor nurse drops in. She puts a hand on my shoulder and smiles.

"Don't worry," she says. "We have every reason to think Gracie is going to be fine. Everyone heals in their own time–brain injuries are tricky. We'll be in later with an ICP monitor which measures the pressure in the brain. We can keep track and notice when it starts to go down. Really, the best thing is that she's sleeping and resting. I'll be back later. I suspect we'll move Gracie out of the ICU shortly. The doctor is making his rounds–he'll be in to talk to you."

"Thank you," I say as I she walks out. Pop is sleeping in his wheel chair in the corner. I need to get him to go home, but he's as stubborn–and as worried–as I am.

"Pop...POP! I raise my voice a bit so he'll wake up.

"Is she up son? What's-a-wrong?" he struggles to sit upright and wake up at the same time.

"Nothing, Pop. Why don't you go...get home, I'll call you and keep you updated." Pop looks at Gracie and back to me, then nods.

Before we can call him a cab, the nurse comes back into the room. "You two have a visitor, but he shouldn't come in here. An Officer Dan? You can go talk in the lounge area."

She sees my hesitation–I don't want to leave Gracie for a second–which I know is obsessive. "We have her monitored, Sal. If there's the slightest change, I'll come get you."

I get to my feet and walk beside Dad as we follow the nurse through the heavy ICU doors and down a short corridor. I spot Dan pouring himself a cup of coffee.

He turns and sees us coming up on him.

"Hey guys," he says, "I got some information to share with you—unless it's a not a good time?"

I shake his hand. "Now's as good a time as any."

"Any change, Sal?" he asks as he swirls the wooden stirrer in the paper cup.

"No, but they keep telling me that's normal. She's stable and comfortable, I hope."

Pop puts his chair next to the small sofa and motions for us to sit down. "Hey —what-a-you got? What happened?"

He takes off his coat and lays it over a chair, then sits so he's between Pop and me.

"Well, where do I start? Umm..Tony–do you remember a Nancy Jamison, who used to clean the Boumont's residence years ago?"

"Si...yes, poor lady," Antonio said, shaking his head.

"Do you remember her little girl?"

"Si...yes, yes... Carolann, I think. She was a little thing-a-with brown hair. Quiet, cute little one."

"Yes, well, she now goes by the name of Camille James. She told us a crazy story last night about her mom and Mr. Boumont–do you know what I am referring to?"

I watch my father's eyes bulge from their sockets as he puts a hand up to his head as if trying to remember was causing him pain and confusion.

"Pop–what's going on? What is it?" I ask him.

"Oh my god," Pop whispers. "She crazy just like her mother. Son, I knew Camille when-a-she was little."

And for the next ten minutes, my father tells me a sad, sad story of a cleaning woman, a selfish man, and a vindictive wife. And, of his role in that story. I watch him age as he remembers things he had no idea would come back to hurt so many he loved.

"Mr. Boumont gave her money and I drove her to get an abortion. Not-a-too long after that, we heard Nancy went insane and got put away. I never knew what happened to little Carolann."

"Revenge," says Dan. "She grew up, got help from the state, changed her name, changed her hair, even got men to pay for plastic surgery and a new nose. Turns out she was stealing from Boumont all along–was gonna take her mother out of the nut house and head to Grand Cayman islands."

"But why try to kill Gracie? She had nothing to do with any of that."

"Gracie has a diamond necklace that was given to Nancy after the abortion, by Mr. Boumont. Mrs. Boumont demanded it back. Told her not to put up an argument or she'd call child welfare, but as it turned out, that happened all on its own."

I think about Gracie laying in a hospital bed attached to monitors–in a coma–and I'm so furious I could punch a hole in the wall.

"Because of all this crazy bullshit," I spit out through clenched teeth, "Gracie almost died! Pop, didn't Richard know who she was?"

"Probably not, son. Richard was away at schools most of the time–he was never home more than a week at a time. He is a little older than Camille–he would not-a have paid any attention to her–she was a little girl."

My fists are clenched tight enough to hurt. "Where is that son of a bitch, anyway? Does he know what he brought into his life–and now ours?"

Dan answers. "He is on his way home now from Boston. He was away on business–but we called him–he knows some, not all."

"It was a necklace..." mutters Antonio to himself.

"What? Pop? You say something?" My eyes flicker in his direction.

"A diamond necklace. I was asked to drop a little present off to Nancy a month or so after her procedure–I didn't know what it was and I no ask. It was-a-the diamond necklace that Luann gave to Gracie."

Pop looks nauseated and very tired after learning about Camille James and her mother. I can't afford anything to happen to him now, too. I rub my hand over my face and put on a small smile. It's the best I can do. I'm tired, too.

"Pop, why don't you go home for a while, get some rest. You know I'll call if there's a change."

"I can take him." Officer Dan offers.

"So tell me Dan, I assume Camille hired the perp to steel Gracie's necklace at the benefit, then?"

"Yep, correct. We also got a full confession. Camille knew you were away, so she went to pay Gracie a visit, took a gun, but just to scare her. But when she got there, she noticed Gracie was already in a bad way, saw the prescriptions and drugged her tea. We're just glad you got there when you did Sal."

"My fiancée is in a coma–I wasn't quick enough," I growl from deep within my chest.

"She's alive, Sal," he answers, "she's going to make it."

Dr. Rosaro, stethoscope draped around his neck, finds us in the lounge and motions at me with his hand. "Gentlemen," he says, "I ah... need to talk to Sal."

My heart stops. "What's wrong?"

The doctor looks at Officer Dan and Pop. "Please excuse us; I need to talk to Mr. Patroni alone. Let's go back down to Gracie's room, Sal."

"That's our cue," Dan says to Pop as he starts for the door. Pop lifts his chin at me to get my attention. "I won't leave yet. I gonna be right-a-outside the door."

I give him a nod as he rolls out of the room.

Back in Gracie's room, two nurses are hooking up another machine. *Oh my god, now what?*

I walk over to Gracie's bedside and touch her fingertips. Dr. Rosaro glances at the nurses. "Go ahead, hook it up" he says.

"Okay, what's this about?" I say, pointing to the new equipment as they are pulling up Gracie's medical gown and gently placing her legs in stirrups. "Doc, you want to tell me what the hell that is?"

"Sal, as we kept checking Gracie's blood I kept getting a reading of high level hormones. That can indicate a lot of things, but the last blood test we did came up positive for a pregnancy. I'm guessing you didn't know."

My legs go weak and I can't feel the floor beneath my feet. My head spins and a choking sob gets caught in my throat. *Pregnant?*

"Nurse, help Mr. Patroni to a chair please. And get him some water." The doctor taps my shoulder. "Mr. Patroni–Sal–can you hear me?"

I nod and swipe at my forehead. "Pregnant? She's pregnant? She thought she couldn't... she had miscarriages...she thought she was a little too old now to..."

"She's right at the cusp–it can happen," the Doctor says, cutting me off. "I'm concerned about the head trauma and the drugs in her system–we want to see if there's a heartbeat. We're going to give her an internal ultrasound–we will be able to detect a fetus and a heartbeat."

I watch, still in shock from the news, as the nurse inserts a metallic wand into Gracie. A black and white screen displays pictures of her uterus. They show me the *womb* and a tiny, black, blinking dot.

"There it is, doctor—we have a heartbeat," the specialist says as she points to the screen. My eyes lock on it—that little spot twinkling at me. I bend over to Gracie and kiss her forehead. *A baby!* I don't know whether to laugh or cry, so I just thank God they are both alive.

Doctor Rosaro eyes the little dot and smiles. "Sal, looks like you're going to be a father—I'd say August, maybe September the latest. She's about nine weeks along. So far we have a good clear heartbeat. All we can do is hope she doesn't miscarry while she's recovering."

CHAPTER 29

I put on a long pale-blue dress with the help of my ladies in waiting. They brush my hair and adorn me with jewels and place a small tiara on my head. The sleeves of my dress are almost long enough to touch the floor and the material floats weightlessly as I walkabout.

I stride through a dimly lit hall made out of massive blocks of stone and the air has a damp musky aroma. There are two guards placed at every entry way and servants scurrying about. My ladies flank me as they escort me out into the castle yard. The air is fresh, the sun bright, and a cool breeze pushes white fluffy clouds east over the sea.

Under enormous gold and maroon-colored tents the servants prepare for the feast. Smoke fills the air with the smell of roasting meats and rows of tables are covered with an array of pastries and fruits.

"Ah, there you are, daughter. Are you ready for the Bishop's feast?"

"Yes, mother–Your Majesty". *I bow before the small dark-haired, blue-eyed woman. My heart recognizes her as Celine.*

"Come along then, your sisters are already seated."

I follow her up a few wooden steps under a tent that has a view of the procession about to begin.

Trumpets sound and men mill about getting into their places. A tall man dressed in a dark cloak and breeches stands on a podium.

"Welcome all, to the Bishop's Feast. Today we honor the Knights Templar for their victorious battle at Malta. Brother Bishop Sabastion will do the honor's."

I smile as I watch my uncle, the Bishop, head to the podium. He is a tall man with dark eyes and when he glances in our direction, my heart recognizes him as Antonio.

"Good Day, ladies and gentlemen and Your Majesty, Queen Josephine de la Guerche. I am pleased to announce our victory in Malta. Our reinforcements from Sicily arrived and we demoralized the Turkish troops and incited them to abandon the siege of the remaining Christian forts!"

Everyone at court stands and cheers the knights' victory. Two big iron gates open and the Knights Templar come galloping in on their horses. They were in white robes, holding shields that bare a Red Cross.

The horses are also draped in white clothes with holes cut around the eyes.. The knights ride in, waving their swords to all. One in particular slows and stops by our area, he trots up close aside me, and he and his horse bow.

"My lady," he announces with a wide smile.. My heart flutters at the familiar, handsome knight for he owns my heart. His long wavy hair and deep brown eyes—yea—even the scruff of his beard. My heart pounds and my soul knows that he is Salvatore.

I nod and return his smile. "M'lord Marsilio," I say as calmly as I can. "Pleasure to see you have returned victorious."

"Will I see m'lady at the feast table and would it please you to be seated at your side?"

"You shall," I answer. He continues to smile as he rides off on his horse. My pulse quickens at the sight of him and I gently put my hand on my belly.

* * *

I wake to the sound of Gracie's heart monitor beeping faster. My head snaps up and I lean over her...

"GRACIE?" I shout, "GRACIE?"

Before I know what's happening, a nurse comes through the doorway and checks on her.

"It's okay, Mr. Petroni, her heart rate sped up a bit but she's okay. Sometimes they get agitated or perhaps she's dreaming–but I see nothing to be alarmed about. Try holding her hand–it may help.

I reach over and gently hold one of Gracie's bandaged hands. I hope she's dreaming something happy. I give her hand a little squeeze and tell her I'm here.

The nurse smiles. "Good, keep it up. She's leveling off."

Gracie's heart rate and pressure returned to normal. Sitting here I feel so helpless I could cry. *Does she know she's carrying our child?*

I think of how scared she must have been, thinking I was going to be killed, when all along it was her we should have worried about. Gracie's premonitions were about *her* safety, not mine.

Later in the afternoon, Pop comes back to the hospital. I ask him to stay with Gracie so I can go home, clean up and pick up some of Gracie's things like warm slippers and a nightshirt. I need her phone so I can call her brother.

Pop comes in and looks over at Gracie. "Hello, mio caro, Pop is here. I gonna stay so Sal can-a-get you some things at home. Toby is well.

Veronica removed the bullet from-a-his shoulder and he is recovering at her place. He is a lucky boy," he says, chuckling as he pats Gracie's leg. Very-very lucky boy."

* * *

When I return to the hospital a few hours later, I get to the ICU door, identify myself so I can be buzzed through, only to be told she's no longer here.

"I'm sorry, what does that mean?" I say to the intercom box on the wall. She was alive and sleeping when I left...

"Ms. Boumont has been moved to a private room."

Before I can pursue it, though, I hear Pop's wheelchair coming down the hallway. He turns the corner and motions me to follow him.

"She's-a still sleeping, but they moved her to a room where we can stay with her without upsetting other patients. Nothing has-a changed since you left." He looks at me. "You look a little better. But you need some sleep, son."

I sigh. "I know, Pop. I'll get some when everything calms down. I had to make some calls, check the house, clean up the storm damage a little."

We get to her new room and I put Gracie's things off to the side, retrieve the cell phone charger, and plug in her phone.

Soon, I see all the missed calls and texts from Celine and Maggie. First, I call her brother and tell him everything I can. He says for me to keep him posted on her prognosis and he'll be home as soon as possible.

As I'm just about to call Celine, she comes busting through the door of Gracie's room.

"Oh my god...Jesus Christ, have mercy! What a nightmare! I called the police because I couldn't get a hold of her – I wanted them to go check on her, and all they told me was she was in the hospital. She looks over at Gracie and starts to cry. "Sal, is she gonna be all right? Look at her... What happened to her hands?"

"She has a concussion and her hands got cut from the barnacles under the pier. Camille pushed her off the pier - she was trying to hold on but the ocean was too rough that night."

Glancing at Pop, then back to Celine, I take a breath. "We got some news yesterday. I want to know if Gracie mentioned that she was pregnant?"

Celine's head snaps in my direction, her big blue eyes as wide as saucers. "PREGNANT? Oh my god! Gracie's pregnant? Sal, she never said anything and I'll be the first to tell you, she didn't have a clue—she thought she was sick because of her nerves—she couldn't keep any food down. You can even ask your father here," she motions with her hand toward Pop. "I was going to take her to the hospital because she wasn't right—she was out of her mind worried about you! I'm glad you're home now. You are never leaving her again, right?"

"No, I'm never leaving her again...Ever!"

"Oh my god, oh my god, a *baby*!" Celine squealed. "Poor thing, she doesn't know yet. How long has she been in a coma?"

"A few days now. She's stable for the most part and the baby's heart is still beating. We're just waiting for the swelling in her brain to go down. Camille drugged her up good. She was too weak to swim."

"That bitch!" Celine barked. "Don't even *say* her name. Just y'all wait till I get a hold of Richard!"

I toss Celine a look. "Me first," I growl.

"Sal, did you call her brother and her girlfriend Maggie? I can do it if you like," she offers.

"I talked to Steve, but I didn't call Maggie yet. That would be great if you can call her–thanks."

"I'm on it." Celine says as she grabs her cell from her purse and walks out into the hallway.

I sit back down next to Gracie and put my head down, close my eyes. "She didn't know she was pregnant, Pop. She didn't know."

"It'll be all right son, it will be all right."

My father's tone is soothing, but I hear it crack just a little.

I lift my head just enough to see Pop keeping watch over us.

"As soon as she is awake and well, I'm marrying her."

* * *

The day's celebration feast was amusing, everyone frolicking about in merriment. Minstrels played music and dancing was enjoyed by all.

Sir Marsilio sat next to me and told me of his journey and victorious battles.

"I am happy thee are safe, m'lord. I've much to tell you since last we've met." I smile and look away for a moment.

He stands and holds out a hand to me. "Shall we walk, Princess?"

I take his hand and we take our leave of the table. We choose the garden for our stroll and as soon as we are out of everyone's sight, he grabs my waist and holds tight, taking my mouth as though he is taking gulps of air. I push back, but just a little.

"My lord!" I breathe.

"Forgive me, Princess, but I have missed these lips and thy smile–it is all I think about. I cannot wait for you to be my wife. Tell me you have missed me, tell me you love me–all I think about is our last night when I snuck into your bed chamber before I left."

I laugh and hug him. "Yes, your grace, I have missed thee and I love thee with all my heart and soul. Our last meeting, you left something behind with me."

"I did?" he replies with a furrowed brow. "I can't imagine what I could have left. Pray, tell me, my love."

I take his hand from my waist and gently place it on my belly. At first, a look of confusion crosses his face, then within a moment, his eyes are wide and he grins. "You are with my child!"

"I am, m'lord. Are you pleased?"

"Am I pleased?" *He echoes, grabbing and kissing me.* "I am delirious with joy! My flesh and blood grows within you. With our love we created life! We must tell the Queen at once—we are to wed immediately!"

* * *

As Maggie made her way to baggage claim at the Jacksonville airport, she noticed how peaceful and empty it seemed to be–like it was the calm before a storm. But of course, the storm had finally passed.

While she waited for her bag and the painting she'd carefully wrapped to come along the conveyor, she sat and turned her cell back on.

She had to try Gracie again. She was very worried she couldn't get a hold of her for days! As her cell chimed on, she noticed missed calls: two from Gracie's friend Celine. The hair on the back of her neck stood at attention! *I knew it–something's very wrong.*

She hit the call back and Celine answered before the ring went through.

"Maggie? Hi, honey. I have something to tell you about Gracie–she's in the hospital."

"HOSPITAL!" Maggie yelled. "What happened? Is she hurt?"

"Well, she's had a head trauma–it's kind of a long story, but.."

"Celine, I'm in Florida. I just landed at Jacksonville airport and I'm waiting on my bags. I knew something was wrong! I felt it–she wasn't answering her phone so Mike put me on a plane as soon as I could get one. I'm here! Where is she? Where is Sal?"

"Maggie sweetie, you stay put. I'm on my way right now to get you. I'll be there in half an hour!" The call disconnected.

Maggie sat frozen in place, stunned. *Hospital? Head trauma? What in the hell had happened?* When she calmed down, she called home and let Mike know what little she knew.

* * *

The Knighting ceremony is beginning. Uncle Sabastion is dubbing the men from the battle.

Everyone is gathered in the great hall. My mother the Queen, my sister Princess Anne, and my step-sister Lady Caterina all arrive and take to their seats.

Lady Caterina gazes upon Sir Marsilio and me as I take his arm. Her icy stare makes me shudder.

"Are you all right, Princess?" Marsilio whispers.

"Yes, I am fine. Shall we sit here?" I gesture with my hand. I can feel her cold glare on me.

I return her stare with my own–and almost jump out of my seat. My heart recognizes her troubled soul–as Camille.

* * *

"She's running a little temperature," the nurse tells me while taking Gracie's vitals. "It's not serious, but we'll keep an eye on it. I'm going to get her a warm blanket."

"Is that normal?" I ask.

"Yes sir–her body is healing. We just want to be cautious with the pregnancy. Don't worry."

I get up and take the few steps to Gracie's bedside. I kiss her forehead and she feels cold to my lips. "Hang in there, Princess. I'm still here waiting." When the nurse comes back with the blanket, she places it on top of her.

"We're going to put a little something in her I.V. I'll come back in a while and take her temperature again."

I watch the medicine slide down the tube and into Gracie's I.V. I touch her upper arm and cheek. "She feels so cold," I say to Pop, who is sitting in the corner with a newspaper.

"Rub her feet, son. Move her legs a little and-a get her blood circulating."

"You think that's all right to do?" I ask. I'm afraid to touch her too much–I don't want to hurt her. Tears well in my eyes. "What if she is already in pain and I don't know it? Pop, I feel so helpless. I can't fix this and it's driving me insane!"

"I know how you feel son. I felt like that with-a-your mother. But, we know Gracie is gonna pull through this. *I* know she will."

After I massaged her feet and gently moved her legs from side to side I re-tucked the blanket. Then I put my ear to her chest. I always do, I love to listen to her heart. I place a kiss on it, then take the chair beside her, resting my head down on the bed.

*　　*　　*

Maggie made it to the hospital with Celine within almost two hours from the time she landed. She followed her through the halls and up to Gracie's room. On the way, Celine filled her in on the whole crazy story

Oh my god, this is bad. Maggie saw Sal laying with his head down on the edge of the bed next to Gracie's bandaged arms. Her breath caught in her throat, and Sal's head snapped up. His hair was a wavy mess—he had deep dark circles under his eyes with what appeared to be almost a full beard. He looked so morose Maggie's heart broke for him and Gracie. A loud sob escaped her chest and she held on to the bed rail. Celine reached for her.

"She's okay, Maggie, she's gonna be just fine, you hear me?" Sal stood up and walked around the bed to greet her.

"Maggie...I'm, Sal."

"I know who you are," she blubbered. "I'm so glad you saved my friend..."

Sal hugged her without saying anything and let her cry on him until someone handed her a tissue. She found a chair and collapsed into it.

Then she noticed Antonio and gave him a hello and a sad smile. She hadn't seen him in years. She took a deep breath, calmed her herself, got to her feet and went to Gracie.

"Honey, it's Maggie. I'm here. I made you a special something and just had to bring it myself..." she broke off as the tears started again. She patted Gracie's fingers gently.

"Celine," Sal said, "Did you mention the.....?"

"No, I believe that's your news to tell since Gracie can't."

"What news?" Maggie asked, her voice still a little shaken.

Sal swiped at his scruffy face then scratched under his chin. He looked away, hesitant to speak the words. He sighed.

"Maggie, Gracie's pregnant. We believe she wasn't aware she was. We're hoping the trauma her body has been through won't lead to a miscarry."

"She's what? How did she not realize...?" Maggie stared into space, then back at Sal.

"You're not blaming yourself, are you Sal? How would you have known if she didn't?"

"I left her," he abruptly stated. "She begged me not to leave–if I stayed we would have found out together. But I left her alone, so terrified something was going to happen to me that she went into such a depressed state she didn't notice. What if she miscarried while I was away? Or it could happen now! I will never forgive myself!"

"Sal, slow it down," Maggie tells him holding her hands up. "Don't do that to yourself please.... She needs you now more than ever. She told me for months that she felt something bad was coming. She thought it was coming for you, but it was her all along–she just got it crossed. You both are *meant* to be.

"Now, Richard," she spit out his name. "*He* was never meant for her–and Gracie always got hurt by him or got caught in his fall out, always! Not this time! I know in my gut and in my soul the baby is going to live Sal, and so is Gracie. This is it, I pointed between them, this...is meant to be!"

* * *

The knighting ceremony went on for an hour as Uncle Sabastion dubbed more Templars, and the Archbishop Reims was there to witness them signing the paper. Marsilio leans over to me to whisper in my ear.

"One of the best days of my life was the day I was dubbed a knight. We were given fortunes after the crusades. Now we are honored with gifts."

I look into his dark brown eyes–he is smiling so big. "What kinds of gifts, Your Grace?"

"I have been given jewels from all over. And, as we speak, my castle in France is just about ready to move in. It will be a wonderful spot for the baby."

"I thought your province was Austria. I would love to see Austria," I say. He chastely kisses my pouting lips.

"Princess, I will take thee to both my castles. We can live wherever you want as long as we are together."

Out of nowhere, Caterina sneaks up behind us. I can smell the mead on her breath. "Sister," she hisses, "you're pregnant!"

Marsilio and I jump and turn to face her.

"How much have you heard, Caterina? Really, it doesn't concern you,". I answer her sharply.

Marsilio takes me under his arm as protection. "This matter is **not** for your concern. I was promised her hand before any talk of a child. Now, be off with yourself. I should not have to endure such foolishness!"

Caterina bows and sashays away.

"She's going to tell the Queen!" I whisper nervously. He eyes me up and down, noting my fears.

"Come, we will tell the Queen first."

The ceremony is over and the handsome Knights are all lined up. As the minstrels played their songs, the knights tried to find a lady to dance with.

Marsilio and I headed over to the throne. We walked properly, heads high, smiles on and holding each other's hand.

"Your Majesty," we bow. I look at her with a small smile. "Mother, may we all talk in private for a moment?"

"Yes, in my chambers." She gets up and motions to the doors to her right. Two guards open them for us and my whole family is already there: Uncle Sabastion, Anne, and Caterina.

We enter with our arms locked. Anne and Sabastion smile at us happily. Caterina gives us an evil glare.

"Come, come. For heaven's sake, you all pick the most unimaginable time to have a family discussion." She turns abruptly and her skirt twirls with force around her legs. "WELL! Out with it!"

"Your Highness, if I may," Marsilio starts, "I am madly in love with your daughter and we came to ask you if we can be wed by the end's week. I must make a trip to France and I would very much like it if Princess Sophia is my wife by then–and by my side."

"Of no doubt you love my daughter and you may have your nuptials in a week's time, but, something tells this old woman there is something else you're not relinquishing. Out with it!" she says sharply.

"Mother," Caterina coos like a contented pigeon. "I do believe I overheard Sophia say she is with child."

The queen holds her head and doesn't even blink. "Whose child?"

Caterina preens, her expression smug. "She did not say–she would not tell me."

Queen mother strolls over to face Marsilio and me.

In a soft voice, she asks, "Who is the father, Sophia?"

"Your Majesty, it is Marsilio's, of course. I have been with no other."

The queen raises her calm stare at Marsilio. "Your flesh is of her flesh–it is your child?"

"Yes, Your Majesty, I am overjoyed."

The queen pursed her lips. "Well then, if you both are happy and content, then we shall get the wedding preparations underway, This is good news!"

CHAPTER 30

Late in the morning Gracie's hospital room door opens and Celine, Maggie, and Pop parade in. Maggie hands me a bag. When I open it there is a bagel, egg and cheese sandwich along with a coffee. I have to admit, the coffee smells really good.

Celine is the first to Gracie's bed. "Hey, Baby Girl, I miss you. But when you feel better, you come on back. Everyone is here: Maggie, Antonio, and Sal. You love Sal, baby–don't let him wait too long now. He's missing on ya real bad.,"

"Gracie," Maggie says next. "I came in for you–we know each other like sisters and I know you're in there fighting to come back. We're all here, we all love you. And, we all miss you like crazy."

"Mio caro, you sleep...you sleeping so peacefully, you take all the time you need to get better. No worries–Toby is-a-fine he gonna be running around soon with you."

BEEP BLIP!

"What was that?" I say and look at everyone in the room. We all stand silent and everything is quiet.

"Pop, say it again. About Toby..."

"Caro, Toby is well–he can't wait to run and-a-jump with you again..."

BEEP BLIP!

"Should we call the nurse or something? Celine asks excitedly.

Then it beeps and blips again... Maggie jumps from her chair. "I'll go get one," she says and she bolts out the door. A few minutes later, she comes back with the nurse.

"What seems to be going on here?"

We all speak at once and it all sounds like gibberish. The nurse puts up her hand like a referee. She points at me.

"Sal, what happened?"

"Everyone was talking to her–and when Pop mentioned Toby, she got extra bleeps. We thought maybe something was wrong."

"No guys, there doesn't seem to be anything out of the ordinary. But all of you've been talking to her?"

We gave her a collective "yes."

"Okay, well, it's a lotta love in this room. Maybe she was just responding. I usually don't allow but two at a time in a room, but, I know you're all she's got and I know I would lose the battle if I tried separating you all."

BEEP BLIP!

"See? See? You heard it!" Did you hear it?" we all chime in like bad students.

"SHHHH..." the nurse says as she checks Gracie's vitals, along with the ICP monitor. "Good news–looks like the pressure in her brain has started to decrease, so maybe she is being stimulated by a dream. Her BP is perfect and the fever is going down. I'll report to the doctor– you'll probably see him later."

Maggie approaches me with another bag–it was bigger than the bagel bag and she places it at my feet. "What's this?"

"That," she points, "are clothes, your tooth brush, underwear and soap. I know you're not going to leave her, and taking a shower here is not great, so, I thought I'd bring you some stuff–

oh and your razor–just in case you want to stop looking like the Brawny guy."

"Thank you, Maggie. How was it sleeping at the house?"

"I chose the small room at the end of the hall and kept the door locked. Truly, I don't know how she lived there alone all these years, so big and empty like the house is sad from its past. Even when dick head was married to her, he was hardly there! Sal, if those walls could talk...." She shakes her head.

* * *

When I get done with a good hot shower, I come out dressed in a fresh tee shirt and jeans with my slippers. I shaved some, and I combed and dried my hair.

"Hey, good lookin'," says Celine. "Now you just got to get rid of the raccoon eyes–you need some sleep, Sal."

"I'm afraid she'll wake up and I'll be out cold–I don't want to miss her. I've got to be there."

"Sal, I don't think you'll miss anything. The bed is big enough–scoot in there and hold her. Sleep beside her–if she wakes she will be in your arms."

I toss a questionable look at Celine then to Maggie–they both nod. "Do you think the nurses will get upset?"

Maggie looks around. "Why? And really what could they say–'Get out of you fiancée's bed? I doubt it.

"Okay, It would be nice to be able to relax, some."

I go to the bed and pull back the covers so I can do the little exercises I do with Gracie every day. I rub each of her feet for a few minutes, and then bend her legs. I slide my palms under her back and roll her on her side to massage her back. How I wish we were home by the sea and that this exercise was foreplay instead of an attempt to prevent bedsores and circulatory problems. I shake those thoughts away.

I catch a glimpse of Celine and Maggie watching me, smiling, but teary-eyed. When I'm done, I sit her up, careful not to dislodge her I.V. or any of her monitor hookups, and slide myself behind her, and lay back down.

Maggie covers us with a blanket from the pile on the windowsill, gives her friend a kiss, and promises to be back later.

Celine gets up, and whistles for Pop who is napping right in his wheelchair. "Come Tony, let's give them some sleepy time. She turns to me and puts her hand on my shoulder. "Sweet dreams, baby. We will see ya'll later."

My breathing slows to match Gracie's. I kiss her and tell her I love her. Then I remember the nurse said she might be dreaming.

"I hope you're dreaming happy things, Princess—all happy things."

I am so comfortable holding Gracie in my arms, I finally relax. Slowly I drift off to sleep.

* * *

"Go! Everyone!" the Queen clapped her hands. "Go–the night is still young and I have two more daughters to find suitors for."

"Wait," Caterina stopped in front of her mother. "I am the eldest, I should have been chosen first."

"You **were** dear, and in less than a year you came home crying! We painstakingly got you a divorce. "It will **not** be that easy to find you a suitor unless he is widowed. Good news is, you should still be young enough to bare an heir."

"But Mother, Sophia's child will be born first. It is not right mine will wait."

"Caterina," Sophia said, "your heir can go ahead of ours. We won't even be living here. Marsilio wants for us to live in France or Austria."

"Oh no, I'm sorry Sophia," the Queen cut in. "If you are first to bear a child, that child will be first in this house. It is the way it has always been done. You may raise the child where you like but know this: upon my demise you will reign until your child is old enough to do so."

"How is this happening mother?" Caterina growled. "I am the eldest!"

"Yes, but you have been divorced, Caterina. The Vatican does not look kindly on divorced Queens. Look at all the trouble that buffoon Henry the VIII caused in England. I'm sorry Caterina, but we will find you a suitable mate and you shall be handsomely titled."

"But Mother!" Caterina whined.

The Queen stood taller and looked at Caterina with searing eyes. "You will listen to me, Princess. You will do as you are told or I will send you away with Archbishop Reins and the Duke and Dutchess of Urbino—and there you will become an old spinster, is that what you want?"

"No, your highness."

"Then hold that wicked tongue that forks in your mouth. And the next time you eavesdrop on any conversation in this kingdom I shall put you on horse duty. Am I clear, Daughter?"

* * *

Celine and Maggie arrived at the mansion around mid-afternoon. The winter wind coming off the ocean was gentle, as though promising better things to come.

"This place is so big and lonely – any chance you can stay, Celine?" Maggie asked as she got out of the car.

Celine thought a minute, then nodded. "Why don't we relax a while, then go out and have a nice dinner–just us girls. We can get to know one another–how's that sound? I can spend the night–I'll just borrow something of Gracie's and make do."

They walked into the kitchen and Maggie turned to Celine. "Cup of tea or a glass of wine?" she asked.

"How about a cup of tea for now. We'll get wine later," Celine replied. She looked out the wall of windows and watched the sea oats sway on the dunes. "So, you said you settled in the small room at the back of the house?" she asked as Maggie filled the tea kettle.

"Yeah, it's yellow and lavender. I like the way it's decorated, but the house is way too big for one person. Rattling around here would make me crazy unless it was full of kids or animals or something fun."

Celine got up off the counter stool in the kitchen and walked over to the brown paper-wrapped rectangle leaning against the wall. "What's in here, Maggie?"

The kettle whistled and Maggie shut it off. "Oh!" she said as she looked at it. "I painted a portrait of Gracie and Sal."

"Really! You paint?"

"I dabble. It's a hobby, really. Would you like to see it?"

"I absolutely would!" Celine insisted.

Maggie gently tore the paper from the painting, then removed the bubble wrap. Then she turned it around and showed Celine. "Well, what do you think?"

"Maggie! Oh my heavens! That is amazing! You're very talented!"

"Thank you," Maggie said. "Gracie sent me two pictures of them via text messaging. One was the night of the benefit and the other was when they were in Napa. The strangest thing though–both pictures felt familiar to me like I'd seen them together before–so I painted what almost felt like a memory."

"Maggie you did a hell of a job. Gracie's going to love it. Sal calls her Princess– did you know that?"

"No, but it's all very strange. I got the pictures and I felt something each time. The hairs on my neck stood up. Just the way they did when I knew something was wrong with Gracie–and...here I am!"

"Lately, Maggie," Celine started, "nothing is strange around here. Gracie having those visions of her and Sal being soul mates for centuries? It's been an eye opener for me–nothing is ever going to freak me out again, I'm a believer"

"Yeah, she mentioned them to me. And a Dr. Brooks...oh did she ever call the psychic back?"

"Yes! Oh god." Celine patted Maggie's arm. Forget the tea–I'll fill you in over dinner and a nice bottle of wine. Let's go!"

"Sounds great! Thank you, Celine for hanging with me."

"Don't mention it. I'm very glad you came and I know Gracie is going to be thrilled to see you."

* * *

Marsilio helps me up on his horse and we ride out to the cliffs that overlooked the ocean beyond the castle grounds. It is quiet and the sound of the feast is in the distance. We sit together and watch the big orange sun as it sinks below the horizon.

"We must be getting back soon–the light is fading–people will notice we're gone."

"You are with me, Princess. You are going to be my wife and the people that matter most already know you are carrying my child. I should think it matters not if we steal away for a while."

He places his hand on my belly, then leans down to put a kiss there. He looks into my eyes then kisses my lips, sweetly at first, then the hungry yearning that is there surfaced as it always does. His tongue finds mine and we fall back on to the earth. I can feel the dewy grass beneath me. I put my hands to his chest and push a little.

"A little air, Your Grace, please," I pant.

With his eyes still locked to mine, he speaks softly. "I cannot wait to have thee with me every day. To wake up in your arms; I cannot wait to see your belly full with our child. I love you more than my own life, Princess—you are the very essence of my soul. I promise you this—I know I will love you through all eternity."

* * *

Two more days drag on. Nurses, technicians and doctors come and go at a pretty steady pace, though mid-afternoons it is quieter and I can sleep some then.

Dr. Rosaro assures me there is progress, but Gracie still seems so far away from me and I wonder if she'll ever wake up. *How will I ever live without her if she doesn't?*

The baby is doing great according to the ultra sounds and blood work they keep doing. I see the little tiny bean on the screen and I'm saving all the pictures. I've got to think positive and remind myself that Gracie will come back to us.

When everyone is gone I crawl up next to her, hold her in my arms and whisper in her ear. I tell her I love her and I am waiting for her. To be strong and get better. I tell her she is pregnant and we are going to be parents and what a wonderful mother she will be, then I fall asleep in her arms.

In the morning, the nurse that has been taking care of Gracie gently wakes me up.

"Mr. Petroni? Wake up, Mr. Petroni."

My eyes flutter open and I'm with Gracie, who is still sleeping.

"We're going to take out those sutures. She's healing up very well. I just need you to move over to the chair now, I'm sorry.." she says, looking slightly embarrassed.

"No no ..sure, I'll get up," I say, sleepily. "I don't want to be in the way."

"It's fine," she says. "I just hated to wake you up. This can be very draining and you need rest, too. Can't blame you for not wanting to leave her—we think it's very sweet how you care for Miss Gracie. You keep it up—we know it's helping."

She unraveled the bandages and again I see the scrapes and tears underneath her forearms and some on her palms. The nurse cleans them, then gently snips the threads used to close the deep gashes. She rubs some ointment on them and rewraps them with new, but less gauze. The nurse catches me staring. "Now you can hold her hand better."

I look up at her—she smiles and winks, then wraps up all of the soiled gauze and trots out the door.

I look back at Gracie and reach for her hand. I grip it, lacing my fingers between hers. I bring her hand to my lips and place a kiss on her knuckles. I smile and gently get back on the bed with her.

* * *

Sitting at a long dark wooden table abundant with breads, fruit, and cheeses, I am assaulted by the glare Caterina gives me as she walks in the room.

"Good morning, sister," I say as pleasantly as I can.

She pulls her chair from the table, dragging it on the stony floor causing a wretched sound. Then she slumps into it and the chair groans with the abuse she has given it.

She ignores me and I'm sad.

"Caterina," I say, "I really don't know what you are so angry about.

"Marsilio and I have been in love for a long time. He was given a choice and he picked me. Everyone knew he would. **You** knew he would. But I did not write the rules. I wish you could just be happy for me. I don't like to see you this way."

She gives me an icy glare. "Sister Sophia, I am well aware of the rules–more then you may think–my marriage arrangement should have been dissolved. I can't believe I was forced to marry that evil Duke of Burgundy. I was in hell, why am I being punished?"

"I am so sorry sister. Please, he is gone–you are here now, safe with us. Why can you not see that your life can be happy without ruling on the throne?" I give her a smile. "So many suitors I saw at the feast eyeing for your company. Go find a nice wealthy one and live a happy life–that's what you truly deserve!"

"Deserve?" she spits, eyes narrowed. "I'll tell you what I deserve. "I was married to the devil himself and I will never be put in that situation again. I demand to be next in line to secure my place–and I don't need a man to do it!"

"What is the meaning of this blasphemous conversation?" the Queen nearly shouts as she enters the room. We both jump to our feet and bow.

"Mother," I plead, "May I speak?"

"No Sophia, I heard the whole conversation." Her eyes trail to Caterina. "As my eldest, and daughter of my first husband, who was not of royal blood, how dare you make demands on what shall never be! You must stop this foolishness, Caterina, it is poisoning your mind. Stop it at once, or I **shall** have you dismissed and cared for elsewhere."

Caterina looks at our mother with the same frozen glare. "It was **you** who made me marry the Duke. He was evil, Mother. I deserve retribution!"

"ENOUGH! What's done is done. You will carry yourself in a dignified manner. And you will go on, Caterina. There are many ways you can help in the kingdom. Many noble causes for your considerable talents. You will be happy for your sister and her child. I don't want to hear any more of this filthy hatred in my house. As your mother, I will not put up with it. As your Queen, I will send you far away to live if I fear you will hurt the family."

Caterina runs from the room and my mother sits in her seat at the table, then looks back at me and smiles. "Sit down Sophia, finish your breakfast. You are eating for two and you will also need your strength to please Sir Marsilio on your wedding night."

"MOTHER!" I squeal.

"Oh my daughter, I **am** a woman—how do you think the three of you got here?" She laughs and I giggle with her.

"Oh mother, I am so very happy but, I wish Caterina..."

"Never mind of Caterina's foolishness. She will come around. No worries my child, you have plans to attend to and we don't want you stressing in your delicate condition."

"Yes mother," I whisper. I wish I could change things with my step-sister, but perhaps I cannot. I give my attention back to the Queen.

"I hear the kitchen is all aflutter with the preparations for the wedding tomorrow—and tonight's wedding eve's dinner. I am excited to meet Marsilio's mother and his brother."

"Yes, all is ready. Mother... Your Highness, I am finished. May I be excused? Marsilio will be here shortly."

"Yes of course my darling, go..go.. oh and for heaven's sake, make sure your sister Anne doesn't hide from the servants. I want that child washed for the celebrations!"

I chuckle. I had seen her dashing off on my way to breakfast. I'd have to go find her. "Yes mother, she is quite rambunctious, isn't she?"

"Yes–I fear she will miss you the most."

"Well, maybe she can come for a while after I have the baby–and stay with Marsilio and me. If that would please Your Highness."

"I think that would be fine, Princess. We will talk of these plans when the time comes." She waves her hand to dismiss me and I leave to meet Marsilio.

As I wait in the courtyard I cannot shake the image of Caterina, cold and so full of anger.

"Princess?"

I turn on my heel. "Marsilio! I'm sorry I did not hear you..."

"Are you ill? You look upset," said he says, thoughtfully.

"I feel well but I am distressed."

"Tell me my Princess, what puts a frown on this beautiful face?"

"Caterina does– I am afraid she has gone mad! Even mother said she would have to her put away if she doesn't stop her anguish. It makes me sad to think she was married to such evil. God only knows what she has really been through–she didn't come back right. She is angry and jealous... I feel it has gotten worse, like a sickness. She scares me, m'lord."

"Caterina, yes..." his answer is hesitant. "She does have some problems but none of this should be of your concern. Worrying is not good for your condition".

He puts his hands on my waist and pulls me close to him. "After tomorrow it will all be done and you won't have to be involved with her—we will be miles away from here. Now, promise me, Princess—happy thoughts only. Tomorrow you shall be my wife—all I want to see is your smile. Let's not allow Caterina to spoil our day."

CHAPTER 31

"The fever has broken, Mr. Petroni. And, the swelling has significantly reduced on the brain. The last scan shows good brain activity. This is all very good news, reports Doctor Rosaro. "Good news indeed. Now we just wait some more. I know this is tough, Sal, but she is better and the baby is fine. Hopefully she'll wake soon."

"Thanks, Doc, I hope so. It's been ten days now. This is the hardest damned thing I've ever been through–and I was a prisoner in a Bosnia prison. I know about waiting."

He gives me a smile. "I get it–that's your heart right there." He gestures to Gracie. "She'll come back, Sal. Hang in there."

And the tenth day forges on like all the days before. My father, Celine, and Maggie come twice a day to sit with us. They bring me food and clothes, and a few days ago, Maggie brought my laptop.

They talk to Gracie and help me brush her hair and massage lotion on her legs and back. We keep the conversations happy and talk of wedding plans and baby names. Some of the names are just awful and the girls laugh loudly at the facial expressions I make.

We're finished with lunch and taking care of Gracie and are on our second round of baby names when there's a knock on the door and we all fall silent and glare at the door.

Richard Boumont slowly enters.

He looks around at all of us, then his eyes rest on Gracie. "May I see her?" he asks quietly.

No one moves. I take a breath. A week ago, I wanted to beat the man to death for bringing Camille into Gracie's life, but I'm not so angry now, though I might feel pretty good about giving him a broken jaw.

He hangs in the doorway not knowing where to look. The girls look to me and I nod. "Come in," I say gruffly.

Celine and Maggie back away from Gracie's bedside and take a seat on either side of Pop, who's staring at Richard. I'm not sure if it's with pity or disgust.

Richard steps to Gracie's bedside. I stay by her and stand up, my hands fisting at my sides. Richard looks down at Gracie and grunts a sob.

"I'm so sorry," he moaned. "I'm so sorry... I wanted to come days ago, I wasn't sure I should..." He switches his gaze to me.

"I'm so sorry, I didn't know....I didn't know Camille was crazy–not in a million years would I have wanted any harm to come to Grace, please believe me!"

I inhale a deep breath and let it out slow–just the sight of him makes my jaw clench tight. Gracie's going to come out of her coma, and we're going to be married and have our baby, she'll hate it if I really hurt him. I look him in the eye.

"I believe that's probably true Richard, but if you weren't so busy being egotistical and self centered, you would have seen what that lunatic was doing right under your nose this whole time. Stealing from you–trying to steal from Gracie. Hired a hit!" I breathe in deep again and try to keep my voice calm.

"Gracie told me how self-absorbed you are. Even when you were married to her you couldn't be bothered to ask if she was having a bad day or felt well. It was all about you.

"People like you should not try to love–you're simply incapable of it. So yeah, I believe you when you say you didn't know. You didn't know you brought shit in–you weren't paying attention to anyone but yourself. And Gracie–an innocent bystander–almost paid for your mistake with her life."

Richard stands there, then wipes at his face and looks around the room at each of us.

"I didn't know who she really was–I didn't know about her mother and my father! My parents never told me...why would they? Truly, I'm sorry, but I don't believe any of this is my fault! I may be a little self-centered but I'm not the bad guy! I was just as in shock as any of you. Antonio, you were there–you didn't even know who she was. I never would have gotten involved with her. And I never wanted anything bad to come to Grace! I want you to believe that."

Antonio nods at him and adjusts his wheelchair so he's in front of the man. "Richard, it's true. She played-a-the game well, pulled the wool right over our eyes. You, Richard, are-a-just like your father in many ways–all business, never put the family first. Your mom was-a-not so happy, she knew of your father's mistresses, but she stayed. She loved you and hoped you wouldn't turn out like him. Your father made a terrible mistake many years ago. Maybe your mother should have-a-told you, maybe you would have been more mindful of things, maybe you would treat people better–maybe you would have loved Gracie better."

An uneasy quiet settles in the room as Richard stands by the foot of Gracie's bed, looking at Pop.

"I think you should leave, Richard," snaps Celine.

Maggie sits beside Gracie, wiping tears from her eyes.

My eyes wander back to Gracie, sleeping so peacefully. I feel a calming wave wash over me-even now while she is sleeping the sight of her calms me. I know she would want to hear Richard's apology.

"Richard, I believe you are sincere and I'm not gonna throw the blame on you. Quite honestly, I don't have the energy to waste on you." I sit back down and take Gracie's hand in mine.

"I love Gracie-she is my world, so, I will accept your apology, but, can I ask a favor of you? When Gracie comes around and is feeling better, you need to apologize to her, yourself. She's the one that needs to hear this from you and decide if she can accept it." I direct my eyes back to him. "Are you man enough to do that for her?"

Richard's eyebrows furrow above his red, wet eyes as he looks at Gracie. He nods. "Yes, I ahh...can do that, Sal. In the meantime, would you please keep me informed of her progress?"

"I will," I tell him.

Richard turns slowly to leave-then peaks over his shoulder at me sitting with Gracie. "I really did love her once, you know. I did."

He has no idea what love is and for that I feel sorry for him. I had loving parents and a great brother and now I have Gracie and her friends in my life. I'm far richer than he will ever be.

I give him a tight smile and a nod –and he walks out the door.

*   *   *

"Welcome my loyal and loving family, and royal subjects, to the engagement celebration of my daughter, Princess Sophia." The Queen announced in the great dining hall. All are gathered for dinner on the night before I am to wed my love, Sir Marsilio.

She continues on, every bit the monarch in her glorious gown with the ruffled collar, and I swallow the butterflies that still dart about my belly.

"We could not be happier of the pending nuptials that will take place tomorrow. I bless this joyous union and wish for healthy heirs these two shall hopefully soon produce."

Mother tosses a glance in my direction and discretely winks. Everyone cheers with joy and the servants usher in the evening's feast on big silver platters.

After we eat, the minstrels play and tables are cleared away to make room for dancing. Marsilio gets up and offers his had to me.

"Dance, Princess?"

I take his warm hand and it gives me tingles. I rise from my chair and he leads me to the dance area. It is our role to lead the evening's festivities.

"Volta!" Marsilio calls out to the minstrels.

Everyone gasps, then giggles at his request. This new dance comes from Rome and Paris and might be considered immoral to some. But it is all in good fun.

The music starts in a three-fourths beat and Marsilio faces me with his hand on my waist.

I put my right hand on his shoulder, and pick up my long skirts in my left hand so it will not get stepped upon.

Marsilio spins and twirls me about several times, lifting me high into a leap and landing me gently, safe and secure in his arms. The court cheers for us every time we leap, and when the dance is over, they stand and applaud for us thunderously.

Marsilio stands arms outstretched, still holding my hand, and we bow low to the floor as smiles and laughter fill the hall.

"Sister, oh sister..." Anne comes skipping over to me and hugs me tight." That was wonderful! You must teach me that dance!"

"Yes, of course, but only if mother will allow it. Anne," I give her a quizzical look, "where is Caterina? She was not at the dining tables and I have not seen her since this morning. It breaks my heart she is not sharing in my happiness."

Anne sticks out her chin. "I tried coaxing her out of her bed chambers before dinner and she would not answer. I told mother and she said for us to pay Caterina no mind, for she probably wants the attention. Mother is not at all happy with her ill manners."

"Poor Caterina," I say. "We truly don't know how hard it has been for her since returning from that evil Duke. I wish there was something I could do."

"Princess, what did I tell you about upsetting yourself?" Marsilio gives me a stern but loving look." Happy thoughts only." He seals his command with a swift kiss on the top of my nose and I giggle.

It is hard not having Caterina around to share in my bliss and I hoped she will be at the wedding. Truth be told, I cannot not stay sad for long. I am overcome by my own joy–marrying the love of my life and being with his child. I beam with delight.

* * *

Night comes again on the eleventh day. Everyone has left the hospital and I'm alone with Gracie like I am now every night. I want so much to hear her voice– need to get lost in her hazel eyes. I can't allow myself to give up hope, especially when things sound better every day. But I miss her so much I hurt.

I wash up, change into a pair of sweatpants and a tee shirt, then reach for a magazine. Planning to sit in the recliner next to Gracie's bed and thumb through it before curling up around her, I lean over to kiss her forehead.

When I look down at her, she appears different–something in her face–she has the smallest shadow of a smile on her lips. I look closer and turn on the bedside lamp.

Holy crap! I gasp and put my hand over my mouth to keep from yelling like a maniac.

"Gracie," I call. I pick up her hand. "Gracie, can you hear me?"

She doesn't respond, but that little smirk on her lips tells me she's surfacing.

I plan to watch her all night, afraid to fall asleep for fear she will wake and I'll miss it.

I don't call for the nurse or anyone–this little victory is mine. I climb on the bed next to her and watch her lips move back and forth all night.

She is in there–she's coming back to me.

*   *   *

Morning comes and I wake with a jolt, realizing I'd fallen asleep.

I glance at Gracie–she's still out but there's still that hint of a smile. I get up as the nurses come in to do their daily routines and check on her.

"Good morning, Sal," says one of the nurses. "How was your night? You seem to be getting a bit more sleep."

"Oh..ahh good, yes, I'm calmer than I was weeks ago. I was running on pure adrenaline then." I point in Gracie's direction. "Do you ladies see a change on Gracie's face? I noticed it last night–I'm hoping it's just not wishful thinking."

The two nurses focus on Gracie. It takes them a minute or two, then one of them gasps, "I believe I see a smile!"

"Yes!" says the other nurse, "it's very faint but it's there—is that what you see?" They ask as they look back at me.

"That's *exactly* what I see," I say, smiling wider than I have in weeks. "That's a good sign, right?"

"Well, any kind of movement is a good sign. Is she responsive at all?"

"No, I tried calling for her last night, and I watched as her lips moved, forming a smile. I know it's a small thing, but I feel good about it like maybe she is on her way back."

"The doctor thinks she is and all the tests seem to indicate that," one of the nurses answers. "Her swelling is way down now and her blood count is normal. Only time will tell."

"She's probably dreaming something happy," says the other nurse. "Maybe about you! Keep talking to her, Sal—I believe she's on her way."

Right before noon, Pop and the ladies show up with a pizza and it smells great. I guess I'm making my way back, too.

"One of Gracie's favorite food groups!" Maggie says with a laugh. She takes her slice over to Gracie and waves it under her nose. "Come on, girlfriend," she coos, "you gotta wake up for a slice." Maggie sits next to Gracie and nibbles at her slice.

"Hey, last night I noticed something new," I say around a mouth full of melty cheese. Everyone turns their attention to me. "Look at Gracie," I continue. Look really close at her face and tell me what you see."

Maggie and Celine lean over, "She looks peaceful," says Celine.

"SHE'S SMILING!" Maggie yells.

"Well I'll be." Celine takes another peek. "She *is* smiling! It's very slight, but I see it!"

"So, it's not the smell of pizza?" Maggie jokes.

"No," I laugh. "It's a small thing I know, but I don't feel so helpless now."

"Let-a-me see, son," Pop says, wheeling himself closer. "Oh mio caro! I see it, son. I see it! Gracie, come back sweet heart," Pop says as he pats her hand. He sheds two tears through a big smile, then reaches toward me and I give him my hand. "It's gonna be all right now, son–it's-a-gonna be all right."

"Oh thank god, a good sign!" Celine says with a wide grin. "You hear me, Gracie? You're a fighter! Now enough is a enough baby girl. You wake your ass up!"

* * *

The morning of my wedding comes with thunder and rain. I am getting dressed with the help of my ladies, and my sister Anne is sitting on the bed.

Lady Beth is helping with my gown when a big crack of thunder rolls across the sky. "Don't worry, Princess Sophia, I hear it's good luck when it rains on a wedding day. They say a wet knot never slips."

"Oh, the rain isn't bothering me. Rain or sun it is my wedding day–maybe it will stop, maybe it won't–but whoo..." I breathe deep. "I must say, I have butterflies in my tummy."

"Butterflies or a baby?" Anne giggles.

"Okay little Princess," Beth chides, "off with you now. Go finish getting dressed, and leave your sister be. Your mother will put me in lock up if you are not dressed and ready on time."

"She's fine, Lady Beth, but I am feeling light headed. Maybe you could fetch me some tea?"

"Yes, Princess and don't worry–it's all a part of the symptoms. Wait till you start purging every

morning–but no fears–its completely normal. I'll just be a moment with your tea."

Lady Beth scurries out and Anne gazes upon my gown, "You are beautiful sister. I shall miss you."

"Oh, no worry's Anne. I have a surprise for you! I've talked about arrangements to have you come to stay with Marsilio and me in France. Would that make you happy?"

"Yes! Oh sister! Really? When?"

"Well I thought right after the baby was born. Marsilio will send for you. You can study and explore and maybe when the time is right we can find plenty of suitors for you to choose from. I also think it be best for you not to be close to Caterina right now. I don't think she is well."

"Speaking of, have you seen her yet"? Anne asks making a sad face.

"No and I have a suspicion I am not going too."

"I overheard mother speaking to the physician. She is going to have Caterina checked. At court they are saying she's gone mad. I'm scared sister–and you will be gone by day's end."

I step over to Anne and hug her close, "Don't be frightened Anne. Stay with your ladies, and try to stay close to mother. You will be all right. If it gets very bad, write me and we will send for you sooner."

"Promise?"

"With all my heart."

CHAPTER 32

Two weeks. *It's been two miserable weeks since I hauled Gracie out of the sea and she's still not even aware I'm here.* Her heart beats steady and so does the little one's. Now I understand how I endured Bosnia. I was there as a result of war, a job I had to do. The price I was willing to pay. Knew it going in.

Gracie was a victim of things that had nothing to do with her. On top of how much I love her, the injustice is killing me a day at a time.

I look out the window at a damp, raw-looking March day. Pop and Celine went and collected Toby yesterday, so life is getting slightly back to normal. They told me he's limping a little but otherwise seems to be doing well. Except he whines for Gracie.

I know how you feel, fella. I know exactly how you feel.

I'm jarred out of my self-pity by a knock on the door. An old man in a light blue "Volunteer" jacket comes in with a delivery of flowers. Just what the room needs, so I smile.

The heavy glass vase is filled with fresh pink and yellow rose buds. I place the heavy arrangement on the bedside table and open the card. It simply says, *Love, Richard.*

Well, at least it's two dozen and the fact he sent anything is a step in a right direction.

I go over to Gracie, who still has a small smile playing on her lips. I place a kiss on her forehead, then on her cheek, then like every day, I put my ear to her chest, listening to the steady rhythm and plant a kiss over her heart.

The morning turns to afternoon and Maggie startles me when she enters the room.

"Holy crap that's a lot of roses! Who sent them?" Maggie points.

I smile and hold up my index finger. "I'll give you one guess–no peeking at the card."

"You shittin' me..." she blurts.

Smugly smiling, I raise my eyebrows and nod once.

"Wow, Richard feeling some heat," Maggie cracks. "You know, I don't think he ever got her flowers when they were married–for any occasion. He would say, 'All that money for what? They just die.' Such an ass."

I shrug. "I just hope he remembers to come see her when she's better, and gives her a proper apology for being an ass. She deserves that much."

"Yes. I agree. But the only problem with that is Richard doesn't know he's an ass. He never thought he did anything wrong." She chuckles shaking her head.

* * *

"Oh, where is Lady Beth with my tea? I am dizzy and now nauseated," I mention to one of the servants.

"I'm sure it's just a bit of nerves, Princess. Just sit here and we will finish dressing you. Take deep, steady breaths, m'lady."

Thunder roars on in the sky. Clips of lightening reflect through the castle windows. The soft knock at the door is my mother. We stand.

"*Come*" I call. She enters my bedchambers and we all bow and greet her as Your Highness.

"*Ahhh... my Sophia. How beautiful you are! Let me look at you,*" she says as she approaches me. "*Lovely, but you look a little peaked, my dear. Are you all right?*"

"*Yes Mother, I think so, but, I do feel a bit dizzy. I believe it might be my nerves. Lady Beth went to retrieve some herb tea, but has not yet arrived. She wanted to make sure Anne was ready – I'm sure she just lost her time.*"

"*Everybody out,*" commands the Queen. "*I want to talk with the Princess alone.*" She claps her hands and our servants scatter like mice.

She comes and sits next to me. "*Daughter, I believe you are having pregnancy symptoms. I know you are not nervous to wed Marsilio. The both of you have been in love for years.*"

"*Yes, I know Mother, it is just what we were saying in front of the servants. I cannot wait to see him – he will calm me.*"

"*Don't worry, the morning symptoms do not last long. I'll see what's keeping Lady Beth and the tea.*"

As she rises from her seat, she smiles and leans over to kiss me on my cheek. "*I am so happy for you. I just wish your father could see this glorious day. Uncle Sabastion will be waiting for you at the front gate of our chapel. He is so proud to have the honor of giving your hand to Marsilio. See you soon, Princess.*"

* * *

Late that afternoon Sal, Antonio, Celine and Maggie were again at Gracie's bedside. They noticed the small smile she had for several days was gone now.

Pop was watching TV while Maggie and Celine were reading and talking. Maggie was reluctantly making plans to return to her family. She'd been away almost three weeks and Mike and the kids needed her back home. She only had a couple of more days.

Sal was getting more quiet every day, wondering what he would do if Gracie didn't wake up. Or what if she woke and didn't remember him?

He prayed day and night for her to wake up. He sat on the side of her bed and held her hand. Then out of nowhere, a glimmer of hope shook him out of his gloom. He looked up–the girls were watching him, wide-eyed.

"Did I hear a slight moan come from her or am I just going out of my mind?" he asked with skepticism.

"No..." Maggie answered. "I thought I heard it, too!"

"I wasn't sure what I heard," Celine said, "but now that y'all mention it, it just might have come from her."

Pop muted the TV and they sat still, looking at one another.

"Sal," Maggie whispered, "Talk to her!"

"Gracie? Gracie, wake up, now."

Looking at her, holding her hand, he spoke softly but firmly. A little sigh escaped from her throat.

Again they all looked at each other like deer caught in headlights.

"Get the nurse! Call the Doctor!" Sal yelled, his heart pounding so hard he thought he'd pass out.

"Gracie...Gracie?"

* * *

Even though I am not feeling good at the moment, I am still overcome with joy. I know the symptoms will pass shortly and it is all part of the little miracle growing inside of me made from pure love.

A knock at my door startles me out of my thoughts. "Come," I call. The door opens slowly and Caterina stands there in the doorway.

"May I enter your chamber, sister? I came upon Lady Beth who seemed frazzled with today's busy chores. I saw the tea and I told her I would bring it to you."

I smile. "Thank you sister, that's very kind of you. I have been waiting what seems like days for that tea."

Caterina strolls into my room and shuts the door. I am happy to see her. She does not have the angry icy demeanor she had yesterday. Instead, her features appear more humble and sorrowful.

"I hear you are not feeling well this morning," she says as she puts the teacup down in front of me on the table. "The herbs in the tea should help."

"Thank you, sister," I smile. "I'm very happy to see you. Please say you will attend my wedding today. I don't want us to part and leave you upset or angry. Thing's will all work out for the best for you, Caterina, I know it. Now, please say you can be happy for me?"

I pick up the tea and sip. It is nice and warm, not too sweet and has just a hint of ginger.

"I am happy for you, Sophia, and yes, I will be in attendance today."

She smiles back at me but it does not reach her eyes. I sip some more on the tea–a warm sensation is numbing my stomach and soon I start to feel very strange.

"Sister?" Caterina asks. "What's wrong?"

"I do not know," I say on a breath. "I am feeling very peculiar."

The warm sensation builds up into my chest and burns at my throat. "Caterina.. go... get help... something is happening to me... something is very wrong!"

I cough and hold my throat which is closing. Caterina makes no attempts to move from her seat. She just glares at me with an evil smile on her face. I know in that moment what is happening.

"You poisoned my tea!" I cough and gasped for air. How could you? Why... sister?"

*My vision begins to spin and fade to black. I hear other voices, like echoes. I heard Marsilio call out, "**Gracie**!" I hear women telling me to wake up but it is so hard.*

I cough again, my throat feels like sandpaper. I can't see but I hear voices talking to me, calling to me–where are they?

I follow the sound but my legs won't move. I feel heavy and I have pain–my head hurts.

* * *

"GRACIE!" Gracie...I'm here–open your eyes! You're okay! Your okay!"

Sal was holding her when the nurses and Dr. Rosaro rushed in the room.. She was coughing and looked like she was in pain.

"Sal, let me see her, it's okay," Dr. Rosaro said as he pushed his way past Celine, Maggie and Sal.

"She's coming around. Gracie," the doctor spoke. "Can you hear me? Open your eyes if you hear me."

They stood around the bed. When Gracie's eyes popped open, she sucked in a big breath as though she'd been holding it for weeks.

She struggled to focus. When she did, her eyes met Sal's. Warm tears flooded his vision when he saw recognition in her eyes, those big hazel eyes.

"Gracie," he sobbed. "Oh, thank God, you're back."

* * *

I'm in a hospital room and not sure why? The headache, maybe?

I look at Sal who looks like he's lost weight and his eyes are bloodshot. I looked around and see Celine and Antonio, both of them laughing and crying at the same time.

Then I hear a familiar voice chime in.

"Hey, Gracie! Welcome back!" I look up and see my best friend Maggie.

Good god, I'm confused. "What's wrong?" I ask. "Sal?" I look around for him.

"I'm right here," he says, taking my hand.

A tall man is on my left side. "Gracie, I'm Dr. Rosaro. How do you feel? Is it difficult to move? Can you sit up?"

I try to sit up and Sal helps but the pain in my head is nauseating. I grab my hand away from Sal and clasp both hands to my head. "OW, my head," I moan.

"Gracie," the doctor continues, "Can you move your feet and legs for me?"

I do as asked. "What's going on? I ask again.

"You were in an accident," the doctor answers. You hurt your head–you've had a concussion causing swelling on your brain. You've been in a coma for almost three weeks. But, you're going to be fine. You're healing. Do you understand?"

"I guess so. An accident?" I ask. "What kind of accident?"

The doctor looks around at everyone then back to me, his brows knit over serious gray eyes. "Gracie, what is the last thing you remember?"

"Ummm, the storm. Home...I was home. Sal... was gone." I look up at him. "You're back! You came back!"

Sal smiles and nods.

"Is that all you remember? The doctor prods.

"Camille... Something's wrong with Camille.." I say curiously.

"That's puttin' it nicely," Celine mutters.

"Okay," Dr. Rosaro says, "I'm going to schedule another CT scan and run some tests. Give her a few hours to let everything sink in. I know this is great and we're all excited to have her back, but let's not overload her right now." He looks at me.

"Give us a little time and we'll get you something for that headache, young lady."

Maggie and Celine take a seat on the small sofa. I glance at Pop, he blows me a kiss, "Welcome back caro." Sal takes me in his arms, pulls me close and kisses the top of my head, then my cheek.

"Gracie, I missed you. I was so scared I lost you!"

I wrap my arms around him. "I'm just so happy that you're home. But, what happened? It's all so foggy."

"Well," he says, glancing at Celine and Maggie, "we'll figure it out. Just tell us what you do remember."

"I remember I was somewhere...a long time ago. I was poisoned by this girl who I felt like I knew her, a sister.. but, she was mad at me....OH! A baby!" As I remember, I touch my stomach. "There was a baby!"

Everyone's eyes get big and the ladies look at Sal.

"Shhh... Gracie, it's all right. You dreamt there was a baby?"

"Yeah, it's fuzzy though. I'm getting bits and fragments. A puzzle with missing pieces."

"Gracie," Sal says. "Don't try to remember anything right now–let your mind rest. In time it will come to you. Just rest, Princess. Just relax."

"Princess!" I blurt.

"What?" Sal says.

"I remember something about being a princess..."

* * *

When I return from my CT scan, only Sal is waiting in the room.

"Where did everyone go?" I ask him.

"Back to your house," he says as he comes over to sit with me on the bed. "They wanted to give us some time."

I sigh. I'm tired and my head still hurts, but it's so good to have him back, scruffy beard and all. I don't want to stay here another minute. "Okay.... what's happened? Please tell me," I plead. "I want to know."

He inhales sharply and lets it out, then scratches at his scruffy chiseled chin and gives me a smile.

"Gracie, I have so much to tell you, but the first thing I need for you to know, is that I love you more than my own life. I'm sorry I left on that mission and I will never leave you alone again. As soon as you are well enough, we're going to get married."

"Sal, there's no rush. You're here now–we'll plan a nice day and.."

"Gracie," he interrupts. "Things have changed a bit and I want to marry you as soon as possible."

I pull away from him–just a little–and see his half smile. I furrow my eyebrows. "What has changed?"

"Gracie," he says calmly, taking my face in his hands and centering his eyes on mine. "Gracie, you're pregnant."

In a flash of a second a million thoughts race through my mind. *Am I still dreaming? Is this a joke? They've made a mistake. That one! I'll pick that one!* "They made a mistake–that can't be possi...bl..?"

Sal shoves a black and white photo of an ultrasound in my face. My eyes go wide and my head pounds. "That's in me? Are they sure?"

"Yes, you're about three months along. And Gracie, I could not be happier!"

I take the picture and study it. "It's healthy? It's all okay? Even with the coma? Is it a boy or a girl?"

Sal laughs and my heart seems to fly.

"Yes, the baby is fine. They don't know the sex yet– but even if they did I didn't want to know until we found out together. You must have gotten pregnant around Christmas time. They tell me you went into a deep depression after I left so you probably didn't recognize the symptoms. You don't remember skipping your period?"

I give him a guilty look. "I kinda do but I thought because I was so upset and couldn't eat anything that it didn't come. Truly never in a million years did I think I could ever get pregnant. It didn't work before."

"Maggie says it worked now because this," he points from me to him, "this was meant to be."

A chill runs over my body after he says those words. "I believe it too!" I cry.

"Are you okay? He chuckles, raising his eyebrows at me.

"I'm *more* than okay..." I tilt my head slowly to the side. "Soooo, Christmas, huh?" I whisper with a big smile. *I got pregnant around Christmas...* I glance at him from the corner of my eye. "Hmmm...must have been that plane ride."

CHAPTER 33

Sal spent the next week at Gracie's side, bringing her up to speed on that stormy night, and helping her gain her strength to go home.

"How's the fear, Princess? Is it gone?"

"Completely gone!" She nodded and reached out to wrap her arms around his neck. "Looks like this time, we made it," she chirped.

Celine and Maggie went on home to take care of their own families, clear that Gracie would make a full recovery and the baby was doing great, too.

Tony made himself scarce, too, only visiting in the evening for a little time.

"I no-a want to leave Toby too long," he told them, always with a warm smile.

On discharge day, Sal walked beside Gracie as she was wheeled out of the hospital to the waiting Viper, this time with the top in place.

* * *

We pull into the driveway and I see an array of vehicles.

"Who belongs to all these car's?" I ask.

Sal smiles big and turns off the car. "You'll see." He helps me out of the car, but I'm doing really well on my own, now.

As we enter my front door, I'm bombarded with family and friends. My brother Steve, Maggie and her husband Mike with their two girls.

I look around and spot Celine and Mimi, my boss Veronica, and of course, Pop. Out of nowhere, Toby ambushes me. Even with a limp he tries to jump up on me. I get down on the floor and Toby whines and squeaks and licks my face.

"He missed you so bad, Gracie," Veronica said. "I'm hoping he'll start to eat better now that his momma is home!"

I fight back tears. "Awww, I missed you too, big guy," I say as I continue to get a dog bath. "You gotta booboo? Lemme see the booboo."

Toby lays down and rolls on his back. I scratch him and tell him what a good boy he is and everybody laughs.

The house is alive with bright flowers and balloons and what looks to be enough food for one of Celine's parties. *A welcome home I will never forget.*

"Is everything okay with Mary and Joe?" I ask Sal. "I wouldn't expect them here, but for some reason, they popped into my mind."

Sal kisses the tip of my nose. "Right you are, Princess. They're at the hospital now. Mary went into labor a few hours ago. Little Anthony will be here any time now."

As the day turns to night and my welcome home party is winding down, the doorbell rings. My brother Steve gets up to answer it and soon Richard is standing in the living room.

I look up at him from the couch and he actually smiles at me—a sight I haven't seen in years.

"I'm glad you're better," he says. "I came to check on you and to talk to you, if I could."

I get up from my seat. "Would you like to go into the study?"

"That would be fine he answers.

While I can't imagine what he could want to say to me, Sal's encouraging smile and small nod take away my fears.

We enter the study and I sit down on a winged-back chair with Richard sitting in the one in front of me.

"Gracie, I don't know really where to start, so I'm just going to say first off I am beyond sorry about Camille. I am sorry I let her make the wedge in our marriage bigger. I know we grew apart. I really did love you in the beginning, that was no lie, but after a while we were just too different. I suppose I could have been at the very least your friend. I thought I was doing the best I could at the time.

"As of lately I found out things about my parents that I never knew. And, I know just saying sorry about everything is too small a gesture, but, I am. I'm so sorry for how I treated you–I'm sorry about it all."

I sit there with my mouth hanging open. I wonder where the real Richard has gone and who this is sitting here with me. "Are you really apologizing to me?" I ask.

"I am. I know it isn't worth much, but I am sorry for all your pain. Before and after Camille."

I smile at him. "I know we did love each other and I don't regret marring you. I am starting to understand now that things happen for a reason. Richard, did they tell you I'm pregnant?"

Richard's eyes open wide. "No–how? And you're fine? Is it healthy?"

I laugh at his expression. "Yes, I'm three months along and everything is perfect. This was meant to be. Richard, I was meant to be with Sal. I have gotten signs that he is my soul mate. I wouldn't have found him if I wasn't here–if YOU hadn't brought me here. I accept your apology,

Richard. I know you would never want to see me get hurt. You may have behaved like an ass, but you're not evil."

For a moment he frowns, then lets it go. "Thanks—I think," he says laughing lightly.

"Thank you Richard, I needed to hear this. It means a lot to me."

He stands and looks a little uncomfortable. "Well, I'm gonna head out. I'm glad you're better and doing well and I'm happy to hear your good news." He started for the doorway and stopped, turned. "You know, I don't have any use for the house. Probably put it up for sale. So you guys can stay as long as you like. I'm not sure what your plans are—and it's none of my business—but just let me know if and when you decide to leave."

"Thank you," I say. "I, umm... not sure. Sal wants to get married very soon. But I will let you know."

I walk him to the door and without another look, he crosses the threshold and is gone. I feel warm eyes on me and turn to see Sal watching from across the foyer. I smile up at him as he makes his way over to me and takes me in his arms. He kisses me and it's fire. Our kisses always are.

His velvet brown eyes look lovingly at my face. "Everything all right?" he asks.

"Yeah, as a matter of fact it is. Not sure what prompted it all, but his apology made me feel good. He's just a mess. I don't wish him anything bad."

"Did you tell him about the baby?"

"Yep. He seemed shocked but happy for me."

"Good, Princess. I'm glad he came and talked to you."

"Ahem... and you wouldn't have had anything to with that would you?"

"Who me?"

He leans in for another kiss. I taste the heat and dive in deeper. He breaks the kiss and his dark eyes burn into mine.

"Tonight, Princess, you're all mine. If you're up to it, we've got some catching up to do."

"I thought you were never going to ask."

* * *

Later that night I was relaxing with Celine and Maggie, while Steve, Sal and Mike cleaned up. Pop sits by a small fire burning in the fireplace with Toby by his side.

"Gracie", Maggie asks. "You said something when you woke up. Something about being somewhere a long time ago–do you remember anything?"

I look at my friends. "I do–I remember a lot–and it scares the hell out of me. I think while I was in the coma I dreamt of a past life. And it was so vivid!"

"Do you feel like you can share it with us baby?" Celine asks. Or do you need some time?"

"No, no, I'm fine as a matter of fact. I couldn't wait to tell all of you."

"Gracie," my brother yells from the kitchen, "do you want anything? We're done in here, but I'll bring you something if you need it."

"No, I'm good, thanks!" I yell back.

The guys come to join us and ask what we are talking about.

"Gracie is going to tell us what she remembered from her coma," Maggie tells him.

Sal gives me a thoughtful look. "It's fine–come sit down–I want you all to hear this."

"Well at first I didn't remember much just a few bits and pieces. But I know with all my heart this was a past life I revisited. Sal, your name was Marsilio, a Knights Templar just home from a battle–I think it was Malta.

My brother Steve jumps up and grabs his laptop. "Wait a minute Gracie, let's see if we can match any of this up."

He powers it up and starts typing away. "Okay, we have a battle of Malta–it was medieval times; mid 1500's."

"Go on, Gracie!" Maggie urges.

"There was a Queen–Celine, she reminded me of you."

"How 'bout that!" she laughs. "Finally I'm in my element!" Everyone laughs with her.

"I had sister's–we were the Queen's daughters. Anne and Caterina– my name was Sophia."

Sal looks at me. "Princess Sophia?"

I nod. "Now I realize why when we first met you felt the need to call me 'Princess', Centuries ago Sal, I'm pretty sure we *were* these people."

I tell them my story and how each of them in some way was there living it with me. "We are all connected and have been for many years on and off."

I told them the details of the castle and the clothes, my blue dress with the long sleeves and the little jeweled tiara I wore.

"You were so handsome in your white robes of the Knights of Templar," I tell Sal. "Your horse was magnificent as well, with his white linen cover adorned with the red crosses."

"And the pageantry was breathtaking, at least from my position as a noblewoman. The huge tents were gorgeous in the burgundy and gold dyes. Celine–you'd have loved it! The castle yards were crammed with tents and animals and people."

Celine turns to Maggie. "Has she seen the..?" she starts to ask Maggie.

"NO!" Maggie yelps, cutting her off, and jumps up from her chair.

"What are you two up to now?" I ask. "Where is she going?"

"I'm not up to anything, but you just wait 'til you see this!" Celine says.

Mike agrees. "I've seen it., This is gonna get freaky!"

Maggie returns holding what appears to be a framed painting. "Gracie, I started painting this right after Christmas day. The first picture you sent me of the both of you was the night you went to the children's benefit. Ask Mike, that picture just haunted me for some reason. Then you sent me another picture of the two of you in Napa in front of that winery that looks like a medieval castle. Again, it was like I was staring at something I'd seen before. Look closely Gracie-you're in a light blue dress and tiara; I painted Sal in white-in the back ground, tents-look what color they are!"

My eyes scour her painting and suddenly I'm transported-I feel a rush of energy surge through me. Goose pimples rise all over my body and I can feel the color drain out of my face as the hair on my neck stands to attention.

Maggie painted a picture from her mind-but with the same exact details from my dream.

Sal looks at me, then the painting, then back to me. "Are you okay?" he asks.

"Yes, I am just fine," I say, smiling from ear to ear. "This," I gesture to her painting, "is total validation! I knew it!"

I pass the painting around so everyone can see for themselves. Pop looks up from the painting. "Your souls never die-your love is-a-that strong."

My brother is still tapping at his laptop. "I can't find too much of your account Gracie, but what I can tell you is the names you've mentioned come up-and there is some connection of royalty-scattered through Italy. Now interestingly enough, there was a battle at Malta with the Turks-and Templar knights, I never heard about it, but it happened-

"For whatever reason, your dreams, this painting, this whole thing–is just beyond us. Let's not question it. I'm just going to believe this was your destiny–like Mags says–it is meant to be."

* * *

Late that night when everyone had gone to bed, Sal and I curl up in each other's arms. I have never felt so loved by a person–I can feel his warmth radiate through me like we shared voltage.

Sal's so happy and relieved to have me home and safe that he breaks down in heartbreaking sobs and my heart knows exactly how he feels. All the weeks I mourned a loss that never happened and almost lost my life. I understand what he means when he says he didn't know how he'd go on if he'd lost me and the baby.

When he settles down, we change the subject to happier talk, making plans for getting married, where we should go to live our lives. Together, we come up with a plan that we will put in motion in a few days, when our guests leave.

Sal hugs me tight and kisses me. We gently and slowly make love.. After covering every inch of my body with tender kisses, he fills himself within me, taking his time and being so careful as if I might break, I almost cry.

But as it always does, no matter how tender the intention, or how gentle the beginning, our desire and hunger spins us into a frenzy that ends up with both of us catapulting over the edge of ecstasy together.

Sal looks into my eyes, and in his I see, my past, present and future in them.

"I will love you forever," he whispers, putting his ear to my chest and listening as my heart slows down.

Placing a kiss over my heart, Sal softly says, "I am right here–always. I promise."

EPILOGUE

Sal and I eloped. We hopped aboard Nick's private plane to Europe where we went to Italy, visited the Vatican, toured Rome, floated in Venice and saw Pompeii.

We spent a week in France and a long weekend in Monaco. We ate fabulous food, stayed in beautiful suites, and saw as many historical sites and museums as possible.

While in England, we toured London and took pictures at Stonehenge, then visited many castles.

No one was at all mad that we slipped away like thieves in the night. Well, maybe Toby–but he was happy staying with Pop. They knew we were together and happy and that's really all that mattered. We were gone for two months. We called everyone weekly just to check in.

By the time we got home, I was going on six months in my pregnancy and my belly was a nice little bump protruding out under all my shirts. Sal told me it was the sexiest thing he'd ever seen, but Celine and I had a blast buying me maternity clothes.

I also noticed since the coma, I wasn't plagued with dreams. Or fear. For whatever reason, they just ceased. Sal and I saw Dr. Brooks a few more times and talked to him about it. We all agreed they had stopped because Sal and I, after centuries, had gotten to our destiny and were finally joined as one.

In those months, Sal's brother Joe, who was enjoying fatherhood, had called a few times and talked to Sal about helping on the winery expansion project. Sal would be a shareholder in the business and he liked that idea.

Sal and I discussed the offer and agreed we were ready to live in Napa Valley. Soon, plans were put to paper. Pop was excited to live in the cottage on Joe and Mary's property and construction on our house just up the road from them was starting. We were excited and ready to start our new life in Napa. Pop was delighted to know he'd be getting to know his two grandchildren, too.

I couldn't believe what a difference a year could make. I'd come full circle. I had been alone with no love and no family—now, I was married to someone who adored me, a baby was on the way, and I'd inherited a wonderful family that was going to live and grow with each other.

Some days I'd wake up and ask Sal if it was all a dream, was this all real? Would I wake and be alone again?

He'd just smile and give me kisses, rub my belly, and over and over reassure me I was not dreaming.

~*~

On September 21st at approximately 2am, I gave birth to a beautiful 6lb. 9oz. baby girl.

Sal coached me and held my hand. He cut the cord and was the first to hold her.

When he finally brought her to me, he placed her gingerly in my arms and kissed the top of her head where sprigs of dark curls poked out from under her little pink cap.

He leaned over and brushed his lips lightly over mine and told me he loved me.

A nurse standing nearby asked us what we were going to name her. I glanced at Sal and he nodded.

"Sophia," I smiled. "Her name is Sophia."

~ Fini ~

ABOUT THE AUTHOR:

Robin H. Soprano was born and raised in Essex county New Jersey. She now lives in Flagler County Florida with her husband. An animal lover, she writes or reads with her loyal dog always at her feet or by her side.

After many years as hairstylist she needed a life change.
On a restless night a few years back she woke and could not get back to sleep. A tiny voice in her head said; "write a book." She thought she was going crazy. But her love for story telling and reading was too big to ignore.

She started to write, and with the advice of a friend found a class in her community. How to Write a Book in Thirty Days. She was very surprised to see she was on the right track and the inspiration from Michael Ray King's program was just the push and direction she needed to keep going.

She has other projects in the works and looks forward to producing many more books to share.

AUTHOR'S NOTE

While writing, my love for music of all kinds kept me inspired. The song list for A Soul Mate's Promise....

Breathe (2am) / *Anna Nalick*
Broken / *Life House*
Right Now / *Van Halen*
Love Comes Walking In / *Van Halen*
Far Away /*Nickelback*
Never Gonna be Alone / *Nickelback*
You Can Talk To Me / *Stevie Nicks*
Just A Kiss/ *Lady Antebellum*
Save the Last Dance For Me / *Michael Buble*
All Of Me / *John Legend*
My Sacrifice / *Creed*
I Won't Give Up / *Jason Mraz*
Bring Me To Life / *Evenscence*
A Thousand Years / *Christina Perry*
Home / *Daughtry*
A Time To Say Good By / *Andrea Bocelli & Sara Brightman.*

There is a little figurine of an Angel on my desk. She sits in a little pigeonhole watching over me. Every day I look up at her and read out loud what it says on the bottom of her gown, its just one word. One little word, so simple with so many possibilities and it makes me smile like a child. That word is....*Believe*...